becoming Jace

TEIRAN SMITH

BECOMING JACE

Copyright © 2017 Teiran Smith

This book is a work of fiction. Names, places, and incidents either are a product of the author's imagination or are used fictitiously. Any resemblance to actual persons, living or dead, events, or locales is entirely coincidental.

ISBN: 0692922504
ISBN-13: 978-0692922507

DEDICATION

To my precious Sasha. You gave more love than I deserved. You were the best friend anyone could ask for. You will always be my baby girl.

The Beginning

Don't look, man. Just don't look.
Do. Not. Look.
Shit, I looked.

My heart races and I forget how to breathe. Mother of God, is this a gift or a punishment?

Sophie Holt hasn't a clue of the danger she's in. Lounging around in a skimpy neon yellow bikini in my presence is a bad, bad idea. I've done my best to keep my distance, but I'm hanging by a thread here.

Look away, Rooter.

Look. Away.

Now.

I squeeze my eyes shut, but the damage is done. The image is scorched into my memory. I'll never survive another summer of this torment.

I remove my helmet and climb off my Harley. With my eyes pinned to my back door, I hurry to my house. I open the back door and Dopey, my pit-bull, bounds out of the house and sprints for the overgrown tree in the backyard.

The urge to look Sophie's way is intense.

I could sneak a peek. She'd never know with my sunglasses on.

But getting caught isn't the problem. My utter lack of self-control is. I've only a scant amount of restraint as it is. Every time I look at her, a little more crumbles away.

But I'm weak. With my body facing the street I glance at her through the corner of my eye. I'm instantly consumed by desire to be near her, to touch her. Her long brown hair is pulled into a ponytail, revealing a slender, elongated neck. She has strong, feminine shoulders, and those legs… so long and lean.

What would it feel like to have them wrapped…

Dopey jumps on me breaking my trance. I stumble sideways with a laugh as he nudges his ball into my hand. As I throw the ball, I see Sophie smiling in my peripheral.

That damn smile… those dimples make me weak in the knees.

It's legendary.

She is legendary.

I want Sophie.

So. Very. Bad.

More than I've ever wanted anything.

Typically, I'm not one to deny myself anything. If I want something, I make it mine.

But I'm also the kind of guy who tries to do the right thing.

It's a tale as old as time. Bad boy meets good girl. Bad boy tries to be better for good girl. Bad boy fails and ruins good girl's life. Bad boy loses good girl and becomes the worst version of himself. Except this isn't fiction. This is real life. Nothing good ever comes of a bad boy, good girl relationship. The odds of us riding off into the sunset living happily ever after are nil. I'd surely ruin Sophie's life. That knowledge is the only thing keeping me away.

But her presence calls to me in a way I've never experienced with any other girl. Sophie emanates a sweet, serene, pure energy that draws me to her. I've felt it since the moment I first laid eyes on her three years ago. It's only gotten stronger. I fear I won't be able to fight it much longer.

The problem is, she's my next door neighbor. I see her almost every day. Over the past three years, I've spent countless hours watching her from my windows. And she watches me. If I'm outside when she's home, I almost always catch her checking me out from her bedroom or dining room window. When she sits on her bed studying at night, she spends more time looking at my bedroom window than at her books.

But Sophie needs me to stay away. She's been through hell in her life. Being involved with a guy like me would only add to her pain and misery.

I'm the Sergeant At Arms of the Double H Motorcycle Club in Halsey, Michigan. As such, I'm involved in dangerous, risky business on a regular basis. I'm frequently in contact with criminals in the—illegal—drug and sex industries. It seems I'm always pissing someone off—people that can and will hurt my loved ones without a second thought if I pushed them hard enough. I walk a very fine line and all it'd take is one wrong move and someone I love could wind up hurt… or dead. It's happened with other Club members, including my best friend, Bear.

Sophie deserves someone better than me. She's an innocent. A sweet, intelligent college girl trying to make a better life for herself. She deserves a normal guy who can offer her a good, safe life. Not a guy who puts her life at risk simply by being with her.

"Goddamn it, Sophie!"

What the fuck?

I spin around and find Mike, Sophie's best friend's brother, standing at their back door. He lives in the house with the two girls. Mike is in serious need of an attitude adjustment, and has been dangerously close to getting one for months now. Today could be the day he gets it.

"What?" she hollers back without looking at him.

"I was supposed to be at work a half hour ago!"

"Then it sounds like you're late."

That's right Babe, don't take his shit.

"No shit! You knew I had to work tonight."

"What's your point?" Unaffected, she nonchalantly holds out her arms and checks for a sunburn. If I wasn't so agitated, I'd laugh.

"Did it occur to you to wake me up?"

Is he kidding? Because he seriously needs to be. He's a grown ass man. Does he really expect her to babysit him?

"Um, last time I checked," she says, "I'm not an alarm clock, or your mother."

Be careful Babe.

Bringing up his mom isn't a good idea. She died last year. He's a whacked out drug addict. It's hard telling what he's liable to do if she pisses him off enough. Though I dare him to try something right now. I'd have my fist through his skull before he could get anywhere near her.

"Worthless fucking cunt!" he hollers and slams the door shut.

I draw in a slow, steady breath to calm myself. One thing I don't put up with is men being disrespectful to women. Calling a woman a cunt is almost as bad a raising your hand to her. The motherfucker will pay for that. No one talks to Sophie that way. Ever. With a clenched fist, I turn to Sophie. Our eyes meet and her breath catches. When she waves at me, my feet move, involuntarily, in her direction.

"Everything okay?" I ask and remove my sunglasses.

"Yeah, he's just a dick."

She stands from the lawn chair and I feast my eyes on the entire length of her firm, flawless body as she approaches me. I shift my gaze back to her eyes, but their intense shade of blue steals my breath. Her close proximity sets my nerve endings on fire.

I'm in trouble.

She's in trouble.

We're both in monumental fucking trouble. I must get a grip on my attraction to her.

"So I've gathered," I say.

She extends her hand and flashes those seductive dimples. "I'm Sophie, sorry about that."

Sophie's eyes sweep over my face, my torso, and the tattoos on my arm. Her expression is soft and her lips parted. When she licks her lips, I have to battle an overwhelming desire to pull her face to mine for a taste.

"No worries." The skin of her hand is soft as a flower petal. If I don't let go quick, I might never. "I'm Rooter."

Mike hollers again, "Where the fuck are my black jeans?"

I shoot him a vicious glare and take a great deal of pleasure in the fear that flashes in his eyes.

Sophie snipes back, "Why would I know where your jeans are?"

"Because you did laundry after me and I had left them in the dryer."

I can tell it's taking all of his strength to stay calm. I wonder how their conversation would play out if I wasn't here? The idea of him hurting her makes my blood boil.

Sophie crosses her arms and scowls. "Well, they weren't in the dryer when I used it."

"Then where are they?"

Back the fuck off, dude, or your missing jeans will be the least of your worries.

"I don't know, Mike," she grumbles, impatient. "I don't keep track of your shit."

"Bitch," he mumbles, no doubt thinking I can't hear him, and goes back in the house, slamming the door behind him.

"Are you sure everything is okay?" I ask with an iron fist hanging at my side.

"He's just a blowhard," she waves her hand.

A blowhard? That guy has serious issues. He could hurt her. Does she not see that? "Seems he could use a lesson in manners."

She agrees with a nod.

"Look, Sophie, you don't know me, but if he ever gets out of hand," I wave toward my house, "I'm right here, just let me know."

I refuse to allow that fuck to hurt her. So even though she's better off not knowing me, I will make this exception in order to protect her.

"Thanks," she says with a smile, "I appreciate it."

"I'm serious. I take that shit seriously." My eyes bore into hers. If she has any trouble with him, I expect her to tell me.

My phone rings, much to my dismay, and I snatch it from my back pocket. It's the Club. I have to take it.

"It was nice meeting you, Rooter," she says and backs away to allow me to take the call.

I could listen to her say my name all day long. "You too, Sophie." Unable to resist, I scan the length of her body again. "Remember what I said."

After diffusing a melee in Brigsby with our rival MC, the Rebels, Bear and I ride out to Sully's, a dingy dive bar on the edge of town, for a beer. I have a little time to kill before I have to be home and after the day I've had, I could use a drink. And tonight, my favorite nineties cover band is performing there.

Sully, the bar owner, still tends the bar even though he's about five days older than dirt. He hollers at us as we make our entrance.

"Hey, Sully," Bear says and takes a seat at the bar. "What's new?"

Sully gives his usual answer, "Fuck all."

The three of us laugh as Sully sets our beers on the counter. We've been coming here so long, he doesn't need to ask what we want.

"Nectar of the Gods," Bear says before chugging half his bottle. He can drink me under the table, and that's saying a lot because I can hold my liquor.

Bear and I grew up together. Both of our fathers are original Club members. I'd take a bullet for him without a second thought and he'd do the same for me. Being that we're both members of Double H, there's a real possibility it could happen. But there's no one else I'd rather have my back. The dude is ruthless. He is a giant with a jaw of steel. I've seen men swing at him only to break their own hands without so much as fazing him.

Forty-five minutes and two beers later I lay a twenty spot on the counter and stand to leave.

"I thought you said you were done with her," Bear says, his reddish-brown hair bobbing up and down to the beat of the rock music.

He's referring to Candace, my former friend with benefits. I recently ended my "arrangement" with her so now we're just friends.

"I am."

"Then why are you leaving?" He cocks a brow. "We've been here less than an hour and this band kicks ass."

In the past, I always used the excuse that I was headed to Candace's when I left early. I no longer have that as a reason and I don't want to tell him the truth. I shrug. "I'm just not feeling it tonight, man."

"Bullshit. You're going over there aren't you?" he challenges with a smirk, tugging on his long beard.

I shake my head, though I'd much rather he think that than tell him why I'm really leaving. If he knew I sat on my front porch four nights a week to make sure my pretty neighbor gets into her house safe after work, I'd never live it down.

Sophie works nights at a local upscale restaurant called The Grand and she'll be home in an hour or so. We live in a shitty neighborhood. For the past ten months I've made sure to be home on the evenings she works.

Bear's entire body shakes with laughter. "You pussy whipped motherfucker."

I flip him the bird and turn to leave, but he's right. I am whipped, just by a different girl.

I make it home by a quarter till midnight and take post in my enclosed front porch. All the windows in Sophie's house are open. No sooner than I sit, I hear yelling coming from within.

Sophie's friend—I can never remember her name—and Mike are going at it again. Their fights have become more frequent and from the sound of it, more violent. Used to be they'd holler back and forth a few times and then it'd be over. But now, once they start fighting it goes on for hours and always ends with her in tears asking him why he hates her so much, and begging him to leave her alone.

I try to mind my own business. I realize brothers and sisters have disagreements, but the way they argue is more like dueling mortal enemies. He calls her "bitch" more than he calls her by her name and the threats he makes aren't that of a loving brother.

His fights with Sophie, however, are an entirely different beast. I'm constantly worried he'll hurt her. She doesn't back down and take his shit the way his sister does. Sophie tells him just where and how hard to shove it. On one hand, I'm glad she's bold enough to stand up for herself, but on the other, it scares the hell out of me. Sophie may not act like it—she may not even realize it—but she's a delicate flower inside as well as out. I'm afraid one day she'll learn that about herself the hard way. I'll be damned if I let that whacked out fuck be the one who shows her.

Nearly an hour later I watch as a pair of headlights come down the street and Sophie pulls into her driveway. When she steps out of her car, she's dead on her feet. I hang my head with the knowledge of what she's getting ready to walk into. The least I can do is warn her. "Hey, Sophie."

At the sound of my voice she jumps and lets out the cutest little shriek. I can't help but laugh.

"Hey, Rooter," she says with a wave.

"Your… friend, Mike, has been on a tear tonight."

"He's not my friend," she asserts with a frown before turning to her front door.

"You might not want to go in there." I warn, trying to deter her from going inside. Perhaps she has somewhere else she can go for the night. It's not a good idea for her to be in the house under the circumstances. The look in Mike's eyes when he yelled at her in the backyard convinced me it's only a matter of time before he hurts her. Tonight could be the night.

She stands quiet and listens for noise from inside, but there's none.

"They've been quiet for the past five minutes," I say, "but it's been like that all night. He screams, she screams back, then it gets quiet again."

She lays her head on the roof of her car, visibly deflated and I feel a pang in my chest. I consider offering for her to stay here tonight, just to keep her away from him, but quickly squash the idea. She doesn't know me. It might freak her out if I suggest she stay here. And if not and she did take me up on my offer, that could lead to a whole other set of problems. Namely the loss of my resolve to keep my distance. No sense trading one bad guy for another in her life.

She stands up straight and takes a deep breath. "Thanks for the heads up."

"If you have any trouble, I'll be here." *I'll reassemble that fucktard's limbs if he hurts you.*

"I appreciate it."

Sophie trudges to her front door. The instant she steps inside, I hear yelling. As I listen, it takes everything in me not to rush over and take matters into my own hands. But that isn't a good idea. With my temper, it's hard telling what I'd do to that worthless pile of shit if I got my hands on him. Besides, it isn't my place.

But if he hurts Sophie, nothing will stop me from massacring him to the point he's unrecognizable.

A loud bang comes from Sophie's bedroom window. I dart to the side of her house and stand below the window so I can better hear.

It's difficult to hear over Mike's incessant yelling, but it sounds like she's on the phone with the police. If Mike gets into her room before they arrive, he could inflict serious harm. I consider going in and dealing with him myself, but if I'm in the house when the police arrives, it'll only make matters worse. If I get my hands on him, I'll inflict serious damage of my own. I don't need that kind of heat from the law. And with my reputation, it would put Sophie in an unfavorable light. I remain below her window, listening to make sure she's okay. If he gets into her room, I'll go in, consequences be damned.

Thankfully the police are fast to respond. When I see the flashing lights of the police cruiser I hurry into my house through the side door. Ten minutes later I watch from my front porch as Mike is hauled away in cuffs. My only concern with them sending him to jail is how he might retaliate. I won't allow it to come to that. I'll be having a talk with Mike as soon as he's released.

Keeping My Distance

I'm in my driveway polishing the chrome on my Harley when Sophie's roommate pulls up with her brother the next morning. I shake my head, incredulous. Does Sophie approve of this? I certainly hope not.

As they walk to the house I catch a glimpse of the girl's face. Her cheek is swollen and bruised. My face goes up in flames and it feels as though all the blood has rushed to my head as my pulse pounds. I inhale a slow, deep breath and continue polishing, but knowing that woman beating pussy is in the house with those girls—with Sophie— is unbearable. I stop working and stand upright. My jaw is clenched as I breathe in and out with long, labored breaths as I stare angrily at their front door.

Suddenly, I'm climbing the steps of their front porch. I turn the doorknob to let myself in, but it's locked. I ring the doorbell and wait, clenching and unclenching my fists. Every muscle in my body is tense. A familiar edginess has fallen over me as my adrenaline surges. This is the feeling I get right before a fight. The door opens and the dickless wonder stands before me. His mouth falls open, and he shuffles two steps back. Seeing red, I lunge forward and swing my fist. When it connects with his jaw, he drops to the floor and I pin him down with my knee.

His sister screams and I hear the sound of footsteps rushing down the stairs. I glance up and see Sophie staring at me wide eyed. This fucker is lucky her face isn't marred or I swear to all that is holy I'd murder him, right here, right now.

"You think you're a man?" I snarl and grind Mike's face onto the hardwood floor. He lets out a shrill cry. His lips tremble as he gasps for air. "Real men don't hit women! If you ever so much as raise your voice to either of these girls, I'll hit you so fucking hard you'll dribble for the rest of your life!"

Keeping a firm grasp on Mike's wrists, I jerk him up from the floor. I look to Sophie. She's staring at me with a dazed expression, her lips parted. She doesn't appear afraid, so much as shocked. *Interesting.*

The other girl won't stop screaming. When I order her to be quiet, and instantly obeys.

I lean in into the pathetic shit's ear and demand he apologize for what he's done.

"I'm sorry," he squeaks, his voice unsteady.

I tighten the grip on his wrists. "Be specific."

He looks to his sister. "I'm sorry I hit you," he says, and surprisingly sounds like he means it. Next, he turns to Sophie. "And I'm sorry for being a dick to you all the time."

His mortified expression gives me a thrill. I demand that he tell them it won't happen again.

"I promise it won't happen again."

I want to take this worthless fuck out in the front yard and beat him until he's unconscious, but I've overstepped my boundaries as it is. When I release his hands, he runs to his sister like the little bitch that he is.

I turn to Sophie who is still gaping at me. I gaze into her eyes longer than I should and in them I see adoration and awe. I want to take her away from here and promise to always protect her and keep her safe. More than anything, I want to take that wet bottom lip into my mouth… I bite my tongue to stop the unreasonable thoughts. "You make sure to let me know if he pulls anymore shit on either of you."

If I don't turn and leave right this second, I won't be able to leave without her. As soon as she nods in agreement I spin around and rush out of the house. I need to get as far away from her as possible. I climb on my Harley, fire it up and tear out of my driveway.

It was wrong of me to insinuate myself into their problems, but I had no control over myself. I have no patience for men abusing women. That Sophie was involved made it intolerable.

I tell myself that I would have reacted the same way had it been any female. But it's a lie. Sure, I would have said something to the dude, put the fear of God into him. But I wouldn't have gone crazy like I did.

What has come over me? What is that girl doing to me?

Being near her stirs something in me I've never felt. I yearn for her in a way that's at once animalistic and pure. I want to hold her hand, gaze into her eyes. I want to taste her kiss and feel her skin against mine. But I want more than physical. I want it all with her. Not only have I never been in love, I've never been inclined to be. But if given the opportunity, I'd give Sophie my heart in a second.

She mesmerizes me. Never have I seen a girl half as beautiful as Sophie. She's perfect in every way. Her long, dark brown hair and don't get me started on her skin—she glows. Her gorgeous blue eyes exude such depth and intensity. She's equal parts tough and delicate. You can tell just by looking at her how strong she is. If you look hard enough, you can see a deep sadness beneath the surface. There are times, however, when she forgets her sorrows and lights up, bright as the sun. She has the most incredible laugh. It's music to my ears. It starts out low and builds in pitch until her shoulders shake and her eyes sparkle, if only for a fleeting moment, before her demons come back to haunt her.

I'd been watching her come and go from her friend's house for two years before she moved in last year. I was already infatuated with her. But when she moved in, I became consumed by her. I suppose I could've introduced myself to her and gotten to know her the normal way. But it was obvious from the beginning that she was an innocent. Unlike the kind of females I normally associate with. So I did a little digging to see what I could learn about her.

I learned a lot.

Sophie had a terrible start in life. Her mother neglected and mistreated her in every conceivable way, physically, mentally, and emotionally. She never knew her father—something we have in common. My biological dad abandoned me, too. She has no siblings or other family.

Unable to endure her mother's abuse, Sophie left home at seventeen. She moved in with her best friend—I think her name is Melissa or Melinda—and her parent's. With their help, Sophie finished high school and has been taking care of herself ever since.

Her friend's mom and dad were like adoptive parents to Sophie. They shared a close relationship. She was devastated when they passed away last year. Now, with the exception of her friend and a few others, she has no one.

My heart bleeds for her. I want to be the one to give Sophie all the things she doesn't have—family, security, love—but it can't happen. As much as I want her for myself, she deserves so much better than me. My life is too dangerous and uncertain. I never know from one day to the next what or who is coming my way. After everything she's been through, it's a risk I'm unwilling to take. If anything were to happen to her because of me, I'd never forgive myself.

She and I can't happen.

Ever.

If I only ever make one good decision in my life, it'll be to stay away from her.

After going for a long, scenic ride, I'm much more relaxed and level-headed. Though I still don't regret what I did—I'd do it again if need be—I've decided I should apologize. While I don't think I scared Sophie, I don't want her thinking I'm a crazed lunatic. Besides, I know I scared her friend.

I pull into my driveway and kill the engine. I glance up to Sophie's window and just as I expect, I find her staring down at me. I motion for her to come out and talk.

I'm oddly nervous as I stand, waiting. I don't know what to expect. She could be furious with me. Fortunately, there's a smile on her face as she approaches me.

"I'm sorry if I scared you earlier," I begin. "That wasn't my intention."

"I wasn't scared." She gazes at me with bright eyes and pulls her bottom lip into her mouth.

"You weren't?" I ask just to be sure.

"Surprised, maybe," the side of her mouth turns up into crooked smile.

Those dimples…

"I bet." I rub the back of my neck, anxious. "How's your friend… What's her name?"

"Miranda. Now, she was scared." She giggles. It's the cutest sound ever.

"I could tell," I admit, and rock back and forth on my heels. I feel the need to explain my actions. "Look, what happened, believe it or not, is completely out of character for me. I'm not some weird dude who busts into people's houses and attacks them. It's just… I have a problem with guys who hurt girls."

"That's an admirable quality," she says with a discernable twinkle in her eyes.

Is she flirting?

"I wish I'd handled it differently. But when I saw him get out of the car... I lost it."

"Well, the good news is, I don't think he'll be attacking us anytime soon."

"You kicking him out?" *Please, say yes.*

She shakes her head. "I just think he'll be too scared to try again. You scared the shit out of him."

I exhale sharply. "Why aren't you kicking him out?"

"He's Miranda's brother, and she owns the house." She looks to the ground then back up at me before adding, "I don't really have a say in the matter."

I shake my head, incredulous. "You should have one if you pay rent to live there."

"It's complicated." Her eyes drop to the ground again.

"No, it's not. He's an abusive ass. He needs to go."

"If anyone will leave, it would be me."

"Maybe you should consider that option." My stare is keen.

"Easier said than done on my income. And Miranda can't afford this house without me." She swallows before continuing. "Besides, I don't think it'll happen again."

Sounds as though she's trying to convince herself more than me.

I laugh mockingly. "Are you kidding me? Of course it will."

"Mike is working through some issues."

"Sophie, do not make excuses for that asshat." I grit my teeth and clench my fist.

"I appreciate your concern, Rooter." She places a hand on her chest. "Truly. But the situation is complicated."

The situation seems pretty cut and dry to me. He's a mentally unstable, abusive drug addict. He needs to go before he seriously hurts one of them. But sometimes, it's easier to see a situation for what it is when you aren't directly involved.

"Well, just know, if I find out he hurts either of you again, I won't be as easy on him as I was before."

"Understood."

My phone rings. A welcome distraction. That asshole staying in the house with them has me enraged. I'm of mind to go in, pack his shit, and toss him out into the street. I pull the device from my pocket and see it's the Club. "I need to take this."

Without a word, Sophie nods and turns to walk away.

But I don't want our conversation to end on that note. I call her name and she spins back around. "If you ever need anything, I'm here.

Dopey nudges his ball into my right hand. My knuckles are swollen, and starting to scab over. The pain is annoying, but not terrible. I have use of all my fingers, so I doubt anything is broken. I toss the ball in the direction of my garage and the dog takes off after it. I hear the rumble of a Harley and turn to find Bear pulling into my driveway. I'm not surprised he's here.

"Hey, man," he says and walks my way. "Thought I'd come by and check in. You all right?"

I throw Dopey's ball and turn to face him. "Fucking perfect."

Today, Andy, one of the Club members called for a vote to revoke my SAA patch. He claimed I violated the Club rule of protecting our members by not defending him against the Rebels. Whenever a member calls for a vote, regardless of their position in the Club or the nature of the issue, it must be carried out. Of course it didn't pass. The fucker should have known better. He knows better now. The beat down he got from Hoyt, the President of the Rebel's was nothing compared to the one I delivered today.

"You almost killed Andy."

"I bet he'll think twice about fucking with me again."

"No doubt," Bear laughs. He dislikes the guy almost as much as I do.

"Pop needs to patch him out. He's trouble for the Club."

The Club has a decent relationship—at least we did before Andy's fuck up—with Hoyt and the Rebels. We had an understanding. They do their thing and we do ours. As long as they keep their drugs out of Halsey, Double H agrees to keep our presence out of Brigsby. The agreement has worked seamlessly for years.

The day before yesterday, the Rebel's had a large Meth shipment coming north and Hoyt asked if we'd allow passage through our town to avoid a toll road. The delivery was to be dropped at a location on their side of the border. Hoyt offered a handsome commission if we agreed.

Mick, my father and the President of Double H, assigned Andy as the escort. All Andy had to do was collect the cash and keep his damn mouth shut. For anyone else, it'd been a simple task. But Andy isn't known for his diplomacy. Just as I expected, he mouthed off to Hoyt. Andy told him not to make a habit of this and then had the nerve to accuse him of being light on the payment. Hoyt called Mick demanding he send someone out for a renegotiation. Mick sent me.

Hoyt gave me two options. Surrender the payment for this passage or collect a one-time payment and allow them continued transit through Halsey. I was furious. Neither choice was acceptable. I apologized to Hoyt for Andy's disrespectful behavior and vowed that it'd be dealt with. But we'd require full payment for this passage only. Hoyt countered and offered to pay half of what was originally agreed upon. He then offered to pay the full amount if I'd allow him to deal with Andy himself. Andy came unglued and dared Hoyt to give it his best shot. Hoyt did exactly that. I didn't step in.

Had I stepped in, we would've forfeited all the cash and our relationship with the Rebels would've been null and void. Defending Andy wasn't worth the cost to the Club. Besides, Andy needed to be taught a lesson. Getting reprimanded by Mick wouldn't have done the job. Mick tends to be overly lenient with Andy, in my opinion.

"Maybe he will after this," Bear says.

I shake my head. "He won't. He's too fucking loyal."

This isn't the first problem we've had with Andy. We've had nothing but problems with him since I was promoted to SAA. He wanted the patch. He felt he deserved it more than me because I haven't been in the Club as long as him. I've asked Pop and our VP, Wrench, to kick him out of the Club. They refuse to turn their back on any member unless that person directly harms the life of another member or their family. While Pop considers Andy a "bit of a loose cannon" he doesn't feel he's done anything to warrant having his patch revoked.

My phone rings. I pull it from my back pocket and see it's Candace. I roll my eyes, silence the ringer and slide it back in my pocket. I don't have the patience for her today.

"So how's that going?" Bear asks with regard to her.

"It's not."

"She take it well?"

"Better than expected."

Bear chuckles. "Just wait. You keep ignoring her and all hell will break lose."

I shrug. "She's harmless."

Just as he's about to protest, Miranda pulls up and parks her old, dilapidated Ford Explorer in front of her house. She looks our way and even with her over-sized sunglasses, I can tell she's scowling. Bear's eyes bulge from their sockets as she walks to her door. Once she's inside, he turns back to me.

"Tell me again why you've been messing around with Candace when you have *that* living next door."

I snort. "*That* isn't my type."

Neither is Candace in all honesty. I'm generally not attracted to voluptuous blondes, which is why they're the only type of female I *associate* with. Going against type makes it easy not to develop romantic attachments.

He points to Miranda's front door. "*That* is every guy's type."

"Well, I guarantee you I'm not hers."

"Yeah, you're probably right." He sniggers.

Bear had a girlfriend once. Her name was Ashley. It was an intense relationship. The guy was certifiably crazy over the girl. It started in their sophomore year of high school and lasted seven years. There's no doubt they'd still be together if she was alive. They'd probably be married with kids.

A hit was placed on Bear for a scuffle his dad was involved in with a drug runner out of Detroit. Bear was home with Ashley when it went down. The hitman broke into their apartment in the middle of the night while Ashley was up getting a drink of water. When she saw the intruder, she screamed, and he shot her between the eyes. The noise from the gunshot tore Bear from his sleep. The shootout that ensued ended in Bear's favor. But he's never been able to forgive himself over Ashley.

Since her death, his only female interaction since has been an occasional drunken hook-up with the Club regulars. But in terms of interest in a girl for an actual relationship, forget it. He swore to never get involved again. I don't blame him. Ashley's death is the very reason I keep my distance from Sophie.

The Warning

Sophie pulls into her driveway a little later than usual for a Monday. From where I sit, I can see dark circles under her eyes. She stands, shoulders slumped, staring at me as though she's waiting for me to say something. When she waves, I return the gesture.

I would say hello, but I can't get in the habit of engaging in conversations with Sophie. Conversations lead to becoming acquaintances, which leads to friendship, which can lead to… more. In our case, I'm positive it'd lead to more. So, I remain quiet and she eventually turns to go inside her house.

I'm beat and ready to call it a night. After getting a quick drink of water, I follow Dopey upstairs. I flip the lights on in my bedroom and the light coming from Sophie's window catches my eye.

It happens so fast that even if I could pry my eyes away, I don't have time to. In a matter of seconds Sophie's in nothing more than a pair of pink panties.

Holy Christ.

I can't breathe.

I can't move.

I can't even blink.

Raw desire charges through me. I've fantasized about her a million times and not once did it come close to how painstakingly beautiful she is. She's tall, and lean, though not without curves. She has a delicate, hourglass shape. Her breasts are magnificent. Small, as I prefer, and pert with mouthwatering rose colored nipples. I lick my lips as I imagine the way they'd feel in my mouth. I bet she tastes sweet as candy. My fingers tingle with the need to touch her.

I glance up and she's staring at me, mouth wide open.

Shit!

I rush to my blinds and snap them shut. I squeeze my eyes closed trying to erase the image of her naked body, but it does no good. It's seared into my memory.

What an asshole!

I can't believe I just stood there, gawking. I invaded her privacy in the worst possible way. Not purposefully, but I could have turned away. I should have turned around the instant I saw her.

Sophie's been through enough. Just last year she was raped by her boyfriend. The last fucking thing she needs is a stalking, peeping Tom living next door. I'm not a peeping Tom, but I can't deny my stalker status.

I spend the night tossing and turning, plagued by conflicting thoughts. Despite my embarrassment and shame, I can't get the visual of Sophie's naked body out of my mind. I dream of kissing her, and touching her… being inside her, possessing her. Christ almighty the girl rouses something in me I've never felt. It's not just about physical pleasure. It's about showing her what it's like to be with a real man who will care for her and worship her for the angel that she is. I could be that man for her. I want to be that man for her.

I know I've vowed to stay away from her. It's for her own good. But what if she never finds a good man? What if she never knows real love? What if she ends up with another guy like her ex? What if she gets hurt again? With me she'd never have to worry about that. I'd never hurt her. I'd rather saw my fingers off than cause her pain.

Stop it! Stop trying to talk yourself into pursuing her.

I glance at the clock. It's five in the morning. I might as well get up. No sense lying here driving myself crazy with my thoughts. Perhaps a run will burn some of my pent up energy.

Five miles and buckets of sweat later, I'm just as amped up.

At work, I spend the entire morning worrying nonstop and wondering if Sophie's angry with me. She must be. I need to make things right with her. Today.

Pop and I are in his office discussing shop financials, but I can't focus. I look at the clock on the wall, eager to get out of here so I can go to Sophie and apologize.

"Everything okay, Son?" Pop asks.

"Yeah." I shake my head, trying to clear my mind.

He lays his pen down and sits forward. "You seem distracted."

I lean back in my chair and exhale. "Sorry, Pop. I just… Have an issue I need to deal with."

His chest shakes as he laughs. "I know that look. Would your issue be of the female nature?"

How the hell does he know such things?

I can never hide anything from my dad. It's as though he can hear my thoughts. I glance at him, unwilling to answer because I refuse to lie, but I won't admit the truth.

I look down at the financial statement in my hands. "We're on track to closing out a great year. We're already eighteen percent ahead of our sales projections for the first half of the year. The only problem is, I'm not sure we have the man power to continue taking on projects at this rate."

"What do you recommend?"

"Unless we're looking to expand, which I don't think we are," to expand, we'd have to hire and we don't hire outside of the Club, "we need to choose our jobs wisely and stop accepting every build that comes through the door."

He scratches his beard. "I hate to turn down work, but I think you're right. I'll talk to the others and let them know."

I check the clock again. Sophie will be leaving soon.

"That's good for now," he says and motions for me to leave. "Go handle your *issue* and be ready to get some shit done tomorrow."

"Thanks, Pop." I stand and open the door. "See you tomorrow."

On my way to the front door, I pass Bear who's installing a gas tank on a build.

"Heading out?" he asks and checks his watch.

"There's something I gotta do."

He stops working and faces me directly. He knows it isn't like me to cut out early unless it's on Club business or an emergency. "Everything all right?"

"Yeah. It's no big deal," I say and lay my hand on the doorknob. Just as I'm about to turn it, the door swings open. If I'd been paying attention, I would've seen the person on the other side of the glass.

Candace. I resist the impulse to roll my eyes. I don't have time for this.

"Hey, Baby," she coos in her low, seductive voice. Her nipples threaten to cut through the tight purple tank she's wearing.

"Hey. I'm just on my way out."

"I was hoping we could talk about my bike."

Mick agreed to customize her Sportster. We're finalizing the design. "Pop's in his office," I tell her and try to push past, but she doesn't let me by.

"Shouldn't you be here, too? To go over the details?"

"He can handle it." I keep my voice steady, trying to hide my impatience.

"How've you been?" she asks and eyes me up and down.

"Not too bad." I answer, and just to be friendly I add, "You?"

"You know me." The corner of her lip turns up, and she plays with my belt buckle. "I'm always bad."

"Find a new boy toy?" *Please say yes.*

"No. I figure you'll be calling any day."

"I might surprise you."

She leans in until her body is flush with mine and grabs my dick; a long time habit of hers. It never bothered me until now. "I certainly hope so."

"That's not what I meant. We agreed to be friends, remember?"

"We can be friends and have sex."

"You are relentless." I smile, trying to keep things light.

"I'll be home tonight, Lover," she whispers, then steps away to let me pass.

When I pull into my driveway, Sophie's car is isn't there, but she pulls up right after me. She gets out of the car and looks my way, but I can't make out her expression. An uneasy feeling comes over me as I approach her. A novelty for me. Sophie's the only girl who's ever had this effect on me. But then again, Sophie isn't just any girl.

I rock back and forth on my feet. A nervous tic. "Hey."

"Hey."

My stomach is in knots with shame and embarrassment. "I'm so sorry about last night. I'd just walked in my room and there you were." I motion up and down the length of her body, trying to push the memory out of my head and failing.

Her face flushes. "It was my fault. I should've closed my blinds. I was just so tired."

I put my hands in my pockets and try to decipher her expression, but come up empty once again. "I don't want you to think I'm a creepy, peeping Tom."

"I don't. Like I said, my fault."

She doesn't seem upset at all. How is that possible? Surely, she must feel some way about it—about me—after everything that's gone down recently. "It's just that, in a year's time, we haven't spoken a word to each other. In the past few days, I've burst into your house, assaulted your roommate, and watched you undress."

Her eyes widen and her lips part diminutively. "Watched?"

Shit. She's definitely mad now. I rub the back of my neck. Another nervous tic. I'm completely off my game. I've been reduced to a spineless pussy. "In my defense, it was kind of hard to look away."

"Did you like what you saw?" she asks as though hoping I did.

Now I've been rendered speechless. My jaw goes slack and I shake my head with disbelief. Not only isn't she upset, but she hopes I liked what I saw? *As if there was any doubt.*

Her beautiful eyes bore into mine, hopeful, innocent, sweet.

Too innocent.

Too sweet.

Too fucking tempting.

I need for her to be mad at me. To be disgusted that I stood there ogling her with dirty, perverted thoughts. I remind myself that I can't have her and dig deep to latch on to the small shred of conviction that remains within me to do right by her.

"Sophie," I start, but my damn phone rings. Perfect timing, as always. I snatch the phone from my back pocket. It's the shop. I have to take it. Sophie takes a step back and I hold up my index finger to stop her from leaving. "Yeah?" I answer.

"I need you to come back in," Mick says. "Greyson is here to pick up his Road Glide. Says he paid in full, but your records show he has a remaining balance."

Greyson has been a pain in the ass since he brought his bike in for customization. I didn't want to take the damn job to begin with, but Wrench insisted. We completed the build three weeks ago. The guy was supposed to bring payment for the last twenty-five percent before he could pick it up. I called him two weeks ago, and he said he mailed it. I told him I'd call him when the check cleared. The check never came. Big surprise.

"I'm on my way. Be there in fifteen." I hang up and turn to Sophie. Her face is flushed, and she's fidgety. "I have to go," I take a step closer, "but to answer your question, yes, I liked what I saw. A lot. And that isn't a good thing for either one of us."

"Why?" she whispers and releases a deep breath.

I scan the length of her body, recalling its flawlessness. I'm right on the brink. If only I could reach out, just once, and feel the softness of her skin. Taste her lips. But once would never be enough. I grit my teeth and swallow. "Because you need me to stay away from you and that was nearly impossible to do *before* I saw you in your panties."

She sucks in a quick breath, stunned by my admission. "It was?"

"You have no idea. If you're smart, you'll stay away from me." If I don't leave this instant, what little resolve I have left will disappear. I turn away and say, "Consider yourself warned."

I mount my bike and fire it up taking one last glance at her before tearing out of my driveway.

Damsel In Distress

Yesterday was a close call. I was about six seconds away from saying "fuck it" and giving in to my impulse to tell Sophie the truth about how I feel. If I hadn't left when I did…

Now I'm avoiding her at all costs, with the exception of making sure she gets into her house safe at night. But no more conversations. Not even a simple hello, wave of the hand, or nod.

Absolutely no interaction whatsoever from here on out.

Period.

Otherwise…

Generally, I stop by my house to let Dopey out to pee on my lunch hour. But not today. It's going on three thirty and he's been locked up in the house since six-thirty this morning. Poor dog. It isn't fair to make him suffer, but I'm teetering way too close to the edge. If I went home to let him out and found Sophie lounging in her bikini again, all bets would be off. I might need to hire a dog walker until I can man up and get a grip on this… this… pathetic weakness. She should've left for work by now, so it ought to be safe to run home.

But as luck would have it, Sophie must be running late for work because when I pull up to my house, she's walking to her car. I pull into my driveway and try not to look in her direction, but fail. The moment I turn my head, she trips and falls to the ground. I hear her scream over the noise of my pipes. I kill the engine and run to her side. Pain is etched into her face as she clutches her ankle.

"Shit, are you okay?" I ask.

When she tries to stand, she cries in pain and sits back down. I crouch to her side and take her ankle into my hands, taking care not to hurt her. "Let me see." I raise her pant leg and carefully remove her shoe to assess the damage. She elicits a groan when I rotate her foot. "Already swelling. If it's not broken, it's a hell of a sprain. You need an x-ray."

Without thinking, I scoop her into my arms and carry her toward her car. She's light as a feather in my arms. I try to be gentle as I open the passenger side door and set her inside, but she grimaces with each tiny movement. "I'll be right back." I dart into my house to get a Ziploc bag of ice to minimize the swelling. Poor Dopey runs to me, tail wagging, but I can't attend to him now. When I glance to my right, there's a puddle of urine next to the plant on the floor in the dining room. I yank my phone from my back pocket and text Bear asking him to come clean up and take care of Dopey. "Sorry boy. Uncle Bear is on his way." I scratch his ear and hurry back to Sophie's car and hand her the bag of ice. "Keep this on your ankle."

Sophie hands me her keys and watches me with slightly raised brows as I back out of her driveway. A moment later she puts the bag of ice down and picks up her purse from the foot well.

"Keep that ice on your ankle."

"I need to call work and tell them I'm not coming." She digs through her oversized purse.

Why do chicks carry such large bags, anyway? I've never understood it. It's like they can't leave their house without a full medicine cabinet, a change of clothes, and a collection of cosmetics. After two minutes of watching her dig, I take the purse from her hands. "Keep the ice on your foot."

The first thing I see when I look into the bag is a thirty-eight special. "She packs," I whisper to myself, stunned. I continue to root around for her phone, but if it's in this thing, I'd have to dump out the contents to find it. "How do you find anything in this trash pit?" I chuckle. I take my phone from my back pocket and look up The Grand. "What's your boss's name?"

"Randy."

A snarky girl answers and I tell her I need to speak with Randy. In my peripheral I see Sophie staring at me wide eyed, mouth agape.

After a short wait, Randy gets on the line. "This is Randy."

"Hey, Randy, I'm calling for Sophie Holt."

"Yeah?" he asks.

"She's on her way to Urgent Care. Might've broken her ankle."

"Okay, tell her to call later and keep me posted." He sounds genuinely concerned. "I'll cover her shift for tonight."

"I'll have her call you when she's out."

I end the call and raise up to slide my phone in my back pocket. "You have a nice boss."

"You know where I work?"

"Mm-hmm." *If you only knew all the things I know about you.*

"And my last name?"

I turn and face her with a raised brow. "Does that scare you?"

"No. It just seems you know quite a bit about me."

"You have *no* idea."

She doesn't respond. Instead, she swallows and holds her breath.

"Does *that* scare you?"

"No."

I can tell she means it. I wish she was afraid. I need her to want me to stay away from her. She seriously needs to give me some reason, any reason of her own, to leave her alone, otherwise, I'm going to lose my battle.

I turn away from her and look back to the road. "Well, it should."

"Why?" Her tone is challenging.

I give a sinister chuckle. This is my chance to scare her away. To make her realize I'm no good for her. "You have heard of my Club?"

"I've heard the rumors."

"Rumors?" I ask, and shake my head, incredulous. "That's what you think they are?"

"Life has taught me to only believe what I see firsthand."

She's much too smart for her age. Not surprising given everything she's seen and endured in her short life.

I come to a railroad track and slow down, trying not to hurt her. I've had a sprained ankle and every little movement is agony. "Well, let me tell you, first hand, they're not all rumors." I cast her a stern look to drive home my meaning.

"Is that what you meant when you said," she lifts her hand to make an air quote, "consider yourself warned?"

I clench my teeth and turn back to the road. "That's part of it."

"If you're so bad, why are you helping me?"

I blow out a breath. She isn't going to make this easy on me at all. "I don't know."

In a way it's a lie, but it's also the truth. I'm helping her because I have an undeniable instinct to protect her. But the more I interact with her, the more likely I am to give in to my feelings for her. I can't help it and I don't understand it. What is it about this girl that has me so captivated? What is it about her that makes me want things I've never been the least bit interested in? I've never been a hearts and flowers guy. I'm not a romantic. But if she was mine, I'd give her hearts and flowers. I'd be romantic for her. I'm so fucking conflicted I don't know whether I'm coming or going. I've never been so frustrated in my life.

"I have a hard time believing you do anything without a reason."

"You're perceptive, you know that?"

She leans in to continue challenging me. "So what's your reason for helping me?"

Perceptive and persistent. She wants the truth. Fine. I'll give it to her.

I pull the car over and turn to face her. She'll never want to see me again once I tell her... That thought scares the hell out of me. "Fuck it, here goes. I've been watching you since I moved in three years ago."

She says nothing. Just blinks.

I continue, "The first time I saw you was when you thrashed the girl across the street."

It was the day after I moved into my house. She was visiting Miranda. A chick across the street attacked Miranda over a parking spot in the street. Sophie stepped in to defend her friend. I was sure the hefty girl would get the best of Sophie and almost stepped in to make sure she didn't get hurt. To my astonishment, Sophie drew back a fist and knocked the girl flat on her ass. I was instantly infatuated.

Still no response.

"The second time I saw you, you came to help Mrs. Frank in the garden." Mrs. Frank is Miranda's mom. It was a warm, late Spring day. Sophie was wearing a pink blouse with white shorts. Her nose was sunburnt. I watched the two of them plant flowers along the side of the house for an hour and a half. I could've watched her all day. "You had the face of an angel."

Sophie's mouth falls open, but she still says nothing.

"I watched as you came and went, visiting the Frank's. You washed their cars and helped around the house. But the day you moved in I decided to learn more about you."

I stop to allow her to digest everything I've just said.

Her voice is barely louder than a whisper, "You watch me?"

I think I'm finally getting through to her. I can't stop now. "More than you watch me."

After laying that bomb, I put the car in drive and pull away. Neither of us speak again as I drive to the Urgent Care Center, but she doesn't take her eyes off me.

As I park the car and turn off the engine, I'm torn. Surely, Sophie's afraid of me now that she knows I've been stalking her.

But did I really tell her because I wanted to scare her or rather because I want her to know how much I want her? Either way, I have to finish what I started.

"Sophie, I wasn't kidding when I said I know a lot about you." I twist in my seat to face her. "I know about your childhood. About your mom. About how you left home after she put a gun to your head." I pause a moment before continuing. "I know about the rape."

The color drains from Sophie's face and she shrinks back into her seat. Her eyes are damp with unshed tears. "You know a lot about me."

What I've just confessed doesn't begin to scratch the surface of everything I know about Sophie. In a moment of weakness, I become lost in her eyes. "You're like a walking contradiction. So strong, and yet so frail."

A tear spills down her check and I battle an automatic reflex to reach out and wipe it away. I hate that I've made her cry.

"Now are you scared?" I ask.

"No."

I don't get this girl at all. I was sure that'd send her running.

I shake my head, get out of the car and walk to the passenger side door to help her out. I lift her into my arms carefully, trying desperately not to cause her added pain as I carry her toward the Urgent Care entrance.

So many times I've wondered what it would feel like to hold Sophie in my arms. This isn't how I imagined it, but I'll take what I can get. She smells incredible. A mixture of flowers and citrus. I commit the moment to memory as I'm sure I'll never hold her again.

Just before the sliding doors open she asks, "How can I be afraid of you when all you do is help me?"

Thirty minutes after being taken back for examination, Sophie hobbles into the waiting room on crutches. She puts a written prescription from the doctor into her purse and heads for the exit. I don't need to ask how she's doing. Her pain is evident.

As I pull out of the parking lot my phone rings. Annoyed, I yank it from my back pocket. "Yeah?" I bark into the receiver.

"Honey, it's Mama. I need your help at the house. Mick can't get away from the shop. Can you swing by?"

"I'm tied up right now. I can be there in an hour." Because I'm not paying attention, I hit a manhole in the road. Sophie makes a face and leans back against the head rest. I turn to her and mouth the words "I'm sorry."

Sounds good," Mom says. "Thanks, honey."

"I'll call when I'm on my way," I tell her and end the call.

"I never knew sprained ankles hurt this bad," Sophie says. "Miranda had one once, and I thought she was such a wuss."

"A wuss?" I chuckle. Do people actually use that word? She's just too cute.

She laughs with me and I feel something squeeze in my chest. I adore the sound of her laughter.

I pull into the pharmacy parking lot and turn to face her. It hasn't escaped my attention that she never asked me to take her to fill it. "Where's your script? I'll go in and get it."

"I'm not filling it."

"What? Why?"

"I'll just take ibuprofen."

She can't be serious. "Ibuprofen won't touch that."

Her gaze drops to her hands, and she sinks into her seat. I immediately understand what's happening here. She can't afford the prescription. My gut twists.

"Give me the script." I snap my fingers.

"I can't afford it," she squeaks.

My heart breaks. "Sophie, you need the pills. Give me the script."

She shakes her head, refusing to make eye contact. "I can't let you buy my medicine."

I'll be damned if she's going to be laid up in misery. I'm buying her those damn pills. I don't care how much they cost. "Give. Me. The. Script."

She turns to me with sad eyes. "You barely know me. Well, I barely know you. You're not paying for my prescription."

I grab her purse and snatch the prescription out before she can stop me. She hollers at me, but it's too late. I'm already jogging toward the store entrance.

When I return to the car and hand her the bag, she asks how much it cost.

"Don't worry about it." It didn't cost much, but if I tell her, she'll insist on paying it back.

Her mouth falls open as she stares. "I want to pay you back."

I shoot her a look. "Sophie, I said don't worry about it."

"Thank you." She holds up the bag. "Again."

"No problem."

We sit in an awkward silence for a few miles. I'm not big on small talk. I figure if you're going to say something, it should be meaningful and important—not just hollow words to fill the empty spaces. I can't afford to have meaningful conversation with Sophie. There's too much at stake for her and I'm hanging on by a thread as it is. Desperate to fill the uncomfortable silence, I hit the power button on the radio. When it comes on, it's so loud I damn near come out of my seat.

Sophie howls with laughter. Of course, the CD she has in the stereo is playing a lame ass pop song sung by a former boy bander. I'm not surprised. It's seems to be all she listens to these days. Last week she had it on blast with all the windows in her house open as she was cleaning. Damn near drove me insane.

"Seriously?" I ask, wondering what exactly she finds appealing about this music.

"It's a good song."

There is nothing good about this song. I feel emasculated just listening to it. I stop the CD and turn the radio on to favorite rock station. "Now this is good music."

"It is."

"You like this?" I've never heard her play this kind of music.

"I'm nondiscriminatory when it comes to music."

I nod with a smile as I take in this piece of new information.

Sophie taps her fingers to the beat. When the song comes to an end she turns down the volume. "This makes three times you've helped me," she points out.

I try to shrug it off. I wish she'd just let it go and not make a big deal out of it. Even if I didn't feel the way I do about her, I would've helped. It's just in my nature to be helpful and do right by people. It's how I was raised.

"Since you know so much about me," she says, "it's only fair you tell me a little about yourself."

I shift in my seat. "You don't want to know me, Sophie. Take my word for it."

"Yes, I do."

No matter what I say, she won't let this go. But I can't give in. I need to get her home as fast as possible and get the hell away from her before I do something foolish.

"I'm waiting." She taps the top of her thigh with her fingertips.

"Give it up, Sophie," I grumble.

"If you can find out things about me, I can do the same."

I throw my head back and laugh. "Go ahead. Maybe you'll learn something that'll convince you to stay away from me."

I only say the words for dramatic effect. I'm sure she's heard quite enough about me to have drawn her conclusion by now. The rumors circulating about me and my Club, although grossly exaggerated, should have been enough to have her running as fast as she can in the opposite direction. Yet, here she is demanding to get to know me.

"Obviously that's not what you want."

I contemplate my response and decide not to deny it. "It's what's best for you."

"But it's not what you want," she presses.

It's not even close to what I want.

What I want is to pull this car over, grab her by the face and kiss her like she's never been kissed by anyone else. To tell her I'm going to protect and take care of her for the rest of her life. The only thing stopping me is fear that it will do her more harm than good. I can protect her better from a distance.

Just keep driving. Get her home and walk away.

No.

Run away.

Fast.

And don't turn back.

Conflicted

S ophie stares at me with knowing, defiant eyes.

What the hell am I going to do now? I mutter an expletive.

"I'll decide what's best for me," she says. "All I'm asking is to get to know you."

"Sophie, I'm a bad guy," I say in what I know is a futile attempt to deter her.

"You keep saying that, but I beg to differ," she argues. "You came to my defense after Mike tried to attack me. You took me to the doctor today and paid for my prescription. Bad guys don't do things like that."

I slam on the brakes and jerk the car to the side of the road. The two boys playing tag in the yard to our right stop and gawk at us upon hearing the screech of the tires. A second before I pull her in for a kiss, I come to my senses.

"What is the matter with you?" Exasperated, I throw my hands in the air. "How are you not freaked the fuck out right now? I've basically admitted that I've been stalking you for three years. I'm a fucking one percenter, Sophie! Any other girl would run in the opposite direction, terrified." Well, not any other girl. I have plenty of girls chasing after me wanting to catch and tie down an elusive bad boy. It's the good girls who run from me. Sophie is definitely a good girl, so this makes zero sense.

"I'm not afraid of you."

I know she isn't. And rightfully so. I'd never hurt Sophie. But how does she know that?

Nothing I say will change her mind. I tip my head back, exhale sharply and count to ten, trying to get a grip on my conflicted emotions, but it's impossible. Without a word, I put the car in drive and pull away.

We pull up to her house and I get her crutches from the back seat before helping her out of the car. When she slips her hand into mine, I make a mental note of how soft, and delicate it is. This'll be the last time I hold it. For her sake, it has to be.

Sophie unlocks her front door. She reaches for her purse and prescription, but I wave for her to go inside. She can't carry them while walking on her crutches.

"What happened?" Miranda asks and shoots up from the couch. Her eyes vacillate between the two of us with surprise.

"It's a bad sprain," I answer.

Miranda looks at me, but asks Sophie, "Why didn't you call me?"

"It happened really fast," Sophie answers and hobbles to the couch. "Rooter was there when it happened."

"Where?" Miranda asks.

"In the front yard on my way to work," Sophie replies as I follow behind her.

"She needs a glass of water to take her pills," I say to Miranda, if only to get her out of the room.

"Sure," the girl says, and goes into the kitchen.

I take Sophie's crutches and help lower her onto the couch. How will she get around and fend for herself once I'm gone? Her roommate seems more concerned with how's, why's, and my involvement than in helping Sophie.

"Thank you," Sophie says once she's seated.

"You gonna be okay here?" My eyes dart toward the kitchen.

"Yeah, Miranda will help me."

I told myself I would drop her off and leave as quickly as possible, but I can't walk away without some peace of mind that she'll be taken care of. I'm the only person I trust to give her the help she needs. "What's your number?" I ask as I take my phone out of my back pocket. She rattles off her number and I program it into my phone. "I'll text you with mine so you'll have it if you need anything."

She tips her head to the side. Her expression is a mixture of surprise and confusion. "You don't want me to know you, but you're giving me your number so I can call you for help?"

"I'm aware of the irony," I smirk, "but I want to make sure you have the help you need."

"I'm sorry, where's the bad boy persona you keep warning me about?"

This definitely hasn't helped convince her to stay away from me. But I'm not sure anything would at this point. "I gotta go."

She smiles and flashes her killer sexy dimples. "Thanks, again."

"See ya, Sophie."

I've always thought Sophie was prettiest in the morning with her wild hair and sleepy eyes. This morning is no exception. But the face she makes as she hobbles to her dining room table with her coffee conveys her pain. Miranda doesn't help even though she's mere feet away and it's obvious that Sophie's in agony. Instead, the girl just stands there running her dick-sucker—probably rambling on about some schmuck she met at Starbucks. It's clear from the look on Sophie's face she wishes Miranda would shut up and leave for work already.

Their friendship puzzles me. They're polar opposites. Sophie is laid back and relaxed, thoughtful, introspective and reserved until otherwise provoked. Miranda is loud, boisterous, opinionated and judgmental. She acts high and mighty, as though she is the epitome of all things moral. While I wouldn't categorize her as a slut, I don't have enough fingers and toes to count the number of times I've caught her giving head or being fingered by her boyfriend on their back porch in the middle of the day. Meanwhile, Sophie would probably still be a virgin had her ex-boyfriend not… Just thinking about it makes me want to track the fucker down and give him another beating. I guarantee he won't be fathering any children. I'd be surprised if his dick still works after being smashed with a brick.

Miranda acts superior to Sophie, and she's not. Not even close. Not that she's a bad person. She's just… typical. There's nothing at all typical about Sophie.

I watch for ten more minutes as Sophie rolls her eyes behind Miranda's back as she continues to yap on and on. Every now and then Sophie gives a one word response to whatever the girl is saying. Sophie's animated facial expressions make me chuckle. Finally, Miranda slings her purse over her shoulder and leaves. The instant she's out of the house Sophie's shoulders relax, and she closes her eyes as she takes a long sip of her coffee.

I pull my phone from my back pocket and stare at the screen for probably three minutes, battling with myself over whether texting Sophie is a good idea. I said I'd cut all communication with her. But I also vowed to keep her safe. Texting is safe. Relatively speaking. It's not the same as talking face to face or even on the phone where I can hear her voice.

Me: I saw Miranda left. Will she be gone long?

I don't know why I ask since I already know the answer. Unless Miranda has made other arrangements with her schedule, she'll be at work until at least five o'clock. I watch as Sophie picks up her phone. Something in my chest contracts as a smile spreads across her face.

Sophie: She went to work. She'll be home after 5:00.

Me: *U gonna be okay while she's gone?*

Sophie: *I think so.*

That's not good enough. I need assurance she'll be okay.

Me: *Do u have everything u need?*

Sophie: *For now.*

Me: *If u need anything, text me.*

She smiles again, and this one is twice the size of the first. I love making her smile.

Sophie: *Okay. Thank you.*

The giddy expression she's wearing excites me like a pubescent boy. I force myself to put my phone in my pocket and turn away from the window. That's enough for now. I've made my point. If she needs me, she'll text me.

I leave for work, but don't make it two miles before remembering Mike is with Sophie. Who knows what he might try with her in a weakened condition. I pull into a parking lot and send Sophie another text: *Will u be alone with Mike all day?*

Sophie: *I'm not sure.*

Me: *If u have any trouble with him text me. I can be there in fifteen minutes.*

Sophie: *And you call me a walking contradiction…*

She's right. I'm sending her mixed signals. Telling her she's better off not knowing me while doing everything in my power to prove myself wrong.

To hell with it. I can't fight this any longer, and I won't. I can't not be in her life. No matter how dangerous it is, I can't stay away. I've known it all along. I was always going to make Sophie mine.

All this back and forth fighting with myself was my way of making myself feel better about it. My way of making myself believe I was putting her best interests above my selfish desire.

A sense of relief falls over me and I let out a deep breath. Tonight, I'm making my intentions known.

You don't know it yet, but you're mine Sophie Holt.

Halfway through the day Pop reminds me it's Sparrow's birthday. The Club is throwing him a party. I'd never skip out on the birthday celebration of one of our guys. Sparrow is a hell of a guy and I've known him forever. But this party is coming at the worst possible time and being held at the worst possible place. The strip club Candace works at. She's not dancing tonight, she's serving, which is worse because it guarantees a lot of interaction and personal attention.

The instant I walk in the door of Mounds and Rounds, Candace comes bouncing over in a shiny red thong and matching pasties. The guys all go wild. They think I should marry her. Well, most of them do. Bear is one exception. Andy is the other. He's had a thing for her for years. It's yet another reason he hates me. If you ask me, it's the biggest reason.

"Hey, Baby," she says and leans in to grab my dick, garnering several hoots and hollers from my crew.

"Candace," I grumble and remove her hand.

She leads me to the round table in the middle of the room which is basically a standalone stage with chairs surrounding it. She pulls out a chair for me and once I'm seated perches on my lap. Here I am, planning to knock on Sophie's door tonight to confess my intentions to her, and Candace is sitting on my lap pressing her tits against my chest.

"Miss me yet?" she coos in my ear and nips at my earlobe with her teeth.

Not at all.

But I need to be careful. One wrong word could set her off and I don't want to ruin Sparrow's party.

"I may be kinky," I tell her and pull away, "but I don't put on shows."

"I can't help it," she whines. "I miss you, Rooter."

"This isn't the time or place, Candace."

"Later?" she asks, her eyes full of hope.

I feel terrible. I don't want to hurt Candace. She isn't a bad person. I should've known better than to get involved with her in the first place. While I don't want to give her false hope, I need to tread lightly. "We'll see."

She lights up with a smile. "Okay."

The table is full with Mick to my right and Bear to my left. Music pulsates through the room and Candace gets up from my lap. Sparrow's favorite dancer Heather comes onto the stage. She's a beautiful girl, but all I can think of is Sophie and how I can't wait to get home to talk to her.

But the night drags on and on. I find myself checking the time on my phone every ten or fifteen minutes. I frown when I see it's going on ten o'clock. Sophie could be in bed by the time I get home. I don't want to wait until tomorrow to talk to her. I want to hear her voice and see those bright, sparkling blue eyes tonight.

"Okay, Brother, time to come clean," Bear says, snapping me from my thoughts.

"What?"

"Who is she?"

I pull my eyebrows together. "Who is who?"

"Come on, man." He grins as he eyes the phone I'm clutching. "You've had bare ass in your face all night and you haven't even noticed."

I try to play it off with a shrug. "I've seen it all before."

"So have I and it's just as hot as the first time." He glances up just as Piper crawls toward him with a pair of swinging double D's. She leans up just inches from his face and squeezes her tits, pinching the nipples. "A man doesn't ignore tits like these unless he's got other tits on the brain."

"You know what? You're right," I come clean, sort of. "I've got tits on the brain. In fact, it's time for me to go see them."

"Alright man. Have fun."

Piper pulls his face into her chest. Bear's the only guy she does that with. She's been hot for him for years, but he won't go there.

While he might enjoy watching her dance, strippers aren't his thing. He prefers good, clean girls. We have that in common.

"You too," I chuckle and stand from my chair.

Candace runs to my side. "Leaving already?"

"Yeah. I have to let the dog out."

"Such a good daddy," she says and rubs my head. I hate it when she does that. I start to walk away but she grabs me by the arm. "I thought you said we'd hookup later."

"I didn't say that."

"Yeah you did, and it's all I've been able to think about." She leans in and grabs my junk, sliding her hand up and down my length. "I saw the way you've been checking the time on your phone. You haven't even looked at any of the other girls. Admit it. You miss me."

I'm in serious trouble here. I take her hand into mine to get it off my crotch. "Candace…"

"Yeah, Baby?"

I squeeze my eyes shut. I don't know what the fuck to do. When I open them, she's looking up at me with sweet, hopeful brown eyes. I'm such an asshole. "I care about you. As a friend. We can't do this anymore."

"You care about me as more than a friend, Rooter. You said it yourself."

What the hell is she talking about? I never said any such thing. "When did I ever say that?"

"About a month ago." She squeezes my hand. "That night you came over drunk and passed out. In your sleep, you said I make you feel things you've never felt and that you want me in a way you've never wanted anyone else."

I remember that night.

Barely.

It was after the Sunday family dinner at my parent's. My mom sat me down to talk. She told me she was worried that being in the Club was holding me back from finding real happiness. That too much of my time was wrapped up in the Club and I needed more out of life to be truly happy. She told me what happened to Bear was tragic, but just because it happened to him doesn't mean it'll happen to me. She and Pop have been together all this time and everyone is fine. She's never felt safer. Being Double H doesn't guarantee a relationship would end in tragedy. She told me I'm too full of love to live a life without it. Wasting my time on casual hookups won't fill the void in my life, and while Candace will always be considered family, she isn't right for me. Mom says I'm a "kind, loving boy who needs to find a good, sweet girl." I don't know about being a kind, loving boy, but Sophie is definitely a good, sweet girl. She's the perfect girl. If my mom only knew I'd already found her…

Our conversation left me torn. When I got home that night Sophie was in her room watching television. Her hair was in a messy bun and she was in a pink sweatshirt and black yoga pants. Every now and again she'd glance toward my window, but my light was out so she couldn't see me. With a bottle of Jack in hand I sat on the edge of my bed fantasizing. I imagined being in her room with her watching TV. I imagined holding her close and breathing in her scent. I thought about what it would feel like to press my lips against hers. Every time her eyes turned my way it pushed me closer to running over and knocking on her door—right to the point that I was on my way, but three steps into her yard my phone rang. It was Candace, of course. Desperate to get my mind off Sophie, I went to her. If I hadn't, I would've knocked on Sophie's door and the rest would be history.

All I can surmise is if I had said those things, I must've been talking in my sleep. I dream of Sophie almost every night and in my dreams, I usually say those exact things to her.

"Candace, I don't know what I said, but—" She cuts me off before I can continue, which may be a good thing because I don't know what I was going to say anyway.

"Why can't you just admit you have feelings for me, Rooter? It won't make you less of a man."

"Candace, we have a lot of history. I don't want to screw up our friendship."

"It won't screw it up. It'll make it better." She leans her body into mine. "Trust me."

I take a step back and look at her apologetically. "I'm sorry, Candace. In time you'll realize I'm right."

"Well, I think in time you'll realize how much you miss me." She crosses her arms like a defiant child. "So I'll just wait until you come to your senses."

I can't get home fast enough. The entire way there, I consider possible scenarios of what I might say and how Sophie might react. When I pull into my driveway and see that Sophie's bedroom light is on, my adrenaline rushes from excitement. I want to run straight to her door, but after spending the past few hours in a smoke-filled strip club with Candace pressed up against me, I feel dirty and tainted. I can't confess my undying devotion to Sophie until I've cleaned up.

After letting Dopey out, I dart up the stairs and flip on my bedroom light. My eyes flit to Sophie's window expecting to see her. But it's not her that I see. There's a guy in her room. I've never seen him before. He's tall with long hair and covered in tattoos. He takes off his shirt and lays down. In. Her. Bed.

What the fuck?

Who is this asshole?

Why is he in Sophie's bed?

A minute later, her door opens, and she walks in. He lifts the blanket, and she crawls in with him.

I shake my head and do a double take.

In the next instant her gorgeous, bright blue eyes meet mine. My heart rams against my chest. My Sophie is in bed with another guy.

This is a sign. This is God's way of stopping me from going to her. I'm not supposed to be with her. She deserves better than me. Maybe mister tall, dark and tattooed can give it to her.

This is a good thing.

Maybe not for me. But definitely for her.

I walk to my window and snap my blinds shut. This is it. I'm done. I'm going to do whatever it takes to get Sophie Holt out of my mind.

Bent Out Of Shape

Of all the shit luck in the world, Sophie is sitting on her porch when I pull up to my house after work. She never sits on her porch. Is she waiting for me? She texted me earlier asking if I was busy and I lied and said I was. She asked me to call her when I was free, but I never did. Maybe she needed help with something. Now I feel like a dick for not calling her back. But if she needed help, why not call the guy who stayed with her last night?

She waves at me as I ride past her to my garage. As I open my back door to let Dopey out, she calls my name. At the sound of her voice, Dopey charges after her. I take off after him, but I'm no match for his speed. "Shit! Dopey, stop!"

Without slowing down, he leaps into the air and knocks Sophie to the ground.

"You all right?"

"Yeah." When she moves to sit up, she bites her lip and sucks in a breath.

I wrap my arms around her to help her stand before handing her the crutches. "Sorry about that."

"It's okay," she says, but she's wobbly on her feet. She flashes a smile. "Really."

"Sorry I didn't get back to you. It was a busy day."

"No worries." She shrugs.

She stole my line. How cute is that? I can't help but smile. "So, what did you need earlier?"

"I don't remember now."

If you don't remember, why were you out here waiting for me? "Oh, okay." An awkward moment passes. "How's the ankle?"

"Hurts like hell. I can't do much of anything for myself."

"Miranda helping you?"

"When she can, but she has her job and school. She hasn't had time to even get to the grocery. Which reminds me why I texted you earlier."

Great. She probably texted me because she was hungry and I ignored her. I'm an asshole. With my hands in my pockets, I rock back and forth on my heels. "Yeah?"

"Would you mind running me to the grocery store?"

Miranda's car is here so I assume she's home. She can't be so busy that she'd send Sophie to the store on crutches. What kind of *best friend* does that? Bear and I aren't roommates, but if he was on crutches, I'd do everything I could to help the guy out. "Miranda isn't able to go?"

Sophie shakes her head. "She's completing an exam online and midnight is the deadline."

I know I told her to call or text if she needed help, but am I really the only person she can ask? I'm trying to forget about this girl. How can I do that if I'm granting favors and spending time with her? Besides, she has other friends. What about the guy from last night? If they're close enough to sleep together, she can ask him for help. "I'm kind of busy, Sophie. Is there anyone *else* who can help you?"

"Not really, but if you aren't able to, I understand. No worries."

There she goes using my words again. She's so damn adorable. I can't say no. "Okay. I'll take you."

"Thank you so much!" she squeals. "You have no idea what this means to me."

I chuckle at her exuberance. "It's not that big of a deal. I'm just taking you to the grocery."

"There's literally *no* food in my house, so yes, this is a *very* big deal."

I pull my eyebrows together in a frown. "No food? Are you serious?"

"Completely."

She must've known this yesterday. One doesn't run out of food overnight. Couldn't she have asked her boyfriend, or whatever he is to take her? They spent the night together doing God knows what, but she couldn't ask him to take her grocery shopping? I can't hide my resentment.

"Why didn't your," I clear my throat, "*friend*, take you shopping last night?"

Caught off guard by my question, she pauses before answering. "He brought me dinner."

"Well, at least he did that much."

She doesn't respond, but the corner of her mouth turns up diminutively.

Being in the confined space of my truck with Sophie has me on fire. Her sweet, floral scent is driving me out of my mind. I can't stop staring. Her upswept hair reveals a long, graceful neck that I bet tastes as good as she smells. And her thighs in those short shorts… I'm going to die if we don't get out of here soon. Then again, it wouldn't be a terrible way to go. If only I could lean in, just once, and breathe her in and taste her skin…

Sophie busts me for staring and I snap my attention back to the road.

I try to make small talk to distract myself, but it hardly helps.

Finally, we arrive at the store. As soon as I've parked the truck, Sophie clutches her door handle. I reach across and place my hand on hers to stop her. A spark travels from my fingertips to my chest. "Wait here," I tell her and slowly pry my hand from hers.

I hop out of the truck, still reeling from the feeling of her hand in mine. How can such an innocent, insignificant touch affect me in such a powerful way? I take a deep breath and remove her crutches from the truck bed before opening her door.

"Turn and face me," I instruct. "Wrap your arms around my neck and I'll lower you to the pavement."

She drapes her arms around my neck and I place my hands on her hips and pull her close. Her body is flush against mine as I ever so slowly lower her to the pavement. This may be the last opportunity I have to hold her this close, I might as well enjoy it.

"Thank you," she whispers, her face flushed.

Inside the store, our first stop is the produce department where Sophie meticulously searches through every package of strawberries for the very best one. After double checking each and every package, she narrows them down to three. She takes one last look at each before finally making her selection. I hold my hand over my mouth to suppress my laughter. When we move on to the apples, she does the same thing. Then again with the grapes, and so on. We spend twenty minutes just picking over the fruit before moving on to vegetables. But I don't mind. It's entertaining.

In the international food aisle Sophie comes to an abrupt halt and her face contorts into an expression of pain.

"You okay?" I ask.

"I'm fine."

"I should've just taken the damn list and come for you." Not long ago I was lambasting Miranda for making Sophie come to the store. I'm no better.

"I'm okay." She gives me a small, forced smile. "I prefer to do my own shopping. I'm picky about brands."

I reach into the cart and hold up store brand mini wheats and generic Hamburger Helper. "Really? Because everything in this cart is generic."

"Not everything." Her face turns scarlet as she points to a block of Velveeta cheese and a six pack of Stewarts Root Beer.

"Pardon me." I can't contain my laughter. "Let's make sure to get brand name processed cheese."

Sophie joins me in a fit of laughter, but the moment of levity is ruined when an impatient asshole hits Sophie's injured ankle with his cart. Sophie whimpers in pain and I grab a hold of the guy. "What the fuck, man? You hit her."

"I—I'm sorry. I didn't mean to hurt your girlfriend, I was just trying to get by."

"The words excuse me exist for a reason shithead." I squeeze his shoulder with all my strength causing him to grimace.

"I'm sorry. Really," he says.

"You're sorry?" I ask. "Did you not see her crutches or didn't that matter to you when you rammed your cart into her?"

Sophie touches my shoulder and says she's okay.

"No, you're not!" I grit my teeth.

The guy's bottom lip quivers as he apologizes again.

"Why are you apologizing to me?" I ask. "She's the one you rammed with your cart!"

He turns to Sophie. "I really am sorry, Miss."

"It was our fault," she says, which infuriates me even more. "We were taking up the aisle."

This was not our fault. "Do not make excuses for him, Sophie!"

"I could've said excuse me," the guy says.

"Yes, you could have," I growl.

Sophie squeezes my shoulder. "It's done now. Let him go."

"Watch where you're going from now on." I let go of the pot-bellied dipshit and watch as he hurries away.

"You act like he took my leg off," Sophie chides me. "It wasn't that big of a deal."

"It was to me."

She tilts her head to the side. "Why?"

"Because it was inconsiderate." I point at her crutches. "He saw that you're on crutches. He could've said excuse me."

"Maybe he thought he could get by."

I pinch the bridge of my nose and exhale sharply. She might be okay with people disrespecting her, but I'm not. I refuse to allow it to happen while I'm around. "He fucked up and deserved to be called out on it."

"The guy was scared to death. I'm surprised he didn't piss himself."

"Now that would've been funny."

Unimpressed, Sophie spins around and walks away. Panic smacks me square in the chest and I reach out and stop her. "I wasn't going to hurt him, Sophie. I was just trying to teach him a lesson."

"I'd say you succeeded," she says flatly.

"Are you mad at me?"

"No." She shakes her head. "I appreciate you standing up for me, but you took it a little too far."

"I'm sorry."

She arches a brow and tilts her head. "Really?"

I can't lie to her. "I'm not sorry about calling him out. But maybe I went a little too far. It's just that he hurt you… It was inexcusable."

"Well, thank you for coming to my rescue." She smiles. "Again."

When we get back to Sophie's house, Mike is sitting on the couch. His eyes flit to mine. He's clearly unhappy to see me, but too scared to say anything.

"We gonna have a problem?" I ask.

"No," he croaks.

I turn to Sophie and tell her I'll be right back. I grab a load of groceries from the truck and as I reach the front door, I overhear Mike talking to Sophie.

"…Miranda was going to the store tonight because you aren't supposed to be walking."

Sophie lied about Miranda being busy? Why? To get me to take her? At first, I'm flattered and even a little smug. But my flattery quickly turns to annoyance when I remember she spent the night with another guy. To my knowledge, he's the first guy she's been with since her ex. She's never brought anyone home and no one, not even her ex ever stayed the night. She must be in a relationship with this new guy. Why go to all the trouble to get me to take her? She should have asked him. I'm sure he wouldn't appreciate his girlfriend making excuses to spend time with another guy. And frankly, I don't appreciate it either. If she's with someone else, she needs to leave me alone.

Sophie shuffles into the kitchen behind me. Burning with curiosity, I turn to face her.

"So, you lied to get me to take you to the store?"

"Rooter, I'm sorry. I just…" Her voice trails off, and she looks to the floor.

"Why?"

"Because it's the only thing I could come up with to get you to hang out with me."

I laugh at the absurdity. "What?"

She peers at me, eyes full of shame and embarrassment. "You're dead set against me getting to know you, so it wasn't like I could call to chat or ask you to come over."

I pinch the space between my eyes and exhale. "Sophie, it's for your own good. Deep down, you know I'm right."

"No, I don't and you won't give me a chance to prove you wrong."

I'm damned close to asking why she's so concerned with proving me wrong if she has a boyfriend? I opt for a different tactic. One that'll hopefully convince her to leave me alone. "What you saw in the store tonight... That's who I am. Do you really want to be around that?"

"You were defending me."

"Why do you constantly make excuses for people?"

"I'm not making excuses," she stands firm. "It's what I believe."

Exasperated, I blow out a breath and back away. I'll be damned if I'll allow her to chase after me when she belongs to someone else. "You know what I believe? You need to forget about me. Forget about me and focus your attention on the guy who woke up in your bed this morning."

I need to get out of here. With impeccable timing, Miranda enters the kitchen. I bark something to her about helping with the groceries and storm off.

Sophie shouts in a panicked voice, "Rooter, last night wasn't what it looked like! Rooter!"

"It really doesn't matter!"

Once I'm inside my house I collapse onto the couch and blow out a deep breath. Rocking back and forth, I drag my hands up and down my thighs, trying to get a grip on the contradicting thoughts spinning through my mind.

I can't keep doing this to myself. I'm the one who decided I can't be with Sophie. Why the hell am I so bent out of shape over her being with another guy? I am not *this* guy. I don't get worked up or jealous over girls. I don't obsess over them and I sure as hell don't stalk them. Women throw themselves at my feet all day, every day. What is it about Sophie Holt that has me bound by the balls? She's just a girl for fuck sake.

This has to stop. Right this instant. If I don't get away from her and put some real distance between us, I'll lose my damn mind.

Perhaps I already have.

Twenty minutes later Sophie's face lights up the screen of my phone—a picture I took of her sitting in her backyard. She was reading a book and must've come across something funny because she threw her head back in one of her full-bodied laughs. It was beautiful. I wish I had captured it on video. Rather than letting the call go to voicemail, I hit reject hoping she'll take the hint.

As soon as the ringing stops, I go to my phone's camera roll to look at the picture again. I stare at it for several minutes before scrolling through the rest of the pictures I've taken of her. My second favorite is one of her in her room looking at my window.

My phone rings. Yet again, I press reject. A few seconds later I get a voicemail notification followed by a text. I don't bother to check either message. The sound of Sophie's voice would break me. I'd just end up calling her back and who knows what that could lead to.

Who am I kidding? I know exactly what it would lead to. It'd lead to me marching over there and telling her to ditch what's-his-name because I'm making her mine.

The voicemail notification on the screen taunts me. I press delete and immediately regret it. Now I'll never know what she said. And if she calls back now, I'll definitely answer. If I answer I'm sure to do something incredibly stupid—something along the lines of ruining her life.

I go to my phone's settings to block her number. Better safe than sorry.

To put the cherry on top of my already stellar evening, Pop calls to tell me Big Boy, the V.P. of the Double H Detroit charter passed away of a heart attack. We are all leaving for Detroit first thing in the morning.

I've known Big Boy since I was a young boy. He was one of the original Halsey members before starting a charter in Detroit with Marx, another former Halsey member. But Big boy never took care of himself. He smoked like a freight train and lived on a steady diet of fried chicken. Last time we spoke, he was so out of breath he could barely talk. His lungs were so congested he couldn't laugh without choking. Recently, there had been talk of him handing over his VP patch due to his condition. Although I knew his health wasn't the greatest, I never imagined he would die so soon. He was only fifty-one years old. Yet another reminder that life is fragile and fleeting.

I toss my phone and it makes a loud clunk when it hits the coffee table. Clutching the back of my head with both hands, I let out a long breath and fall back onto the couch.

Normally when I go out of town, Mama or Isa takes care of Dopey for me. But Isa is in Chicago with a friend. Mom and all the Club wives will be attending the funeral. It's too late tonight to arrange boarding and I won't have time in the morning. Dopey is my main man, my buddy. I don't trust him with just anyone.

As I wrack my brain for ideas, my phone pings with a text. It's Candace. I hadn't considered asking her. While she isn't my first choice, I trust she wouldn't put my boy in harm's way. She's watched him in the past when I've been in a pinch.

Candace: *Hey sexy. I know u miss me. Come over.*

Me: *Can't. Headed to Detroit in the AM. I was wondering if I could hire u to watch Dopey for me while I'm gone? $100 a day. Shouldn't be more than a few days.*

Candace: *I'm happy to help, but I can't bring him here. My new landlord doesn't allow dogs.*

Under normal circumstances, I'd never allow anyone other than family or Club members to stay in my house. But these aren't normal circumstances and I've known Candace forever.

Me: *Stay at my house. I'll leave keys under the mat on the front porch.*

Candace: *I can come by tonight.*

Me: *Big Boy died today. I'm heading out at first light. Got a lot to do between now and then. If you can get to Dopey by late morning, that would be perfect.*

Candace: *I'm so sorry, Rooter. I know he meant a lot to you. I'll be there in the morning. And don't worry about your boy. You know I'll take good care of him.*

I don't remember falling asleep. Last thing I remember is putting the TV on after texting Candace. I check my watch for the time. It's late, or early depending on how you look at it. Dopey lies in front of the stairs like he always does when he's ready for bed. He won't go up without me. With a groan, I stretch and push myself up from the couch to finish off the night in the comfort of my bed.

I walk into my room and flip on the light. Sophie's bedroom light is on. I'm surprised to see her awake at this late hour. The instant she sees me she throws her window open and hollers that she needs to talk to me. The entire neighborhood can probably hear her. I consider opening my window, but decide against it. It's the middle of the night. I'm physically and mentally exhausted and in a few hours, I'll be on my way to Detroit to say goodbye to a dear friend. I walk over to my window and snap the blinds shut. I know it's rude, but I just can't talk to her right now.

The mattress shakes as Dopey circles round and round at the foot of the bed trying to get into the perfect sleeping position. "Dude, pick a spot already."

As I try to fall asleep, Sophie's words play on repeat, "Last night wasn't what it looked like." What the hell does that mean? That she didn't fuck the guy? Even if she didn't, she must be seeing him. Why else would he spend the night? I grab the pillow next to mine and smash it against my face and groan.

If Bear was acting like this, I'd tell him to man up and grow a pair. Either stake his claim on the girl or drop it. Stop with the drama. But it's easier said than done. If I was deciding based on my own desire, I'd pursue Sophie, but I'm trying to do what's best for her.

As upset as I am over Big Boy's death, this trip couldn't be coming at a better time. Maybe time away will do me some good.

Hopefully I can return with a fresh perspective and with my thoughts and emotions in check. I can't continue to drive myself crazy with this back and forth nonsense. While I'm gone I will decide, once and for all, what I'm going to do. Either I'll stake my claim or I'll drop it.

The Mistake

The pain in my head is like an icepick being repeatedly rammed into the side of my skull. Even worse than that is waking up to Candace's naked body draped over mine. Dread and regret are like a thousand pound weight on my chest. I'm such an idiot.

She's going to assume this means I've changed my mind. I haven't. Even if I explain that last night was purely alcohol induced, it won't matter. All that'll matter to her is that we had sex, and I allowed her to stay the night. Something I've never done no matter how drunk I've been.

But last night I was more than drunk. I was in a full blown existential crisis. Big Boy's death took a toll on me. It got me thinking about the life I lead and the things I've done… my mortality. If I died today, God wouldn't welcome me into Heaven. I wouldn't deserve it. What about Big Boy? I considered him a good man, but did God? Big Boy and I led similar lives being in the Club. We both lived by the same moral code and made similar choices. If I'm not worthy of Heaven, how could he have been?

Those thoughts led to many more questions and no answers. What is meaning of life and what is my purpose? Are my circumstances the result of freewill or is my life predestined? Does my existence hold any value? Will I grow old or die young? Will I have enough time to earn God's love and forgiveness? Will I ever try to earn it? Or will I just go on doing the same thing day in and day out? Why was I born into this particular life? Why did my biological father abandon me? Should I be angry or grateful? Would I be different if he hadn't? Would I be a better man?

I love Mick. He has been there for me my entire life. He raised me as his own and loved me as though I am his blood. I am proud to call him my father and to be a member of Double H. I wouldn't want it any other way. I can't imagine life without my Club brothers. I can't imagine being anyone other than who I am. So why do I harbor such guilt and uncertainty?

Perhaps it's because I know that one day, I will answer to God for the things I've done. Though I only inflict pain on the wicked, it doesn't make it right. I am no man's judge or jury, yet I have deliberated several men's guilt, laid out many sentences. I have taken it upon myself to act as their God. And I'd do it again if only because it kept children from becoming drug addicts, girls from becoming prostitutes, and saved the lives of the innocents we have vowed to serve and protect. When my time comes, I will admit to it all and I'll ask for forgiveness. It's all I can do. The rest is up to Him.

By the time I returned home yesterday, I was completely mind fucked. Candace was here and saw the state I was in. She poured me a drink which led to several more, which led to poor decision making on my behalf.

I crane my neck to check the time and when I do, Candace stirs. She looks up at me with sleepy, but satisfied eyes. "It's early, go back to sleep."

Eight-twenty may be early for her, but it's late for me. I never sleep this late. And Dopey's standing at the door, shuffling from paw to paw, waiting for me to take him out. He's usually out before seven. I can't expect him suffer because I put one on last night.

"I gotta let the dog out," I mumble and nudge her off me.

When I sit up, the throbbing in my head intensifies a thousand times. Once the whooshing subsides, I grab my jeans from the floor and slide them on. Dopey races down the stairs ahead of me and whines by the back door as he waits impatiently for me to open it. Even with sunglasses, the bright morning sun is excruciating.

I glance at Sophie's window. Her blinds are drawn. Another wave of nausea strikes as I recall the disgust in her eyes when she saw me with Candace in my room last night.

While away, I was also able think about my situation with Sophie. As I deliberated my life and the dangers that come with it, I concluded I was right to stay away from Sophie. If I'm not good enough for Heaven, I'm not good enough for her. I hate that she saw me with Candace, but maybe it's a good thing. Maybe now she'll realize I'm not worth the trouble and leave me alone.

Speaking of trouble… Candace is still in my bed. I hope she won't stay long. It's been a tough few days. I need some time alone. If I was a complete dick, I'd wake her up and tell her to leave. But I allowed her to spend the night. The least I can do is let her sleep.

By the time Candace wakes up, I've taken a shower. My head is no longer banging thanks to the two ibuprofen I took, but I'm still hung over. Candace on the other hand, looks perky as ever as she bounces down the stairs with a smile. Her long blonde hair is pulled into a sleek ponytail and her face is make-up free. I've never seen her without her face painted. She looks almost wholesome, except for her outfit.

"Last night was amazing," she says and sits next to me on the couch.

I don't have the energy to shrug her off. I definitely don't have the energy to discuss last night. A mistake I will pay for dearly, I'm sure.

"You have such a comfy bed," she says after I don't answer. "I could've stayed in it all day."

My only response is a nod.

"What do you want to do today?" she asks and leans into me, propping her feet up on my coffee table. "I say we lounge around and take it easy."

This is where I should explain that last night was a drunken mistake. That it doesn't mean we're together. But she'd get all worked up and I don't have the patience for it. That talk will have to wait for another time. "Can't. I have to get going. Got work to do."

"You're much too responsible for your age."

Responsible? If I'd been acting responsibly, I wouldn't have taken that first drink from her, or at the very least, I'd have stopped there. I knew exactly what'd happen if I got drunk with her, yet I did it anyway. What does that say about me? Nothing good, that's for damn sure. It certainly wasn't *responsible*.

Perhaps in my subconscious I did it on purpose. I needed something to take my mind off Sophie and the stress of the past few days. Candace was here, and the booze eased my conscience. Now here I am the morning after facing heavy consequences.

"I don't want to be rude," I pat Candace's leg, "but I need to get going."

I stand from the couch and Candace follows suit.

"Will I hear from you soon?" she asks as we walk to the back door.

I grab my keys from the kitchen counter and open the door. The answer is yes, but only so I can deliver the dreaded talk. Again. "Yeah. I'll get in touch."

Days have passed and I haven't laid eyes on Sophie once. Her blinds stay closed at night and she no longer spies on me from the windows of her house. Out of curiosity I unblocked her number in my phone to see if she would call or text. She hasn't. Oddly, this feels like a breakup. I don't like it. At all. It's driving me mental. I'm like a tweaking junkie. At the sound of every car door closing I break the speed of light with how fast I run to the window.

And the disappointment in her eyes when she saw me with Candace that night. I can't get it out of my mind. Nothing against Candace or the time we've spent together, but the last thing I want is for Sophie to think I'm with her. It's too late for that now, I suppose.

The only way to relieve the twisted, sick feeling in the pit of my stomach is to go to Sophie and explain everything, including my feelings for her. But I won't. I'll let her think I'm with Candace and hope for her sake she's completely disgusted with me. Sure, I'll be fucking miserable, but if it keeps her away from the likes of me, it'll be worth it.

"What did that pen do to you?" Bear asks with a chuckle and closes my office door behind him.

I look down at the mangled pen in my hands and drop it onto the desk. "Just having a bad day."

I'm supposed to be working on the shop's quarterly finances and though I've been sitting here for two hours, I haven't accomplished a damn thing.

"You know I'm not one to pry," he takes a seat in a chair on the other side of the desk, "but is there something going on? You're not yourself lately."

I close my eyes and inhale long and deep, debating what to tell him. Part of me wants to talk to him about my issue with Sophie. But the other part wants no one, including my best friend, to know. What would he think of me if he knew I've been stalking my neighbor for the past three years and that I've fallen for her? That by forcing myself to stay away from her I'm driving myself insane?

"It's nothing, man. Just a bad week."

"I'm not buying it, Rooter." He shifts forward in his seat, his hazel eyes probing mine. "I know you. Something's going on."

I've never been able to bullshit Bear. He catches me every time. I shift forward, resting my elbows on the desk and rub my eyes.

Detecting my hesitance, he continues, "Just tell me this, does it affect the Club? Your family?"

I shake my head.

"Your health?" he presses.

"My mental health, maybe," I laugh sarcastically.

He looks at me, skeptical.

"I'm fine, man," I insist. "I'm just in a funk."

"Well, I'm here if you need me." Not one to overstay his welcome or to say more than is needed in any given situation, Bear stands to leave. "What time should we be at your house tonight?"

"What?"

"Your turn to host. You forget?"

Shit! I did forget. Every month, one of the Club members hosts a party. We're not expected to attend every party, however every member in the Club is required to host, and we are on a strict rotation. Mick thinks it's an important part of keeping our brotherhood alive by letting loose and bonding outside of work without the interference of Club business. The only time you're allowed to skip your turn to host is if you're in the hospital, or dead. I'm neither, so whether I want to or not, I'm throwing a party tonight.

"Tell everyone to be there by six. I'll need you and a couple other guys to leave with me at five to help set up."

As I pull up to my house with Bear, Sparrow, and Darren in tow, Sophie and Miranda are walking to their front door. My heart lodges itself in my throat. Sophie's no longer on her crutches. She looks incredible with her long hair blowing in the wind, oversized, dark sunglasses, and tight white capris. I silently pray for her to look my way, but she doesn't.

As the hours pass, I can't stop staring at Sophie's house. I look from window to window hoping to find her looking out at me, but she isn't there. I know she can hear us out here with the loud music and hollering. There was a time not long ago when she would've been glued to a window watching me.

I've finally done it. I've driven her away. I never really had her so she wasn't mine to lose, but it feels like a loss just the same. I knew it would suck, but I didn't know it'd feel this *wrong*. I try to comfort myself with the fact that she's better off. But there's no comfort to be found.

I take a long swig of my beer when Candace appears before me. She never misses a Double H party.

"Hey, sexy," she says and flips her hair. If her skirt was any shorter, there'd be no point in wearing it.

Like the saying goes, if you can't be with the one you love, love the one you're with. So for now, I'll hold off on having that conversation with Candace.

Perhaps I won't have it at all.

Jealousy

Today was Sophie's first day back to work since twisting her ankle so I'm out on my porch waiting for her to get home. She pulls into her driveway and the car behind her pulls up to the curb in front of her house. I stand at once, ready to take action. But then I recognize the car. It belongs to mister tall, dark, and tattooed. While I'm relieved no one means her harm, I'm not exactly happy it's him. When she gets into his car and leaves with him, I'm overcome with jealousy.

I guess that's that. They're together now. I've succeeded in pushing her into another man's arms. I want to punch myself in the face. But what did I expect? She's a beautiful girl. She wasn't going to stay single long. I never staked my claim on her. She's free to be with whoever she chooses. I lost my chance. He gained his. End of story.

Two hours later, I give up on sleep and turn on my television. Knowing Sophie's with another guy, right now, doing God knows what… Images of them together, him touching her, her kissing him, stream through my mind. My body is soaked from head to toe in sweat. I'd rather someone drive nails into my arms or have acid thrown on me than to endure another moment of these thoughts.

I finally start drifting off around five in the morning. I shut off the television and sleep until almost ten. Rather than waking up exhausted, I'm full of repressed energy. I throw on a pair of shorts and my running shoes and hit the pavement.

I run five miles. Usually, I alternate between sprinting and walking, but today I just run, fast and hard. I take my usual route, out of habit, but I don't acknowledge or really even notice the passersby. I'm so focused on thinking about anything other than Sophie that I nearly cream a little old lady walking her dog.

Like salt to a fresh wound, Sophie and mister wonderful pull up just as I approach my house. She steps out of the car looking perfectly tousled, her hair in a messy bun, wearing last night's clothes. Our eyes lock for an instant before I look away. I can't look at her because when I do, I'm accosted by visions of his hands on her body. It's enough to make me want to ram his face into his steering wheel. And when I hear her call him "Babe" it's like a kick in the gut.

Babe pulls away. To hide the fact I'm watching her, I stretch my quad, pulling my leg up behind me. Sophie glances my way, but doesn't acknowledge my presence as she walks to her house. I should leave her alone, but I can't.

"Hey, Sophie," I say, hoping she will reciprocate.

She mutters a "Hey" in return before walking into her house and closing the door.

Frustrated, I stand staring at her door. I can't turn away and yet I can't run after her the way I want to. How did I think I could do this? Did I honestly believe I could live next to Sophie and not talk to her? Not be a part of her life? Now, I don't have a choice. All evidence points to the fact that she doesn't want anything to do with me. I don't blame her. Sometimes, I don't want anything to do with myself. This is one of those times.

Pop calls me over to help him hang a new television. A distraction will do me some good. I've done nothing but stare at the white siding of Sophie's house all day.

Just as I swing my leg over the seat of my bike, a slick black BMW pulls up in front of Sophie's. At first, I don't think much of it. I assume it's a guy here to pick up Miranda. But then both the driver and passenger doors open and out step two guys.

My next thought is they are here for Mike, but I quickly squash that idea. The guys he hangs with don't drive brand new BMW's and they definitely don't wear dress clothes. These guys are dressed for dates.

Dates.

Plural.

But Sophie has a boyfriend. She called the guy "Babe." They spent the night together. Twice. Now she's going out with another guy? What the hell? She woke up with one guy this morning and now she's going out with someone else? Who is she? This isn't the Sophie I know.

Then again, I don't really know her. I've spent very little time with her. I know her mostly through my research. Maybe she's not the sweet, innocent girl I figured her to be. My stomach churns.

The guys stand at the door. The one who drove flashes a smarmy smile. He reeks of arrogance with his perfect posture. And what's with the tie? What do women see in guys like him? They think he's got swag. He doesn't. Not even close. Men who drive that kind of car and dress like him are only pretending to be confident when in fact they are spineless, insecure little punks. And the other guy, with his shoulder length shaggy hair and fitted sweater… Please. I'm not sure which is worse.

Which one of these losers has Sophie agreed to go out with? The anticipation is killing me as I tighten the strap on my helmet. Finally, Sophie steps forward, and the driver takes her by the elbow and leads her to his car. She's too stunning for words. I've never seen her so beautiful.

That dress…

It has an open back that is cut low. Too low. And it's much too short. If she bends over... Why would she wear that? If you ask me, girls who dress like that are asking for it. I gag in utter disgust and she turns my way. My stomach knots up at the sight of her face. She's so pretty it hurts. That guy will never appreciate her beauty the way I do. He won't appreciate *her* the way I do. He'll take advantage of her if she lets him.

What if she wants him to take advantage of her?

As she lowers herself into the car, with her eyes still on mine, the right corner of her lip turns up in a sneer.

She's taunting me! She knows exactly what this is doing to me.

Fuck!

To make it clear that I know that she knows what she's doing to me, I start up my bike and rev the throttle full boar before tearing out of my driveway.

My curiosity is eating me alive. Will Sophie come home tonight? Will that slimy scrote stay with her? I swear to all that is holy if she sleeps with that assclown, I'm officially done with her. I'll never be able to look at her the same again.

When I pull up to my house, all the lights in Sophie's house are out. They must still be gone. I sit in my usual spot on the porch as I wait. It offers the best vantage point. I don't care if she sees me. I've got nothing to lose.

Less than twenty minutes later the black BMW pulls up to her curb. That it's early is a good sign the date hasn't gone well. I certainly hope it didn't.

Sophie throws her door open and hurries out of the car. Rich boy runs to her side of the car to help her out, but it's too late. Another sign things haven't gone well. A smile spreads across my face. I straighten up at once when she seeks me out and her eyes land on mine. She quickly averts her gaze and smiles at her date. When he offers her his arm to walk her to the door, she takes it.

Bile rises in my throat. Maybe it wasn't a bad date after all.

They're talking about something, but I can't make it out, and Sophie's still smiling. I think he's going to kiss her. I'm on pins and needles waiting to see if she'll let him. And then she leans in and closes the distance between them. My body tenses and I clench a fist. I can't tell what kind of kiss it is. I seriously hope she didn't accept his tongue in her mouth. The bile in my throat raises a little higher. I hear her tell him the night was lovely before he walks away.

Then she turns and shoots me a look that says, "Take that, Fucker."

Wait. What?

Evidently, this is a game to her. She's putting on a show for me, to get my attention.

She has it.

And she knows it.

But I don't play games.

I'm overwhelmed with frustration, shock, desire, unease. Part of me wants to call Sophie or better yet, go over there and call her out on her bullshit. But the other part of me begs me to let it go.

An intense wave of adrenaline hits and I can't sit still. I pace my living room floor while Dopey looks at me like I'm a crazy man. I feel crazy.

Physical activity always helps put my mind at ease. Since I already went on a run this morning I go into my workout room to lift weights. I put the stereo on blast and lay on the weight bench.

Thirty minutes later I'm covered in sweat and physically spent. But my mind is still spinning. I don't know what to make of all this. First, Sophie tells me that the other night with mister tattoo wasn't what it looked like. Then tonight she puts on a show for me with BMW boy. But I can't let it get the best of me. I have to ignore it. Or at least pretend to. I have to make her think I'm not affected by any of this. The best way to do that is turn a blind eye. Or better yet, face it head on with a smile.

But what I really want to do is drop the pretense. I want to go to her and tell her there's no need to play games. If she wants me, I'm hers.

I'm right back to where I was before—driving myself insane with wanting Sophie but not allowing myself to stake my claim. Something has to give before I snap. Why does doing the right thing have to be so damned hard?

I drag myself to the shower for a quick rinse. When I step out of the bathroom, I see Sophie's bedroom light turn on.

She's not alone. *"Babe"* is with her.

What the fuck?

If the other night wasn't what it looked like what is this? It looks to me like Sophie's a girl with a revolving door. Her eyes widen when she sees me and she hurries to close her blinds. Disappointment, revulsion, and jealousy tear through me as I snap my blinds shut. I really thought she was better. I thought she was something special. Yet she's gone and proved me so very wrong. Candace may be a stripper with somewhat questionable morals, but even she wouldn't do this.

I'm done.

Fucking D.O.N.E.

The next morning, I receive a phone call from Pop telling me the clubhouse was vandalized overnight. I'm in my driveway getting ready to leave when Sophie walks *Babe* to his car. Even though their kiss doesn't linger, it makes my stomach flip. I can't believe she spent the night with him after going on a date with another guy. What has gotten in to her? I wonder what this guy would think if he knew. Maybe I should tell him.

"See you tomorrow, Babe," he says before opening his car door. His voice is deep and he has a British accent.

"See ya, Babe." Sophie stands and watches as he drives away. When she turns around, she glances at me before walking to her house.

I can't keep my opinion to myself. "I really didn't take you as the revolving door type."

She freezes and whirls in my direction. "What did you say?"

I set my helmet on my handle bar. "Fucking one guy, going out with another a couple days later, then calling the first guy over after being dropped off by the second. That's high traffic if you ask me."

Her mouth falls open. "I didn't ask you, Rooter, so fuck off!"

I shrug, not at all sorry for my candor. If she's going to be one of *those* girls, she needs to learn to handle the criticism that comes with it.

She rushes over to me, anger dances in her eyes. "And who the hell are you to judge me? I've seen the skanks you run with."

I toss my head back and laugh, sarcastic. "Apparently you aren't any better than them."

"I'm not a slut."

I hate to break it to her but... "Your actions would prove otherwise."

"You have no idea what you're talking about."

"No? You fuck," I make air quotes for effect, "*Babe*, go out with another guy, kiss him, agree to another date then bring *Babe* over to fuck again? Pardon me, but that is a perfect definition of a slut!"

If looks could kill, her glare would be lethal. "For your information, not that it's any of your damn business, but," she mocks my air quotes, "*Babe*, the guy you think I'm fucking, is *gay* you asshole!"

All the air has been sucked out of my lungs. I stumble forward unable to wrap my mind around what she just said. "What?"

"That's right. *Babe* is one hundred percent take it up the ass *gay*! I'm not fucking anyone and I'm *not* a slut." She spins on her heels and starts to stalk off.

I'm a total ass. I was completely off base. She is the sweet, innocent, perfect girl I thought she was. She was putting on a show for me last night when she kissed that guy. I have to make this right. But how? What do I say? I don't know, but I have to stop her from walking away. I grab her by the elbow, twirl her around to face me and press my mouth to hers. Her lips are so soft and warm but I don't have time to savor the kiss because she breaks away and slaps my face with all her might.

"Don't touch me!" She yells.

Suddenly I'm back on planet earth. My face stings from her blow. "I'm sorry. I shouldn't have—"

"You're damn right you shouldn't have." Like mine, her chest heaves as she breathes in and out. Her eyes vacillate from my eyes to my lips and back before she turns around and hurries into her house.

Should I go after her? If I did, what would I say? I misjudged her so badly, and even if I had been right in my assumption, it was none of my business. She's not my girl. I have no claim on her. She's free to do whatever she likes with whoever she chooses. And she's right about me. The girls I run with are skanks. Who am I to judge her?

To kiss her against her will was a bad, bad move on my behalf. If I went after her right now I'd just say or do something else to make matters worse. I should give us both time to calm down. Besides, I'm needed elsewhere.

The Rescue

The day drags on as we clean up the aftermath of the vandalization. The clubhouse has been demolished. It's hard to tell if anything is missing, though it doesn't appear anything was taken. But every room in the place has been decimated. Not one item has been left untouched. Furniture has been torn into, the drywall busted. Whoever was here was looking for something in particular.

I find it convenient this happened only days after confiscating a kilo of heroin from Kip, one of Halsey's best known marijuana dealers. Kip is nothing more than a spoiled punk living off his rich daddy. He refuses to be a productive member of society and instead sells pot. His father knows about it, but turns a blind eye. We did as well when it was only weed.

Double H doesn't take offense to recreational marijuana use. The majority of our guys are known to toke a joint now and again, Bear included. I used to, but I stopped a few years back. I didn't care for the paranoia it induced.

I don't believe Kip is the vandal. He's scared shitless of Double H. When we took his heroin, we put the fear of God into him. We told him if anyone came for the drugs or if the police were tipped off, he would be suspect number one and we would come for him.

My money is on Andy. He's had a chip on his shoulder since I kicked his ass. He's been MIA for two days.

He knows we have the drugs, just not where. It's been moved to a secret location that only me, Pop, and Wrench know about. It's where we keep anything that could possibly link Double H to any crime.

Pop called him in today for the Club meeting to discuss the vandalization. To my surprise, he showed and appeared to be shocked and angry. He immediately pointed fingers at Kip and Hoyt. I'm not buying his show of solidarity. But until I can come up with concrete evidence, I need to keep my suspicion to myself. Pop can be loyal to a fault. Because of my turbulent relationship with Andy, he will dismiss my concern as prejudice.

When I pull into my driveway, I see Sophie eating at her dining room table. I need to apologize for this morning, but now isn't the time. I'm still caught up in my fury over the vandalization and my suspicion of Andy's guilt. I'm in no condition to try to talk to her. It's best if I take a few minutes to unwind and shift gears. I can't be thinking about the destruction at the clubhouse when I speak with her. Besides, I haven't had any time to consider what to say.

A few minutes turns into a couple hours. Shaking my anger and calming down isn't easy an easy feat. All I can see is the destruction of the clubhouse and Andy's smug face as he tore the place to shreds.

I still haven't come up with anything good to say to Sophie. There's no justifying my words or my actions. Sure, I was upset after Pop called and seeing Sophie with her friend sent me into a jealous rage. But it's no excuse for what I did.

For the first time in my life, I'm afraid to talk to a girl. Does she even want to talk to me? Probably not. If I knocked on her door, she'd probably slam it in my face. But I can't put it off out of fear of rejection.

As I sit on the edge of my bed I see Sophie with Miranda in her room. With a big bowl of popcorn, it looks like they're watching a movie.

It kills me to know how deeply I've offended her. I can only imagine how badly I hurt her feelings. My guts churn as I consider the consequence of my actions. I'm cloaked in shame and regret.

I lean forward with my elbows on my knees and head in my hands. I'm in uncharted territory. I've never had a problem admitting when I've made a mistake and trying to make amends. But I've never cared so much about the person's reaction. What if she rebuffs my apology?

After taking several deep breaths I look up. Her eyes meet mine and it gives my heart a start. The anger I'd expected to see in them isn't there. Instead I see her usual sweetness and thoughtfulness.

Go over there now.

I feel faint. I don't have the balls to knock on her door.

I'll send a text and see how she responds to it.

I type out the text and my heart pounds as I press send.

Me: *I promise to leave u alone, but I want to tell u I'm sorry. For everything.*

Sophie leans over to get her phone from the bedside table. My hands tremble as she reads my message. A long moment passes and I almost think she'll ignore it. Nervous, I stare at my phone, praying for a response. No response at all would be worse than a "Go fuck yourself." Even if she told me to fuck off, I could work with that. A response, even a negative one, means the lines of communication are open and there's a chance of a reconciliation. No response means there likely is no chance.

My already roiling gut does full on somersaults as the second's tick by. *Please respond, please.* Sophie begins typing and my heart accelerates with anticipation. When my phone pings I'm jolted by a mixture of relief and fear of what she wrote. I blow out a deep breath before reading her words.

Sophie: *Thank you for your apology. I haven't decided whether or not I want you to leave me alone (and I will be the one to make that decision). I'll let you know when I do.*

I shake my head and grin at her message. It's just like her to assert her will. At least she doesn't hate me.

Me: *That's fair.*

A short while later, I turn out the lights and slide into bed, ready to call an end to this day. Sophie is still in her room with Miranda. Unable to resist, and wanting her to know I'm thinking about her, I send her another text.

Me: *Good night Sophie.*

A warm sensation spreads throughout my body as her lips curl into a smile. I wait eagerly as she types her reply.

Sophie: *Good night Rooter.*

A blood-curdling scream rips me from a sound sleep. It's Sophie. The light from the hallway outside her room is just enough that I can see a masked man dragging her from her bed. Following them is a second man with Miranda.

I jump out of my bed and call Bear. He answers on the first ring.

"At least two armed men broke into the house to the right of mine and are attacking the residents. I'm going in now. I need you to get the van and bring Tank, Jonesy, and Cartwright."

"On my way, Brother."

I grab my gun off the nightstand and run to Sophie's house. I'm tempted to bust into the house, but that could prove detrimental. First things first—assess the situation. In a situation such as this, never go in blind and try to use the element of surprise to your advantage.

Carefully, I climb their front porch stairs and peek through the window. I see the two masked men. Mike is tied to a chair with his mouth duct taped while Sophie and Miranda are kneeling on the floor. There doesn't appear to be anyone else inside.

I need to get inside as inconspicuously as possible. The kitchen window stays open night and day. I run to my garage and grab a box cutter so I can cut a flap in the window screen. Standing on a lawn chair, I poke my head inside to listen and survey the area. The window sits above the sink where dishes are piled high. One wrong move and they'll know I'm inside. Grabbing the edge of the counter to balance myself, I slide slowly inside. My left hand brushes a bowl, almost knocking it off the counter, but I catch it just in time.

Once I'm on my feet, I tip toe to the doorway leading to the living room and peer around the corner. Sophie and Miranda are still on their knees. One assailant stands next to Miranda. The other one must be on the other side of the room. If I go in from this direction, he'll see me coming. The dining room is my best bet. I dart into the dining room and from that doorway I see the second intruder next to Mike. The guy says something about Mike knowing where to get the cash. I grab him by the throat and put my gun to his head. The man standing by the girls reaches for his gun.

"Move another inch," I snarl, "and I'll put a bullet through this fuck's skull."

This is a precarious situation. He could grab one of the girls for leverage. I guarantee I care more about their lives than he does his accomplice.

Thankfully, he doesn't budge. Without taking my eyes off him, I order Sophie to go get her gun. I hate to make her do this, but as it stands, they have the upper hand with two guns to my one.

Sophie jumps up from her position on the floor and bolts up the stairs. A moment later she hurries back down and points her gun at the goon across the room.

"Keep it on him," I tell her and push the guy I'm holding to the floor. I look at Miranda who's still perched on her knees and tell her to tape his feet together. She jumps up and grabs the roll of duct tape from the coffee table. I look to him, "If you even think about touching her, I'll blow your brains all over this floor."

Once Miranda's is finished with his feet, I instruct her to tape his hands behind his back. When she's done, I go to the other guy, my gun aimed at his heart.

"I've got him," I tell Sophie. "Go watch the other guy."

I tell Miranda to tape this guy up, same as the other. She works quickly. When she's done, I put the men, side by side. I kneel and put my Double H tattoo in their faces. Horror flashes in their eyes.

"That's right bitches, I'm Double H. And that girl right there," I growl and point to Sophie, "the one you snatched out of bed in the middle night to do God knows what with, she's mine. You fuck with her, you fuck with my Club. I'm sure you've heard what happens to people who fuck with my Club."

"I didn't know she was your girl, man," the thug on the left says.

I smash the barrel of my gun into his temple. "So what? You think it's okay to go around hurting innocent women?"

"We didn't hurt her, man," he screeches.

"There's blood on her face!"

"That's my blood. The bitch bit me!"

I glower at him and slam the butt of my gun into his cheekbone. "Do *not* call her a bitch. Why are you here?"

The guy on the right nods in Mike's direction, "He owes Viper three large. He sent us to collect."

I turn and glare at Mike. *Of course.* I hop to my feet and saunter over to him, ripping the duct tape from his mouth. "This true?"

The little bitch nods, humiliation and fear etched onto his face.

"You're fucking pathetic. I'll deal with you later."

"I should call the police," Sophie says.

"No!" I yell and turn to face her. "The police can't help you. Viper will just send someone else to finish his dirty work. I need to handle this."

Her mouth falls open and she gasps. "Do you know Viper?"

I know him very well. We had an altercation a couple years ago when he and his crew were trying to set up shop in Halsey. "Yes, and we need to finish this shit tonight."

"What are you going to do?"

"I'm going to send Viper a message." I scowl at the men on the floor. "That this house and its inhabitants are under Double H protection, and that the debt will be considered paid in full for the attack on you."

In the next breath, the front door swings open and Bear and the guys walk in. Gun in hand, Bear takes in the scene. When he sees Miranda in her skimpy pajamas, he grabs the throw blanket from the back of the couch and hands it to her.

"Everyone okay?" he asks.

"We're good. Put these two in the van," I motion to Viper's men. "Take them to the warehouse."

As they carry out the first guy and I turn to Sophie. Her hand shakes as she keeps her gun pointed at the remaining guy.

"You okay?" I ask and take the thirty-eight from her hand and put it on the table alongside my nine millimeter.

She doesn't answer. Her face is ashen and her lips quiver. I draw her to my chest and hold her close. She drapes her arms around my hips and leans into me. After a few beats her breathing begins to slow and her body stops trembling.

My men haul the second guy out to the van. The sound of Miranda screaming takes me by surprise.

"How could you do this to us?" She slaps her brother's face. "What the hell is the matter with you?"

He whimpers an apology.

"If it wasn't for Rooter, we could all be dead right now!"

Bear walks back into the house. "They're loaded," he says. "You staying?"

"Yeah. I'm not quite finished here." I nod in Mike's direction.

"All right. Need anything else from me?"

"I've got this. Take care of them," I say, referring to Viper's men. "I'll catch up with you when I'm done here."

"All right, man." He nods and exchanges a glance with Miranda before turning to leave.

"Okay, everyone have a seat," I begin. "We're going to have a little family meeting."

I gesture for Miranda to take a seat on one side of the sofa before leading Sophie to the other. Once both girls are sitting, I drag the chair Mike is sitting in so he's facing the three of us. I take a seat in between the two girls, draping a protective arm around Sophie's waist.

"Are you going to leave me tied up?" Mike asks.

"You will speak only when I've given you permission. Do you understand?" I command and point at him. "You are moving out first thing in the morning. I don't care where you go or if you even *have* anywhere to go, but you are leaving."

The little weasel opens his mouth as if to speak, but doesn't. It's a good damn thing. Any argument from him would result in the worst ass kicking he's ever received.

"Do you have a problem with this?" I ask Miranda, fully expecting a rebuttal on her brother's behalf.

She casts her eyes downward. "I agree that he needs to go, but…"

"No but's," I snap. "I won't allow him to be here if Sophie's here. Do you want Sophie to leave instead?" In my peripheral I see Sophie staring at me bug-eyed.

"No," Miranda answers.

"Then he's gone. First thing." I look back to Mike. "If I need to, I'll personally see to it. I don't want you coming anywhere near this house or Sophie without my prior knowledge."

"That's a little extreme," Miranda whines.

"Extreme?" I shout. "He almost got you both killed tonight or have you already forgotten?"

Miranda cowers into the couch. "No, but he's my brother. This is my house. I'll decide whether he can come here."

Sophie glares at Miranda, her nostrils flaring. "How long are you going to accept the shit he puts you through? The shit he puts both of us through?"

"You're acting like I should write him off." Miranda sniffles. "I can't do that. He's the only family I have left."

Sophie stares in disbelief. I'm not surprised Miranda would choose that waste of space over Sophie. But Sophie doesn't need her. She has me and I will protect her.

"Fine." I pull Sophie closer. "Sophie will move out first thing in the morning."

"What?" The girls ask in harmony.

I turn to Sophie, resolute. "I won't have you here if he's here."

Sophie gapes at me with wide eyes. "Rooter, it's not that simple."

The hell it isn't. I'll have her things moved into my house within an hour. If she doesn't want to stay with me, I'll find somewhere else safe for her to go.

"It is that simple, Sophie." I turn back to her so-called friend. "So who's it going to be? Your loving, reliable best friend or your precious brother who almost got you both killed?"

Miranda wipes her tear-stained face and looks at her brother. She speaks in a soft, apologetic voice. "You have to go, Mike."

Mike starts to protest, but when I leap from my seat he quickly shuts his mouth.

"You heard her. You're out," I tell him. "And I better not hear of any retaliation against these girls over it."

I cut away the tape that's securing Mike to the chair and he runs straight up the stairs. Miranda stares at the ceiling.

"You're doing the right thing," I assure her.

Her only response is a hesitant nod.

I understand this is difficult for Miranda given how recently she lost her parents, but it must be done. She may not realize it, but she's better off with Mike gone. His being here puts her at risk. Maybe she's aware of the danger and is willing to take that risk. But I won't take that chance with Sophie's wellbeing.

"Thank you for helping us tonight," Sophie says. "I thought we were dead."

"Thank God your window was open or I might not have heard your screams." I shudder at the memory of the sound. I reach out and tuck her loose hair behind her ear.

Miranda mumbles that she's going to talk to her brother. The ungrateful little shit doesn't offer me any thanks before disappearing up the stairs.

You're welcome.

"I've never been so scared in my life," Sophie says with a quivering voice, and I pull her to me. "I can't believe what just happened."

"It's okay now," I murmur. "Those guys won't come near you again."

She peers at me with the sweetest eyes I've ever seen. "How can you be so sure?"

"Viper won't mess with the Club. He knows better."

"Care to elaborate?"

"Trust me. After telling those guys you're mine, I wouldn't be surprised if you receive a handwritten apology from Viper himself."

Sophie glances at the clock on the wall and moans. "Shit."

"What?"

"I have to be at work in less than six hours."

Tonight's events have been traumatic for her. The last thing she should do is go to work, but she probably can't afford not to go. "You should try to sleep."

She nods and rubs her eyes. "I doubt I'll be able to, but I should try. I'm working a double."

I should get to the warehouse. I doubt Mike will try anything after my threat. "I need to go deal with… things."

Sophie's posture stiffens as though she's afraid. Her voice shakes as she speaks, "Will you stay… a little while until I calm down?"

If she intends to go to work, she needs rest. "Sure, but I thought you were going to try to sleep?"

"It's just that I'm completely on edge and won't be able to sleep until I calm down. Your being here… makes me feel safe."

If she needs me here to feel safe, the situation at the warehouse can wait. "Okay. I'll stay."

Sophie slides her tiny hand into mine and I lead her up the stairs. The light from the street lamp illuminates the room as I close the door behind us. I pull back the sheet, holding it up as she gets into the bed. Sophie lays facing the wall and I slide in behind her, pulling her back to my chest.

"Is this okay?" I ask.

"Yeah." Her body trembles as she begins to cry.

I hold her tight and murmur in her ear, "It's okay, Sophie. I'm here."

"I thought I was going to die," she sobs.

Please don't cry, Baby. "I'll never let anyone hurt you."

"My life is so fucked up. This is the kind of shit that always happens to me. No matter how hard I try to get away from it, it finds me."

"It'll never find you again. I won't let it."

I keep her wrapped snug in my arms as continues to cry. After a short while, her body relaxes and her breathing evens out. I press my lips to the back of her head. "Everything will be okay, sweet girl. I promise."

Staking My Claim

Once again, I'm torn from my sleep, but this time it's by the world's loudest and most annoying alarm clock. Sophie and I both jolt upright in the bed.

"Shit, what time is it?" I roll over to silence the noise. According to the clock it's only seven. I could use a few more hours of sleep, but I need to get to the warehouse. If Viper doesn't hear from his men soon, he'll send someone here to look for them.

Sophie lays back own and pulls the blanket up. "Let's go back to sleep."

"I should go deal with things at the warehouse." I hover over her and smooth the wild hair from her face.

Sophie doesn't respond. She appears transfixed with her eyes pinned on my bare torso.

"You sure about working today?" I ask, pretending to be unaffected by the fact I just busted her for checking me out.

"I have to."

"I'll send one of the guys to escort you there. What time are you off?"

"You don't need to do that." She starts to sit upright but I place a hand on her shoulder to stop her.

"It would give me peace of mind."

Her lips part and her eyes widen, conveying fear. "I thought you said nothing else would happen."

"It won't once I get word to Viper." *Which I need to do soon.* "Right now he's probably wondering where his guys are."

"This is so messed up," she groans.

"Yeah." *But I'll make sure it never happens again.* "I'll come get you from work. Are you getting off at your normal time?"

"Yes."

"Damn, that's a long day." *I wish she'd take the day off to rest.*

"Got to pay rent somehow." She shrugs, but I can see in her eyes how much she wishes she didn't have to go.

"You're very strong, Sophie."

She laughs once, a cynical sound. "Yeah, right."

"You are," I declare and lie on my side to face her. Longing to touch her, I graze the soft skin of her arm with my fingertips. *God, I adore this girl.* "You've been through so much. And you were great last night. So calm, collected. Did everything I told you to."

"I was freaking the fuck out."

"It didn't show. You know, that's one thing I've noticed about you. You have a great poker face. You never give anything away."

"From years of practice."

Her words break my heart. The poor girl has been through more in her short life than most people experience in an entire lifetime. If I had the ability to go back in time, I'd rewrite her history and give her a normal, happy life.

Tears pool in her eyes and she turns away, trying to hide them.

She needn't be ashamed or embarrassed to be vulnerable in front of me. I want to be the one to comfort and care for her. I turn her face back to mine. "You don't have to hide from me, Sophie."

She shakes her head and a tear spills down her cheek. "Sometimes, I wish I could hide from myself."

I take her into my arms and kiss the side of her head. "I didn't mean to make you sad."

Sophie wraps her arms around me and snuggles close. With her face pressed tightly against my chest, she inhales a deep breath.

The urge to kiss her is overpowers me. But just as my lips are about to touch hers, I stop. Last time I kissed her, it didn't go over well. "Is this okay?"

She whispers, "Yes."

Slowly, I close the distance between us and press my lips to hers, taking my time to give her a tender, closed mouth kiss. My chest swells with emotion. I might feel more for this girl than I realized.

When I walk into the front room of the warehouse, Tank is fast asleep with his head down on an old wooden work bench.

"Hey, Brother," I pat him on the back to rouse him. "I got it now. Go home and get some sleep."

He nods and stretches his arms over his head before standing. "They're in the back. Had to tape their mouths to shut 'em up."

"Thanks man," I say as he heads to the door. "Don't worry about going in to the shop today. I'll tell Pop I sent you home."

"Cool." He yawns. "See you later, Brother."

The front door swings open and Bear walks in. He steps to the side to make room for Tank to leave. With a lopsided grin he asks, "Time to have some fun?"

"Oh, yeah." I rub my palms together. Let the games begin.

Bear follows me to the far back room where both men are propped up against the wall, sleeping. I flip the lights on and holler as loud as I can.

"Wake up bitches!"

Both men jerk upright, their eyes full of fear.

"Sleep well, Princess?" Bear taunts the guy on the left.

"We have some unfinished business to attend to." I glare at the guy on the right, the one who called my Sophie a bitch. The memory of it makes me want to ram his nose into his brain. "Which of you wants to go first?"

"We weren't going to hurt the girls, I swear to God," he says.

"Bullshit!" I yell and feel my face heat up. "And even if that was true, I don't care. They are two innocent women. You broke into their home and snatched them from their beds in the middle of the night. That shit is *not* okay with me."

"I'm sorry, man," the man on the right whines. "Viper sent us. We didn't have a choice. We're sorry your girl got caught up in it."

The memory of Sophie lying in bed crying herself to sleep only hours ago, fills me with a blind rage. Thoughts of what might've happened to her had I not been there send me over the edge. I kick him as hard as I can in the ribs. "You think you're sorry now? Just wait until I'm done with you."

An hour later Viper's guys are bloody from head to toe and can barely stand. Bear and I stand, both of us huffing for breath and drenched with sweat. The beating we gave them was quite a workout. I retrieve one of their cell phones to find Viper's phone number. Before calling, I take their picture and text it to him.

"Who is this?" Viper snaps after answering on the second ring.

"We've met before. I'm the one who left you with that pretty little scar above your eyebrow."

There's a brief pause. When he speaks, he's much calmer, yet I detect an undertone of fear. "I remember. What is this about?"

"This is about your men breaking into my girl's house and snatching her from her bed in the middle of the night."

"What? I didn't send—"

I don't allow him to finish. "Maybe the name Mike Frank rings a bell?"

There's a brief pause. "Yeah, he owes me three grand. I sent my men out for him."

I take a seat at the desk Tank had been sleeping at when I arrived. Bear leans against the wall opposite me with his arms crossed. "Well, as luck would have it, he lives in the same house as my girl."

"Shit," Viper sighs. "Look, man, I'm sorry about your girl getting mixed up in all this."

Sorry doesn't cut it with me. And that Sophie was involved isn't my only issue with the incident. I poke my tongue into my cheek and inhale a long breath. "The problem here, Viper, isn't just that *my* girl was involved. The problem is that Double H doesn't condone the mistreatment of *any* women. Ever. Your men have paid for what they've done. But if I hear of any more of your men attacking innocent women for any reason, next time, I'll come for you and you'll be left in a lot worse shape than the last time we met. Do you understand?"

"Yeah, I understand."

"One more thing. You'll consider Mike's debt paid in full for the attack on my girl and her friend."

"Done."

"Good," I stand and walk to the back of the building where the men lie on the floor. "I'll drop your men at the corner of Third and Wabash in fifteen minutes."

Bear and I haul the men to the van. After loading them up, we stand at the front bumper. Bear stares at me with an amused smirk. "Seems you been withholding some very interesting information, my friend."

He's referring to Sophie. I shrug.

"Hey, I think it's great man." He pats me on the back. "I'm happy for you. She's cute."

"Sophie is more than cute, Brother. She's the sweetest fucking girl I've ever met."

"Would she be the reason for your weird behavior lately?"

"She would be," I chuckle.

"Everything straightened out now?" he asks.

"We'll get there."

Bear looks me in the eye and raises his chin. "She's the kind of girl I always pictured you with. I never understood why you fucked with girls like Candace. They aren't your style."

Ashamed of the truth, I drag a hand through my hair and look away. "That's why I fucked with them. To avoid attachment."

"I get that. I've been guilty of the same." He blows out a breath. "But I was never happier than when I was with Ashley."

"I don't know what I'd do if Sophie gets hurt because of my shit." I lean my weight against the van. "I don't want to bring trouble into her life."

"That's life, Rooter." He kicks a rock across the parking lot. "No one can avoid trouble. We might as well live in a way that makes us happy. None of us are gonna get out alive, anyway."

I arch a brow. "Ever consider taking your own advice?"

"Every day, and speaking of, do you think you can arrange a little get together for me with her hot roommate?" He winks.

I snort. "I seriously doubt it."

Tonight, I plan on making my intentions with Sophie perfectly clear. It's only right that I set things straight with Candace beforehand, so I called and asked her to meet me at Rosen's Park.

I sit on the top of a picnic table with my feet on the seat, elbows resting on my knees when she pulls up. The smile on her face tugs at my heartstrings. She thinks I invited her here to hang out.

"Hey there, sexy," she says, hips swaying in an exaggerated fashion as she approaches me.

"Hey." I smile halfheartedly.

"It sure was a nice surprise getting your invitation."

I nod and clear my throat. My stomach churns. Consumed with guilt, I look away. *Please, please, please let this go well.* "I called you here so we could talk."

She takes a step back. "Are you dumping me again?"

We were never really together, but no sense debating that point. "Candace, I'm so sorry."

She takes a small step back and crosses her arms. "Why?"

"It's just not a good idea for us to be involved."

"Bullshit. Tell me why and don't tell me it's because you're worried about jeopardizing our friendship. I know you better than that. You wouldn't have gotten involved with me to begin with if that was the case."

She knows me too well. "We agreed no strings attached, remember?"

"And my feelings for you have been obvious for a long time now. What's changed?"

"I'm just trying to do the right thing."

Her eyes widen and her lips part. "Oh my God, you're dumping me for someone else."

I shake my head. "No."

"Yes, you are. It's the only thing that makes sense."

"This is about you and me. No one else." Yes, I want someone else, but my ending this has nothing to do with that.

"Are you seeing someone else? Don't you dare lie to me," she chokes and starts crying. "I deserve better than that."

Making eye contact is excruciating. "I've met someone," I admit with a nod, "but that's not why I'm doing this."

"I can't believe this is happening." She stumbles forward and I catch her before she falls. "How can you do this to me?"

"I'm sorry."

"We grew up together." Tears pour from her eyes. "I've loved you since I was fourteen years old."

I take her into my arms. I knew this wouldn't be easy, but I didn't expect this. If she's loved me for that long, I never knew it. She never told me, never gave any inclination. I thought her feelings for me began during our arrangement. "I didn't know, Sweetheart."

"Please don't do this." She leans back and peers into my eyes. "Whoever she is, she'll never love you like I do. She'll never be able to give you what I can. I've known you your whole life, Rooter. I understand you in a way no one else ever could." She pulls my face to hers and presses her lips to mine, but when she tries to deepen the kiss, I pull away.

"I never intended to hurt you."

"Hurt me? This isn't hurting me, it's killing me." She sobs. "It's killing me. I can't live without you. I won't."

"Don't say that." My chest tightens. "We'll always be a part of each other's lives, Sweetheart."

"That's not the same. I need you, Rooter. You're all I have. The Club is the only family I have. Without you, I have nothing. I'll die. I mean it, Rooter, I can't live without you."

"You won't be without me. I'll always be here. The Club will always be here. Things will be exactly the way they were before…we…"

She shakes her head. "I don't want that. I don't just want to be someone you know. I want to be… more."

"You *are* more than just someone I know. Like you said, I've known you my whole life. I just can't give you what you want."

"Yes, you can. Please, Rooter, give me a chance. Give *us* a real chance."

"I truly believe in time you'll find you're better off without me. You'll find someone better who can give you what you want."

"There isn't anyone better than you. All I want is you." She collapses into my arms. At least fifteen minutes pass before her sobbing subsides. When she looks up at me, her faced is streaked with black eyeliner and mascara. "Please?"

"I'm sorry."

It's after midnight and I'm sitting on my bike waiting on Sophie to come out of the restaurant. I think back to this afternoon as I watched Mike carry his things out of Sophie's house. I'm worried about what he might do to the girls, especially Sophie. He'd likely be more inclined to hurt her than his sister especially since he probably blames Sophie for getting kicked out.

The back door of the restaurant opens and Sophie walks out with the guy I accused her of sleeping with. There are dark circles under her eyes from lack of sleep, but her face lights up with a smile when she sees me.

"Hi," she says.

"Hi." I get off the bike and extend my hand to her friend, feeling ashamed once again for the accusation I made. How could I ever have thought such things? Does he know? "I'm Rooter."

"Ryan," he says and shakes my hand.

"Nice to meet you, Ryan."

"Same here," he says without a trace of visible judgment before turning to Sophie. "See you tomorrow night."

"See ya."

"What happened to *Babe*?" I ask once he's out of earshot. It's nice to joke after the stressful day I've had. When she smiles, those adorable dimples of hers light up my world.

"Well, I didn't want you to get worked up again."

Embarrassed, I rub the back of my neck. *I so don't deserve this girl.* "Now that I know he's gay, I'm sure that won't be a problem."

She laughs and it's music to my ears.

"Ready to go home?" I ask.

"Yeah." She eyes my bike with an excited gleam.

"Want to ride with me?"

She looks over my shoulder to her Toyota. "What about my car?"

"I'll bring you to pick it up in the morning." I fasten my helmet to her head. It's too big, but it's better than nothing. I mount the bike and have her get on behind me. "Put your arms around me like this," I say, and wrap her arms around my waist before instructing her to hold on tight.

I wonder if she's ever been on a motorcycle before. "If you get scared, let me know."

"I will."

"You ready?"

"Yeah." The enthusiasm in her voice thrills me.

I take it slow the entire way home, something I never do. But tonight, I'm carrying precious cargo. When we pull into my garage and dismount the bike, I ask her what she thought about the ride.

"It was amazing!" Her smile is infectious.

"I love riding," I say after helping her remove the helmet. "I can barely tolerate being in a car anymore."

"I can see why." She stares in awe as she ever so lightly grazes the gas tank with the tips of her fingers. "Maybe I'll get one of my own."

I'm all for women riding, but the idea of Sophie on a motorcycle by herself ignites panic inside me. "Whoa, whoa, slow down. One step at a time."

"It's not like I can afford one, anyway." She shrugs.

"How'd you do today?" I ask as we walk down my driveway toward her house.

"I was fine until the halfway point, but I persevered."

"I'm not surprised."

"Gotta do what you gotta do."

"One day, life will be easier." Especially if I have a say in the matter, and I intend to.

Her expression slackens as do her shoulders. "I've been telling myself that for years."

"It will, I promise you." I take her hand and squeeze, hoping to convey my meaning. I never want to let go.

"Thank you. For everything."

"No, Sophie," I shake my head, "it's I who should thank you."

"For what?" She pulls her eyebrows together in surprise.

I look down at our clasped hands. Though it feels so right being here with her, there's a nagging in the back of my mind that I'm not good enough for her. "For giving me a chance when I didn't deserve one. I've been awful to you."

"What?" She comes to a sudden stop. "You've done so much for me. I don't even want to think about where I'd be right now if not for you."

"I don't want to think about it either. But I've done some pretty nasty things too."

She tugs on my hand to make me look at her. "You've also done some pretty great things. You saved my life."

Thoughts of what may have happened to her had I not heard her screams give me a chill. Yet I'm thankful because it brought us together, in this moment. Now that I'm here with her, I can't imagine being anywhere else. "I thought you were better off without my influence, but now I believe you might actually be better off with me around."

"I've always believed that," she breathes.

Sophie's intense stare makes me nervous and surprisingly diffident. After a moment of unusual reticence, I pull myself together to make my declaration. "I'm done trying to stay away from you, Sophie. When I told those guys you were mine, I meant it."

She gasps, but says nothing.

"I intend to make you mine."

"I think you'll find that won't be very difficult," she murmurs.

I remind myself to take things slow. I have to be sure not to move too fast for her. And, I want to savor every single moment as our relationship unfolds. I bend forward slowly and press my lips to hers. Sophie pulls me against her in an attempt to deepen the kiss, but I pull away.

"I want to do this right." I pause and take a breath before saying words I've never said. "This will probably sound juvenile, but… will you go on a date with me?"

"I'd love to go on a date with you, Rooter."

Thank God she didn't laugh. I blow out a breath I hadn't realized I'd been holding. "When's your next day off?"

"Wednesday."

"Then Wednesday it is."

"So, how did today go for you?" she asks as we resume walking.

"It was fine," I answer, hoping to leave it at that, but her expression conveys concern. No way am I telling her what I did to Viper's men. "I've taken care of everything. Don't worry."

"I was just curious."

"It's done now." I kiss her hand. "You rest. We'll talk tomorrow."

Betrayal

There are few things in life I enjoy more than a hot shower after a morning run or workout. The sensation of the hot water cascading down my neck and back relaxes and calms me. It's one of the only times in the day that I'm truly at ease, physically and mentally.

After an hour long extreme cardio session, my shorts are soaked and sweat rolls off my face and chest. I turn on the shower and wait until steam filters into the bathroom before stepping in. I close my eyes and lean forward with my arms against the wall and let the scorching water roll down my back. My eyes grow heavy and I nearly drift off to sleep until my phone rings.

I assume it's Sophie calling for me to take her to her car. I grab the phone from the back of the toilet, disappointed to see it's not her. It's Pop.

"Yeah?" I answer.

"Get to the clubhouse," he says. "Andy left his patch here last night and a note saying he's joining the Henchmen."

Fuck. I hang my head. I didn't see that coming.

The Henchmen are the largest outlaw biker club in the Midwest and they're nothing but trouble. They wreak havoc everywhere they go. They've been known to wipe out entire thriving cities. If a Henchmen charter sets up shop in your town, you leave and don't look back. The only thing keeping them out of Michigan is the combination of Double H and the Rebels. We're too much of a force here. But as the Henchmen have continued to grow, we've been concerned that they might try to push their way in.

That Andy joined them tells me two things. One, he intends to use them hurt us. Two, they're on their way here.

This is a big, big problem.

I tell Pop I'm on my way and end the call.

As I stare at my reflection in the mirror, gone is any trace of the peace and calm I felt only moments ago. Now all I feel is rage.

I can't ever have a fucking minute to just breathe. In my life, it's always something. A Club deal gone wrong, the cops breathing down our necks, or another MC provoking Double H. I've never known true peace. Even when I was young, there was constant drama. I remember visiting Pop in the hospital after he was shot in the leg by a rival MC member. That's the nature of the life I live as a member of Double H. With my rank in the Club, I'm involved in everything that goes on, good or bad—but especially the bad shit.

I go to my room to throw on some clothes. After zipping my jeans I cast a glance at Sophie's window and see that she's awake. She's still in her bed while Miranda stands before her. Whatever they're discussing, Sophie doesn't seem happy about it. Once Miranda is gone, I dial Sophie's number.

"Hello?"

The sound of her sleepy morning voice has an immediate calming effect. "I'm surprised you're up so early."

She turns to her window with a smile. "Stalking me?"

"Always," I chuckle, taking myself by surprise given my circumstances. "I saw you talking to Miranda."

"Yeah, she and I got into it last night. She begged me not to move out."

What? "You're moving out?"

Sophie rakes her fingers through her messy hair. "I doubt it."

"You doubt it?" I ask, unsettled with her answer. If she's moving out, I need to know when and, most importantly, where to. I won't have her living anywhere I deem unsafe.

"It was a stupid fight. We'll get over it. We always do."

"Let me guess, it had to do with kicking Mike out."

"You guessed it."

"And she blames you and me." I grind my foot into the floor then shift from one foot to the other. It's difficult to hide my frustration. Miranda seems like a serious pain in the ass. I can't imagine why she's Sophie's best friend.

"You guessed it again," Sophie confirms. "You ready to take me to my car?"

"That's why I called. I need to run an errand. Shouldn't take longer than a few hours."

"That's cool," she flashes her gorgeous dimples. "I could use a few more hours of sleep. Maybe you can take me to work later. I don't go in until four."

"That'll work. I'll call you when I'm done, okay?"

"Okay," she says with a yawn.

Though Sophie doesn't seem concerned about her argument with Miranda, I am. The idea of her no longer living next door is unsettling.

When I arrive at the clubhouse, I find Pop and Wrench sitting at the Club table. No one else is here. Why would they call me in alone when this concerns the entire Club?

"Where's everyone else?" I ask.

"I'll call them in later," Pop answers and motions for me to sit. "I want to talk, just the three of us."

This is unlike Pop. He isn't one to hold secret meetings or keep things from the other members.

Interest piqued, I rub my jaw and take my seat to his left, across from Wrench.

"Andy is seeking retribution." Pop hands me a letter. It's written in Andy's barely legible chicken scratch. "The Henchmen are starting a charter here in town."

In his letter, Andy talks about not being recognized for his contributions to the Double H and not being given the respect he's earned. It's time for him to move on to a real MC where he will be appreciated. He goes on to say Double H's glory days are over. The Henchmen are taking over Halsey. They want me patched out of the Club, effective immediately, or there will be hell to pay.

Heat flushes through me. I stand and kick my chair across the room. "That motherfucker!"

"We're going to have to consider an alliance with the Rebels." Pop's voice is voice thick with reluctance. "Hoyt doesn't want the Henchmen here anymore than we do."

I shake my head with disbelief. "That'll mean allowing their drugs into Halsey."

"It's the only choice we have, Rooter," Wrench says. "It's either their drugs or the Henchmen's. The Rebel's are the lesser of two evils."

"I'll kill him." With my hands clasped behind my head, I pace the room. "What's the plan?"

"We have to play this smart," Wrench says. "We don't have the manpower to go up against the Henchmen on our own."

"By joining forces with Hoyt's crew," Pop starts, "we can keep them from getting a foothold here in Halsey. Ivan won't stay where it isn't profitable." Ivan is the President of the Henchmen.

"And what about Andy?" I ask. "I want him to pay for what he's done."

"Ivan won't tolerate Andy's shit the way we did," Pop declares. "It's only a matter of time before he cuts Andy loose. Once he does, we'll take care of him."

Pop is right, but I'm impatient and I don't want to wait for vengeance. I want that piece of shit to pay now. And though I detest the idea of an allegiance with Hoyt's crew, it's the only chance we've got. I pick up my chair and retake my place at the table. "When are you meeting with Hoyt?"

"I'll call him after we've told everyone what's going on."

"Here's the thing, Rooter," Wrench starts, "Andy's out to get you. Once he finds out we haven't cut you from the Club, we expect him to make a move on you."

Pop shifts toward me and says, "I expect shit to get real ugly, real fast. Don't let your guard down and watch your back at all times."

"I know the drill," I say. I've been through this before, just never as the main target.

"Ivan and his crew are ruthless, Son. They'll come at you anytime, anywhere."

"I can be just as ruthless," I remind him.

I know all about Ivan and what his men are capable of. I'm not afraid. At this stage in my career as a Double H member, I've accepted the realities of what can happen. I'm always prepared.

But what if Sophie's with me when they make their move? The Henchmen are savage. She'll be nothing more than collateral damage to them. This is exactly what I was afraid of and why I tried to keep my distance from her. I knew this would happen.

I'm sure Andy has been keeping an eye on me. He's probably seen me with her. I can't allow Andy and the Henchmen to use her as leverage against me. I must protect her.

I'm so anxious to see Sophie I can hardly sit still as I wait for her to get home from work. I'd considered escorting her home, but thought better of it. I don't want to give her any cause for concern. After what seems like eons, though in reality it's only been twenty minutes, she finally pulls up.

Her face lights up at the sight of me. "Hi."

"Hi." Having her near eases my anxiety. I kiss her cheek before taking her hand and leading her toward her door. "How was work?"

"Kicked my ass." She continues before I can respond. "Can I ask you something?"

"Of course."

"All this time, you sitting on your porch when I get home from work, have you been doing it to make sure I get in safe?"

I rub the back of my neck. "Yes, I have."

"You truly are amazing."

"This is a bad neighborhood. I don't want anything to happen to you." If only a bad neighborhood was my only worry…

"My own personal bodyguard." She looks up at me with bright eyes full of admiration.

"I guess I am."

We're at her door, but she doesn't move to unlock it. She's waiting for me to kiss her, and trying not to be obvious about it.

With a chuckle, I ask, "You going to unlock your door or do you want to hang out here all night?"

Her eyes dart from me to the ground and back again as she fiddles with her keys. "I'm waiting for my good night kiss."

I lean in and kiss her cheek, knowing full well that's not what she meant.

"That's all I get?"

After a moment of watching her squirm, I lean in slowly and press my lips to hers in a delicate, chaste kiss.

"I want a real kiss," she whimpers.

I shake my head. "I'm not kissing you until after our date."

Her eyebrows scrunch together as she frowns. "Why?"

I squeeze her hand lightly and run my thumb across her knuckles. Her skin is so soft. "Because I want to do this right."

Technically, we've already kissed, but the first time was a catastrophe. The second time I was caught up in the moment and it wasn't even an open mouth kiss. I want our first *real* kiss to be memorable, special.

"Okay." She unlocks her door, seemingly happy with my explanation. "Thank you for walking me to my door."

"My pleasure. Good night, Sophie."

"Good night, Rooter."

First Date

I've never been as excited about anything as I am about taking Sophie out on our date. I've never taken a girl on a proper date. Before Sophie, I thought I never would. As I press the doorbell, I realize I forgot to bring flowers.

The door opens and I'm surprised to see Sophie dressed for the Harley. She looks incredible in her black blouse and tight skinny jeans, it's just not what I expected. I imagined her wearing something similar to what she wore on her date with BMW boy.

She looks me up and down, evidently as surprised by my appearance as I am by hers. Tonight I've ditched my cut. I even bought a new outfit for our date, dark wash jeans, a long sleeve gray shirt, and new boots.

"I wasn't going to make you ride the bike tonight," I say.

She looks down at her outfit. "Is this not appropriate? I can change."

"You look amazing, but I don't want you to think you always have to dress for the bike."

She exhales, noticeably relieved. "Rooter, you hate being in cars. Of course I dressed to be on the bike."

"This is our first date. I'd be happy to take my truck."

"I like riding with you on your bike."

She really is the girl of my dreams. "You are too good to be true."

"No cut?" she asks as I lead her to my garage to get the Harley.

"Not tonight."

"It wouldn't bother me."

I turn to face her. "That's not why I chose not to wear it." Feeling a little off my game, I swallow. "Sophie, there's more to who I am than the Club. Tonight I just want to be a guy on a date with his girl."

She smiles. "As long as you aren't doing it for me. I don't have that kind of expectation."

Of course she doesn't. This girl never ceases to amaze me. I place my helmet on her head and fasten it. "We need to get you a helmet of your own."

Her eyes light up and she bounces on her toes. "So, where are you taking me?"

I shake my head and grin, unable to hide my excitement. "Have to wait and see."

Sophie climbs onto the Harley behind me and wraps her arms around my waist. Just as I'm about to start the engine, she leans in to my neck in breathes in. My heart jumps at the unexpected show of affection. It feels incredible, her being this close, holding on to me.

Forty-five minutes later, we pull up to our destination—my aunt Pam's beachfront cottage. It's just like the pictures you see in magazines of beach-side living. High ceilings, light, beachy furnishings, dark floors, and tons of windows. If I had to guess, the place is easily worth a million bucks, but the setting is what's truly phenomenal. It's the reason I asked Pam to let me borrow it for the evening. The look on her face when I asked was priceless. She stared at me with big eyes and asked, "Did I hear you right?" She, like everyone else, considered me the consummate bachelor.

When we get off the bike, Sophie fusses with her hair, but I'm eager to show her what's waiting for us. I tell her it's perfect and take her by the hand.

I open the front door of the cottage and step aside to let Sophie enter first.

Her eyes are wide and her mouth hangs open as she takes in our surroundings. "Wow."

I tug her hand. "Come."

I escort her through the living room to the French doors that lead to the backyard to reveal my surprise. A beach-side candlelit dinner. Aunt Pam put out her best china and finest crystal and I draped the pergola in white curtains and red roses. Romantic music streams through the outdoor speakers.

"Rooter, this is…" Sophie starts, but pauses. "There are no words for what this is."

Her reaction is exactly what I was hoping for. I place a kiss on her hand. "I'm glad you like it."

"I more than like it. I've never…" her voice cracks and her eyes glisten as though she might cry.

Even though they're happy tears, I pull her close. "I want to give you the things you deserve, Sophie." I tilt her face up by her chin so I can see her eyes. "This is what you deserve."

Her voice is barely more than a whisper, "Rooter, please kiss me."

I lean in close. "I'm going to kiss you Sophie."

She stares at me with pleading eyes and sucks in a breath, waiting for me to follow through.

I hover close and speak in a hushed yet determined tone. "I'm going to kiss you like you've never been kissed in your life. Like you'll never be kissed by anyone else ever again." Her lips part in anticipation, but I pull away with a smirk. "But not until the end of our date."

She gasps. "That's cruel."

"Anticipation makes it better." I wink, still smirking.

"I've been anticipating it for a year, a few more hours can't possibly make a difference." Her face turns bright red at her admission.

"Have you now?" I mock.

"I—I..." She stutters and looks away.

I chuckle at her sweetness. "I've been anticipating it for three," I admit and turn her face to mine. "Stalker, remember?"

"I remember."

Taking her by the hand, I guide her to the candlelit table that awaits us. After helping Sophie into her chair, I take my seat and wave for Pam who I know is watching from inside the house. She has agreed to be our server tonight.

"What will you be drinking tonight?" Aunt Pam asks once she reaches us.

Sophie glances my way, her forehead wrinkled. This is obviously someone's home, not a restaurant. She could ask for any kind of soda, beer or mixed drink and we'd probably have it. I went all out for tonight wanting to make sure we'd have whatever she might want.

"I'll have a Corona," I say to my aunt and turn to Sophie. "You like whiskey and beer, right?"

"Yes." Surprised, she blinks and her mouths parts a little.

"I had them stock Jack Daniels for tonight." I know it's her favorite. "Have you tried Corona?"

She nods and looks to Pam. "I'll have Jack on the rocks and an ice water, please."

"Sure thing," Pam says and leaves to retrieve our drinks.

Sophie tilts her head to the side and smiles. "You really are something else."

"What?" I play dumb.

A moment later, Pam reappears with our drinks in hand. "Would you like to order now or do you need a few minutes?"

Sophie pulls her eyebrows together in confusion before noticing the menu placed in front of her. As she reads, her eyes go wide. All three of the menu options are her favorite meals. I really do know a lot about her. Things I shouldn't know at this stage in our relationship.

"Give us a few minutes," I say to Aunt Pam.

"Wave when you're ready," she says before going back into the cottage.

"Just how close of attention have you been paying?" Sophie asks.

I shrug as though knowing so much about her isn't at all strange and inappropriate.

Sophie brings the glass of Jack to her lips for a sip. She closes her eyes and lets the whiskey linger on her tongue a moment. "Thank you, Rooter. This is perfect."

"I aim to please," I say with a wink.

"Mission accomplished." She winks back and it might be the cutest thing I've ever seen.

Sophie looks around, taking in our surroundings. Her hair blows in the breeze and she closes her eyes, leans back and inhales.

As breathtaking as our view is, it's nothing compared to her. I can't take my eyes off her. I could sit and watch her for hours. Days even. I've never been as happy as I am in this moment. Seeing the smile on Sophie's face and knowing I've put it there makes me feel like a king.

"Can I ask you a question?" she asks, her tone serious.

"Of course." I sit up straight and ready myself for whatever she might ask.

"What about the blonde? Are you two still together?"

That's not quite what I was expecting. I thought she was going to ask about my life in the Club or something of that nature. Regardless, I'm prepared to be one hundred percent honest with her. "We were never together, Sophie. That should've *never* happened."

"She stayed at your house while you were gone and then with you. I've never seen any other girl at your house before, so I must assume you've known her a while."

She really has been paying attention if she noticed that I don't bring women to my house. I can see how that'd make her think my thing with Candace was more than it was. "I've known Candace a while, but we were *never* in a relationship. It was just…" I stop mid-sentence, cringing over the fact that I'm talking about sex with another woman while on my first date with Sophie.

"Sex," she finishes the sentence for me.

I close my eyes and cringe again. "Yeah, but it's done, Sophie. You have nothing to worry about."

She says nothing.

Her unsettled expression sends me into panic mode. "Sophie," I wrap my hand around hers. "I'm not the kind of guy you need to worry about. I'd never hurt you."

She opens her mouth to speak, but closes it abruptly and shakes her head. "Never mind."

I scoot my chair closer to hers. "No. Say it. I need to know what you're thinking."

She opens her mouth and closes it again and takes large gulp of her whiskey. "I can't."

No, no, no. Whatever it is, I need to know so I can reassure her. I won't have her worried that she can't trust me. "Well, you have to because I won't let this go until you say it."

"I don't want to ruin this." She motions at our romantic setting.

"You won't ruin it," I assert. "Sophie, I want you to always be honest with me. Tell me what you're thinking."

She stares into my eyes intently as though she's trying to read me. Finally, she speaks. "She and I are nothing alike. If that's the sort of thing you go for, how can you possibly be attracted to me?"

Oh, God no. Please don't think that, Baby. "Sophie that's *not* the sort of thing I go for. She was just… available."

She recoils from my choice of words, but there was no other way to put it. I want her to know, without a shadow of a doubt, that Candace is not, never was, and never will be what I want. It was just sex. It meant absolutely nothing.

"I don't know how I feel about that."

The disappointment in her eyes scares me. Perhaps I shouldn't have been so honest. "Sophie, you must believe me. I have never wanted *anyone* the way I want you. Tonight is a case in point. I have never dated. *Ever.* You make me want things I've never wanted."

Her mouth drops. "Never dated? How old are you?"

"Twenty-five, and no, not even in high school."

She blinks. "How do you go twenty-five years without dating?"

"I was never interested in relationships," I answer honestly once again and hope she can handle it.

"Oh." She finishes her whiskey.

"Like I said, you make me want things I've never wanted. I want to date you." I shake my head because that isn't right. I want so much more. "No. I want to make you mine."

"Why me?" she asks in a soft, disbelieving voice.

"Because you are unlike anyone I have ever met," I shift forward in my seat. "You're everything I never knew I always wanted. And I knew it the moment I first laid eyes on you."

Sophie gasps and raises a hand to her chest. "I feel the same way."

Last First Kiss

Hearing Sophie say those words thrills and excites me. I lean in close to tell her she's safe with me, that I'll protect her and never hurt her the way others have. But before I can utter the words her stomach roars and we break into hysterics.

"Hungry?" I ask jokingly.

Her lips spread into a bashful smile. "Starved."

"Let's order."

I wave for Aunt Pam to come take our order. Luckily, all the food on the menu, with exception of the steaks, has been prepared in advance. We won't have to wait long to eat. But I ask Pam to bring out some bread and butter so Sophie can have a little something to nibble on while we wait.

"It occurs to me," Sophie begins after we've ordered, "I'm on a date with a guy whose name I don't know."

I furrow my brow, confused. "You know my name."

"Your real name."

"You know my real name."

She cocks her head to the side. "You were born with that name?"

I chuckle because she's just too cute. "What? You don't like it?"

"Of course I do," she answers emphatically. "I just… assumed it was a road name."

"You're right. It isn't my birth name. But it is my real name." She stares at me with a confused expression so I continue my explanation. "Birth names are chosen for us before we figure out who we are. Our road names are chosen when we become men. After we learn who we are."

"So, your road name is based on who you really are?"

I laugh because she looks even more perplexed than before. "My road name was chosen for me by Bear, my best friend. You've met him."

"Does it have a meaning?"

"It does."

"Which is?" she presses.

I had hoped this conversation would come after she gets to know me better and won't be so shocked by the answer. I wag my finger. "Privileged information which you must earn."

"Seriously?" She raises a brow.

"Dead serious."

"Then at least tell me your birth name."

That I can do. "Jace Alexander Russo."

Her lips curl into smile. "I like it. You look like a Jace."

"You like Jace better than Rooter?" No matter how crazy I am about her, she can't call me Jace.

"No. I think both suit you well." She seems to mean it.

"Good, because no one calls me Jace."

"Not even your parents?"

I shake my head. With Pop, it was no issue. He understands road names. Mama on the other hand took it a little harder. She raised me with the name Jace and was—and still is—sentimental about the name. "It took a while for my mom to accept the change, but I've gone by Rooter for years now."

Pam arrives with the warm bread and butter. Sophie immediately reaches for a slice and slathers it with butter.

"I can't imagine going by a different name than I was born with," she says, and takes a bite.

A bit of butter sticks to the corner of her mouth and I wipe it away with my napkin. I can't take my eyes off her, she's flawless. "I couldn't imagine you with any other name. A beautiful name for a beautiful woman."

She blushes scarlet and looks to her lap. "Thank you."

"Hey," I say so she'll look up at me. "I mean it."

She nods. "I get the feeling you don't say anything you don't mean."

"You're right. I don't." Not usually anyway. But I'm human. In the heat of the moment, I've been known to say some pretty nasty things to drive home a point, though I can't imagine ever doing that to Sophie. It'd kill me to hurt her.

"So, tell me about yourself," she says and takes another bite of the bread.

"What do you want to know?"

She shrugs as she considers my question. "Everything."

I chuckle. "That's a lot of information to fit into one evening."

"Start with the basics. Family? Brothers and sisters?"

That's a loaded question. One I'm not up to answering fully. I have a younger brother and sister through my biological father, and while I know who they are, they don't know me. They likely never will. But that isn't first date conversation.

"I have a little sister, Isa. She's a senior in high school. She's a great kid. We're very close. My mom's name is Camilla, Pop's name is Mick, but you probably already know that."

Sophie nods. Almost everyone in town knows who Pop is.

"We're very close the four of us," I add. "I have a great family. We're not like you'd imagine. The media gives us a bad rap."

"I don't imagine anything. They say only believe half of what you see and none of what you hear."

"That's good advice."

"I don't have family, but you already know that. I was close to Miranda's mom and dad before they passed. Miranda's all I have left. She's the sister I never had."

I don't get her relationship with Miranda. Perhaps in time I'll come to understand. "You've been through so much at such a young age."

She shrugs, not as though it isn't a big deal, but because the subject makes her uncomfortable. "What are some of your favorite things?"

"My family, obviously. My dog, my bike… you." I wink.

She blushes and shakes her head. "Those are obvious answers."

"How do you know you're one of my favorite things?" I tease.

"I—I didn't," she stammers, her cheeks turning a deep shade of red. "I meant about the other stuff."

I love the effect I have on her. "Hmm, let's see… I like working out, but again, you probably know that… Thirty Seconds To Mars is my favorite band, and gray is my favorite color."

Her eyes crinkle as she laughs. "I only know one song by Thirty Seconds To Mars."

"The Kill?" I ask.

She nods. "I like it. But I've never heard anything else by them."

"You're in luck." I wink. "I'm just the guy to educate you on their greatness."

"Take a walk with me?" I ask once we've finished eating and Pam has cleared the table.

"I'd love to."

I lead Sophie down the stairs to the private beach. There's nothing better than a private beach. No litter, no throngs of teenagers, and it's quiet. The mixture of the sound of the water and the breeze is soothing. I've been known to pitch a tent and sleep out here on the weekends.

I lift our joined hands and marvel at how small hers is in inside mine. "You have the softest hands."

Sophie blushes and shakes her head, modest as usual.

"You don't take compliments very well."

She turns away, gazes at the lake before coming to a stop. Even though she's turned away, I can tell she's frowning. After a moment, she turns back to me, but remains quiet.

If only I could read her mind. "Where'd you go just then?"

"Nowhere I want to be."

I take a step and we return to walking. I sense that she keeps her thoughts and feelings bottled up inside. Doing so is a recipe for disaster. One day it'll all rise to the surface and she'll explode. I know because I've done it. "I'm a fantastic listener. You can talk to me about the things you think about. Your memories."

"I don't want to talk about them," she says, her tone sad. "I don't want to think about them, although I do."

"I respect that. I'm just throwing it out there so you know you can if you ever want to."

"Thanks." She gives me a small smile. "So, tell me more about yourself. When did you join the Club?"

"My pop started the Club with his best friend, Wrench, when they were nineteen, so it's been a part of my life forever. I started working for them at eighteen and became an official member when I turned twenty-one."

"Growing up, did you always want to be a member?"

"Off and on. There were times when I thought it was more trouble than it was worth, but those guys are my family, so I suppose it was inevitable."

If I had decided I didn't want to join Double H, Pop would've been fine with it. When I was sixteen, we discussed it. He told me he'd support me in whatever I chose to do with my life. He'd be proud of me no matter what I did. I always wanted to work with him at the shop, but I found the idea of being a member of the MC daunting. I wasn't sure I'd be able to live up to the expectations. But in the end, it's where I belong.

"Was there anything else you wanted to do?" Sophie comes to a halt and bends down to pick up a rock in the sand. She inspects it with a smile and puts it into her jeans pocket.

"Not really," I say as we begin walking again. "I always wanted to run the shop with my pop. Everything I know I learned from him and Wrench."

"Can I ask you a question?"

I stop walking and turn to look into her eyes. "Sophie, you don't have to ask if you can ask me things. Just ask. I'll tell you anything I can."

She nods, understanding, but hesitates before asking her question. "Your shop is successful. Makes a lot of money. Why get involved in other… bad things?"

I've been waiting for this question. Everyone not affiliated with the Club asks it eventually. "It's not exactly what it seems. All we've really done is fight to keep drug dealers and prostitution out of Halsey. That was the reason for the Club's inception. To do what the cops can't do. What they don't have the balls to do. But they can't possibly have the locals knowing we're doing their job better than they are, so they have the media spin it a different way to make their tiny little dicks look bigger."

Sophie pulls her brows together and bites her lower lip. "But you even said you do bad things. It was why you wanted me to stay away from you."

"Sophie, to keep this town safe, we get involved in very risky shit with extremely dangerous people on a regular basis. Anyone who is involved with us is a target. Being with me means wearing a bulls-eye. That's why I was reluctant to get involved with you."

"But you changed your mind." The corner of her mouth turns up.

"I still think this is dangerous," especially considering my issue with Andy and the Henchmen, "but I can't not be with you."

Her breath hitches and she whispers, "I can't not be with you either."

With all the stories that go around about me and the Club—most of which are exaggerated but not entirely inaccurate—I'll never understand how she's not afraid to be with me. "I don't get your interest in me at all. Explain it to me."

A moment passes before she answers. "You make me feel something I've never felt."

"What's that?" I ask.

"Safe."

I was *not* expecting that. The last thing I'd expect is for Sophie to feel safe with me. I shake my head and chuckle.

"What's funny?" she asks.

"I just told you that being with me could be potentially dangerous to your health and you feel *safe*?"

"Rooter," her voice is low, seductive even, though I doubt she realizes it. "I've always felt safe around you."

Astounded, I lean my forehead against hers. "I will always do everything in my power to make sure no one ever hurts you."

"I believe you."

This is the moment I've been waiting for. For Sophie to be looking at me just as she is now, happy, hopeful, trusting and with longing. I place my hands on each side of her face and widen my stance so I'm eye to eye with her. "You can always believe in me Sophie. You've been through so much. You've been hurt and mistreated so badly by those who were supposed to love you. I promise you I'll never hurt you."

If there's one thing I'm sure of, it's that I will never hurt Sophie. I'm not capable of it. Just the idea of her being upset or sad is unbearable. I can never be the one to make her feel that way.

"I hope not," she whispers, seemingly accidentally. A lone tear slides down her cheek.

I've never experienced such intense emotions. As I stand before this incredible girl, my chest aches as my heart races. Does she notice my fingers trembling? I brush the tear from her cheek. "You are safe with me."

I want to remember every single detail, every second of this kiss. Mesmerized by the light in Sophie's eyes I lean in slowly. I feel as though my life is just beginning. Maybe it is. All I know is nothing will ever be the same for me now that I have Sophie. *I* will never be the same. It's as though she's my reason for being—that everything I've done in my life has been leading me to her. Sophie closes her eyes in anticipation of my kiss, but there's one thing I need to make clear first. I don't care if it's too soon. She needs to know. I tell her to open her eyes. "Once I kiss you, you're mine, Sophie. Do you want to be mine?"

"I've never wanted anything more." Her tone is solid and sure.

Finally… Sophie Noelle Holt is officially, formally, legitimately mine.

I've never been nervous about kissing a girl, but I've never had so much on the line. This isn't just a kiss. It isn't just lust. In fact, for the first time in my life, it isn't about lust at all. Although I desire Sophie more than anyone before her, this kiss isn't about that. It's about giving myself, heart and soul, to another human being. It's about wanting to earn her heart and soul in return.

We may have only just begun, but the one thing I'm sure of is I'll never let Sophie go. From this moment on, this girl is the single most precious thing in my life. She is my reason. For everything. She is my sun and my world revolves around her. I am hers. Entirely.

I lean closer and Sophie closes her eyes, waiting for me to make her mine. With this kiss, I intend to deliver on my earlier promise, to kiss her like no other. To rock her fucking world and erase all others from her memory. With my hands still on each side of her face, I bring my mouth to hers slowly. I trace her bottom lip with my tongue asking for entrance, but she doesn't grant it. I can't tell if she's teasing me or if she's nervous. Impatient, I take her bottom lip between my teeth and bite gently. Her lips part and I can't stifle my groan when her tongue slides along mine. Her taste is sweeter than I imagined and damn, the girl can kiss. She moans as I kiss her long and hard, then soft and sweet. She whimpers into my mouth and drapes her arms around me, pressing her body against mine.

"Oh my," she murmurs after I pull away.

With my hands still cupping her face, I stroke her cheeks with my thumbs. "Even better than I imagined."

"Best first kiss ever," she breathes.

"Your last first kiss."

She smiles and pulls her phone out from her back pocket. She pulls up the camera and hands it to me. "I want to record this moment."

I hold the phone up and take two photos, one of us smiling into the camera and a second of us kissing. Once I'm finished, I text both pictures to myself. The one of us kissing will be the new screen saver on my phone.

"Good first date?" I ask a couple minutes later as we sit in the sand, her back to my chest. I smell the sweet scent of her shampoo as her hair blows in the breeze.

"My last first date."

Damn straight it is. I chuckle and place a kiss on her temple. "Good answer."

Mine

I shouldn't be smiling right now. I just got my ass reamed by a client. His custom Slim was supposed to be delivered today, but thanks to Andy's bullshit we've fallen behind on the job. More than half our crew is out either keeping surveillance or with Pop and Wrench as they try to convince Hoyt to form a temporary alliance with Double H. At this rate, we'll be lucky to finish the build and get it delivered in time for the weekend.

I had to give the client a twenty percent discount on the build to calm him down. He accepted it, but was still furious. Said if he doesn't have his bike by Saturday morning, he isn't us paying a dime for the work we've done. But worse than the lost money is the possible dent in our reputation. We've never been late on a build. Never. Looks like Bear, Darren, and I will be here all night working on it. We'll probably be here all day and night tomorrow, too.

Yet as pissed as I am, I still have a smile on my face. I can't get Sophie off my mind. I keep replaying our date and the kiss on the beach, over and over.

As I join Darren and Bear at one of the picnic tables in the back lot of the shop I hear a familiar voice. I turn to my left to find Candace walking our way, her blonde hair bouncing with every perky step. Ever since our meeting, she's been texting and calling non-stop telling me she's not letting me go without a fight.

"Hey, Candace," Darren says when I fail to greet her.

She looks like her usual, chipper self in short shorts and tight pink tank top. She scans the empty lot and yard, "Where is everyone?"

"Club business," I answer.

Darren and Bear strike up a conversation about the slim and where they'll pick up once we go inside. I'd chime in, but Candace doesn't give me a chance.

"Must be major if it's taken everyone away from the shop." She raises a questioning brow. "Why are you here?"

"Overseeing a build while Pop and Wrench are out."

Satisfied with my answer, Candace nods and sits on the small piece of remaining bench to my left. She could've sat on the other side of the table in the empty spot next to Darren. With Bear to my right, I've no room.

"I'm trying to eat," I complain.

Bear stands and moves to the other side of the table to sit next to Darren. I scoot as far to the right as I can, but Candace sidles up right next to me, her chest pressed to my arm. She drags her long, pink fingernail up my denim covered thigh and leans into my ear. "Did you like the video I sent you?"

I'd done a good job of forgetting all about it until this moment. Last night, when I failed to respond to her one thousand two hundred and fifty seven texts, she sent me a video of her pleasuring herself. "It looked like you enjoyed making it," I evade.

Her hand is now resting at the junction of my thighs with her index finger brushing the head of my cock. She whispers, "Nobody gets me off like you do."

Darren chokes and gets up from the table and Bear follows. The girl has zero modesty.

Candace rubs her hard, silicone filled tits on my arm. "You've ruined me for other men, Rooter. If I can't have you, I don't want anyone else."

Candace's rocklike chest on my bicep makes me think of Sophie and how soft and natural she is. It also makes me wonder how Sophie would feel if she knew another girl was rubbing against me. If the situation was reversed, I'd be seeing red. "Candace, it isn't happening. I'm sorry."

"You honestly think you can resist me forever?" She licks the rim of my ear.

Yep. "Trust me, sweetheart, you're better off without me. This is for the best. We've been friends too long to risk jeopardizing it."

"They say friends make the best lovers," she presses. "And gauging by the way I make you scream, I'd say you agree."

I admit the sex was great. Phenomenal even. But for me it was just sex. It wasn't anything special. "We had some good times," I allow.

"How about I remind you how great it is? I'm thirsty." Candace reaches for my belt buckle.

I yank her hand away. I don't have many inhibitions, but getting a blow job outside in the middle of the day, where anyone passing by can see is where I draw the line. Besides, I'm taken. "Candace, stop."

She looks at me with wide eyes. "Since when do you turn down head?"

"Since now."

"Is she as good as me?"

I clear my throat and shift in my seat.

There's a spark of humor in her dark brown eyes. "She isn't, is she?"

"I'm not talking about this Candace."

She tosses her head back and her entire body shakes as she laughs. "The girl you chose over me can't fuck right. I love karma."

Heat instantly floods my body and my nostrils flare. "Be careful, Candace."

"We're meant to be together, Rooter." She folds her arms over her chest making her cleavage pop out more. "You know it as well as I do."

With a sigh, I turn away. "You're just making this harder than it has to be."

She grabs me by the chin and turns my face to hers. "It's you and me. Always will be."

I shake my head.

"It's just a matter of time before you show up on my doorstep."

I squeeze my eyes closed. "I guess we'll see."

The back door swings open and Bear sticks out his head. "Rooter," he says, "I need you to come look at something."

"I'm coming." I stand. "I have to go inside."

"I meant what I said," Candace says. "I won't let you go without a fight."

"I guess you gotta do what you gotta do." I throw what's left of my lunch in the trash can beside the door.

I'm standing in Sophie's driveway as she pulls in. I open her door to help her out. "Hi," I murmur and kiss her softly.

Her eyes crinkle at the sides as she smiles at me. "Hi."

"How was work?" I stroke the top of her hand with my thumb.

"Good. Made a ton in tips." Her eyes stay on me the entire walk to her door. "Want to come in?"

You have no idea. "Wish I could. I have to be at the shop by six. We're running behind on a build."

She bites her lip and looks to her feet. "You didn't need to wait up on me."

I tilt her face up so I can see into her eyes. "I'll always wait up on you, Sophie. Your safety is more important than sleep."

She places her tiny hand on my cheek and brushes her thumb over my stubble. "But you'll be so tired tomorrow."

I lean into her hand. This moment, right here, is well worth lost sleep. "No worries. I napped earlier."

"Thank you for walking me to my door."

"Maybe we can grab lunch together tomorrow. I'll call you around noon."

Her blue eyes sparkle. "Okay."

Sophie's breathing picks up as she awaits my kiss. I move in at an excruciatingly slow pace. She licks her lips and her breath catches just before my lips graze hers. Her full lips are warm against mine as I kiss her soft and gentle. It takes every ounce of strength not to devour her. But I like teasing her, testing her to see how she'll react. I pull her bottom lip in between my teeth and flick it with my tongue. The sound of her moan turns me on. Thoughts run through my mind of all the ways I could illicit that sound.

Sophie clutches my head with both hands and pulls me into her, trying desperately to deepen the kiss. I almost give in, but I'm having too much fun driving her crazy. I open my mouth just slightly and flick my tongue against hers. She whimpers into my mouth and pulls me tighter. I pull away and take her hands into mine.

"Don't tease me," she whines, breathless.

"But it's so much fun."

"Not for me."

"No?" I lean down and softly graze her cheek with mine. My own heart is racing and my nerve endings tingle at the thought of kissing and touching her. "I think you like it. Look at how you're responding."

Sophie's face is flushed and her lips are slightly parted. She stares at my lips with pleading eyes. Feeling smug at how much she wants me, I chuckle.

"I hear payback is a bitch."

I lean back and cock an eyebrow. "Is that right?"

"Yeah." She smirks, suddenly confident.

"And exactly how do you plan on paying me back?"

"Maybe next time, I won't *let* you kiss me." She flashes her eyebrows, trying to taunt me.

"Oh Sophie," I lean in just inches from her face and twist a lock of her hair, "we both know better than that."

"Guess we'll have to wait and see."

Indeed we will, Babe. "Good night, Sophie,' I say with a wink and walk away.

The morning drags. Every ten minutes that passes feels like an hour. I told Sophie I'd call her at noon. At this rate, I'll be fifty when twelve o'clock finally rolls around.

It's another lean day in terms of on hand personnel at the shop. Since Bear and Darren are home for the day, it's just me, Sparrow and Tank. A two man crew isn't going to cut it. Especially those two. I love the guys, but they don't work with the same zeal as Darren and Bear.

I help where I can with heavy lifting and sometimes paintwork, but when it comes to frame and bodywork, I'm useless. Then again, someone has to manage this place, balance the checkbook, pay the bills, and cut the checks for the guys. Not the most manly of jobs, but no less important.

Pop had been doing it for years and began grooming me for it when I was still in high school. When he's ready to retire, I will become the official owner of the shop. I'll need to know the ins and outs of the business behind the scenes.

But at times like this, I wish I was out there on the floor welding or doing anything with my hands. Thoughts of Sophie consume me. I need busy work to keep my mind off her. Now that we're "together" I want to spend every waking moment with her. I may have spent the past year digging into her past, but there's so much more to know. I want to know what she thinks and how she feels about everything, including the mundane. What are her dreams, hopes, and darkest secrets? What makes her tick? What moves her? What is she most passionate about?

At five minutes till twelve, I turn out the lights in the office and tell the guys I won't be returning before hurrying outside to call Sophie. I tell her I'm on my way and twelve minutes later, I pull up in front of her house. I don't even have time to get off my Harley before she comes running out of the house with a giddy smile on her face. The entire world seems brighter and more colorful at the mere sight of her.

"Happy to see me?" I ask.

She shrugs, playing off her enthusiasm. "Just hungry."

"Is that right?"

"Yep."

"Well, I'm *very* happy to see you." I lean in for a kiss, but she steps back. *Game on.* "Playing it like that, huh?"

"Just giving you a taste of your own medicine. How is it?"

"Pretty damn good from what I can remember." I wink and wait for her reaction.

Her face flushes and the corner of her mouth turns up into a faint smile. "Well, that memory is going to have to hold you over a while."

I tilt my head back and shoot her a playful grin. "We'll see."

"Yeah, we will."

I like playful, flirtatious Sophie. I take the helmet from my head and place it on hers. Once it's secured, I motion for her to climb on behind me. She wraps her arms around my waist and I pick up her right hand and bring it to my lips, flicking my tongue across her palm. Sophie sucks in a surprised breath. I'm a creative guy. If she won't let me kiss her on the mouth, I can find other places.

Hand in hand, we walk into Skyles, Sophie's favorite restaurant. With her tight budget, she doesn't get to eat out often. I figure I might as well take her somewhere she likes. I like it here, too. Great food, decent service. Only problem is it's a popular hangout for obnoxious frat boys, which I have zero tolerance for. I've had to come here on behalf of my little sister quite a few times to put a stop to their harassment.

The moment we're inside, the owner and bartender, Joe Skyles, recognizes Sophie. There's an unmistakable twinkle in his eyes as he looks at her.

"Hey, Joe," Sophie says as I lead her to a high-top table near the bar.

"Hey, Soph." Joe places menus in front of both of us. He looks at Sophie, to me, then back to her again.

"Joe, this is Rooter," Sophie says and motions toward me. "Rooter, this is Joe."

"Nice to meet you, man." I extend my hand. The last time he and I spoke, he was escorting me, along with the frat boy whose face I'd just mangled, out of his bar.

"I've seen you in here before," he acknowledges in a neutral tone as he shakes my hand. "Nice to meet you. What can I get you to drink?"

"I'll have my usual." Sophie flashes him her adorable smile.

It's obvious they know each other well. Ridiculous as it is, their familiarity and the way she's smiling at him perturbs me. "I'll have a coke."

Joe goes back to the bar to get our drinks, but can't take his eyes off Sophie. Poor guy looks like a five year old who lost his favorite toy. He fills my cup too high, and the soda spills onto the counter and I chuckle.

"What's funny?" Sophie asks. She gets the cutest little wrinkle between her eyes when she's confused.

"Joe doesn't seem very pleased to see you with me."

She shrugs. "He's probably just surprised. I usually come here with Miranda."

Who does she think she's kidding? She must know he's completely smitten with her. "Yeah right. That poor man is heartbroken."

"One sweet tea and one coke," Joe says and sets our drinks on the table. "Ready to order or do you need a minute?"

"Give us a minute," I answer. When it comes to business, I can decide with a moment's notice, but when it comes to eating out, I can't make a decision to save my life.

Joe lingers at our table, gazing at Sophie as though memorizing her face before finally turning and walking away.

"And I thought you came here for the food," I joke.

"I do!"

This is too much fun. I lean forward and goad her on. "Yeah, that and the exceptional service."

"Jealous?"

I shake my head. I'm proud to be the man sitting here with her, but most of all I'm astonished. "Not at all. I simply find it interesting."

"Find what interesting?" She furrows her brow.

I take her by the hand and brush her knuckles with my thumb. "The fact that you can have any guy you want and you chose me."

What could she possibly see in me that she doesn't see in Joe? He's a successful business owner. He's known locally as a good guy—donates food from the bar to the local homeless shelter every week, he's involved in the community. And I'm secure enough in my manhood to admit he's a good looking guy. She'd be safe with someone like him. So why choose me?

Sophie stares at me, processing what I've just said. Clearly, she doesn't agree. "You should remember that next time you think about teasing me."

I lean in close and speak in a hushed tone, "That a threat?"

She moves forward to close the space between us. "Try me and find out."

"Sophie, if you want me to kiss you, I will. Right here. Right now." And it wouldn't be a soft, gentle kiss either. It'd be borderline porn tongue.

Her face turns pink and her breath catches, but she falls back into her seat and crosses her arms trying to seem unaffected. "You just want to mark your territory."

"You and I both know I don't need to."

"What does that mean?" She tries to sound offended, and fails.

"Simply that I know how much you want me."

"You're so full of yourself!" she scoffs with a smile.

"Just telling it like it is."

Sophie shoots me a dirty look and shakes her head, but can't hide the desire in her eyes.

I lean in again. "I want you just as much Sophie. And mark my word before this day is over I will kiss you."

Phenomenally Beautiful

My favorite quote is by Voltaire, "Man is free the moment he wishes to be." I believe that's true. Nothing in this life has more power over you than you allow it to have. You are free to be whoever and whatever you choose. Most people, sadly, don't have the confidence or the courage to do or be what they really want. They'd rather follow the societal "norm" than risk not fitting in.

Life is too short to waste a single moment. I refuse to pretend to be anything I'm not. I am who I am and if you don't like it, fuck off. I live my life unapologetically. When I walk, it's with confidence and pride.

I've earned my reputation of a criminal. I've done bad things, I've hurt people, but only for the greater good. Everything I do, is with the big picture in mind. Sometimes a little suffering for a few is worth the long-term happiness of many. It's never an easy decision to make, though necessary.

These are the thoughts on my mind as Sophie and I ride out to the Westlake Boardwalk after lunch. Since Sophie is riding with me, I take the longer, scenic route along the lakeshore.

When we arrive, Sophie's shivering and covered in goosebumps. "Were you warm enough? I wasn't thinking about how much cooler it is along the lakeshore when I took that route."

"It was p-perfect," her teeth chatter. "So beautiful."

"We'll take the main roads home." I take her by the hand and guide her to the left, away from the public beach entrance. The long walk to the private beach should warm her up.

"I thought we were going to the boardwalk." She motions to the entrance.

"Going in the back way."

"There's a back way?"

No. Just a different way. But I don't say as much. I just give her a sly smile. I'm not surprised Sophie doesn't know about the private beach. She's a good girl. Using a private beach that she doesn't have permission for isn't her style. Breaking any law, no matter how small, isn't her style. She can probably count on one hand the number of laws she's broken. I couldn't begin to count the laws I've broken. My first offense, though I wasn't caught, was stealing a street sign with my last name. I was only thirteen.

Letting go of her hand, I wrap my arm around Sophie's waist to draw her close as we walk. A thrill shoots through me when she returns the gesture. I've dreamt of being with her for so damn long, never thinking it would actually happen. Yet, here we are.

She's mine.

I repeat it in my mind again and again, but I doubt I'll ever get used to it.

From the looks we're garnering by the passersby, I'd venture a guess they're even more stunned than I am that Sophie's with me. Their mouths fall open and they glare at me with cold eyes when they see my arm draped around her. The men glance from her to me with disdain. They can't possibly imagine what she sees in a piece of shit like me. They probably assume I'm taking advantage of a young woman's naiveté—that I'm corrupting her. But right now, I couldn't care less. I'm on cloud nine to have this beautiful girl by my side.

But Sophie isn't as jubilant. She looks ill at ease with a frown as she chews the inside of her mouth. It occurs to me she might not be as unaffected by the gawking and unspoken judgments. As we pass a few more disgusted onlookers, her posture stiffens.

She's embarrassed to be seen with me.

My throat constricts painfully at the realization. I come to a halt and when I do, Sophie falters in her step. "Do you want me to take you home?"

"Why would I want that?"

"Please, Sophie," I groan. "I can see how uncomfortable you are."

"What? No."

"Yes you are," I tear my hand away. "Everyone's staring and judging you for being with me and it bothers you." Insulted, I back away from her.

"No. Rooter." She grabs my hand and squeezes it. "I don't care what anyone thinks about me being with you. I don't like the way they're looking at you."

I turn to face her. "What?"

"These judgmental assholes are looking at you like they're better than you and it's pissing me off!" Sophie ferociously stares down an ogling bystander, ready to pounce. It's completely adorable.

Swathed in relief, I laugh and sit her down on the bench to our right. "Whoa, killer. Back down." I take her by the arms and pull her close. "It doesn't matter what they think."

"But they're wrong!"

"Again. Doesn't matter. Don't let it bother you. I don't."

"Never?" Her eyes are filled with disbelief.

"I don't care what strangers think of me."

She raises her voice. "It doesn't piss you off even a little that they're looking down on you when they don't even know you?"

"They're strangers, Sophie," I speak with a gentle, easy tone. "I'll never see any of them again, so why should it bother me?"

"Yeah, but it still pisses me off." She presses her lips into a thin line and glowers at a nosy spectator.

I smile and lean my forehead against hers. "I like protective Sophie."

For a long moment, I stare into her eyes. This incredible creature continues to surprise me. She's like a protective mama bear. I'm not used to being the one being defended. I pull away and bring her hand to my lips. She licks her lips and leans forward infinitesimally. She wants me to kiss her. It's very tempting. But… the game is still on.

I give her a wink and stand from the bench, holding out my hand.

We resume our walk to the beach, but every time someone frowns at us, Sophie becomes tense. I fear she might attack someone.

"I have an idea," I say. "Something my mom taught me."

"What's that?" she asks through gritted teeth.

"Every time someone gives us a dirty look, smile at them like you're happy to see them."

"What?"

"It's a great way to call them out. It says, I see you judging me, and guess what, I don't give a shit."

She purses her lips, doubtful.

"Like the guy in the blue shirt coming our way," I nod in his direction. When we get a little closer, I meet his stare and smile wide, pulling Sophie close. He quickly looks away, tripping on his feet.

Sophie beams. "That was hilarious. His face turned bright red."

"It works every time."

A few minutes later, we reach the entrance to the private beach. It's not much of an entrance, per se. It's just a beaten down path that has been worn in between a pair of tall sand dunes.

"This is a private beach," Sophie whispers when she sees the no trespassing sign.

"No one ever says anything," I assure her with a smile and a squeeze of the hand.

There's hardly anyone here, anyway. The woman reading a novel under her beach umbrella is almost always here, in the same spot. There's also a few couples, one with a young boy running around with a ball. One of the couples briefly glance our way.

"You come here often?" Sophie asks.

"Mostly in the winter."

"The winter?" Her brows are pulled together in surprise.

Few people are brave enough to come out here in the winter. Winters on Lake Michigan are not for the faint of heart. They are brutal. There's usually a foot or more of snow on the ground January through the end of February. Since I can't ride in the winter, I spend a lot of my time at the beach, taking in the view of the ice-covered lake. "Yeah. When the lake's iced over, the sunset here is phenomenal. Have you ever seen it?"

She shakes her head emphatically. "Not much of a cold weather person."

Not surprised, I chuckle. "Well, I'm bringing you here this winter. You must see it."

Sophie blanches and shakes her head. "Take a picture."

"No pictures," I insist. "You have to see it in person to really capture the beauty of it."

She giggles, but doesn't say what she finds funny.

"What?" I ask.

"You and phenomenally beautiful sunsets seem like a bit of an oxymoron."

"What?" I clutch a hand to my chest and act insulted. "I'm not phenomenally beautiful?"

She looks at me with a thoughtful expression before answering. "Actually, you are."

I take her face into both hands, my eyes fixed on hers. "I think you're phenomenally beautiful."

Sophie's breath catches, her expression a silent plea for a kiss. Just as I'm about to give in, she's hit in the head with a fly away beach ball. The little boy I saw when we got here stands before us looking up at her.

"Sorry," he says and takes off running with the ball.

Both of us laugh and Sophie glances back at me through thick eyelashes, desire evident. But I fix my gaze on the lake, pretending to be unaffected.

Sophie removes her shoes and walks toward the water. As I follow behind, I smell her perfume in the breeze—feminine and sweet, just like her. I fight an intense urge to pull her against me and bury my face in the crook of her neck. We stand on the edge of the water, just close enough that the waves don't reach our feet. Sophie closes her eyes and basks in the warmth of the sun as the wind blows through her hair.

"I could spend all day here." She turns to me with a smile.

"I'm game."

I take a seat in the sand and Sophie follows suit, lifting her face to the sky. I'd be content to sit here, staring at her all day long.

"I wish I could," she says, "but I have this thing called a job and unfortunately I need said job to pay another thing called rent."

I'm half tempted to tell her to forget her job. To quit and stay here with me. I'll pay her bills and make sure she's taken care of. The thought surprises even myself. I've never been inclined to take care of a woman before Sophie, with the exception of my mom and little sister, but that's different. They're family. Obviously I'd take care of them. Nothing would please me more than to take care of Sophie and provide her every need and desire. However, it's much too soon to be making such a declaration. I lace my fingers with hers and smile. "I'll bring you back when we can spend an entire day together. Preferably with you in that yellow bikini."

Her face turns crimson. As she leans in for a kiss, her phone rings, but she doesn't answer it.

"I thought you weren't kissing me," I jest and lean in a bit closer.

"I changed my mind." Her phone continues to ring.

I raise a brow. "Is that right?"

She leans in another couple inches. Her breath is warm on my face. "Yeah."

"Well, so have I." I pull away and feign disinterest.

"What?" She stares at me, blinking rapidly. Finally, her phones stops ringing.

"I'm going to make you work for it."

"Work for it?"

"Yeah." I nod. "You're going to have to earn it."

At first she looks at me, dumbfounded, but then folds her arms over her chest. "I won't go out with you again until you kiss me."

I lean in close and linger like I might just kiss her. I look from her eyes, to her tempting lips, and back to her eyes. "Sophie, be realistic. You know you can't stay away from me."

Sophie falls back and props herself up on her elbows. "You so need to get over yourself."

I follow, hovering above her. "Actually, I think it's *you* who can't get over me."

Her breathing has picked up. Our faces are mere inches apart and she leans in until I can almost feel the softness of her lips. "Kiss me," she begs.

Sophie's phone rings again and I pull back with a smirk. She answers the call.

"Hello?" She listens to the caller. "What happened?"

I turn in her direction as she listens with concern to whatever her caller is saying.

"I'm on my way." She ends the call and turns to me, panicked. "I need to get home."

"What is it?"

"Mike just called Miranda and threatened her."

Too Far

When we walk into the house Miranda is on the couch crying. Her body shakes as she stares at the cell phone on the coffee table.

"Has he called back?" Sophie asks and takes a seat next to her.

Miranda sniffles and shakes her head in response.

"What did he say?" I ask and sit in the chair next to the sofa, resting my elbows on my knees.

"He said this is his house as much as it is mine," Miranda answers with a shaky voice, "and I had no right kicking him out. And said I was wrong to choose Sophie over him and he's going to make both of us pay for it."

Sophie looks my way. "He can't be stupid enough to try something. You warned him to stay away."

"He was seriously pissed off," Miranda says. "And you know how he gets when he's high."

"If he's doped out, there's no way of knowing what he might do," I say and shift upright in my seat. "He probably won't come here, but he could show up somewhere else. I wouldn't put anything past him."

If he shows up here, he'll get a very unpleasant surprise.

"He's never sounded like this," Miranda mutters, her voice thick with fear. "He was serious."

I grab Miranda's phone from the table and hold it out to her. "Unlock it."

She takes it, but hesitates, her eyes glued to the screen. "What are you going to do?"

"I'm going to call him." *What the hell do you think?* I snap my fingers.

"That'll only piss him off more," she argues, "especially if you call from my phone. He'll think I had you call him."

"That's the point," I explain, holding my hand out for her phone. "If he thinks you called me for help it might scare him enough to drop it."

Finally, she unlocks the device and hands it to me. I understand her trepidation, but this must be done. I need to make it perfectly clear that I'm here and he'd better not even *think* about harming these girls.

I scroll through her long list of contacts until I find Mike's number. On the second ring he answers, screaming expletives. "Stop talking and listen fucker," I snarl. "Did I or did I not say no retaliation against these girls? If you want to keep your limbs, you will *never* threaten these girls again. Do you understand?"

Miranda clutches Sophie's hand and her eyes are big with fear. She need not be afraid. I won't let her brother harm her. I may not have much of a relationship with Miranda, and she's not my biggest fan, but Sophie loves her, therefore I will protect her with my life the same as I would Sophie.

After no response from Mike, I roar, "Tell me you understand!"

"I understand," he mumbles, fearfully.

"Good. Now promise me you will stay away from them…"

"I'll stay away."

"Good boy." I end the call and set the phone back on the table. I turn my attention to the girls. "I think he got the point, but to be sure, either me or one of my guys will keep watch over you both for a while."

"Thank you," Miranda says through tears. "I never believed he'd actually hurt me, but now I'm sure he will."

"I won't let that happen," I promise.

"It'll be okay," Sophie reassures her.

Miranda falls against Sophie and sobs. "No, it won't. I've lost my entire family."

Miranda isn't my favorite person, largely in part to her obvious antipathy for me, but hearing those words and watching as she falls apart in Sophie's arms is heartrending.

"I know it feels like the end of the world to you, but it will be okay," Sophie pledges. "Your parents may be gone, and Mike is messed up, but you're not alone. You will never be alone, Miranda."

"What would I do without you?" Miranda snivels and squeezes Sophie tight.

"You'll never have to worry about that."

Mike would have to be a complete moron to come anywhere near these girls, but then again, he is an idiot. I can't trust that my threat will be enough to keep him away. I need to put a plan in place that will protect both girls. I can be with Sophie when she's not working, but I can't be with Miranda at all times, and I suspect she's the one he'd come after. I rise and go into the kitchen to call Bear.

"Hey, Brother," he answers.

"I need a favor." I drag my fingers through my hair as I pace the room.

"Name it."

"I have to run Sophie to work in a bit and I need you to keep watch over her roommate."

"What's going on?"

"The roommate's brother made a threat. I called him and warned him not to try anything, but I'm feeling a little uneasy. Better safe than sorry."

"When do you need me there?"

I check my watch. Sophie needs to be at work in an hour. "Half hour."

"I'll be there."

Back in the living room, I tell Sophie and Miranda that Bear is on his way. I turn to Miranda. "He'll stay with you while I take Sophie to work."

"Is he the scary one with the beard?" she asks Sophie.

Sophie and I both laugh.

"That's the one," Sophie confirms.

"Good," she swallows. "He'd scare the shit out of Mike."

"He scares most people," I admit and chuckle again.

Sophie glances up at the clock on the wall. "Speaking of work, I need to get ready."

Though I've been in Sophie's room before, I don't remember much about it. Given the circumstances, I wasn't inclined to pay much attention. One's personal space can tell you a lot about them. Sophie's room is tidy, bed is made in a quick job kind of way—the blanket is pulled up and pillows stacked. There's no clutter, no dishes or trash lying around. I'm not surprised. She's usually the one mowing the lawn and working in the yard trying to keep things looking nice.

Above her bed, there's a very telling phrase stenciled onto the wall, *I crave a love so deep the ocean would be jealous.* Sophie deserves a love that deep. I've no idea what the future holds for us in terms of our relationship, but our love would be epic.

On her nightstand, I spy a romance novel with an image of a half-naked couple on the front. Unable to resist, I pick it up and take a seat on her bed and turn to a random page. The protagonist is talking to her best friend about the hot guy she has a thing for. The best friend tells her he's bad news and she needs to stay away. I flip to another random page where the heroine is losing her virginity to the bad boy. I nearly choke while reading the paragraph detailing the girl's life altering, earth shattering, toe curling orgasm.

"Have a thing for bad boys?" I ask with a grin.

A flush sweeps across Sophie's cheeks and her ears turn red. "I thought that was obvious."

I set the book back on her nightstand and walk over to the wall across from her bed. It's covered in postcards of different places throughout the world. There's no rhyme or reason to them.

"What are these?" I point to one of the postcards featuring a tropical beach.

"Places I hope to visit one day."

"There's a lot of them here."

Her voice is tinged with hopelessness when she says, "I dream big."

"That's a good thing," I try to encourage her.

She taps one of the postcards and sighs long and slow. "Yeah. Good for setting myself up for big failure."

"Don't say that." I turn to face her. Her shoulders are slumped and there's a distant look in her eyes. "You can do anything you want with your life. You're strong enough to make your dreams come true."

"Yeah, well, strong or not we don't always get what we want in this life."

I can't argue that. "You're right, we don't. But the fact you have these on the wall proves you haven't given up hope."

"Sometimes, I feel like hope is all I have." Her voice trembles ever so slightly.

If only she could see herself through my eyes. Outside of hope, she has intelligence, capability, and strength. "You have so much more, Sophie," I reach up and stroke her cheek, "but hope is one of the most important things to have. My Nona always said that without it, we have nothing."

"She sounds like a wise woman." She steps away from the wall, dejected.

"She was." I regard her thoughtfully as she walks to her dresser. "You remind me of her."

"I do?" Her eyes flit to mine, full of surprise.

I slide up behind her close enough that my chest rests against her back and she shudders. I speak in a low tone, "Your demeanor is the same. Incredibly sweet and strong."

"I'm not that sweet."

I bow down and press my face to her neck and inhale her delicious, feminine scent. She smells so damn good, I could devour her. I wrap an arm around her waist and place a wet kiss just below her jawline. "And you taste even sweeter."

She drops the items she's holding and spins around to face me, desire blazing in her eyes. She presses her lips to mine and kisses me hard and fast. With her arms around my neck, she pulls me flush against her. Her tongue rolls with mine in a quest for dominance. My hands travel down her back and rest just above the curve her ass. I'm tempted to reach lower, but I'm unsure how she might react.

As we continue to kiss, she reaches beneath my cut to explore my chest and abs. I feel the warmth of her hands through my shirt. Her touch is like fire, igniting my desire. I reach down and grip her ass. With my free hand, I take a fistful of her hair into my hand and pull, though not hard enough to hurt her.

A lustful groan escapes her lips and her hands travel down to the waist of my jeans just above the button. Taken by surprise, I'm not sure what to expect next. She lifts the hem of my shirt and grazes the skin just above my belt buckle.

Fuck.

Her touch is electric. My head rolls back and I moan in pleasure. Sophie continues to explore my bare skin with her fingers. Desire burns in her eyes and her lips are swollen, her face is flushed.

I remind myself I must tread lightly, take things slow. But the look on her face says she wants me to take her right here, right now.

I guide her to her bed and lay her on the mattress. Hovering above her, I kiss her lips before moving to the soft skin of her neck. She arches her back in response. Leaving a wet trail, I lick and nip my way up to her earlobe and take it into my mouth. She gasps for breath and clutches my waist. My breathing is fast and shallow and my fingertips tingle with the need to touch every inch of her body.

I let go of her hair and lift her legs and wrap them around me. I slide my hands along her outer thighs until I reach her hips and clutch tightly. Overcome with hunger, I groan her name and grind my hardness between her legs.

Sophie gasps and jerks away. The desire that I had seen in her eyes only moments ago has been replaced by fear.

"Shit!" I jump up from the bed. *What the hell was I thinking?* "I'm so, so sorry, Sophie. Are you okay?"

Sophie crosses her arms and nods, but doesn't speak.

"Talk to me," I plead gently. "I need to know you're okay."

"I'm fine," she murmurs and covers her eyes with her arm. "I'm sorry."

"Hey," I lean down and tug her arm away so I can make eye contact. "You have nothing to be sorry for. I let it go too far."

"I don't know why I reacted that way."

"Because you're not ready for this, that's why." I shove away from the bed and stride to the other end of the room, facing the opposite direction. "I can't believe I did that."

"It was my fault. I started it."

I spin around to face her. "Don't make excuses for me Sophie. You should be able to kiss me without worrying about me jumping you. I just..." I rub the back of my head. "I'm not used to... having to control myself. That's not an excuse. There is no excuse." I hurry over to her and fall to my knees. "You know I wouldn't have... let it go any farther, don't you?"

"Of course I do."

"Sophie, I'd never do anything you aren't ready for. Shit." I jump up again. "What am I saying? I just *did* something you weren't ready for. I promise, it won't happen again. I never want you to be afraid of me."

"I could never be afraid of you."

"But you were, just then," I wave at the bed where she's still sitting, "when you jerked away. I scared you."

"No." Sophie shakes her head. "I wasn't afraid of you. I was…" she pauses. "It was a stupid memory."

I wince and close my eyes. The last thing I want is for Sophie to compare me or anything we do together to her rape. I hate that what we just did brought forth that memory because I would never force myself on her.

I hear her stand from the bed just before she takes hold of my hand.

"Listen to me," she urges, "I'm fine with what happened."

She sounds convincing, but I scan her face for any indication that she's lying to make me feel better.

"I am," she asserts. "Actually, I really liked it and I feel stupid for freaking out."

"Of course you freaked out, Babe." I brush her cheek with the back of my hand. "That was way too much, way too soon."

She leans into my hand. "I didn't exactly do anything to stop you."

"I know." I drop my arm. "But for the first time in my life, I want to be with someone. In a relationship. But I want to do it right and I'm already screwing it up."

"You haven't screwed anything up."

"I told myself I'd take things slow with you. One step at a time." I rub the back of my neck and rock on my heels. "But when you kiss me, it's like I can't think straight. All I can think about is how *good* it feels."

Her eyes widen, though infinitesimally and when she speaks she sounds almost shy. "I feel the same way."

I smile, but only for her benefit. "You're trying to make me feel better."

"Yes," she admits and flashes her dimples, "but I mean it."

What happened to Sophie was traumatic. I knew there was a chance that sexual behavior would bring forth memories. I pull her to me and kiss the top of her head when there's a knock on her door.

"Bear is here," Miranda says.

"You should get ready for work." I let Sophie go and turn to the door. "I'll go downstairs."

"Hey." She tugs my hand and I twist in her direction. "We okay?"

"Of course, Babe." I wink like all is perfect in the world and leave her to get ready.

When I get to the top of the stairs, I realize my phone isn't in my pocket. It must've fallen out when we were on the bed. I tap on her door, but there's no answer so I open it just a crack. When I do, I find her face down on her bed wriggling and kicking like an overexcited toddler.

"Um?" When I chuckle, her body freezes. "I left my phone."

She doesn't move a muscle and remains lying face down in the mattress. I reach down and pick up my phone.

"You might want to hurry," I say, unable to hide my amusement. "We need to leave in fifteen minutes."

"Mm-hmm." She waves me off and I laugh on my way out.

Downstairs, Bear stands by the front door.

"Thanks for coming, Brother," I say.

"No problem. Happy to help."

My cell phone pings with an incoming text. I check the screen and see it's from Pop asking me to swing by the clubhouse. I send a quick reply letting him know I'll be a little while.

"Pop needs me at the clubhouse. You okay to stay here for a while?"

Miranda shifts on her feet, chewing a nail as she looks back and forth between the two of us.

"As long as you need." Bear looks to Miranda who quickly averts her gaze to the opposite wall.

"Bear will take care of you," I assure her.

She nods and pads to the recliner where she continues to gnaw on her thumbnail.

A few minutes later, Sophie comes bounding down the stairs. I stand from the sofa and go to her side. Miranda sits in the recliner with her legs pulled to her chest, observing Bear with an uneasy expression as he sits on the couch texting.

Sophie whispers in my ear, "I don't know if this is a good idea."

"What?"

"Miranda is scared to death."

I find it comical that Miranda is afraid of a guy who—because I have asked him here—would give his life to protect her. Yes, he can be ruthless and deadly when need be, but Bear's a big softy to those who know him. "Bear won't hurt her."

"I know, but look at her." Sophie motions in Miranda's direction.

"She might as well get to know him. He's my best friend, and he's going to be around. Besides, I talked to him and told him to be a little less—"

"Scary?" She interrupts.

"I think I used the word *intense*."

Sophie observes Bear who is still texting. "I mean, does the guy ever smile or is he pissed off all the time?"

I snort. "He's not pissed, Sophie. He's just a very serious individual."

She rolls her eyes. "I'd say."

I take her hand into mine and peer into her eyes. "He's a good guy, trust me."

"I do trust you."

"Good." I glance at my watch. "We really need to get going."

Sophie checks the clock, looks to me, then to Bear. "I'll be right back," she says and goes over to Bear and asks to talk.

Miranda and I watch as they go into the dining room. I can't hear their conversation, but when they emerge a couple minutes later, Sophie appears satisfied. She walks over to Miranda, crouching in front of her.

"I have to go to work. Bear is going to stay and make sure you're safe in case Mike shows up."

Miranda looks from Sophie to Bear, who stands behind Sophie. "Okay," she squeaks.

"I won't let anything happen to you," Bear assures her.

She nods and looks back to Sophie, still skeptical.

"I'll be back in a little while," I tell Miranda, hoping it'll offer some relief. She may not care much for me, but she's more familiar with me. "I have an errand to run after I drop Sophie off. I shouldn't be too long."

"I love you," Sophie tells her. "I'll see you when I get home."

Protecting Sophie

When I get to the clubhouse, I find Pop sitting with Wrench in the meeting room. "What's up?" I ask and take my place at the table.

"We received a threat from the Henchmen."

"What did they say?"

Wrench lays three pictures on the table in front of me. One of Mama, one of Isa, and one of Sophie. Next, he hands me a piece of paper. A note that says, *Cut Rooter from Double H or we will cut one of these women.*

I clench my teeth and ball my hands into fists. "I'll kill him."

"Your mom and Isa are going into lockdown at the house," Pop says. "There'll be a minimum of three guys with them at all times. I suggest you bring your girlfriend."

I shake my head. If Sophie knew about any of this, it'd scare her. That's too much reality, too soon. "I don't want her knowing about this. I can protect her when I'm with her, but I'll need someone to keep watch when I'm not able."

Both men nod.

"Of course," Wrench says.

"She works at The Grand," I say. "I'll want surveillance when she's there and I'll need someone to follow her home at night when I can't."

"Just let us know what you need and when," Wrench says.

"Have you had any luck with Hoyt?" I ask regarding our proposed alliance.

"He wanted time to consider our request," Pop answers with a sigh. "Said he would let me know tomorrow."

I take a deep breath. With my elbows resting on the table, I clasp my hands in front of my face. "Maybe I should leave the Club."

"That isn't happening," Pop insists.

"It'd put an end to this shit."

"No one tells us how to run our Club," Wrench slams his palm on the table. "You're not going anywhere."

"Even if you left," Pop starts, "Andy would still be out for you. And the Henchmen have been after us for years. You leaving won't change that."

Wrench adds, "This Club needs you, Rooter. And you need the Club."

When Sophie and I arrive at her house after her shift, it's an entirely different scene than it was when we left this afternoon. Bear and Miranda are sitting side by side on the couch with Miranda in hysterics. There is a smattering of empty beer bottles on the coffee table.

"Oh my God, Sophie, you have to see this!" Miranda slurs and waves Sophie over. "I found out why he never smiles."

"I think it's time for me to go," Bear says, and tries to stand, but Miranda grabs hold of him and keeps him in place.

"Show her," Miranda whines. "It's so cute."

I'm not surprised that they are getting on so well. Bear and I have been texting throughout the day. Miranda spent the first couple hours in her room "sorting laundry." Bear knocked on her bedroom door and asked if she was hungry. Over pizza, Bear struck up a conversation with her about school and her ambitions. Afterwards, he took her for a ride on his Harley to get ice cream which led to beers and a movie.

"See?" I whisper into Sophie's ear. "I told you she'd be okay with him."

"Show her," Miranda commands, standing with her hands on her hips. Bear looks at her with a tight face. She flutters her eyelashes at him and grins. "Please?"

"Okay," he huffs and shakes his head. "But you have to make the face."

Miranda follows his orders and makes the most ridiculous face, crossing her eyes, sucking in her cheeks and sticks out her tongue. Bear smiles. Wide. Putting on display the whitest teeth anyone has ever seen. Sophie and I burst out laughing. Bear never smiles because when he does, it freaks people out. He's this gruff, scary looking dude, with a smile of perfect, unnaturally white teeth.

"I care about dental hygiene, okay?" Bear grumbles.

"Is that seriously why you never smile?" Sophie asks through a fit of giggles.

"Yes," I chortle. "The guys all call him Pearl."

Bear flips me off. "I think it's time to go."

Miranda, still latched onto his arm makes a sad face and pleads, "Stay a little while longer."

"Can't," he says. "I have to be at the shop early."

"Boo." She makes a pouty face. "You're no fun."

"How did this happen?" Sophie whispers to me.

While I had every confidence Bear could win Miranda over, I hadn't expected this. "I have no idea."

"I'll come back after work tomorrow," Bear assures her.

"But who will protect me tonight?"

"Rooter is right next door." Bear points toward my house.

"Actually, I'll be staying here tonight," I chime in. Sophie twists and faces me with big eyes prompting me to explain. "I'm not leaving you alone until I'm sure this thing with Mike has blown over."

Even if not for the Henchmen's threat, I would have insisted on staying tonight. But now that I have them and Mike worry about, I'm not asking, I'm insisting. I'll sleep on the couch if Sophie prefers, but no way in hell am I leaving this house.

Before leaving, Bear helps take Miranda upstairs to bed. Once he's gone, I rush home to get Dopey and change into something I can sleep in.

Miranda hollers as I reach the top of their stairs with Dopey at my side. Sophie is sitting on the bed next to her.

"Thank you for int-introducing me to my future husband," Miranda says.

"No problem," I snigger and go into Sophie's room to give the girls more time to talk.

I flop onto Sophie's bed and sit, resting my elbows on my knees waiting for her to come in. Dopey plops down next to my feet. A couple minutes later the door creaks as it opens.

"Future husband?" I ask with an arched brow. I'll be sure to tell Bear tomorrow. He'll get a good laugh out of it.

"I think Maxim has created a monster." Dopey jumps up and runs to her side. "Hey, boy."

"He told her his name?"

"Yeah."

"He doesn't tell *anyone* his name." Outside of the Club and his previous school teachers, no one knows it.

Sophie shuffles to her dresser with Dopey on her heels. "Maybe he likes her, too."

"Evidently."

"I didn't see that coming," Sophie echoes my earlier sentiment.

"Me neither." I shake my head.

"I'll be right back," she says, holding a pair of pajamas and disappears from the room before I can offer to give her privacy.

I fall back onto the mattress, lying with my hands under my head. My thoughts drift to Andy's betrayal and the Henchmen's threat, but I force them away. I want to enjoy my time with Sophie rather than dwelling on a situation I can't rectify tonight. To help clear my thoughts, I glance around the room at all of Sophie's pictures. There are quite a few. Miranda is in several of them, along with other friends. In each one, Sophie's genuinely happy. No trace of the sadness that usually lingers in her eyes. There's one with just her and Miranda. She's smiling so big her eyes are squinted to the point they're almost closed. I wish she was always that happy and carefree.

A few minutes later the bedroom door opens. In walks Sophie wearing the most hilariously adorable pair of Wonder Woman pajamas—a tank top with the Wonder Woman symbol and a pair of shorty shorts covered in stars. A laugh rumbles deep in my chest.

Her face turns crimson. "They were a gift."

"Indeed, they are," I say through my fit of laughter.

"Shut up." She slaps my arm and pushes me over so she can fit in the bed.

"You're too cute. Where's my phone?" I reach over her to get it from the nightstand.

"No pictures!" She yanks the phone from my grasp and tucks it beneath her.

"That isn't going to stop me," I sneer and reach beneath her. She fights me, trying to keep me from getting to the phone. She's strong and puts up a good fight. But I'm determined, so I change tactics and start tickling her.

She shrieks. "I give up."

But I'm having too much fun to quit.

"I said I give up!" She arches her back to give me clear access to the phone.

A blast of cold air blows through the window and Sophie's body is instantly covered in goosebumps. I gasp at the sight of her hardened nipples in the skin tight tank top, but quickly avert my gaze. After what happened earlier, I don't want to make her uncomfortable.

"You cold?" I ask and back away to put space between us.

"A little." She pulls the blanket up to her shoulders.

"I'll close the window," I say and reach up to pull it shut.

"No." She pulls on my arm. "I like it cool at night."

"You won't be too cold?"

"No." She smirks and leans into me. "I like to cuddle in the blankets."

I lift the blankets and snuggle against her. "Me, too," I say though I can't recall a single time I've ever cuddled. But I like the idea of cuddling with Sophie. I roll onto my back, taking her with me so her head rests on my chest. We lay a moment, neither of us saying a word. *Yeah, I definitely like cuddling.* I press my face into her hair and inhale a deep breath. "You smell so good."

She scoffs. "Yeah, like garlic and onion."

I inhale again. It's true, she does smell a bit like the restaurant, but she also smells like Sophie. "Sweet, like flowers."

"I like this," she says, drawing circles on my chest with her fingertips.

Hypersensitive to her touch, my heart races and I hope she doesn't notice when I shiver. "Me, too."

"It kind of makes me glad Mike called."

"Look at me," I say and wait for her eyes to meet mine before I speak again. "You never need an excuse to be with me, Sophie. Want me to stay here, ask. Want to stay with me, tell me. Okay?"

"Okay," she says in a small voice. Her eyelids are heavy.

"It's late." I press my lips to her forehead. "Let's get some sleep."

When I wake up, I'm alone in Sophie's room. I'm overheated and my chest is slick with sweat so I kick the blankets off. Not only am I not used to sharing a bed, I prefer to sleep in the nude or at most in a pair of boxers. Last night, I slept in a pair of sweatpants with Sophie curled up against me. Not that I'm complaining. I glance around the room and see that Dopey's gone too and get up and find them.

The living room is empty so I head for the kitchen. As I fill a glass with water, I see Sophie with Dopey outside through the window. He runs and jumps trying to entice her to play, but she just stands and smiles. A couple minutes later they come in. Dopey runs over and paws at me to get my attention. I pat his head and turn to Sophie. Her eyes are glued to my bare waist with her mouth hanging open.

"My eyes are up here," I joke and point at my face.

Her face lights up and she turns away, bashful.

"Good morning, Babe." I walk to where she stands and wrap my arms around her. This is a great way to start the day.

"Good morning."

"Sleep well?" I massage her back.

"Amazing."

"Me, too." I lean down and kiss the top of her head. "You're an excellent spooner."

"I am?"

"The best." We stand in place, holding one another. Just as I'm about to ask what she has on tap for the day she pulls away.

"Coffee," she grunts. "Must have coffee. Should I make enough for you?"

I shake my head. I can't stand the bitter flavor. The only time I drink the stuff is when I need it to keep me awake. "What are your plans for today?"

She glances down at her outfit, a pair of black yoga pants and a loose t-shirt. "Don't have any plans, but I seriously need to do laundry."

"That's cool." I chug the rest of my water and put the glass in the sink. "We can hang here for a while. I need to run by the shop later. The three of us can grab lunch."

"Rooter," she folds her arms across her chest, "you don't need to babysit me."

"I'm not." I wrap her in my arms and try to act nonchalant. "I'm just hanging out with my girlfriend on her day off."

My girlfriend. I've never so much as thought the words, let alone said them, and yet it feels so natural—so right.

She cocks her head to the side. "You're babysitting me."

If she knew everything that's going on, she'd understand why. "I'm spending time with you and in the process making sure you're safe. That's what any good boyfriend would do."

The word boyfriend slides off my tongue just as easily as girlfriend. By her expression, she appears to like it as much as I do.

"Well then, you can help with the laundry." She smirks.

"I'd love to fold your delicates."

"I bet."

Just as girls wonder whether we wear boxers or briefs, guys wonder what kind of bras and panties girls wear. Cotton bikini style panties, or lacey thongs? Padded bras or see through? I figured Sophie for the type of girl who wears cotton until she chucks a basket full of freshly cleaned bras and panties onto her mattress. There isn't a scrap of cotton here. It's all lacy and sheer. I don't even think there's a pair of full ass bottoms in the pile. I swallow and try not to imagine her in any of it. Last thing I need is to be standing here with a raging hard-on. I try to focus on anything else until I notice the large quantity of bras in the heap.

"Do you really need this many bras?" I chuckle.

"Yes, I do. They all go with their own matching panties."

My cock twitches at the sound of her saying the word "panties." I clear my throat. "This is something I didn't know about you."

When she picks up a bra and folds it, I grab one and try mimicking her. This is pure torture. What have I gotten myself into? I pick up a purple thong and it nearly kills me to know where it's been. Now that I know this is what she wears under her clothes, I'm certain

I'll never again have a coherent thought while in her presence. "Do you actually fold these?"

"Yes," she takes the thong from my hands and shows me how she folds it. "Like this."

"Seriously?" I don't see the point. It's a waste of time. "There isn't enough material to bother with."

"I prefer things to be neat and in order," she explains. "Makes it easier to find when I'm trying to pair things together."

I pick up another thong and fold it the way she did. Again, I'm assaulted by the thought that I'm folding underwear that has been between her legs. *Jesus.*

We stand in silence and fold. When I come across a red, see through bra with black laces on the cups, I hold it up and draw in a sharp breath. "Shit. You actually wear this just to wear it?"

"Yeah," she answers with a small voice.

"Go put it on," I demand.

Her jaw goes slack. "What?"

"Knowing you have it on will be hot as hell." I wink.

This girl is going to be the death of me.

First Fight

"Ready to grab lunch?" I stand next to Sophie while she empties the washing machine and puts the wet clothes into the dryer.

"Sure, I could eat."

"Afterward, you both can come with me to the shop. Bear and I are doing a favor for a friend of the Club. I need to see if he's ready for me to paint."

"I'd like that." Sophie smiles and tosses a dryer sheet in with the wet garments. "It'd be cool to see where you work and what you do."

"I don't actually do much work with the bikes," I admit and pick up the basket of freshly dried clothes from the floor so I can carry it for her. I don't want her doing laundry alone anymore. Carrying these baskets up two flights of stairs could be dangerous. "The only time I work on bikes is as an extra pair of hands."

"So what do you do there?" She starts up the basement stairs ahead of me.

"I mostly work in the office managing finances, writing quotes, and making sure jobs get done on schedule."

"Sounds like a lot of responsibility."

"It is. Pop's grooming me to take over ownership of the business when he retires." Sophie opens the door leading into the kitchen and steps to the side to let me by. "There's still a lot to learn. At some point, I need to learn more about the design and building process."

"I couldn't imagine running a business. Way too much pressure for me."

"What do you want to do?" I ask and start up the stairs to Sophie's room with her following behind. "Any dreams or ambitions?"

"This is going to sound bad, but no. I never really dreamt of doing anything specific like being a lawyer or doctor. All I ever cared about was earning enough money to be self-sufficient." She sits on the bed as I set the basket on the floor. "When I envision my future career, I guess I see myself in an administrative role like office management."

"I think that sounds great," I take a seat next to her and clasp her hand. "I never understood the concept of going to college straight out of high school. Who the hell knows what they want to do at that age?"

"Exactly!" She twists her body in my direction. "That's why I thought a degree in business management was a good idea. It's a professional degree that won't leave me feeling pigeon holed into a certain career."

"It's a good plan."

Miranda comes bouncing out of her room where she's been all day, recovering from her hangover. She stops in front of Sophie's door when she sees us on the bed.

"Want to go with us to eat and then go by Rooter's shop?" Sophie asks her.

"Yes!" Miranda answers, overexcited. Undoubtedly due to the prospect of seeing Bear. "I'm starving."

I follow the girls downstairs and on the way out the front door, Sophie offers to drive us in her car.

"I'm driving," I say and hold out my hand for her keys. Sophie eyes me like she might argue or ask why. Before she can, I explain, "I have an aversion to being a passenger in cars."

She stops walking and tilts her head. "An aversion?"

The three of us stand in the middle of the yard, Miranda looking back and forth at us with a bemused smile.

"I was involved in a car accident when I was seventeen." I don't want her to think I have control issues or that I'm chauvinistic. Admittedly, I can be controlling at times, but only when necessary. "The driver was fucking around flirting with some girls next to us, went left of center and hit an oncoming car head-on. Broke my collarbone, some ribs, my arm and my foot. I haven't been a passenger since."

She tosses me the keys. "Okay, you drive."

When I open the door, a blast of heat rolls from within the car. On days like today where it's unseasonably warm, my usual attire of jeans, boots, and my MC cut isn't practical. On the Harley it isn't an issue. I'd wear shorts more often if it wasn't for the fact that almost everywhere I go, I go on the motorcycle. The only time I drive my truck is in inclement weather and in the winter. Hell, I've been known to ride well into October when the temperature can get down into the thirties.

I turn the keys in the ignition and Sophie's typical annoying pop music comes blaring through the speakers. I jump high enough that I almost smack my head on the roof of the car. "Shit!" I stab the power button.

Sophie and Miranda roar with laughter.

"Do you ever listen to anything else?" I ask.

"Occasionally," she answers with a shrug and turns the radio back on, but at a lower volume.

No way can I tolerate listening to this crap. Frankly, I can't comprehend how it gets made in the first place. "I seriously need to educate you on what real music is."

"Oh, really?" She turns her body toward me.

"Nirvana," I hold up my index finger to count as I pull out of the driveway, "Radiohead, Soundgarden, Alice in Chains. Four of the greatest rock bands of the nineties."

She wrinkles her nose and squints. "Nirvana? No, thank you."

"What?" I can't believe my ears. "They are *legendary.*"

She curls her lip in disgust. "They're greasy and grungy, and that guy, Kirk whatever, couldn't even sing. All he did was scream."

No fucking way! I stare her in the eyes. "Do. Not. Ever. And I mean ever, hate on *Kurt* Cobain. The man was and always will be a legend."

"Pay attention to the road." She turns my face back to the road.

"Where do you girls want to eat?" I ask.

"Let's go see Joe at Skyles," Miranda proposes.

"You in love with him, too?" I ask jokingly and look at her through the rearview mirror.

"He is hot in an old guy sort of way," she states, making Sophie laugh. Miranda scoots up to Sophie's seat. "Poor Joe will be heartbroken when he sees you have a boyfriend."

"He already knows," I say and shoot Sophie a wink. I was right about the guy after all.

Following lunch, the three of us head over to the shop. As I drive, Sophie and I hold hands and steal glances at one another. In the backseat, Miranda primps, trying to look good for Bear. First, she touches up her makeup, applying way too much lipstick. Luckily, Bear prefers overly done up girls, so it'll be fine. Next, she fusses with her hair and when she's finished, it looks the same as it did when she started. Watching her is comical and makes me laugh. She smacks me on the arm and warns me that if I say anything to him, she'll castrate me.

"This bike will be sick as shit when we're done with it," I boast to Sophie as I turn into the lot. My jovial mood is instantly ruined when

I see Candace's glossy red Mustang parked at the main entrance. "Fuck."

"What is she doing here?" Sophie asks as I pull into a spot by the alternate entrance on the other side of the lot.

"Probably checking on her bike," I lie and step out of the car. Yeah, we're still working on her bike, but that's not why she's here.

Candace has been texting me all day. She knows better than to show up at my house uninvited, but there's nothing stopping her from coming here. Pop keeps an open door policy at the shop. I knew Sophie and Candace would eventually come face to face. Due to Candace's connection to the Club, it was inevitable. But I'd hoped it'd be far into the future after Candace had moved on. If they meet today, it'll be ugly and I'm not prepared for the possible fallout.

There's a large window next to the main entrance. If Candace is near that window, she'll see me out here. Miranda takes forever to crawl out of the back seat. My muscles twitch and I have a sick feeling in the pit of my stomach. Once she's out, I hurry toward the alternate entrance and usher the girls inside. I survey the area making sure the coast is clear before moving on.

I guide the girls down the hall to the conference room. There's virtually zero chance of Candace coming in here. I flip on the light and tell Sophie and Miranda to wait here.

"Where are you going?" Sophie asks. Visibly tense, she taps her foot.

I speak in a calm, reassuring tone, "I'm only going to see what she wants."

"Why can't I go with you?" She juts out her chin and crosses her arms.

"It's just business, Sophie."

"Then why are you hiding me in here?"

"I'm not hiding you."

"That's what it looks like to me," Miranda pops off and I turn to her and glower. "Sorry."

"Look," I turn back to Sophie, "I told you that was done and I meant it."

"And yet, you're stowing me away in a conference room."

I blow out a breath and drag a hand through my hair. "You don't want to come with me, trust me."

"Why not?" She presses with her arms still folded across her chest and her head tilted to the side.

"Sophie, it was just weeks ago that she and I…" I won't say we were together because we weren't. We were just sleeping together.

"Were fucking?" she completes my sentence.

Hearing her say the words is disconcerting, causing me to flinch. "Yes. And I don't think she'd appreciate seeing us together."

"Too bad," she challenges me with narrowed eyes.

"Sophie, please," I beg. "Trust me."

Sophie shakes her head with a sigh and stares into my eyes as though trying to decide whether she can trust me. I know this looks bad, but she has nothing to worry about. I wish she'd have a little faith in me.

"I'll be five minutes," I say. "I promise."

"Fine." She rolls her eyes. "Go."

This may be my first relationship, but I've seen my mom give this look to Pop on several occasions. It's not a good sign. "You're pissed."

"Yeah."

"I'm sorry." I'll find a way to make this up to her later. I lean in and kiss her on the cheek. "I'll be right back."

With hands balled into fists and a clenched jaw, I stalk down the hall to the front of the shop. I want to ring Candace's damn neck. How many times and how many ways can I tell her no before she finally accepts it? I realize I'm partially to blame here. I never should have gotten involved with her to begin with, but I've made myself clear several times. Enough is enough.

Still yet, as much as I want to tell her off, I won't. It wouldn't be right. Besides, this isn't the time or place. She'd either lose her shit and cause a scene, or she'd break down crying. I don't have time for any of that. I need to get back to Sophie fast as possible. I don't know how long she'll stay put in the conference room. Right now, I just need to appease Candace and send her on her way so I can get back to Sophie.

I round the corner into the shop work area and find Candace standing next to Bear and Darren. The moment she sees me, she prances toward me.

"Hey there, sexy," she purrs.

"Candace."

"I've been texting you all day, but you're ignoring me. Figured I'd find you here."

"I'm not ignoring you. I've been busy. I would've returned your calls when I had a chance."

She snorts and stares at me through narrowed eyes. "Bullshit. I know you. If you want to talk to someone, you talk to them. You don't care what's going on."

She's right. I look to the ceiling and blow out a breath. I can't stand here and argue with her. "What's up?"

"Did you not read my texts?"

"Not yet."

She rolls her eyes. "I have a problem with a regular at the club." She's referring to the strip club. "He's there every night when I work. Started following me to my car at the end of my shifts. He won't leave me alone."

Now I feel like an ass for ignoring her texts. "Have you told Brad?"

"Yeah, but this guy is a big spender. A corporate attorney who brings his rich clients in on the weekends. Spends thousands. Brad just told him to take it easy which didn't do any good. If you talked to the guy, I know he'd leave me alone."

Brad, the owner of Mounds and Rounds, is a good dude, but he's greedy. Always has been. The written policy at the club is that the patrons can't touch or harass the girls. But that only stands for the average Joe's. He allows his rich regulars to do as they please. This isn't the first time I've had to step in and deal with a problem customer. Last time, I told Brad I wouldn't tolerate this shit. My subtle threat must not have registered.

"All right. I'll handle it. When do you work again?"

Her eyes linger on mine as she smiles. "Tomorrow night. He usually shows up about ten o'clock."

"Okay, I'll be there." I glance toward the hallway where Sophie waits. "I really need to get to work."

"You okay?" she asks and reaches up to cup my cheek.

"I'm good. Just got a lot of work to do."

"You sure that's all it is? Work has never stressed you out."

"I'm sure." I take her hand into mine to get it off my face. "And I need to get to it."

"Okay, I'll go." She heads for the exit. "But thank you for the help. I really appreciate it."

"No problem."

She turns to face me before I can open the door. "I can tell by looking at you she's not giving you what you need. All you have to do is call and I'll take care of you."

"Thanks for the offer."

"I'm serious."

"I know."

"You miss me, Rooter. I see it in your eyes."

I close my eyes and swallow. I'd been hoping our conversation wouldn't take this turn. I reach for the door handle and she puts her free hand on mine. "I'll see you at the club tomorrow night."

"I'm the woman for you, Rooter. I'll never give up on you."

"You're relentless as ever."

"You haven't seen anything yet. I'm in serious withdrawals. By the looks of you, you are too."

I laugh to keep things light, but she's not far off the mark. Going from getting laid on an almost daily basis to not getting it at all is a shock to the system. Especially for a guy in his sexual prime.

I walk her outside to her car. I'm almost in the clear and my heart is racing. Just as we reach her car door, she leans into me, grabs my crotch and kisses me. I jump in surprise—more so from the kiss than the crotch grab. Grabbing my junk has been a habit of hers for longer than I can remember, but she never kisses me. The only time we've ever kissed was during sex. It was one of my rules.

Candace lets go of my crotch and leans into my ear. "Call me when you realize how much you miss pounding this tight pussy."

She pulls back with a naughty smile and wags her eyebrows. I smile in return. She's too much to take. I've never met a girl with a mouth as dirty as Candace's. After she pulls away, I fix my gaze on the end of the building where Sophie waits for me.

"Man, that could've been ugly," Bear says when I walk back in. "I saw you sneak Sophie and Miranda in the end of the building."

"I have a feeling it's still going to be ugly. Sophie knows Ca—"

Bear cuts me off and points at the window. "They're leaving."

I spin around and see Sophie back out of the parking space. "Shit!" I run as fast as I can out of the building. I hadn't been thinking when I walked Candace out. There's a window in the conference room with a view of the parking lot. Sophie probably saw what just went down between me and Candace. I scream Sophie's name as she speeds out of the parking lot. I continue running until I reach the end of the block, but she's out of sight.

"*Fuck!*" I yank my phone from my back pocket and call her, but she doesn't answer. "Sophie," I say through a labored breath, "Baby I'm sorry. Just let me explain. Call me or come back to the shop, please."

I race back to the shop and grab the keys to the company van. No one says a word, but they all watch in astonishment as I run out of the building.

I speed to Sophie's house, although I doubt she'd go there. There's no way to hide from me there. But I don't know where else to go. As I drive, I call her phone repeatedly, but she doesn't answer. I careen into my driveway and slam on the brakes. My heart pounds and my mouth is dry. I have to fix this. Sophie has to hear me out. I call her again and plead aloud that she'll answer this time. This time she answers on the fourth ring.

"Stop calling me," she screams and hangs up, denying me the chance to explain myself.

I'm at once panicked and pissed off. I know what happened looked bad. I can only imagine what she thinks she saw, but damn it I deserve the chance to explain. I dial her number again, but it goes straight to voicemail. I raise my phone to throw it, but change my mind. Instead I leave a voicemail. "Babe, I know you think you know what you saw, but it's not what you think. You need to call me back. Now."

I hang up and pace her lawn with my hands clasped behind my head. *What the fuck am I going to do?* My initial response is to get on my bike and go looking for her, but I don't even know where to begin my search. Driving around town aimlessly is pointless.

"Damn it!" I kick a fallen tree branch, sending it flying across the road and nearly hit a pedestrian. The guy comes to a halt and shoots me a dirty look. The instant he sees my cut he turns away and keeps walking.

Sophie is out there somewhere pissed off and hurt by what she saw and I have no way of getting to her to make it right. All I can do is wait. I'm completely powerless and I fucking hate it. The only comfort I have is knowing that she can't avoid me forever. She has to come home, eventually.

A half hour passes and I call her again. Just as I expect, it goes straight to voicemail. "Sophie, since you turned your phone off, this is gonna be my last message. I understand what you think you saw. If it was me I'd probably be pissed, too. But I wouldn't run away from you." I pause and momentarily consider begging, but change my mind. "You can't hide from me forever so when you get this message, call me."

Dopey trots after me as I pace every room in my house. He whines and paws at me to get my attention, but I can't play right now. I'm too busy freaking the fuck out. If only Sophie would give me the opportunity to explain myself, I could make her understand and repair the damage.

Minutes tick by and I hear a car pull into Sophie's driveway. I dart out of the house through the side door and see Miranda stepping out of Sophie's car.

"Where is she?"

"None of your damn business." She hurries to her door.

Desperate, I rush after her. "Miranda, it wasn't what it looked like."

"No?" she challenges and crosses her arms. "Because it looked a hell of a lot like some skank kissing you with her hand on your dick."

"I was just as surprised as you when it happened." It's not a total lie. I hadn't expected the kiss.

She shifts her weight to one foot and flips her blonde hair off her shoulder. "You didn't do much about it."

I rub the back of my neck and rock on my heels. "It's complicated."

She stares daggers at me and I half expect her to slap me. "No it's not. Either you're with Sophie or you're not. You can't have both."

"I don't want both. I only want Sophie."

She puts her key in the deadbolt and turns it, but doesn't open the door. "I'd say you've just lost your chance."

"Look," I take her by the arm and spin her to face me. "I know how it looked and I get why you're both pissed, but it really wasn't what you think."

"I'm not the one you need to explain it to."

"Actually, you are. I need for you to talk to her."

She shrugs away from me. "Oh no. You're on your own."

"If you heard the story from Bear, would you believe it?"

She opens the door then turns back to me, considering my proposal. "I might be a little more inclined to."

A half hour later, Bear arrives and I tell him to explain my situation with Candace to Miranda. He obliges and without me asking, he also explains his take on my feelings for Sophie. Bear tells Miranda I've never been in a relationship before and he's never seen me so crazy about a girl. He promises Miranda that my feelings for Sophie are the real deal.

Miranda sits in silence as she considers everything she's just heard. "Okay, I believe you."

"Thank God!" I leap from the couch. "Now will you please call Sophie and tell her to come home?"

She picks up her phone and dials Sophie's number, but it goes to voicemail. "Sophie, I talked to Rooter. It was all a huge misunderstanding. I think you should call him when you get this message."

"Thank you," I breathe.

"Don't expect to hear from her tonight," she says. "I seriously doubt she'll turn her phone on until morning."

"If I promise not to go after her, will you tell me where she is?"

"I get the feeling you couldn't keep that promise."

She's got me there. With everything that's going on, I don't like the idea of Sophie staying where I can't protect her. "At least tell me this, is she safe?"

"Completely."

It's not enough to calm my nerves, but it'll have to do. I just pray Sophie will turn her phone on and call me after she hears Miranda's message.

While Bear and Miranda hang out I take Dopey up to Sophie's room. To pass the time, I put away the clothes we left in the basket on the floor. I have a good idea of where things go from helping her earlier today. I open her sock drawer and inside I find a picture of a woman who resembles Sophie. I suspect it's her mom. In the picture, the woman cradling an infant that I assume is Sophie. Inside the drawer are a few more pictures of the woman. It's sad that the memory of Sophie's mom brings her such grief she has to keep the pictures tucked away. It's a testament to Sophie's ability to love and forgive that she even keeps them after everything the woman put her through.

I can't imagine not being close to my mom. Then again, I can't imagine my mom ever putting me through the things Sophie endured by the hand of her mother. My mom loves me and Isa unconditionally. She'd protect us with her very life. Even now that I'm an adult and can take care of myself, my mom would take a bullet for me.

That's what you do for family and loved ones. You love and protect them no matter what the cost. I doubt there's anything I could say or do that would change my mom's love for me. I can't understand how a parent could love her child any less than that. It baffles me that Sophie's mom didn't understand the gift she had in her daughter.

I put the pictures back inside the drawer and close it. The clothes are all put away. Needing something to keep my mind busy, I scan the room. On her dresser are various pieces of jewelry and hair accessories. I pick up the ring she wears the most and slide it onto my pinky. It's a delicate gold band with intricate etching. It looks like an antique. I wonder how she came to have it. Is it a family heirloom, was it handed down to her from Miranda's mom, or did she perhaps find it in a vintage clothing store?

As I look around the room I'm reminded of how much I still don't know about Sophie. Just like this ring, there are several items here that all have stories of how they came to be. Like the picture of her with two other girls in a bar. They're wearing party hats. Was it a birthday party? If so, whose? One of Sophie's? Which birthday?

A few hours pass and my eyelids become heavy. I've resigned myself to the fact that Sophie isn't going to call or come home. Although I know it won't do any good, I call and leave her another message.

"I'm lying in your bed, and I hate that you're not here." I clutch her pillow to my chest just as I would hold her if she was here. "I hate that you're out there somewhere so mad at me that you won't talk to me. Sophie, I swear to God I'd *never* do anything to hurt you." I pause and take a breath. "I care so much about you. Knowing that you're sad because of me is killing me Baby. Please come home and talk to me."

Forgiveness

Why the hell hasn't Sophie called? It's late morning. She's had to have listened to my messages by now. I was sure Miranda's message would've convinced her to get in touch with me. She must be angrier than I assumed. I'd call her again, but I doubt she'd answer. I'll just wait for her to come home. I don't care if I have to sit on this couch for days on end, I'm not leaving here until we talk. Sophie's going to face me whether she likes it or not. She *will* hear me out and we *will* make up.

A car pulls up in front of the house. From the couch, I see Ryan's car. Suddenly uneasy, my pulse races and my palms become slick. I've never been nervous to talk to anyone about anything. It's a foreign feeling. But my relationship with Sophie is on the line. I have to be sure to say the right thing in precisely the right way to make her understand what she thinks she saw yesterday was a huge misunderstanding.

The key turns in the deadbolt and the door opens. Everything moves in slow motion as she steps into the room. "Sophie."

"What are you doing in here?" she barks and tosses her purse to the floor.

"I've been waiting for you to come home." I stand and rub the back of my neck.

She walks to the chair and stands behind it in an obvious attempt to keep distance between us. "Couldn't you have waited at your own house?"

I move toward her in a slow fashion. "I was afraid you'd avoid me." When she doesn't say anything, I continue to walk toward her. "Sophie, I'm so sorry."

She rolls her eyes. "You're only sorry you got caught."

I take another step closer and she shoots me a look warning me not to come any closer. "That's not true."

"You just stood there and let her…" She imitates the way Candace grabbed me.

"Listen to me, I know how it looked and I'm sorry but—"

She slams her fists into the top of the chair and shouts, "Stop saying you're sorry!"

Fire rages in her eyes, prompting me to step back.

"And don't you dare say it wasn't what it looked like!" She points in my face. "You fucked up."

I hold my hands up in front of me and slowly shift forward. "But, it wasn't what it looked like, Babe."

She curls her lip and recoils. "Don't call me that! I'm not your Babe."

"Yes, you are," I insist and reach for her. "And I'm yours."

"No." She pulls away with pursed lips. "If you were mine, you wouldn't have let her touch you that way."

I clutch my hands above my head. If only I knew what to say. "I should've handled it differently, it's just that…"

"No justs, no buts." She wags her finger. "It should've never happened. How'd you like it if you saw some guy do that to me?"

The thought of some guy groping Sophie causes heat to flush through my body and my muscles become tense. "Honestly, I'd probably massacre the guy."

"Exactly, but now I'm supposed to say, oh, don't worry, it's okay."

"No, you're not," I groan, growing restless with this conversation. "That's why I'm trying to explain it to you."

"Please, by all means, let's hear why you let your ex-slut kiss you and grab your dick."

When she puts it that way, I realize there is no way to justify it, yet I have to explain. "What she did is something she's always done—"

"So since she's always done it she might as well keep doing it? Is that what you're saying?"

"No. Sophie," I'm not saying the right thing, "will you please let me speak without interrupting?"

"Fine. Go ahead." Sophie walks around me to the front of the chair and takes a seat. Her overly perfect posture is cold and unwelcoming.

I take a seat on the couch to her right. "I've known Candace all my life. We grew up together. Her dad was one of the original Club members. When he died a few years back, she ran off with a guy from school. About a year ago, she moved back here after he nearly beat her to death. We started hooking up a few months back.

I stop and give her time to digest what I've just said. She seems to take it well so I continue. "We made a deal. It was just sex. No strings attached. If either of us met someone new or if one developed feelings and the other didn't feel the same, we'd stop. So, after the night of your break in, I ended it with her. She put two and two together and figured I'd met someone. She flipped out.

I squeeze my eyes closed and inhale. "She admitted she was in love with me. Begged me to give her a chance. She threatened to kill herself. Said I'm all she has. The Club is her only family. I knew that if she saw me with you, she'd lose her shit. She's not stable. She could've hurt you or herself. I was taking the path of least resistance."

Sophie raises a brow. "And part of that path is continuing to let her kiss and touch you inappropriately?"

"No. I told her it had to stop."

"Then why were you both smiling?" she challenges.

"What?" I don't remember smiling.

"After she grabbed you, she said something to you that had you blushing."

I look to the floor to avoid her penetrating stare. "I don't remember."

"Bullshit," she growls and moves in close. Her voice is low and angry. "Do *not* lie to me or you can leave right now."

My eyes flit to hers. "She said to call when I realize how much I miss her."

Sophie shakes her head. "That wouldn't have made you blush. Tell me what she said."

"You don't want to hear it."

She pounds the arm of the chair. "Yes, I do!"

She's won't let this go, I might as well be honest. I think I might throw up. "She said to call her when I realize how much I miss pounding her tight pussy."

She stares into my eyes as she processes what I've just said. I expect her to go ballistic, but instead she closes her eyes and quietly asks, "Do you miss it?"

"No." That she thinks so lowly of me is offensive.

"Of course you do!" she blows up. "Who are you trying to fool? Me or yourself?"

"You want honesty? I'll give it to you. If sex was all I was after I'd probably be with her right now. But that's not what I'm after, Sophie. I want something real." I kneel before her and rest my hands on her thighs. She leans away. I can't believe what I'm getting ready to say. "I never thought I'd be saying this, but I want to be with someone I can fall in love with. That's you. I want to give you my heart and I hope you'll give me yours."

Sophie gasps and blinks rapidly. My heart might explode from my chest as I hold my breath waiting for her response. But it doesn't come. She just slumps into the chair and rubs her face. I clutch her legs, fearful that I'm not getting through to her.

I plead, "Please don't let one mistake ruin everything."

"That's just it!" She blows out a breath. "This probably isn't even the first time something like this has happened and I seriously doubt it will be the last."

"I'll handle her." I don't know exactly what to do, but I'll make damn sure nothing like this ever happens again.

"Like you did yesterday?" She shoves my hands away.

"Sophie, please," I breathe, defeated.

"Your situation with her is a lot more involved than you led me to believe. You've known her your entire life which means she'll always be around."

I lean toward her again, but this time she holds her hands out to keep me at a distance. "You have absolutely nothing to worry about, I promise."

"I believed that until yesterday."

I grab her hands so she can't push me away and move in close. "I won't let that happen again. Sophie, please give me a chance."

A moment passes as she considers my plea. "I need time to think."

I shake my head. "No."

"No?"

"That's right. No." I lean in even closer. "You want to pull back and be distant and pissed off, go ahead. But I'm not going anywhere. I'm going to stay right here and prove to you that this is where I want to be."

Her jaw slackens, and she stares into my eyes, astonished.

When she doesn't respond, I continue, "So you go ahead and do what you need to do and when you're done being pissed at me, let me know."

I've spent most of the day surveilling The Grand. About fifteen minutes ago, I pulled into the parking lot to greet Sophie when her shift ends. There's a good chance she won't be happy to see me. As per usual, I texted her throughout the day to let her know I'm thinking of her, but she never responded. I'm not surprised, but it still cuts a little. The longer I wait, the more nervous I become. I've had guns held in my face and not been this anxious. It's not a feeling I enjoy.

When the door opens and Sophie steps outside, our eyes lock. I'm relieved she doesn't appear upset to see me, though it could be because she knew I'd be here.

"How was work?" I ask and dismount the Harley to greet her. I want to reach out and pull her into my arms. Would she push me away? I reach back and rub the back of my neck. When I do, Sophie's eyes dart to my exposed midsection. A faint flush appears on her cheeks. Hope springs inside me that she's no longer angry with me, or at least, not *as* angry with me.

"Slow and very boring," she answers.

"Want to ride home with me?" I ask, hopeful. With my hands in my pockets I rock on my heels.

She shakes her head and my heart plummets to my stomach. "I have my car."

"I can bring you back to get it tomorrow."

She opens her car door. "I have a doctor's appointment in the morning."

Doctor's appointment for what? "Everything okay?"

She nods. "Just an annual. But it's an early appointment so I'll need my car."

"Okay, I'll follow you home." I take my chances and lean in for a kiss. She gives me her cheek and there's a pang in my chest.

I follow closely behind Sophie on the way to her house. We turn onto her street and I notice she's not slowing down as we approach her house. At the last minute, she hits the brakes and skids into her driveway, coming close to knocking over her trash can. Once she's out of the car, I joke about her forgetting where she lives.

"Wasn't paying attention," she answers, nonchalant.

We walk side by side to her door, but I don't reach for her hand like I normally would. I'm afraid she'd pull away. Tension radiates from her and as she unlocks her door, she blows out a deep breath. As she steps into the house, I remember I forgot Dopey at home. The one and only time I left him alone overnight, he shredded my pillows and comforter.

"I'll be right back," I say.

She spins around to face me with wide eyes. "Rooter, you don't need to stay tonight. Mike won't come around here."

"Sophie, you don't know that." Although, Mike is the least of my worries. My staying the night has much more to do with the current state of our relationship and my wariness over Andy.

"Yes, I do. And so do you." She looks down. "The only reason you want to stay here is because of what happened."

"Fine, you're right," I admit and lift her chin. "I told you I wasn't going to give you space."

"No," she backs away infinitesimally, "you said you wouldn't give me time to think. You didn't say anything about space."

Lamenting the distance between us, I step in to lessen the gap. "Well, I'm definitely not giving you space."

"Well, you can't stay in my house without my permission." She presses her lips into a thin line and glares at me with narrowed eyes. She's cute when she's angry.

I jut out my chin and widen my stance. "I won't let you push me away."

"I'm not pushing you away. I'm tired. I want to go to my room and go to sleep."

"Fine, then let's go to your room and sleep." I inch forward. "We don't have to talk and I won't lay a finger on you."

"Rooter," she slumps and rests her head on the door jamb, "just go home. Please."

"That's what you really want?"

She hesitates. "That's what I want."

"There's really very little I wouldn't do for you," I say before turning around and going home.

Her hesitation said so much more than her words. She doesn't want me to go, she's just frustrated. Rather than fight about it, I let her think I'm leaving her alone for the night when all I'm doing is running home to grab Dopey. If she doesn't want me in her room with her tonight, that's fine, I'll sleep downstairs on the couch. But with everything that's gone down with Mike, Andy and the Henchmen, and between me and Sophie, I need to be in the house with her. I need to make sure she's safe and I also need to make sure she knows I meant it when I said I'm not going anywhere.

Sophie and Miranda keep a spare key to the front door in a fake rock in the mulch bed in front of the house. Being that Mike knows it's there, they should get rid of it or at least change the hiding place. But right now I'm glad it's still there. Otherwise I'd have to devise another plan to get inside the house.

I let Dopey into Sophie's room first so she'll know it's me and not an intruder.

"What the—" she starts, but I silence her by placing my fingers on her lips.

"Remember me saying there's very little I wouldn't do for you?" She nods and I continue. "Well, I refuse to give you time or space."

"So you break into my house?" Propped up on her elbows, she tries her best to sound mad, but I detect relief in her voice.

I chuckle. "I didn't break in. I used the hide-a-key."

She shakes her head. "I honestly don't know what to say."

"Don't say anything. Let's go to sleep." I plant a kiss on her forehead and crawl over her to the side of the bed against the wall.

She remains propped up and stares at me, incredulous. I scoop her into my arms and pull her against me. "Good night, Sophie."

"Good night, Rooter."

The alarm is set to go off in one minute. Sophie is tucked into me with her face pressed against my bare chest. Her long, smooth legs are tangled with mine. For the past twelve minutes I've been dreading the alarm sounding and stealing her away from me. I don't know what kind of mood she'll be in when she wakes up, but I doubt she'll want to be snuggled up against me. I press my face to her hair and inhale, relishing the comfort of holding her close while it lasts.

The alarm goes off and Sophie jumps, but she doesn't immediately pull away as I anticipated. I take it as a good sign that she's not disgusted by being in my arms. Instead, she breathes in deep and snuggles closer. When I reach over to shut off the alarm, she tries to roll away, but I pull her back to me.

"Stay here a little longer," I whisper and massage her back. She lets out the cutest moan. "I like waking up like this."

We lie this way for a few minutes, me rubbing her back, before she says she needs to get up. This time I let her go and prop myself against her headboard and watch as she hunts through her cluttered closet for something to wear. Based on how she's dressed, I'd say she wasn't expecting me to come back last night. She's in a pair of tiny boy shorts and a tight tank top that leaves little to the imagination. I force myself to think of anything other than how incredible she looks.

"What time is your appointment?" I ask.

"What?" she asks and walks to her chest of drawers.

I repeat the question.

"Nine thirty." She holds the shirt in her hand up to a bra to make sure it matches.

I can't help chuckling.

"Want to grab lunch afterward?" I ask and swing my legs over the side of the bed. I know it's a long shot, but it's worth asking.

"What part of I'm mad at you do you not understand?"

"I understand it perfectly, Babe." I extend my hand and pull her over so she's standing between my legs. "What part of I'm not giving you time or space do you not understand?"

She rolls her eyes, but I can tell she's amused. "You're not going to be one of those possessive, clingy boyfriends are you?"

"So you're saying you're still my girl?" I sneer and brush my hands along the back of her thighs. A simple, innocent touch yet it's enough to ignite my desire.

She cocks her head to the side as she looks down at me. "Do I have a choice?"

"No."

Her breath hitches as I continue to softly graze the backs of her legs. "I'm meeting Ryan after my appointment."

My hands come to a halt. "For real? Or are you blowing me off?"

"I really am meeting him." She grins. Her eyes roam my face appreciatively before settling on mine. "We're going shopping for Miranda's birthday."

"Oh, okay." Relief washes over me. I pull her to me and rest my face innocently against her chest. *Please don't pull away.* She brushes her fingers through my hair. Her soft touch gives me goosebumps and I hum with pleasure. "Please don't stay mad at me long, Babe."

"Look at me," she demands and I don't hesitate. "Seeing you with her like that hurt me."

My fingertips sink into her hips as I clutch her tightly. "I can't begin to tell you how fucking sorry I am."

"I need for you to set her straight on what is and is not acceptable behavior."

"I promise, I will." *God, I'll do anything you say, Babe. Just forgive me.*

She pulls my hair, not so much that it hurts, and holds my head in place. "I also need you to promise you won't let her or any other girl kiss or touch you."

"I promise." I don't want to be touched by anyone but this beautiful creature.

"Do you also promise to be loyal to me?"

"Always, Babe."

She pulls my hair again and this time it stings enough to make me wince. "And do you agree that I reserve the right to castrate you if you break any of those promises?"

"Happily." I smile wide. "I'll even provide the knife."

"Okay. I forgive you."

Thank fucking God! I growl in satisfaction and pull her onto the bed with me. Entwining my legs with hers, I place a slight kiss on her collar bone. "Thank you."

Another Fight

It's been a couple days since the blow-up over Candace. After the morning in Sophie's bedroom, we were back on track. Everything was going great. But Candace has been calling and texting nonstop. I told her to give it a rest—that no amount of phone calls or text messages will change my mind. But that only added flame to Candace's fire.

Sophie and I are at Skyles having lunch when my phone beeps. Another text from Candace. Sophie doesn't want me ignoring the messages in her presence. She wants to know what Candace is texting.

Yesterday Sophie and I were hanging out in her living room when my phone kept beeping with one text after another. Sophie eyed me suspiciously and said she couldn't imagine Candace bugging me so much for no reason. I have nothing to hide so I handed her my phone and let her read the messages. My transparency made her feel better, but Candace's suggestive messages didn't. I assured Sophie there's nothing to worry about. I don't want to be with Candace. There's nothing Candace can say and no text she can write that will change my mind.

I open the text and when I do, I choke. It's a picture of Candace in pink lingerie with a caption that reads "Remember this?" I remember it all too well. She once showed up to my office on a rainy day wearing only that under a pink raincoat.

"What does it say?" Sophie asks.

I desperately want to tell her it's nothing and not to worry about it, but that won't fly. I consider deleting the photo, but that'd make matters even worse so I hand her the phone.

"Fucking slut," Sophie growls and tosses the phone back to me. "She's seriously on my last nerve with this shit."

"I'll talk to her, Babe."

She rolls her eyes and tosses her fork onto her plate. "Like that'll do any good. Why don't you just change your number?"

"Can't with the Club and the business."

"Then block her number," she huffs. "I'm sick of this, Rooter."

I take Sophie's hand into mine and squeeze gently wishing she wouldn't let Candace get to her. "If I block her, it'll just make things worse. Trust me."

"How can it possibly get worse?"

"Do you want her showing up all hours of the day and night? If I block her number that's what'll happen."

She jerks her hand away. "Then find a way to make her to stop. I've had it."

"I'm trying, Babe." Since my talk with Candace has only intensified her pursuit, I've decided the best approach is to ignore the messages. Sophie doesn't agree, but she doesn't know Candace like I do. "She'll get tired of this eventually. We just have to wait it out." My phone pings with another text and I put it in my pocket.

Sophie cocks a brow. "Put yourself in my position. How would you feel?"

"She's harmless, Sophie. There's nothing she can say or do to come between us."

She folds her arms across her chest. "Answer my question."

I drag a hand through my hair. "If I were in your position I'd probably lose my shit."

She shifts forward in her seat. "But I'm supposed to just put up with it?"

"It won't last forever."

After lunch, Sophie tells me she has chores to catch up on before work. I suspect she's lying to get rid of me and the never-ending ringing of my phone. It's not just Candace calling. It's Pop updating me on the status of Andy, Mama calling to ask me for a favor, and Bear asking me to help swap out his old washing machine with a new one. Typical life in the Club. Someone always needs something, and it's not often we turn each other down.

Later that evening, I go into the café across from The Grand to keep surveillance on the building. Throughout the evening I text Sophie funny meme's and sweet messages to let her know I'm thinking of her. Towards the end of the night, she tells me she's not sure when she'll get off and I shouldn't come to the restaurant to see her home. I want to believe her, but I can't help but wonder if she's telling the truth. She could be making an excuse to avoid seeing me. But if she is making it up, perhaps I'm better off leaving well enough alone. I don't want to further upset her by showing up against her wishes.

But given the situation with Andy, I'm not comfortable leaving her unprotected. Before leaving the café, I call Darren to come take my place and make sure she gets home safe. The great thing about Darren is he's stealthy. He can follow you for a hundred miles and you'd never know it.

I'm sitting on Sophie's front porch steps when she pulls up awhile later. Dopey takes off after her the moment she steps out of the car. Upon her approach, I give her a contrite smile and hoping she's not as irritated with me as she was this afternoon.

"How was your night?" I ask as she unlocks her door.

"Fine." She pauses and keeps the door closed. "I don't think you should stay here tonight," I start to argue, but she doesn't let me, "and not just because I'm mad."

I cross my arms and tilt my head to the side. "Why then?"

She sighs. "Because, we don't live together and it's not a good idea to get into the habit of spending every night together."

I clutch her hips and pull her to me. "I think we should definitely get into that habit."

"I'm serious," she groans and nudges me away.

"So am I." I tug her to me again. I'm trying to keep things light, but she has me worried.

"You're not staying here tonight," she steps back. "Mike hasn't been an issue, so there's no need."

If only she knew the real reason I've been staying with her. I drop my hands and take a half step back. "This is because you're mad."

"Yeah, I'm mad," she admits, "but I don't think we should spend every night together."

I consider her words. It is a bit soon to be spending every night together. The only reason I've insisted on it is for her safety.

Maybe that isn't true. Even if it wasn't for Mike, Andy, and the Henchmen, I'd try to spend the nights with her, anyway.

"Too much, too soon?" I ask.

"Yeah," she whispers.

"Okay, I understand." I snake my arms around her waist. "Just so long as you aren't pushing me away because of Candace."

"Thank you for understanding."

That she doesn't say Candace isn't the reason concerns me, but if she doesn't want me to stay, I'll respect her wishes whether I want to or not. I comfort myself with the knowledge that I live right next door. Still yet, I'll keep my window open and listen for any sign of trouble. I likely won't get much sleep tonight. "Are we still spending the day together tomorrow?"

She nods with a small smile. "Yeah."

"Okay," I lean down and kiss her cheek, "get a good night's sleep."

The night was torture. I bet I didn't get more than two broken hours of sleep. Every time I'd nod off, I'd jerk awake, scared that something might have happened to Sophie while I was sleeping. Each time, I'd not been asleep more than fifteen minutes. I'd then spend the next hour listening for signs of trouble.

Tonight is the Club's annual party. As the Matriarch, Mama hosts it every year. As SAA, I am expected to attend, but I've been trying to get out of this one. I explained to Mom and Pop the issue between Sophie and Candace. They can't both be there. They reminded me that Candace is considered family and as such, she is always welcome. If the girls can't get along, Sophie will have to sit this one out. I voiced my concerns about leaving Sophie unprotected, but Pop came up with a solution for the evening. We will have a few of the guys rotate hourly shifts so they can each spend some time at the party.

After working at the shop for a few hours, I head to Sophie's to let her know we can't spend the day together as planned. I could tell her on the phone, but I want to see her, even if it's only for a few minutes. When I get there, her front door is open and through the screen door I see her sitting on the sofa. When she sees me, a smile lights her face, and she stands to greet me as I let myself in.

"How'd you sleep?" I ask.

"Good. You?"

"Terrible," I grumble and wrap my arms around her. "I missed you."

"Yeah?"

"Did you miss me?" I lean in like I might kiss her, but hold back.

"Maybe," she taunts with a gleam in her eye.

"Maybe?" I playfully throw her to the floor and tickle her until she's screaming for me to stop. "Still a maybe?"

"Yes, I missed you!"

"How much?" I continue to tickle her.

"A lot!" she squeals.

"Be specific."

"I missed you so much I barely slept at all."

If that's true, she just made my day. I stop tickling her and stare into her eyes. "Really?"

"Yes," she pants.

"Does that mean I get to sleep with you tonight?" I know I should give her space. It's not my intention to force myself on her. But with everything that's going on, I can't be away from her at night. If something happened to her because of me, I'd never forgive myself. Impatient, I press her for an answer. "Hmm?"

"Rooter—" she starts to protest, but I ensue tickling her again before she can.

"All you have to do is say the words I want to hear and I'll stop."

"Okay, okay!"

I stop tickling. "Yeah?"

She sits up slightly. "On one condition."

"Which is?"

"That we sleep in your bed."

I quickly agree. We'll fit better on my king-size mattress. I help her up from the floor when my phone rings. We can never have uninterrupted time together. I check the screen and see it's Mama calling. "Hey," I answer and turn away.

"Where did you disappear to?" Mama asks but doesn't give me time to answer. "You're supposed to help set up for the party. Are you coming?"

I resist the urge to sigh. I was hoping to spend an hour or two with Sophie before heading back, but I can't leave my mom hanging. "Yeah, I'll be there in thirty minutes."

When I turn back to Sophie, she's eyeing me inquisitively. I hate lying to her, but I can't tell her the truth. If I tell her about the party without inviting her, she'll put two and two together and figure it's because Candace will be there. "I know we said we would do something today, but something came up with the Club and I can't get out of it."

"That's okay," she says. "Miranda asked earlier if we could do something when she got off work."

"I'm really sorry, Soph." I bow my head with a guilty conscience.

"Hey, it's okay." She takes my hand and I look into her gentle blue eyes. "I understand. I just can't believe you drove all the way here from the shop to tell me. You could've just called."

"I wanted to see you before I left." I brush her knuckles with my thumb. "You were so mad at me yesterday."

"Yeah, yesterday wasn't the greatest." She looks to the floor.

I tilt her face up by the chin to make eye contact. "You believe me when I say you don't have to worry about Candace, don't you?"

"Of course I do," she sighs. "I just wish she'd go away."

"You understand why I can't write her off?" While I'll continue to make it clear that I'm with Sophie, I can't turn my back on Candace. I really fear she might try to hurt herself if I do and I couldn't live with that. I may not be *in* love with Candace, but I do care about her. She deserves better from me after all these years.

Sophie turns away and folds her arms across her chest. "Yeah, I guess."

"You guess?"

After a moment she turns back around. "I realize you've known her forever and there's history there, but put yourself in my shoes." She flips her long brown hair from one side to the other. "What if a guy I'd known forever who was in love with me was calling me and throwing himself at me constantly? Would you be able to sit back and be patient until he decided to stop?"

"Probably not." I pinch the bridge of my nose in frustration at myself, Candace, and Sophie. Sophie's always throwing hypothetical questions in my face. The answer is, if the shoe was on the other foot, I'd hate it. I probably wouldn't handle it well at all. Even so, as guilty as I feel over what I'm putting both girls through, I can't hurt one to satisfy the other. Candace is already hurting because of me. I don't want to deepen the wound.

"I'm willing to give it a couple weeks and see what happens, but if she hasn't let up by then you'll need to do something about her."

I hold my right hand to my chest. "I know I'm asking a lot of you, but she's hurting right now Sophie, and it's all my fault. I should've never…"

"Had sex with her," she finishes my sentence.

"Let's just see what happens." I stroke her cheek with the back of my hand. "I promise we'll figure it out.

I check my watch for the thousandth time. I was supposed to have called an hour ago. I tried to sneak off to make the call, but Candace has been following me around like a lost puppy all night. When I go to the bathroom, she waits outside the damn door. I had hoped to get out of here around ten to meet Sophie back at my house. When I tried to leave, I was pulled into a corn hole competition with Bear, Pop, and Wrench. It's me and Bear against the old guys. The rule is we play until one team has two wins in a row. I didn't think it'd take long for me and Bear to beat them, but for the past seven games we've traded wins.

Pop leaves for a bathroom break and my phone rings. It's Sophie. Since I've been playing corn hole, Candace has been hanging with Mama. She isn't looking my way so I answer the phone and tell Sophie to hold on a minute. I sneak around the corner of the house. When I speak, I keep my voice low. "Hey, Babe. What's up?"

"Where are you?" she asks drunkenly.

I'm caught off guard and instantly concerned. "Are you drunk?"

I thought she was out playing dodgeball with her friends. She told me she and Miranda were going home when they were done. I told Sparrow to come back to the party when they left, assuming she was going back to her house and I'd soon be joining her. With no one watching her, she's completely unprotected.

"A little," she hiccups. "When are you coming home? I missssss you."

Thank God she's home. No matter what it takes, I'm getting the hell out of here so I can go be with my girl. "I'll be there in a half hour."

"I'm not at home and we're all drunk."

Shit. I need to get to her now. "Where are you? I'll come get you."

"I'm at," she starts to tell me when Candace appears before me.

"Rooter, what are you doing over here all alone?"

I hold my phone to my chest and pray to God Sophie didn't hear Candace's voice. "I'm on the phone, Candace."

"I see that. Talking to your girl?"

I stalk away and warn Candace not to follow me. When I put the phone back to my ear Sophie is screaming my name. She obviously heard Candace.

"Sophie—" I start, but she cuts me off.

"Are you with that bitch?"

"Babe, listen—"

She cuts me off again, screaming so loud I have to hold the phone away from my ear. "Fuck you! I'm not listening to shit. You're with her! You lied to me. It's over. It's fucking over!"

Trouble In Paradise

"**S**ophie!" I holler, but she's not there.

No, no no no no!

I jump to call her back, but it rolls to voicemail. Instead of leaving a message, I call right back. Again, it goes to voicemail.

"Fuck!"

"Trouble in paradise?" Candace asks.

Ignoring Candace, I take off for my bike. My heartbeat thrashes in my ears as my heart races. I have to find Sophie so I can explain.

Candace runs after me, but can't keep up in her heels. But by the time I secure my helmet and start my Harley, she catches me.

"Goddammit!" I scream. "Leave me alone!"

I tear out of the driveway, but have no idea where I'm going. Halsey is filled with bars. I wrack my brain trying to imagine where Sophie is most likely to go before I remember Skyles. I get there in record time, but she isn't there. I pull up a picture of her on my phone and show it to the bartender. He tells me she was here earlier, and that Joe took her and her friends home.

I speed all the way to her house, but she's not there. I sit on the porch stairs and call her number again, but it goes to voicemail. I hang up and squeeze my phone hard enough that it makes a popping sound.

This can't be happening.

It isn't long before a car pulls up in front of the house. In it I see Joe and Miranda, but no Sophie. I race to the car.

"Where is she?" I yell as Joe walks to the passenger side door to help a tipsy Miranda out.

"I don't want any trouble, man," he says. "I'm just trying to get the girls home safe."

I get in his face and growl, "Except Sophie isn't home. Where did you take her?"

"She's safe," he tells me as Miranda steps out.

"I'm going to ask one more time, where is she?"

Miranda says, "She doesn't want to see you."

"Where is she, Miranda?" I ask.

She shakes her head in refusal. "You had me fooled for a minute, but not anymore. Sophie's done with you."

I follow her and Joe to the front door. "Miranda, it isn't what you think."

"Whatever, Rooter. Take your bullshit lies somewhere else."

"I'm not lying, dammit! Where is she?"

Miranda drops her keys and huffs in frustration. "I really don't care! She isn't here and I'm not telling you where she is, so leave or I swear I'll call the cops."

"Call them! I don't give a shit. I'm not leaving until you tell me where she is."

Miranda takes her phone from her purse and starts to make a call. Assuming it's the police, I yank the phone from her hand and throw it into the front yard. Fear flashes in her eyes and I immediately regret my actions. Joe steps in between us.

"I'm sorry," I say. "I didn't mean to scare you."

"I think you should leave," Joe says. He picks up Miranda's keys, but doesn't open the door.

"You gonna make me?" I ask.

"Like I said, I don't want trouble."

I step forward till we're nose to nose. "Tell me where the hell Sophie is, and there won't be trouble."

"She's safe… Just leave her be."

I know where she is. I grab him by the shoulder. "Let's go."

Joe tosses Miranda's keys to her as I drag him down the porch stairs. "I won't take you to her."

I keep walking until we reach his car. "I can figure out where you live on my own."

His chin falls to his chest, and he sighs. After a hesitation, he opens his door and slides inside.

"I'll follow you," I say. "If you take me anywhere other than to where she is… you'll be sorry."

A few minutes later, we come to a stop in front of what I assume is Joe's house. I jump off my bike, following Joe to his door. "Sophie!"

Joe unlocks the door and I push past him into the house. I stride over to Sophie. Her posture is tense and her nostrils flare. Without a word, she smacks me in the face hard and yells, "What are you doing here?"

"What are *you* doing here?" I holler back. She could have gone home with one of her other friends. Hell, I'd even been okay if she went to Ryan's place for the night. Why come here? Unless…

No, I can't allow myself to think that. If I do, I'll go ape shit.

"Trying to stay the hell away from you!"

I toss my head back and cackle. Has she forgotten who she's dealing with? "That's never going to happen. Let's go. Now." I yank her toward the door where Joe stands.

She jerks away and shuffles several steps back. "I'm not going anywhere with you! Go back to your skank."

I inhale a deep breath and stalk over to her. "Do you really want to do this here?"

"I don't want to do it at all." She points to the door. "I want you to leave!"

My voice is low and foreboding. "I'm not leaving without you."

"Well, I'm not leaving!"

Every muscle in my body is coiled tight as I stare her down. "Yes, you are."

Defiant as ever, she crosses her arms and juts out her chin. "No, I'm not!"

My lips curl into a devilish grin. "I'll carry you out of here if I have to."

"Touch me and Joe will call the cops."

I glare at Joe. "Fuck the cops! Call them. We'll be gone before they get here."

Tears slide down Sophie's cheeks as she pleads, "Just go, please."

Pain rips through my chest at the sight of her crying, knowing it's my fault. When I speak, my voice is quiet and calm. "Sophie, it's not what you think."

She clutches the back of her head and groans. "I'm so fucking sick and tired of you saying that! How dumb do you think I am?"

So much for calm. "I know what it seems like, damn it! But it really isn't what you think!"

She crosses her arms and squeezes her biceps. "I don't care what it is, Rooter. I want this to be over."

I take a step forward. "Well, that isn't happening."

She wipes away her tears and her lip trembles. "Why are you doing this? Is this some sick joke to you?"

"Baby, no. God no!" How can she possibly think that? Haven't I told her time and again that she's all I want? Why won't she believe in me? I reach out to stroke her face.

"Stay away from me!" She slaps my hand away and moves backward, taking notice that she's running out of room. "Just go!"

I make a steeple with my fingers, covering my nose and mouth. "Sophia," I sigh and drop my hands, "you have two choices here.

You can hear me out the easy way or you can hear me out the hard way."

Her mouth drops open. "Rooter, don't you understand that I'm tired of hearing you out when it comes to her?"

"Yes, I do. But I'm telling you, what happened tonight was completely innocent."

"Innocent or not," she points at my chest, "you lied to me. You said you had Club business, and you were with her!" She glances at Joe and a strange expression crosses her face. A look of longing or the very least, wondering *what if.*

I turn her face back to me and demand that Joe leave us alone. I need her to hear me out without distraction.

"Sophie, I didn't lie. I was with the Club. I was at our annual summer party." I look to the carpet and rub the back of my neck, nervous. "My mom throws it every year. I knew Candace would be there, so I tried to get out of it. But it's something my family does for the members and with my rank in the Club I had a responsibility to be there."

"Why didn't you tell me the truth?"

"I wanted to, but with everything that's gone down the past couple days with her, and you being pissed off at me…" I pause and rub my face. "I wanted to take you, but we both know what would've happened if I did. If I would've told you the truth about what was going on, it would've hurt you. I was protecting you."

"So again, she wins."

"What are you talking about? Wins what?"

"No matter what, she'll always be around because of her history with the Club. She gets to be there and I don't. I won't be in a relationship with you like that."

"Sophie, this shit with her ends tonight. I'm putting a stop to it. I'll tell her no more phone calls or texts. It's done." Even though I say it, I'm not sure it's the truth. Yes, I'll have another talk with Candace, but I have to be delicate with her. But in this moment, I'm desperate. No way will I let Sophie break up with me over something this stupid.

She laughs, sarcastic. "Like that'll matter. She's not going anywhere."

"She'll always have ties to the Club, yes, but not with me."

"Yes, she will." Sophie pulls away and walks to the picture window keeping her back to me. When she speaks, she sounds defeated. "She always will."

"Sophie, I'm asking you to trust me." I walk up behind her and as much as I want to take her in my arms, I refrain from doing so. "Trust me that nothing is going on between her and me. Yes, I run into her from time to time and I probably always will, but it doesn't mean anything. She's just somebody I know."

"How can I trust you when you lie to me?"

"I didn't lie."

She spins around and jams her index finger into my sternum. Fire dances in her eyes. "You lied by omission!"

Surprised, I recoil and take a step back. "Can't you understand why I felt uncomfortable telling you?"

"It's too much, Rooter. I can't deal with this." She tries to walk past me, but I hold her in place.

I glare at her through narrowed eyes. I won't let her walk away from me. "Well, you'll have to deal with it because I'm not going anywhere."

"Fuck!" she screams with her hands clenched at her sides.

"Babe," I speak as delicately as I am able, "there's nothing Candace can say or do to change the way I feel about you. You're the one I want. The *only* one."

She screws her eyes shut and chews her bottom lip. I keep a hold of her arms should she try to get away again, but instead she takes a slow, deep breath in and says, "If I leave with you, I want you to take me home and leave me alone for the night."

"There's no *if.* You *are* leaving with me."

Her eyes fly open. "You don't control me. I'll do what I want, Rooter. If I want to stay here, I will."

I laugh because she really thinks she will—that she can. I'll never allow my girl to stay the night in another man's house, especially when that man wants her for himself. "I don't think so."

Sophie tries hard to pry free from my hold on her, but I'm too strong. Eventually, she gives up. "You can't stop me."

"From staying the night with another man? Yes, the hell I can."

She rolls her eyes and huffs. "I wouldn't be staying with him, Rooter."

"You won't be staying here at all." In fact, we're getting the hell out of here right this instant. I let her go and grab her purse from the kitchen counter and point at the front door with it. "Let's go."

She shakes her head, but not in protest. "Let me go tell Joe I'm leaving."

Fuck that. You aren't going anywhere near him.

When she starts for the hallway, I hurry past her and cut her off. "I'll tell him," I say and give her the purse. "Wait here."

We don't say a word the entire ride home. When I turn the engine off Sophie jumps off the bike, hands me my helmet and hurries to her house. I follow after her.

She unlocks the door and steps inside.

"We need to talk," I say, "but not until we've both had time to calm down. I'll call you in the morning."

She nods and without a word closes her door.

Oddly, I have no desire to spend the night with Sophie. I'm pissed. Why the hell did she go to Joe Skyles' house? I get that she thought I was with Candace and that I'd lied to her, but she could have gone home with one of her other friends. Did she go to Joe's to get back at me? Was she planning to dump me to be with him? Had he coerced her or was it her idea? I bet he coerced her—used the situation to his advantage to get her alone so he could convince her to give him a shot.

Well he lost his shot. For tonight anyway.

First thing tomorrow morning, I'm going to get to the bottom of why Sophie chose to go there. She'd better have a damn good explanation. I won't put up with any girl of mine going home with another man, ever, for any reason. If Sophie and I are going to stay together, she'd better learn quick that when she has a problem with me, she'd better come to me about it. I won't tolerate her running off with other guys.

And it's damned well past time for her to learn that she can trust me. If she won't trust me, this will never work.

I barely sleep and at a little after six, I roll out of bed for a run. Running always helps to clear my head and relieve my stress. I need to burn some pent up energy before talking with Sophie.

Just before nine, I call her. When it goes to voicemail, I assume she's still asleep and send her a text telling her to call me the moment she wakes up. Twenty minutes pass with no response. Impatient, I call and text again. When she doesn't respond, I dart upstairs to see if her blinds are open yet. They're not. I peer into the dining room windows and see Miranda moving about, but no sign Sophie. I can't shake the nagging suspicion she's avoiding me.

By ten thirty I can't take anymore and go to her house. Miranda opens the door and gives me an unsure look, but I push past her.

"Come on in," she says snidely.

"She awake?" I ask.

"She's in the shower."

I knew she was avoiding me. "I'll wait for her in her room."

In her room, I pace back and forth while she takes the longest shower in history. When her door opens, I saunter to her, stopping just inches away. "Is there a reason you're ignoring me?"

She furrows her brow. "Ignoring you?"

"I've been calling and texting all morning," I bark.

"Shit." She smacks her palm to her forehead. "I don't have my phone. I threw it across the parking lot after talking to you last night."

My tensed muscles instantly relax. "Oh. I'm sorry."

Sophie looks down at her towel covered body. "Can you give me a minute to get dressed?"

Consumed by my anger I hadn't even noticed her state of dress, or undress. But now as I eye her from head to toe, thoughts about her going to Joe's take a backseat. Her long hair is dripping wet and her shoulders and chest glisten. I fantasize licking the water droplets on her shoulder and then working my way... *Snap out of it Rooter.* Sophie stares at me as though she can read my mind and I smirk. "I'll wait in the hall."

Out in the hallway I lean against the wall with arms crossed and one foot propped up on the wall. While I wait, I remind myself why I'm here. I hear Sophie shuffling about in her room and a couple minutes later she opens her door. She looks just as incredible in a battered black concert t-shirt and denim shorts as she did the towel. Hell, she'd look good in a burlap sack.

"Come in," she says and takes a seat on the side of her bed.

"How are you this morning?" I ask as I sit next to her.

"Tired and hung-over." She rubs her forehead.

Before I start in on my irritation about her going to Joe's, I want to know where she's at in all this. "You still mad?"

She blows out a breath and drags her fingers through her wet hair. "Yes and no."

Her answer grates on me. Either she's mad, or she's not.

She continues, "I understand why you felt you couldn't tell me the truth. But I need for this issue with Candace to go away."

She's no longer mad about what I did, she's angry about Candace in general. I can work with that. "I get that and I told you last night it will."

"Okay, but how?" She twists her torso to face me. "How will you make it go away?"

"I'm going to talk to her."

She cocks a brow, skeptical.

"Today," I say. "I'll tell her the phone calls and texts must stop."

"And if they don't?" Her posture tenses and she grips the edge of the mattress.

I rub the back of my neck. "I don't know. But I promise I'll figure something out."

"Fair enough." She turns the rest of her body in my direction, resting her knee on my thigh. "And do you promise not to withhold things from me in the future? Even if you think it'll hurt me or I'll respond badly to it?"

"Yes, I promise." I swallow before saying my next words. "But you need to understand that Candace is someone I'll always know. I can't make her disappear."

"Rooter, I need to know I can trust you."

She seriously didn't just say that.

Sophie continues, "You sympathizing with her and allowing her to come between us makes it hard for me. Especially when you withhold information from me."

I take a slow breath in and exhale. "I get it, Sophie. It won't happen again."

She plops back on the bed and grumbles. "I hate that I'm turning into one of those crazy jealous girlfriends."

Crazy jealous, huh? I can definitely work with that. I chuckle and lean over top of her, propped up on one elbow. My lips are only inches from hers. "You have nothing to be jealous about. I'm yours."

Her eyes dart to my mouth and she licks her lips. Her breathing speeds up and her hands are clenched at her sides. When her eyes meet mine again, they plead for me to kiss her. She leans in, but I pull away. I refuse to kiss her until I know where she stands. Until I know she's really and truly mine and until she understands exactly what that means.

Unexpected

"Are you mine?" I growl.

Sophie stares at me with wanting eyes, and answers without hesitation. "Yes."

"Say the words."

"I'm yours."

I move in close, so very tempted by her full, pouty lips, but I'm still not satisfied. If she's mine, and she truly wants to be with me, why did she look at Joe the way she had? How could she be tempted by him? Why did she go to him? There isn't a woman on this planet that could charm me away from Sophie. My loyalty lies with her. There's nothing any woman—including Sophie—can do or say to sway me. My decision has been made. I need to know Sophie feels the same way. "I saw the way you looked at him last night. Do you want him?"

"No."

"Don't lie to me, Sophie."

"I'm not lying—"

I cut her off. "Were you going to let him kiss you? Were you going to sleep in his bed?" My body shudders at the thought of her with him—of what may have happened had I not gotten to her.

"No!" she hollers, offended.

My chest burns as disgusting thoughts invade my mind. Images of his mouth on hers, his hands on her body, but worse is the vision of her enjoying it. Anger blazes through me. "Just the thought of his hands or his mouth touching you makes me crazy."

"He didn't touch me."

"And he never will." My eyes bore into hers. "No one will ever touch you, but me."

Sophie returns my fierce glare. "Then no one had better be touching you, either."

"You're the only one I want to touch me."

Her stare softens and her body goes slack beneath mine. She whimpers, "Kiss me, please."

I still have questions that I require answers to, but her begging is my undoing. The desire in her eyes pulls at me, fueling my own. Unable to fight it any longer, I claim her mouth with my own and we moan simultaneously. "You taste so fucking good," I rasp and place a trail of kisses from the corner of her mouth to the sensitive area just below her ear. When I nip her earlobe, she arches her chest into mine.

Sophie kisses and licks the skin just above my collarbone and I groan at the warm, wet sensation. She kisses me again in the same place, swirling her tongue and sucking at the skin. *Jesus, her mouth feels good.*

She whispers in my ear, "Do you like that?"

"Hell yes."

She wiggles her hands that are still pinned above her head. "I want to touch you."

I release her wrists and prop myself above her with my elbows. I'm not sure what she means by wanting to touch me, but I'm eager as hell to find out. I want her hands all over me.

First, she places her hands on my biceps, then moves them up to my shoulders and down to my chest that rises and falls with fast, shallow breaths. She tugs at the hem of my shirt. "Take this off."

Eager for her touch, I quickly discard it.

Sophie pulls her bottom lip into her mouth as she takes in the sight of my bare torso. "Roll over."

Holding her close, I roll the both of us over so that she's straddling me. My breath hitches the instant her warm fingers make contact with my chest. With her eyes on mine, she begins to lower her body and I shoot her a look of concern. If she so much as sinks another inch, she'll feel how hard I am. I don't want a repeat of what happened last time.

"It's okay," she affirms and takes a hold of my hands before slowly lowering until she's firmly pressed against my erection.

My breath catches as she rocks back and forth on my cock. I pull my bottom lip into my mouth and grip her hips as I grind myself between her legs. "Fuck, that feels good."

I've had a lot of sex, been inside my fair share of women. Nothing has felt as good as being between Sophie's legs, both of us fully clothed. That she's allowing me to touch her in this way excites the hell out of me.

Her warm hands graze my chest down to my waist. I clutch her ass as her mouth travels from my neck to my nipple. The instant her tongue makes contact I grasp her hips. She sucks and flicks the sensitive tip before circling my nipple with her tongue. Watching her makes my cock twitch. My fingers dig into her hips as I hiss with pleasure.

Fuck, this is so hot.

She reaches up and traces the outline of my lips with her index finger and I take it into my mouth and suck. Before I have time to register what's happening, she sits upright and pulls her t-shirt over her head. My stomach flutters. Hers are the most perfect tits I've ever had the good fortune of seeing up close. I can't tear my eyes from her chest. All I can think about is having those rose colored nipples in my mouth.

But before I can ask permission, she flashes a devilish grin and whispers, "My turn."

"Christ, Sophie," I groan through labored breaths. "Are you sure?"

"Yes." She rocks back and forth over my cock once more.

If she keeps this up, I'll explode. I flip us back over so that she's lying beneath me. "You're so beautiful."

I lean down and press my lips to her neck, skimming the soft skin with my tongue. She quivers as I blow on her wet skin. My right hand travels down her side to her ass as I softly kiss her collarbone. Her deep, throaty moan sets me on fire. I grind into her again and again until my balls tighten. With orgasm threatening, I draw back and gaze at her bare chest. I take one into my hand and sweep my thumb delicately across the nipple. Her body shudders and she elicits the tiniest of a whimper.

"I've fantasized about touching you." I bow my head and lick my lips, ready to take her into my mouth. "About feeling you against my tongue."

"Me, too."

With my eyes locked on hers, my mouth hovers just above her breast, ready to taste her sweet skin. Before I do, I need for her to be absolutely sure she wants this. "You're sure?"

"Yes," she breathes.

Keeping my eyes on hers, I graze the tip of her nipple with my tongue. She arches her back, pressing her breast to my mouth.

"Again," she purrs.

Ever ready to please her, I slowly circle Sophie's nipple with the tip of my tongue before capturing it with my mouth and sucking. I moan in satisfaction as I work her with my tongue. Being able to touch and taste her is so much better than I imagined. Her hands roam over my shoulders, back, and arms as she writhes beneath me, moaning wildly.

"So soft." I draw back and blow on her hard, wet nipple. Goosebumps cover her skin and she shivers. "You like that?"

"Mm-hmm." Sophie grasps my shoulders, pulling me down for more.

"Should I kiss the other one?"

"Yes, please."

"Open your eyes, Babe. I want to watch you watching me."

It was so hot seeing her suck my nipple and I want to return the favor. Once her eyes are open, I swipe the other nipple with my tongue and then blow on it. "I've laid in bed so many nights," I rock back and forth between her legs, wanting her to feel how hard she's made me, "looking at your window, fantasizing about what it would be like to touch and taste you."

"Me, too."

"Yeah? And is it as good as you imagined?" I flick her nipple again.

She gasps and her eyes roll back into her head. "So much better."

"I agree." I move to the other breast and brush it with my tongue. She likes it when I tease her with feather-like licks.

"Rooter," she moans and pulls my face against her breast.

Her calling out my name is my undoing. My cock twitches in my jeans, a familiar, almost painful pressure building, begging for release. I grip her ass with both hands and grind myself against her pussy. *Is she as wet as I am hard?* "Do you like feeling me against you?"

"Yes," she whispers and wraps her legs around my hips, drawing me closer. She rakes her nails up my back and moans as I rub myself against her again and again, rotating my hips in a circle. I take her earlobe into my mouth and nip and suck, calling her name. Her body quivers beneath me and her face and chest is flushed. She calls my name and shouts, "Oh, God yes!"

I pull back and gaze into her glossy eyes, continuing to rock against her. "Yeah?"

"Yeah," she groans and bites her bottom lip. Lost in the heat of the moment, she closes her eyes.

Shit yeah. I want her to come undone for me, but I want her eyes open when it happens. I yearn to see the depth of her desire and for her to see mine as we come together. I stop thrusting and her eyes snap open. "Keep your eyes open."

Eyes locked, I rock into Sophie again and again, rotating and thrusting my hips. She clutches my biceps and sucks in a breath. Way past the point of return, I'm right on the cusp.

So. Damn. Close.

She needs to come. Now.

"Let go, Baby," I encourage her. "I want to watch you come for me."

I push against her once more and she screams my name as her body quivers beneath mine. The sweetness that usually resides in her eyes has been replaced by pure, animalistic need.

The sight of Sophie getting off does me in. Digging my fingers into her thighs I push myself into her and sudden, intense pleasure tears through me.

Fuck, I'm coming.

I feel it everywhere, even my fingers and toes tingle. Staring into Sophie's eyes, I grunt and call her name as my cock pulses inside my jeans. A wave of sweet relief crashes over me and everything fades to black.

Moments later I collapse on top of her with ragged breaths. I lay this way for several moments trying to catch my breath and collect the strength to move.

I've never gotten off by grinding myself against a girl fully clothed. If you would've asked even a day ago, I would've told you it'd be impossible. Yet, I've just experienced the most intense orgasm of my life.

I've had guys tell me they've experienced orgasms so strong they bordered on pain. I thought it was bullshit. I stand corrected.

"Holy shit," Sophie mutters, breathless.

"I second that," I say and roll onto my back. "That was hot as hell."

Sophie clasps her hand over her face and covers her breasts with the other.

"Are you embarrassed?"

A nod is her only response.

I lift her hand from her face so I can gaze into her sweet eyes. "Why?"

Her face flushes red. "Because I just… You know. While you watched."

"So did I." *She is too cute.* I smile and brush away a lock of damp hair from her forehead.

"You did?" She glances at the wet spot on my jeans and her eyes widen. "Oh."

"It's so cute how quickly you switch from bold to bashful."

"I'm glad I amuse you."

"Now what am I supposed to do about this?" I point to my wet crotch.

"You do live next door." She points to my house.

"Miranda is downstairs."

"Forgot about that." She giggles.

"Shit. All right." The only way I can clean up is to go home. I crawl over top of Sophie to get out of the bed. "I'll be right back."

I run down the stairs as fast as my wobbly legs will carry me. Miranda is sitting on the couch watching television as I sprint to the front door. She looks my way with a surprised expression as I hurry out of the house. Hell, I'm just as surprised as she is. I'd fully expected another argument and for Sophie to tell me to get lost. I definitely didn't imagine what just happened. I thought it'd be weeks or even months before Sophie and I got to this point in our relationship.

After a quick rinse in the shower, I'm able to think clearly once again. I still have questions about last night. I need to find out why Sophie went to Joe's house and I need to make it perfectly clear that I won't tolerate her going home with other men. Ever. I don't care how pissed off she gets at me.

Without knocking, I let myself into Sophie's room. She's perched on her bed, knees pulled to her chest wearing a dazed expression. Before I move on to my questions, I should acknowledge what just transpired between us. We've taken our relationship to a significantly higher level. Sophie trusted me enough to be intimate with me—something she's never done with any other guy.

I take a seat on edge of the bed, turn to face her. "That was amazing, Babe."

"Yes." She blushes and rests her chin on her knees.

I reach out and brush her cheek. "But we need to finish the conversation we were having before I got distracted."

She blinks. "We weren't finished?"

I shake my head. "I need you to tell me why you went home with Joe Skyles."

Her body tenses and she sighs before she hangs her head. "Because I was mad at you and didn't want to come here."

"That's the only reason?"

Her head snaps upright and there's a spark in her eyes. "Of course. Why would you even ask me that?"

"Out of all your friends, you had nowhere else to go?" I ask as calmly as I can, trying my best not to sound accusatory. "No one else to call?"

"You don't trust me."

"Sophie, you told me it was over, refused to talk to me," the volume of my voice escalates. "Next thing I know, you're at another guy's house."

She rolls her eyes. "It was late, Rooter. He offered me a place to stay. That's all it was."

"I believe you. But, Sophie, I won't tolerate you going home with other guys." I place my hand over her mouth when she tries to interrupt me. "I don't care how mad you get at me. You don't go home with other men. Ever." Just the thought of it causes my body to shake.

"I said it wasn't like that."

"I get that and I don't care." I take a deep breath and pinch the bridge of my nose as I try to calm down. "You don't go home with other men."

Sophie throws her hands in the air and hollers, "I thought you cheated on me!"

Here we go. I take a deep breath. "Because you wouldn't hear me out. Which is another thing we need to work on." I pause and rake my fingers through my hair. "This is all new to me, Sophie, and I'm trying, but you can't run off and refuse to talk to me every time I piss you off."

She straightens her legs out in front of her and leans forward. "It's not just because I was pissed it was because of the *reason* I was pissed."

I squeeze my eyes shut and exhale sharply. "I'm going to tell you one more time, and I seriously hope it will be the last." I open my eyes and stare into hers intently. "I'm completely loyal and faithful to you. I will never cheat on you. If you ever doubt me or have questions, talk to me. Don't assume because I promise you'll be wrong every time." I scoot over to her and take her face into my hands. "There's no way I'd ever risk hurting you or losing you. If you knew how damn much and for how long I've wanted you, there's no way you'd ever think I would."

She swallows and stares at me, incredulous. When she speaks, her voice is barely louder than a whisper. "I'm sorry." She leans close. "I promise, I won't ever go home with anyone again."

"Do you also promise that you'll hear me out next time you get pissed?"

"I promise."

I rest my forehead on hers and peer into her intense blue eyes. "I'm crazy about you."

"Me, too."

I lean in for a kiss, but my damn phone rings. Not surprisingly, it's Candace. "Should I answer it?"

"You did say you'd talk to her."

Reluctantly, I pull away and answer the call. "Yeah?"

Keeping my eyes on Sophie's, I gauge her expression while Candace tells me her car broke down and she doesn't know what to do. She needs a ride to her friend's house. I draw soft circles on Sophie's inner thigh with my fingertips causing goosebumps to raise on her skin.

"I'll send a tow truck and meet you at Molly's Auto," I say to Candace.

"Thank you," Candace says. "I'll see you there."

"All right," I tell her and end the call.

"What was that about?" Sophie asks.

"Her car broke down."

She arches a brow. "So she called you?"

I shrug, nervous. "I'm sort of the one she's always called when she needs help."

Sophie sighs and rolls her eyes. "You're going to tell her that has to stop, too, aren't you?"

"Yes, Babe." I rub the back of my neck.

"Are you going there now?"

"Want to come with me?" I offer.

"Really? Are you sure?"

This may very well blow up in my face, but it's a necessary step to proving to Sophie that she can believe in me. "I'm done letting Candace come between us. I'm going to show you, once and for all, that you can trust me."

Threatened

I play out the scene at Molly's in my mind. One thing is certain. Candace will flip out and Sophie will be more than ready to put her in her place. I fear this is a nightmare getting ready to come true. But it's the only thing I can do to prove my loyalty to Sophie and get Candace to face reality.

Candace hears my bike and looks our way. A scowl is fixed on her face and she stands with her hands on her hips as Sophie and I approach. "I thought you were taking me to Nicole's."

"Bear's coming," I say and prepare for the introduction. "This is Sophie. Sophie, this is Candace."

Candace's eyes sweep over Sophie. Unimpressed by what she sees, she shrugs and turns back to me. "You can't be serious, Rooter."

Sophie's body tenses beside me.

"Candace, be nice," I order.

"Be nice? Seriously?" She motions to Sophie. "You bring the bitch you dumped me for and expect me to be nice?"

Here we go.

Sophie lunges for her, but I grab her by the arms before she gets to Candace. "You better watch who you're calling a bitch, skank."

"You better watch who you're calling a skank!" Candace yells.

I spin Sophie around so she's facing away from Candace. Candace had better be careful. I've seen how well Sophie can handle herself—she'll obliterate the girl.

"Let go of me!" Sophie screams and flails, trying to get free.

"Stop it, now!" I bark, having a difficult time keeping a hold of her.

"Why would you bring her here?" Candace gripes in a high pitch, whiny voice. "Are you trying to hurt me even more?"

"Bitch please—" Sophie starts, but I stop her.

"Sophie, stop it," I demand and hold her tight against me as she continues to try to pry free from my grasp. I crane my neck to address Candace. "No, I don't want to hurt you. You're the one who called me for help. We were together when you called."

"You better stop calling!" Sophie threatens.

"Sophie," I roar, growing impatient.

Candace laughs snidely, "I'll call him anytime I want."

"Rooter, tell her," Sophie urges.

I take a deep breath and count to ten to calm myself. "Candace, you can't keep calling and texting me pictures."

"Come on, Baby," Candace coos. Sophie opens her mouth to speak but I cover it with my hand while Candace continues. "We both know exactly how this is going to go. The moment the novelty wears off, you'll get bored with her and call me like you always do."

Candace is skating on thin ice. If I should lose my grip on Sophie, she'll get her ass beat.

"It's not like that with Sophie," I insist. "I'm with her."

Candace cackles, oblivious to the danger she's in. "Yeah, this month."

"Candace, if we're going to stay on good terms you need to respect my relationship."

"Oh, you mean the way you respected me?" she asks with crossed arms and sticks out her hip. "One day I'm sucking your dick, the next I'm out with the trash?"

I cringe. First, she's not entirely off base. Second, I've hurt her deeply and feel horrible over it. Third, I don't want Sophie hearing it.

"You *are* trash!" Sophie screams. Her body shakes and I have to grip her tighter.

Candace lunges at Sophie, but I keep the girls separated with my back to Candace and Sophie pressed against my chest.

"Sophie, damn it!" I holler, all patience now gone.

One of the mechanics watching from inside a garage bay sprints over to us. "You need some help man?" He looks from me to Candace.

"Put your hands on me and you'll be eating your balls for dinner," Candace threatens him.

He ignores her and chuckles. "Got a pair of feisty ones on your hands."

No shit. I nod in agreement. I lean into Sophie's ear and murmur, "Sophie, will you please go inside and let me finish talking to her?"

She gasps. "Are you kidding me?"

"We're not going to get anywhere like this." I speak gently and place a kiss on her temple. "Please? Five minutes."

Her body relaxes and I allow her to twist in my arms so she's facing me. "The last time you asked for five minutes it ended with her tongue in your mouth and her hand on your dick."

I cringe again. Sophie shoots Candace a threatening glare so I turn her face back to mine. "I promise that won't happen."

Sophie gazes into my eyes for several moments before answering. "Fine."

"Thank you," I say but before letting her go, I give her a look warning her not to try anything. Once I'm sure she won't attack Candace, I look to the mechanic. "Take her to the office, man?"

The instant Sophie is inside the building, Candace smarts off. "I seriously can't believe you brought her."

"I already told you, we were together when you called."

Her shoulders droop and her expression is a mixture of anger and sadness. "Do you have any idea how bad this hurts?"

"I'm not out to hurt you, Candace," I say gently, "but you need to accept that our involvement is over. I'm with Sophie now."

"I just don't get it." She glances toward the building. "What do you even see in her? She's not your type at all."

If only she knew how very wrong she is. "I came here to help you, not to argue."

"I'd rather still be stranded on the side of the road." She looks away and pouts.

"Well maybe you should call someone else next time you need help."

She jerks her head back in surprise. "You told me everything would be the same as it always was. Of course you're the person I called for help."

"And I'm here to help you."

She stomps her feet. "You just don't get it!"

If I wasn't so irritated, I'd laugh at how ridiculous she looks. Bear pulls into the parking lot and I motion for him to go into the building where Sophie's waiting.

"I hate to tell you, but you're the one who doesn't get it. You need to accept that we aren't going to be together. We never were."

"You used me until something better came along."

I start to tell her that isn't true, but she speaks again before I get the chance.

"Actually, no. That's not right. You just used me, because that mousey little plain Jane in there," she points to the office, "will *never* be better than me."

"I did not use you, Candace," I sigh and look to the sky. "For the millionth time, you and I had an agreement. Just Sex. No strings. It wasn't meant to last."

"Whatever, Rooter. Go ahead, be with your little princess who can't fuck right, but don't bother calling me when you get bored with her."

I throw my hands in the air and turn away. "I'm finished with this conversation."

"Fine!"

"I can't believe her," Sophie grumbles as we walk in her house.

"I'm sorry about that, Babe, but it pretty much went the way I figured it would."

"If you hadn't been holding me, I'd have rearranged her face," she says with gritted teeth.

"I figured that, too."

She tosses her purse and keys onto the coffee table. "What I don't understand is why you were yelling at me to calm down instead of her."

"You were the only one I stood a chance with. There's nothing I could have said to control Candace."

"I guess that makes sense." She falls onto the couch. "So do you think it did any good, her seeing us together?"

"Time will tell," I say and take a seat next to her.

"That bitch is out of time with me. If I run into her again and she gets in my face," she balls her right hand into a fist, "I'm going to put my fist through her skull."

I take her fist into my hand and stroke her knuckles until she relaxes her fingers. "Don't concern yourself with Candace. She isn't worth your aggravation. I told you where I stand with that."

My phone rings. Perfect timing, as always. It's Pop. "What's up?"

"Get to the clubhouse, now. Got a package from Andy. You're not gonna like it."

My shoulders tense and a tremor runs through me. "I'm on my way." I hang up and glance back at Sophie. "Club business."

She nods. "I have to get ready for work, anyway."

I lean down and give her a soft kiss. "I'll see you tonight."

Apart from Bear and Sparrow, everyone is at the clubhouse when I arrive. Bear will be here as soon as he drops Candace off at her friends. I've tasked Sparrow with making sure Sophie gets to work safely.

"What's going on?" I ask the moment I walk inside.

Pop motions for me to follow him into the meeting room. "Come with me."

We take our usual seats and he hands me a manila envelope. I open it and remove a letter and several photos. A sudden rush of heat floods my body and there's a pounding in my ears. The first image is of Sophie in her front yard. Based on the outfit she's wearing, this picture was taken just a couple days ago. The rest of the pictures are of me and Candace in various compromising positions in my office at the shop and at her house.

"Read the letter," Pop urges.

Rooter,

Turn in your patch and walk away from the Club or I will send copies of these pictures to that pretty new girlfriend of yours. I understand Sophie doesn't care much for Candace. I don't think she'd appreciate seeing these pictures, especially the one of your face between Candace's legs. If you want to keep your girl, you better do as I say.

A

"I'll kill that motherfucker!" I roar and send a handful of the photos flying across the room. "Fuck the consequences, I'm going after him."

Pop takes a hold of my shoulder. "I figured you'd say that. But Rooter, we have to be smart and not let anger get the best of us."

"Too late for that," I seethe.

"Listen, I've got a plan."

That doesn't surprise me. For all I know Pop's been in possession of these photos for hours, waiting to reach out to me until his plan was formulated. I arch an eyebrow, waiting to hear what he has to say.

Pop scratches his beard. "First, you should know Hoyt has agreed to the alliance."

"With his crew and the extra manpower from our charters, we can take the Henchmen. Let's get this shit going."

"Rooter, even with the odds in our favor, it'll be bloody and could cost lives."

I struggle to keep from hollering. "If we allow this to continue, it could cost lives anyway."

He nods, but pauses before speaking. "I'm going to reach out to Ivan. Tell him of the alliance and what he'll be up against." Pop stands and paces to the other end of the room and back before finishing. "One thing I know about Ivan is he won't risk losing if there's another way out. I'm going to propose a trade."

"A trade?" I ask, curious yet skeptical.

"We'll pay Ivan to hand Andy over to us and to stay out of Halsey."

I shake my head. It'll never work. "We don't have the kind of money it would take to make that trade."

"I'm going to offer one-fifty," he means one hundred and fifty grand, "but I suspect he'll counter with at least two-fifty, maybe more."

We don't have that amount of money lying around. We pay our crew generously at the shop and for their contributions to the Club. Pop might have that much saved up. I sure as hell don't. I have decent savings, but nowhere near that much. If we asked for donations from our guys, we could come up with it, but we'd never ask our guys to tap into their savings.

"How are we going to come up with that kind of cash?"

He sighs. "I'll ask Hoyt to cover half. I'll pay the other half."

I laugh even though it's not funny. "He'll never do it. Why should he pay for my problem?"

"He wouldn't know about any of that. As far as Hoyt will know, it's to keep Ivan out of Halsey. It's not a lie."

"And if he finds out the real reason we're proposing this deal?"

"We'll deal with that if it comes to pass. I'd rather go up against Hoyt than the Henchmen."

"Good point." I blow out a breath. "Do you think Hoyt will go for it?"

"Only one way to find out."

I've been on pins and needles for the past two hours waiting for Pop and Wrench to return from their meeting with Hoyt. Bear sits next to me when they pull into the parking lot.

"What'd he say?" I ask the instant they walk into the building.

"He's in on half," Pop answers and sits in a chair across from me. "But only up to a hundred grand. The rest is on us."

"How do we come up with our end?"

"Your mother and I have savings."

"Pop, I can't ask you—"

He holds his hand up to stop me. "You didn't ask. This was my plan. And it's not just about you, Son. It's about the Club, our families, and this town."

With Pop it's always about the bigger picture.

"I have some money saved up. I can give you fifty grand."

Pop shakes his head. "Keep your money. Like I said, this was my idea. I'll pay."

Bear asks, "So when do you reach out to Ivan?"

Wrench answers, "Now."

There's no direct access to Ivan. The number we call goes to a low ranked member who sends our message to his boss, who determines the importance of the message before deciding to pass it up to his boss. In the end, our message will go through as many as eight men before it reaches Ivan. Most messages don't make their way to him. Luckily, those coming from the President of a rival club usually do. Still, it could be hours or even days before we hear back. For now, it's a waiting game.

I don't do well with waiting.

The Red Door

With everything that's gone down, and the uncertainty surrounding Andy and the Henchmen, the last thing we should do is hit up a night club. But Sophie asked that I go with her to the Red Door to celebrate Miranda's birthday. Fortunately, Bear's going as Miranda's date—at least he assumes it's a date since she didn't specify. I've also asked Darren and Bones from the Detroit charter to tag along to help keep an eye on things. With the four of us keeping surveillance, we should be able to keep the girls safe from any potential harm.

But the moment I step into Sophie's living room, any thoughts of Andy and the possible danger he presents is forgotten. I hardly recognize Sophie as she stands before me in a barely there red dress. The neckline plunges so low I can damn near see her belly button. As if that wasn't enough, she's wearing a gold body chain that lies in the middle of her chest. My cock stiffens at the sight.

"Goddamn," I say as I walk toward her. My eyes travel the length of her body up to her eyes.

"What do you think?" she asks with a hint of uncertainty in her voice.

"It's so unlike you." I blink and eye her up and down again. Her entire look, including the heavy make-up and eye shadow, differs vastly from her typical style. "You're hot as hell, Babe."

"Really?"

I lick my lips. "Oh yeah."

"See, I told you he'd like it," Miranda tells her before ushering us out of the house.

As if there was any doubt I'd like it.

Inside the limo, I can't take my eyes off Sophie. Between those long, lean legs and that sexy as hell body chain, I'm entranced. I didn't want to go to the club before and I damn sure don't want to go now. Though for entirely different reasons. If I had it my way, I'd turn this car around and we'd go to my place where I could have my way with her. Well, perhaps not. I doubt she's ready for what I'd like to do to her. But either way, we'd have a hell of a lot more fun in my bed than inside a crowded dance club.

I drape an arm across her shoulders while caressing the top of her thigh with the other. Her skin is so damned soft and she smells incredible. Imagining tasting the inside of her thigh, I bite my bottom lip and suck in a breath. I lean in and murmur in her ear, "You look… Fucking edible."

"I might hold you to that," she breathes and takes my earlobe into her mouth and sucks.

Her words take me by surprise and the warm wetness of her mouth shoots straight to my cock. "Keep doing that and we won't make it out of this car."

"That would be okay with me." She nips and sucks my earlobe again.

"Christ, Sophie." Suddenly all that matters is to get my hands and mouth on her body as fast as I can in hopes she'll return the favor. I lean all the way into her and slide my hand up her thigh, under her dress, and squeeze her ass.

Miranda clears her throat, reminding us we're not alone. Reluctantly, I pull away from Sophie and try to straighten up in my seat. I shift a couple times trying to get comfortable, but it's impossible with the raging hard-on in my jeans. My chest rises and falls rapidly as I look over at Sophie who's smirking at me smugly.

Fucking hell. This is going to be a long night.

Inside the Red Door, we each flash our ID's to the bouncer before heading down a dark corridor to the bar and dance floor. The place is packed, shoulder to shoulder. Men and women grind against one another to the sound of provocative dance music. The small of Sophie's back is cool to the touch as we follow Miranda and Bear to the VIP area. The girls are greeted by their friends, no less than two dozen guys and girls. Ryan sprints over to where Sophie and I are standing and pulls her into a hug.

"Babe!" he shrills.

"Babe!"

I don't know Ryan, but I'm good at reading people and I like him. He puts off a good vibe and seems to be a genuine friend to Sophie.

Ryan pulls away, clasping Sophie's arms. His jaw slackens at the sight of her. "Holy fuck! You put every bitch in here to shame."

I concur, "Yes, she does."

Sophie spins in my direction with a dubious stare.

"It's true," I tell her and extend my hand to Ryan. "Good to see you, man."

"You, too."

It takes forever for Sophie and Miranda to greet all their friends. When they're finally finished, Sophie and I take a seat on a red leather love seat. One of their guy friends ogles Sophie's exposed thighs. When he realizes I've caught him, he turns gray and averts his gaze. I chuckle and pull Sophie close. It doesn't bother me that other guys check out my girl. It makes me proud. Sophie could have her pick of any guy and she chose me.

"Do you want a drink?" I ask her.

"Jack on ice."

I should've guessed. I wink and watch desire pool in her eyes before waving at the VIP waiter to come take our order. "Two double Jacks," I tell him. "One on ice, the other neat. And whatever those two want." I point at Bear and Miranda. "I'll start a tab for the four of us."

Sophie's two friends Jess and Abby—the girls she was with the night of our epic argument at Joe's—are here. "Glad to see you two patched things up," Abby says.

"Yeah. It was just a huge misunderstanding," Sophie tells her.

"So, Rooter," Jess leans in and licks her lips, "you're in that motorcycle gang, Halsey Hellions."

"Double H isn't a gang," I correct her. "It's a club."

I can't count the number of people I've had to correct on this subject. Most people view us as a gang because that's the way we're portrayed in the media.

She raises her eyebrows with doubt. "But you do… dangerous things."

"Sometimes."

"Your Club was involved in that shootout with that drug dealer…" Abby interjects, "what's his name?"

I shake my head. "I can't discuss Club business."

"Your Club is in the news a lot," Jess says.

I shrug. "Comes with the territory I suppose."

Abby gets ready to say something else, but Jess beats her to the punch. "So, is it like they show it on TV, being in a motorcycle club?"

"Depends on which shows you're watching."

"You know, the ones with the hot chicks running around half dressed, and lots of fights and danger."

I laugh. "Sometimes."

"I think it's so hot—I mean cool." Jess turns bright red and looks to Sophie apologetically.

Sophie laughs it off and drags her fingers up my thigh. "It's okay. I think it's hot too."

It turns out all of Sophie's friends are curious about the biker life. After answering their questions, Sophie and I relax on the loveseat. My fingers skim the top of her thigh, back and forth, as I gaze into her eyes. She trembles at my delicate touch. I should be on the lookout for Andy, but I can't tear my eyes away from Sophie. She tosses back what remains of her second glass of whiskey and Miranda leans into her ear to say something.

"The guys said there's been no sign of Andy," Bear tells me.

"The fucker better not show up here," I bristle, but after a second I reconsider. "Then again, if he did, it'd give me the opportunity to handle him once and for all."

"True," he tosses back a swig of his beer, "but wouldn't want the girls to witness that kind of brutality."

He has a point. I'm sure they have an idea of what we're capable of, but to observe it first hand is totally different.

Sophie stands and begins to follow Miranda, but I tug her hand before she gets away. I hate to come across as overbearing, but better safe than sorry in the event Andy is lurking somewhere around here. "Where are you going?"

"Miranda and I are going to say hi to a friend."

I can't tell her no so as the girls walk away, Bear and I get up to follow. We don't trail on their heels, but stay close enough that we can get to them should anything go down. They stop at the DJ booth and the DJ's eyes bug out of his head at the sight of Sophie. He pulls her in for a hug and grabs her ass. My nostrils flare and I press my lips into a thin line.

Not cool, buddy.

Sophie pulls back from him and looks around, probably for me. I come up from behind her and snake a possessive arm around her waist letting the guy know she's mine. He looks petrified at the sight of me and my scowl.

"Mario, this is my boyfriend, Rooter. Rooter, this is Mario."

Keep your hands off my girl's ass, Mario. I jut out my chin as my only means of greeting.

"Nice meeting you, man." He holds his hand out to me. The same hand that was just on Sophie's ass. I glare at it a second before shaking it.

I turn to Sophie. "Want to dance?"

"You dance?" She gapes.

I hold a hand to my chest faking offense. "I've been known to on occasion."

"Well then let's do it." The side of her mouth curls into a smile and she takes me by the hand, leading the way to the dance floor.

My eyes are trained on Sophie's ass, swaying left and right, as I follow. Guys stop dancing with their girls and do a double take the instant they see her, but they don't stand a chance. She's mine.

Sophie picks a spot on the jam-packed dance floor and turns to face me. As crowded as it is, when people see me in my cut, they step back to make room for the two of us. I step up close to Sophie, place my hands on her hips and move to the beat of the song. She watches me, impressed by my skilled dance moves, and I shoot her a cocky smirk.

My mom being Puerto Rican loves music, dancing, and singing. From the moment I could walk, I remember dancing with her. The woman can move. Everything I know I learned from her.

The next song is slow and I pull Sophie flush against me. I reach around and cup her backside with both hands, and lean in to her ear. "You have a fantastic ass."

"I'm glad you think so." Her voice is husky.

"Every man in here thinks so."

She shakes her head. She's far too modest to agree.

I pull back just enough to look her in the eyes. "Every guy in this place wants to be me right now."

She presses her pelvis against me and murmurs in my ear with a deep, sensual voice, "You're the only one I want."

Hearing those words lights a fire in me that is nearly impossible to contain. The world falls away, and it's just the two of us on this dance floor. I spin Sophie around and thrust against her backside. With a hand on her hip and another on the chain between her breasts, I sway in time to the beat. Her body slackens against mine as she allows me to take the lead. The smell of her perfume is intoxicating, reminding me of the day on her bed. The way it felt to be between her legs. The complete and utter trust I saw in her eyes. I kiss her shoulder and work my way up to her ear.

"I have never seen anything as beautiful as you," I confess.

Sophie's long brown hair brushes the side of my face and I lean in to inhale its sweet scent. In a trance-like state, I'm completely fixated on her. With her body pressed firmly against mine, we continue to dance. My hands roam from Sophie's hips, to her chest, back down to her waist. The entire length of her body is pressed against mine and yet, I'm nowhere near close enough to her.

A faster tempo song comes on and Sophie bends over, grinds her ass into my crotch and flips back up. She sashays around me, caressing my ass as she makes her way to the other side. She grinds against me once more before taking it low and working her way up the side of my body. I want to get the hell out of here, take her home, and put my mouth everywhere that she'll allow.

I tug Sophie against my chest and place a lingering wet kiss on her neck. As we continue to dance, my eyes remain trained on the body chain. I'm jealous as fuck of an inanimate object.

"You like?" she asks.

"One day," I reach out and trace the chain on her chest, "I want to see you in just this, a thong, and these heels."

Her lips graze my ear as she speaks, "I'd be happy to show you tonight."

My breath stalls. *Does she really mean it?* "You're killing me, Babe."

Bear and Miranda join us on the dance floor, but I'm in need of a drink. If Sophie keeps talking this way, there will be a hell of a lot more than dancing going on between us. Taking Sophie by the hand, I lead her back to the VIP seats and order another round of drinks. Sophie perches on my lap, and she either doesn't notice my arousal, or she's choosing to ignore it.

A few of Sophie's friends, including Ryan, join us for small talk, though I wouldn't call what I'm doing conversing. It's more like I'm on autopilot, nodding and agreeing where it seems appropriate. Regardless of who's talking or whom I'm responding to, my eyes never wander from Sophie. The combination of dancing, her words, and my libido has me on fire.

A bead of sweat rolls down my neck and hunger flashes in Sophie's eyes. She leans in and licks it away. "You taste so good," she murmurs into my ear.

My cock jerks. I've been hard damn near since we left her house and my balls ache. I ache. For her.

"You two need to get a room," Ryan teases.

"Yes, we do," I agree. *And the sooner, the better.*

Once we're in the car, it's on. Sophie straddles my lap and whispers for me to touch her. Happy to oblige I put one hand on her ass and cup one breast with the other. Remembering we have company, I look to Miranda and Bear, but they are in a similar position, not paying any attention to the two of us.

Sophie whispers in my ear, "I want your mouth on me."

"Not here, Babe," I say gently.

"Why not?" she whines.

"Because we're not alone," I remind her. Otherwise, we'd be naked already.

She looks back at our friends then back to me. "I don't care."

I chuckle. "I do."

She groans sticks out her bottom lip.

"We'll be home soon," I whisper and give her ass a gentle squeeze, "and then I'll do whatever you want me to do."

Her eyes light up. "Whatever I want?"

"Anything."

"Strip for me?"

"If that's what you want." There's nothing I wouldn't do. All I want to do is please her.

She sucks in her bottom lip. "That's what I want. I want to see all of you."

She's clearly drunk, but I've always believed we're more honest and forthright when drinking than when we're sober. At least I know I am. I don't have many inhibitions, but when I'm drunk, the few I have fly out the window. Evidently, so does Sophie's. I doubt she'd ask me to strip if she was sober.

"Be careful what you ask for," I warn, teasingly. I don't want to do anything she might regret in the morning.

"Oh, I want it, trust me." She rocks her hips and presses herself into my hard cock. Her fingertips graze the skin just above my belt buckle. "I've wanted it for a *long damn time*."

I moan, enjoying the friction of her body moving against mine. "Yeah?"

"Ever since I moved in."

"You want me, Babe, you got me."

The Good Stuff

Sophie's naked body is draped across mine, her head resting on my chest. The sheet lays across her just low enough to expose the dimples in her lower back. Her breaths are long and slow as she sleeps peacefully. I'd be content to lay here holding her all day. But Dopey is at the side of the bed whining for me to take him out.

"Babe," I say and brush my fingers through her hair.

Nothing.

I continue running my fingers through her hair trying to rouse her. "Babe."

Sophie's eyes open a smidge. "Hmm? Where are we?" She looks around the room before her eyes settle on mine.

"Sorry. I need to let the dog out."

"The dog?" She blinks and looks around again.

"I'll be right back." I plant a kiss on the top of her head and scoot out from under her. Upon my standing, Sophie gasps. I crane my neck to find her staring at my bare ass, mouth hanging wide open. I wag my eyebrows and shoot her a smirk before pulling on my jeans and walking out of the room.

Eager to get back to Sophie, I don't take the time to play ball with Dopey the way I normally do in the morning. As soon as he does his business, I usher him into the house and speed back to my room.

There's nothing sexier in this world than the sight of Sophie lying naked in my bed. Even hung over, she's sexy as hell.

She spots the hickey she left on my hip and licks her lips.

Correction.

There's nothing in this world sexier than Sophie, naked in my bed, and panting at the sight of me. If only I could read her mind.

"How do you feel?" I ask and crawl into the bed alongside her.

"Not bad at all." She scrunches her eyebrows. "How is that possible?"

I gaze into her eyes and brush her cheek with the back of my hand. "I fed you a cheeseburger, two ibuprofen, and made you drink two glasses of water before we came up to bed."

"Thank you." There's an unspoken question in her eyes.

"So you don't remember last night, do you?" I say playfully as I stroke her palm with the tips of my fingers.

"Not all of it." Her voice is small. Shy.

"What's the last thing you remember?"

Her face turns a light shade of pink. "I remember showing you my double sided tape at the bar."

I shake my head and cackle. That happened about an hour before we left. A lot happened between that time and when she passed out. "Would you like me to fill you in?"

"I think you better."

I scoot up and prop myself up with a second pillow. "First, you should know, we did not have sex."

"We didn't?" She seems relieved.

"Of course not." I wouldn't have allowed it to go that far no matter how hard she tried to convince me otherwise.

She raises a questioning eyebrow.

"Babe," I gaze into her eyes, "our first time making love won't be when you're trashed."

I've never used the terminology "making love" before and I'm surprised by how naturally the words roll off my tongue. I shouldn't be surprised though because when it does happen that's exactly what it will be. Making love. It could never just be sex with Sophie.

"Okay, so why don't you fill me in on what did happen?"

I roll onto my side to face her. "Do you want a play-by-play from the bar, or just the good stuff?" I ask with a chuckle. There was *a lot* of good stuff.

"The good stuff," she answers.

I decide to skip the stuff in the limo and the heavy petting in the club. As fun as it was, the really good stuff happened when we got back to my place.

"All right then. After we got home and ate, you told me you had something you wanted to show me and dragged me in here," I point to the bottom of the bed, "where you proceeded to strip."

I give her a moment to let that sink in and allow myself to remember it in detail.

"And this is where it gets interesting," I go on, "because of the tape. Apparently, it hurts when you try to remove it, which of course I was more than happy to help you with."

"Of course you were." She grins and bites her lip.

Standing at the foot of my bed she began her rendition of a strip tease which as I recall wasn't too bad. A bit wobbly from the copious amounts of alcohol she'd consumed, but still hot. She lifted the halter strap over her head, but the tape held the front of her dress up, covering her breasts. She tugged on one side and cried out in pain. Sexy dance ceased at once, but she insisted on getting the dress off so I helped her gently peel the tape away from her skin. It took a few minutes, but we were able to peel the tape away without doing any damage. Not exactly the sexy strip tease she'd wanted to put on, but that didn't matter to me.

"So after getting you out of the dress and carefully removing the tape," I reach over and grab the body chain from the nightstand and hold it up in front of her, "I got my wish."

"Okay, go on," Sophie says, her face a deep shade of red as she picks at her fingernails. Her eyes follow my hand as it slides into my jeans and I readjust my rock hard dick.

"Babe, let me just say, hottest lap dance ever."

She covers her face with her hands, embarrassed, but I pull them away with a chuckle. Her face, ears, and chest are flushed. Embarrassment aside, something in her eyes conveys curiosity and excitement. A hint of the confident, sexy, determined woman from last night. Perhaps I can help her to remember. I pull the sheet down, exposing her breasts and point at the hickey I left alongside her nipple.

"That's when you told me to put my mouth on you. A request I couldn't possibly refuse." I bow down and lick the mark.

Just as I'm about to take her hardening nipple into my mouth, she says, "Let's not get distracted," and turns my face to hers.

"I thought a reenactment might help you to remember." I wink and prop myself back upright.

"Just tell me. You can show me later," she says, but doesn't cover herself up.

I rub my hands together as I prepare to tell her the rest. "This is when it gets really good." Unable to resist, I trace the outline of her hickey with my fingertip and recall her standing before me nearly naked in those come fuck me pumps. My balls ache. This may well be the worst case of blue balls I've ever suffered. "You told me you wanted to touch, kiss, lick, and suck every inch of my body and ordered me to get naked. I stripped down to my boxer briefs, and that's when this happened," I point to my own hickey. I can still feel the heat of her mouth on my skin.

"Go on," she insists.

I sweep a lock of hair away from her face and look deep into her eyes. As much as I wanted her, and as good as her touch felt, I somehow found the strength to put on the brakes. "I told you I thought we should stop. Save the rest for later. You said you were tired of waiting." I point to my straining hard-on. "You grabbed a hold of my dick and said you hated that other women have touched me and you haven't. You all but ripped my boxers off," I snicker and brush her arm with the back of my hand. "Do you want to know what happened after that?"

Bashful, she turns away, but nods.

"Nothing," I answer.

She takes in a breath and with her fingers pressed to her lips, looks back to me. "What?"

"It was so cute." I kiss her palm. "You were staring at my cock with eyes wide as saucers and then you passed out cold."

"Oh my God," she grumbles and rolls over onto her stomach.

"Babe, it's a good thing you passed out because I honestly don't know how I would've stopped if you'd touched me."

"I'm *never* drinking again." Her voice is muffled by the pillow.

"Hey," I caress her shoulder, "look at me."

She turns her face my way, but remains lying on her stomach.

"Don't be embarrassed," I say and massage the small of her back.

"I'm not embarrassed. I'm mortified."

"Sophie, you have *nothing* to be embarrassed about. Last night was one of the best nights of my life." Hands down, and I didn't even get laid. That says a lot.

She starts to protest but I shoot her a stern look. If I say it, it's so. She needs to trust the words I say.

"I need coffee," she says, changing the subject.

I stand and reach for her, but she wraps her arms around herself, self-conscious. I go to my chest of drawers and find a t-shirt and pair of sweat pants for her to wear. They'll be too big, but the pants have a drawstring. After laying the clothes on the bed I tell her I'll start a pot of coffee and leave the room to give her privacy.

While Sophie gets dressed, I make the coffee and relive the events of last night. The best part for me was lying in bed with her. After removing her body chain and heels, I slid into the bed next to her and watched her sleep. A half hour later she rolled over, rested her head on my chest, and mumbled that she loves being held by me.

As I pour myself a glass of orange juice, I hear the water kick on in the bathroom upstairs. A foreign sensation comes over me. Contentment. I like hearing Sophie moving about in my house. I like going to bed with her and waking up next to her. There was a time when I thought I'd never like such a thing. I liked having my space to myself and couldn't understand how people could stand being married and around someone all the time. But now, I get it. When you find the right person, you want them around.

It's hard to imagine I went from hating the idea of sleeping next a woman to it being the thing I most look forward to. If it was up to me Sophie would be in my bed every night, but sleeping together every night is basically living together. I doubt she's ready for that.

When Sophie enters the kitchen, my heart stutters. She's fresh faced and cute as can be in my baggy clothes. As hot as she was last night, I prefer her this way. Natural. Sweet. Soft.

"I don't have creamer," I point to the milk and sugar I left on the counter for her. "Will that be okay?"

"It's perfect." She pours coffee into her mug. "Thank you."

Sophie looks around the kitchen, taking in our surroundings, but I can't make out her expression. "I was thinking about making breakfast. Would you like some?"

"That would be great."

On my way to the refrigerator, I place a kiss on the side of her head. Her hair still smells fresh as if she'd just stepped out of the shower.

"I used your toothbrush," she says softly. "I hope that's okay."

"Sure."

Another first for me. I've *never* shared my toothbrush. If anyone other than Sophie said they'd used it, I'd throw it out. But using a toothbrush after Sophie doesn't bother me in the slightest. I'm a completely different person with her.

Sophie watches me from the dining room table as I get the items together to make bacon and eggs. I don't eat it often, but bacon is one of my favorite cheats from my usually healthy diet. On an average morning, I have oatmeal with fruit and egg whites. But with Sophie here, I'll splurge.

"Can I help with anything?" she asks.

"No. Enjoy your coffee."

As I stand at the stove frying the bacon, my thoughts turn to my plans for the day. I want to spend it with Sophie, but it's Sunday. Mama and Pop are holding the weekly Russo family dinner. My attendance has been hit and miss lately. Mama called yesterday and told me she expects me to be there and won't accept any excuses.

Sunday dinners are sacred to my mom. We've been having them my entire life, but they took on a different significance when I became an adult and moved out of the house. Now that her children are growing up and creating lives of their own, Mama still wants to keep us close. She would like for us to attend each week, but realizes life can get in the way, so only two Sundays a month are mandatory. I make most Sundays, but since hooking up with Sophie my attendance has been less than exemplary.

Last night I considered inviting Sophie. But attending the family dinner is a big deal. It's called a family dinner for a reason. *Only* family is allowed. Friends, girlfriends, and boyfriends are not permitted unless it's a serious, long term relationship or engagement.

My relationship with Sophie is new, but I know she is *it* for me. I can't explain how I know other than to say I feel it. She is the one I'm meant to be with. My other half. Since being with her, I feel… whole. It's as though something has been missing from my life for all these years and it turns out, it was her.

Essentially, by bringing her to the family dinner, I will be bringing her *into* the family. It's an enormous step, but I don't need more time. I've never been more certain of anything in my life. We may not be married or even engaged, but she's mine and I'm hers. I consider her a part of my family. It's time my family knows and by bringing her with me they will understand, without explanation, her importance to me. She is my future.

I glance at Sophie whose eyes are fixed on the hickey she left just above my hip. She's holding her cup up with her lips parted slightly. I chuckle. "Penny for your thoughts?"

Her face turns a deep shade of red and she looks down to her mug. The bacon pops and grease splatters on the bare skin of my rib cage, reminding me I have a job to finish.

Once the bacon and eggs are done, I make plates for the both of us and carry them into the dining room. After setting one plate in front of Sophie, I take the seat across from her. She takes a bite of the bacon and closes her eyes as she chews.

"This is *so* good," she says. "Thank you."

"You're welcome."

Bear's Harley fires up and Sophie's head spins toward her house.

"Bear stayed with Miranda?" Sophie asks in a high-pitched tone.

"Yep." Her jaw slackens and I laugh. "Apparently we ruthless bikers have rubbed off on both of you."

"Apparently." She looks at her house through my kitchen window.

There's no time like the present to ask her to join me for the Russo family dinner. "My parents are having a cookout this afternoon. Mom texted and asked me to come."

She doesn't say anything, but her expression conveys what she's thinking.

"Candace won't be there," I assure her. For all intents and purposes, Candace is considered family, but she has never attended the Sunday family dinner.

Sophie shoulders relax and she exhales a breath of relief. "Good."

I swallow a bite of bacon. *Here goes nothing.* "I'd like for you to come with me."

Her eyes widen. "To meet your parents?"

I shrug as though it's no big deal. "Yeah, why not?"

"Okay."

Neither one of us speaks again for a couple minutes. I eat and try my best to act cool. Sophie has no idea how big of a deal it is that I'm taking her. She doesn't know what it means to me—of what she means to me.

"Should I get dressed up?" she asks.

I shake my head. We're not a dress up kind of family. "It's just a backyard cookout, hamburgers, hot dogs. We'll ride over on the bike."

"What time?"

I glance at the clock on the wall. "We need to leave in an hour."

Sunday Family Dinner

My parents have a nice spread on the edge of town. Their log home sits on a wooded lot, surrounded by a large pond. You can see it from any window in the house. The garage door is open as usual and when I turn off the bike, I hear their signature classic rock coming from the backyard.

I lead Sophie through the garage to the backyard. Mama is watering the flowers in one of her many gardens. Mama is obsessed with gardening. She talks to her flowers when she waters them. It's hilarious. But she believes flowers benefit from being talked to. Something she probably read online.

Isa is sunbathing on a chaise lounge with her iPod on. I look around for Pop, but he's nowhere to be seen. He's probably in his office. Holding Sophie's hand, I guide her over to my mom to make the official introduction.

I called Mama when Sophie went home to get ready to let her know I was bringing her. To say she was pleased is an understatement. She squealed loud enough that she almost blew out my eardrum.

The moment Mama spies us, she hurries to us and pulls me into a bear hug. She hugs me whenever she sees me, but not with this much exuberance.

"Hey sweetie," she says in her heavy Puerto Rican accent as she squeezes the breath out of me. When she finally pulls away, she beams at Sophie. "You must be the reason he's missed the last few Sunday dinners."

Sophie looks my way with a question in her eyes before extending her hand to my mom. "I'm Sophie."

Mama ignores her hand and pulls her in for the same type of hug she gave me.

Geez ma, take it easy on the girl.

"I'm so happy to meet you," Mama squeals and pulls back to take a good look at Sophie. "I'm Camilla, but call me Mama."

Isa runs to us with a smirk plastered on her face. "Rooter, what do we have here?"

As if she doesn't know. I know damn well Mom told her about Sophie the moment we hung up.

"This is Sophie—" I begin, but Isa cuts me off.

"I'm Isabel, but everyone calls me Isa."

"It's nice to meet you, Isa." Sophie holds out her hand.

"We don't shake hands in this family," Isa explains and wraps her arms around Sophie for a quick hug before hugging me. She whispers in my ear, "Good choice, she's pretty."

I shoot Isa and Mama a look warning them to take it easy on Sophie. This is her first visit. I don't want them to overwhelm her any more than she already is.

I steer Sophie to the deck by the pond and we sit on the wicker sofa. With Sophie to my right, Isa sits to my left.

"I'll go get Papa," Mom says and disappears into the house.

Next to me, Sophie chews on her bottom lip and picks at her cuticles. I give her an apologetic smile and gently squeeze her leg for reassurance.

"Did you wear a bathing suit?" Isa asks Sophie.

Sophie shakes her head. I hadn't thought to tell her to bring one. I was too caught up in the excitement of bringing her to meet my family.

"You can borrow one of mine when you're ready to get in," Isa offers and points to the beach area of the pond.

"Thank you." Sophie gives Isa a small smile, but I can tell she's uneasy. I don't blame her. We as a group are a lot to digest when you first meet us.

After what seems like forever, Mama and Pop emerge from the house. Pop looks from me, to Sophie and back to me again. When he gives me his nod of approval, my shoulders relax. I hadn't realized how nervous I was until this moment. This is the first time I've brought a girl home, and she isn't just any girl. She's *the* girl. It's important that they like and accept Sophie. I stand to greet Pop and Sophie does the same.

"Pop, this is Sophie."

"Hey, pretty lady," Pop says, "I'm Mick, but everyone here calls me Papa." He pulls her in for a hug the same as Mama had which takes me by surprise. He's usually more reserved with his affection. But when he pulls back, I see excitement in his eyes. Not only does he accept that I've brought her, he's happy about it.

"It's nice to meet you," Sophie says.

"We're happy you could make it," Pop replies.

Mama asks Sophie if she likes gardening to which Sophie replies she doesn't have a lot of time for hobbies between school and work. Mama goes on about how relaxing gardening is, but that it's time-consuming. When Isa and I were both young, she had to give it up because she didn't have the time to devote to it.

Before I know it, the three girls are immersed in conversation. While the girls chat, Pop and I talk about the old Harley he and I are restoring. Every now and again I make eye contact with Sophie to make sure she's okay. All signs of her earlier apprehension are gone.

"So, how did you two meet?" Mama asks, glancing back and forth at me and Sophie.

"Sophie lives next door," I explain.

"Lucky you." Pop winks.

I agree with a nod and a chuckle. *Lucky indeed.*

"We're very happy to meet you, Sophie," Mama says to Sophie with a wide smile and pats her on the hand.

My family are all ears as Sophie tells them a little about herself. She tells them about Miranda and the Frank's. She admits her mother passed away, but doesn't say how. When Mama expresses her condolences, Sophie simply says thank you and leaves it at that. Thankfully no one presses for details and I'm relieved when Mama asks Sophie about her college studies. When the conversation wanes, Isa suggests we all go for a swim.

I glance to Sophie. "Are you up for it?"

"Sure," she smiles, completely at ease.

"Come with me," Isa tells her and tugs her by the hand. "I'll get you a bathing suit."

The instant the girls leave Mama says, "She's very beautiful, Son."

"Yes, she is," I proudly agree.

"But it seems things are moving rather quickly."

I shrug. "I've known her a while." It's not a total lie. Sophie may not have been in my life for very long and our relationship is new, but it has been a long time in the making.

"And the thing with Candace?"

"It's done."

Pop clears his throat and says, "I hear she isn't taking it very well."

"She'll get over it."

"Be gentle with her, Rooter," Mama warns.

"I'm trying, trust me. She isn't making it easy."

"That girl has been in love with you forever," she says. "I had a feeling this was going to happen when you two got involved."

"If I'd known, I never would've hooked up with her."

"What's done is done." Mom sighs and smacks the tops of her thighs before standing. "I'm going to put on my bathing suit."

Pop gets up from his chair to join me on the wicker couch. Through the corner of my eye I see Isa jog to the beach. Sophie must still be in the house.

"This was a surprise," Pop says, referring to me bringing Sophie to the family dinner.

"I know. I'm surprised, too."

"You're sure about this? About bringing her into the family?"

I look him square in the eye. "Absolutely."

He nods. "Okay then. It's done."

I exhale a long breath. "This means a lot to me, Pop."

"Son," Pop bumps my shoulder with his. "She seems great and sure is pretty."

"Yes, she is."

"But I gotta say, I thought I'd never see this day come."

"Me either, Pop." I pat him on the back. "There's just something about her."

"Hey, Sophie!" Isa hollers and waves from the pond.

When I turn around, Sophie's standing behind us on the deck. Isa's bikini top is a tad big, but Sophie is still a sight to behold. I wonder if she heard our conversation, but her expression gives nothing away.

"If I was twenty years younger and single, you'd have some serious competition, boy." Pop jokes and bumps me roughly on the shoulder.

"This one's all mine," I assert and pull Sophie onto my lap.

While the girls are in the house cleaning up after dinner, Pop and I sit in wicker chairs on the deck and talk Club business. I watch Sophie through the sliding glass doors.

"Son, now that you've brought Sophie into the family, you should tell her what's going on."

He's referring to the situation with Andy and the Henchmen. I blow out a breath. "I don't want to burden her with that shit."

"She needs to understand what it means to be affiliated with the Club. The danger it presents."

"She has a good understanding of what life in the Club is like."

"Then why not tell her what's going on?"

I glance back at Sophie who's washing the dishes. Seeing her smiling alongside my mom and my little sister makes me happy. "Because we just got together. I don't want to give her a reason to be scared already."

"I get it, Son." He scratches his beard. "But her being unaware puts her at greater risk."

"How?" I turn in his direction. "Whenever I'm not with her, I have eyes on her."

"You know as well as I do, you can't prevent an attack when your eyes aren't open or when you're unaware. By telling her, she can be on the lookout."

I shake my head. "I can't put that on her. It isn't right."

"You put this on her when you chose to be with her," he sighs. "I can't make you do anything, but I will tell you right from wrong. You're wrong to keep this from her."

I lean forward and rest my elbows on my knees. "I just can't Pop."

"If you think she can't handle it, why get involved with her?"

"It's not that. I know she can handle it." I slump back into the chair and rub my face with both hands. "I'm just not ready to burden her with it so soon. I want to enjoy being together for a while."

"I respect that. Just remember, most often, the hard choice is the right choice."

I cock my head to the side. "Coming from the man who almost always chooses the path of least resistance."

"Touché. But this is different. I've never hidden anything from your mother."

"This is just shit timing."

"The shit that goes down in the Club always happens at a shit time. It's the nature of life in the Club."

He's speaking the truth. "I want to break her into the life slowly."

"I've always said, the best way to test the water is to jump in. Otherwise, you may never go all in. You want her to be all in, right?"

"Of course."

Pop leans in my direction. "At some point, she'll have to jump in and the sooner the better."

"Yeah, but me throwing this on her right now is more like pushing her in."

He shrugs. "In the end, the outcome is usually the same."

The whole way home, Pop's words play on repeat, "The best way to test the water is to jump in." Maybe so, but sometimes you jump in and the water is too damn cold and you jump right back out and refuse to get back in. What if I pushed Sophie in and the water is too cold? She already knows the gist of my life in the Club. I told her early on that it's dangerous. It was the reason I pushed her away. She knew the risk, and she chose to be with me, anyway. So, even though I'm not telling her about the issue with Andy and the Henchmen, she knows danger lurks about. She knows something could happen at any given time. There's no reason to scare her with this shit.

"My family loves you," I tell Sophie after we pull into my driveway. Before we left, my mom pulled me to the side and told me what a lovely young woman Sophie is. Isa talked her ear off most of the night. Isa doesn't fake it when she doesn't like someone. And like me, she has great intuition about people.

"I think they're pretty great, too." A genuine smile spreads across her face. "I'm glad you took me."

Not only did Isa spend the night attached to Sophie's hip, she also told Sophie the significance of my taking her to dinner. Isa laid that tidbit on me when she hugged me good night. Initially, I was furious.

But after some thought, I was glad to be off the hook. And honestly, I suspected Isa might say something. I didn't expect her to come outright with it, but I figured she would plant the seed in Sophie's mind that tonight was more than just a fun family dinner. I clear my throat and rock back and forth, heel to toe, digging for courage to bring it up. "Isa told me she spoke with you."

"You mean in regards to the significance of taking me to the Russo Sunday family dinner?"

"Yeah," I say with my hands crammed in my pockets.

"I would've rather you told me."

Looking down at the garage floor I see a bottle cap and kick it, sending it across the bay. "I was afraid you would think it's too soon and refuse to go."

Sophie nods. "Everything about us is happening really fast, but, it has been a year in the making. So…"

Relieved, I blow out a breath and rest my forehead on hers. "I want to give you all the things you don't have. You have a family now, Sophie."

Sophie gasps and her eyes gloss over. "I don't know what to say."

With a hand on each side of her face, I kiss Sophie's lips softly followed by her cheeks, nose, and eyelids. I trace her bottom lip with my tongue until her mouth parts. With my hands still cupping her face, I kiss her long and languid. I lose myself in the kiss—in her—as her tongue rolls with mine. Sophie moans softly and her body falls into mine. Every nerve ending is on fire with the need to be as close to her as possible. What I feel goes so far beyond want or lust. I *need* to be with Sophie. Tonight. By the look in her eyes, the feeling is mutual.

I take her hand and lead her to my back door. The instant I swing the door open, Dopey leaps out, jumping on me with excitement. I motion for Sophie to go inside and tell her I'll be right in.

Once inside, without a word, I take Sophie by the hand and lead her up the stairs to my room. I turn on the lamp on my nightstand

and stare into her eyes. Tonight, I'm going to touch and kiss every single inch of her body that she'll allow me access to. If she tells me to stop, I will, but something tells me she won't be saying anything but yes.

I take off my t-shirt and then tug at hers, asking for permission to remove it. She raises her arms and I pull it over her head. Her chest rises and falls with fast, shallow breaths as her greedy eyes scan my naked torso before finding my eyes once again. She licks her lips and bites her bottom lip.

Yeah, she wants this as much as I do.

I give her a teasing wink as I loosen my belt. She licks her lips again and takes a step back so she can watch as I unzip my jeans and let them fall to the floor. So sweet and innocent, she gasps as though seeing me for the first time. It does crazy things to me having her look at me this way. It makes me want her all the more, but reminds me to take it slow.

I step forward and reach around her to unclasp her bra. Sophie removes it the rest of the way and I take her left breast in my hand. I'll never get used to touching her. "So beautiful."

I flick her hardening nipple with my thumb before bringing my free hand to her other breast and repeating the act. I'm in heaven. Sophie tosses her head back and whimpers at my touch.

"I love looking at you and touching you," I murmur.

With our eyes locked, I unzip her jeans and slowly push the denim down her hips and thighs. She clutches my shoulders for stability as she steps out of them. As I rise, my hands skim the outside of her thighs.

"I want you so much." I gently stroke her face. "Are you ready?"

She bites her lip and nods.

"I need to hear the words, Baby."

"I'm ready," she whispers sweetly and I feel an indescribable pang in my chest.

I pull the comforter back and lay Sophie on the mattress. My chest swells with emotion as I hover over her. For the first time in my life, I'm being led by something more than sexual desire. I bow down and kiss her neck just beneath her ear. Sophie wraps her arms around me and arches into me until her chest is pressed to mine. Knowing what she wants I press myself between her spread legs before circling her nipple with my tongue.

"That feels so good," she murmurs and brushes her fingers through my hair.

The sound of her sultry voice shoots straight to my cock, igniting my flame. "Yeah, Baby, talk to me."

I take her breast into my mouth and flick the nipple back and forth until her body quivers. "You're perfect."

I grip myself through my boxers as I place a trail of wet kisses from her chest down to her belly button. I stroke myself as I lick her from one hip bone to the other. Sophie bites down on her bottom lip and moans. With my eyes on hers I dip my fingers into her panties, teasing the edge of her sex with soft strokes. She watches me with eager eyes as I slowly make my way closer to her slit. I finally reach my destination and I'm pleased to find her wet and ready. My fingertip brushes the tip of her clit eliciting a raspy moan. I circle the swollen nub in a slow, steady rhythm.

"God, yes," Sophie breathes. "Keep doing that."

The desire in Sophie's voice spurs me on as I drag my fingers up and down her wet folds. There are so many things I want to do with and to her. I want to make her come in every way before I'm inside her. "You're so wet, Babe. I want to taste you."

Without answering, Sophie closes her eyes. I take my hand out of her panties to remove them, and my fingers are red. Tonight's fun has come to an end. But now how to handle this? She's going to be humiliated.

"Babe," I say gently.

Sophie looks at me and I hold my hand up for her to see. Her face turns ashen and her body goes rigid. She clutches her face to hide from me.

"Hey," I speak gently and lift her hands away from her face, but she keeps her eyes squeezed closed. "It's okay."

Her body shakes as she cries and it breaks my heart. She needn't be embarrassed. Not knowing what else to do, I scoop Sophie up from the bed and carry her into the bathroom so she can have a moment alone to get cleaned up. Once I put her down, I turn on the sink faucet and clean my hands. She stands as still as a statue with her legs pressed together and her arms covering her breasts.

"Tell me what you need," I say. "I'll go to your house and get it."

Her eyes fall to the floor and she clears her throat. Her small voice trembles, "Tampons, clean underwear—the cotton kind—and something to sleep in. It's all in my dresser."

I lift her chin and kiss her lips. "I'll be right back."

Sophie is in the shower when I get back to my house. I place her things on the bathroom counter and close the door behind me. In the bedroom, I find a small spot of blood on the bottom sheet. I change it so she doesn't see it when she comes back in the room.

The water shuts off and a lot of time passes. She should have come out by now, but she's probably too embarrassed to face me. I go to the bathroom door to check on her.

"Babe? Everything okay?"

"No."

"Are you dressed?"

"Yeah."

When I open the door, she's perched on the toilet seat with her head in her hands. I crouch before her. "Hey, don't be embarrassed."

Sophie refuses to look me in the eye. "I'm sorry, I didn't know."

"You have nothing to apologize for," I assure her. "It's a fact of life, Babe. Not that big of a deal." Not that I would tell her, but this isn't my first experience at this particular rodeo. I stand and extend my hand.

Sophie looks up at me studying my expression before taking my hand and following me to the bedroom. I crawl into the bed and motion for her to join me. Once she does, I wrap my arms around her and hold her close. "Are you comfortable? Do you need anything? Tylenol, ibuprofen?"

"I'm okay," she squeaks.

"Close your eyes and sleep," I whisper and kiss the back of her head.

We lie in silence for a while until her breathing finally evens out, and she falls asleep.

Bad News

"Hey man," I hear Bear's voice from behind me as I stand in the backyard playing fetch with Dopey. I turn in his direction. He appears exhausted yet relaxed at the same time with bags under his eyes and zero tension in his stance. "I was just coming to get you."

"What's up?" I raise my chin.

"Mick texted. Wants everyone at the clubhouse."

"Now? Did he say what it's about?"

Bear shakes his head. Dopey shoves the ball in his hand and he throws it.

I glance at Sophie's house then back to Bear. As he stands before me with disheveled hair and wrinkled clothes, he wears the smile of a well-satisfied man. "So… another night with Miss Priss?"

"She's not a priss."

"Could've fooled me."

"She's a cool girl."

"I gotta say, I didn't see that one coming."

He grins. "No girl can resist me when I turn on the charm."

I shake my head in disbelief. How Bear of all people won that girl over I'll never understand. "I'll go say goodbye to Sophie and I'll be on my way."

When I round the doorway into my bedroom, Sophie is still in bed, but awake. If not for Pop's request, I'd crawl back in with her. I stretch my arms over my head and yawn. "There's a problem at the shop." I lie, but only because it's easier than saying I have Club business and I don't want to give her reason to worry. I grab a t-shirt and a pair of clean boxers from my chest of drawers. "I'll grab a quick shower and head over there. You can stay here and sleep."

She sits up and swings her legs to the side of the bed. "I'll go on home. I have a lot to do today before work, anyway."

"Okay." I bend down and kiss her forehead. "I'll see you when you get home from work."

She looks at me, unsure, fidgeting with her fingers, but remains quiet. She's thinking about what happened last night.

"And stop freaking out about last night," I insist. "No worries, okay?"

Her smile is small and timid. "Okay."

"Anyone know what this is about?" I ask Darren and Sparrow after pulling into the lot of the clubhouse.

They shake their heads and follow me into the building where Pop, Wrench, and all the other Double H members are sitting in the front room.

"Hey, Son," Pop motions for me to come to where he's standing by the bar.

"What's up?"

Pop looks around the room before addressing everyone. "We've got news on Andy."

We all stand in silence as we await the news.

"He's dead," Wrench says in a solemn tone.

Gasps fill the room.

"Dead?" I ask.

"Evidently," Pop begins, "he pissed off a couple gang members in a bar in Kalamazoo Saturday night."

Sounds like Andy. "You're sure about the intel?"

Wrench answers, "Came directly from Ivan."

"We will not celebrate Andy's death," Pop declares. "Regardless of the fact that he was no longer one of us, and despite the trouble he caused, this is not a happy day. I ask that you not remember the Andy of recent, but the Andy of old. Remember the man who made sure your children got to and from school safely. The man who helped around your house. The man who stood up and took a fist for you. Remember the good in him, not the bad." Pop turns to me. "Because there was good in him. Andy was a deeply troubled young man whose demons got the best of him. We all have demons. Not one of us in this room is perfect, myself included. So I'm going to send a prayer up that he has found peace. I hope each of you will do the same."

One of the biggest lessons I've learned as a member of Double H is there is nothing on earth more precious than human life. Each life is invaluable and once it's snuffed out, it can never be replaced. Be it a friend or as in this case a foe, death is not to be celebrated under any circumstance. While I won't mourn this loss, I will not take delight in it either.

I'm not shocked by the news. I don't have the details, but I've always expected Andy's mouth would lead to his death. The guy acted as though he was invincible. Either he believed he was, or perhaps he was looking for a way out.

As with any death, Andy's leads me to ponder my own mortality. I could be gone tomorrow. Hell, I could be gone in an hour or after my next breath. The one thing I'm sure of is my end won't come gently.

My life is filled with enemies who'd be happy to see me perish. The only thing that would make them happier is to be the one who pulls the trigger. I never know from one moment to the next if someone will come for me, but it'll happen one day. I can only hope I'll be prepared.

Speaking of enemies, I wonder how Andy's death will affect Ivan's intentions for Halsey? Will it affect Pop's proposition for a trade?

I find Pop in one of the back rooms staring out a window.

"Do you have a minute?" I ask.

He turns and asks, "What's up?"

"I was wondering if you're still going forward with the trade proposition."

"We have to keep Ivan out of Halsey. Hoyt and I are meeting with him later today."

Pop turns back to the window. Andy's death seems to be affecting him more than I'd have guessed.

I walk over to where he stands. "You all right?"

"You know how I get when shit like this happens."

"Yeah, I do." I put a hand on his shoulder and squeeze. "But Pop, you can't beat yourself up over this. It isn't your fault."

"Isn't it?"

"No, it isn't. Like you said, Andy's demons got the best of him."

He turns to me. "How did I not see this coming?"

"No one can see the future," I say, even though I saw this coming a long time ago.

"I let Andy down and put the Club at risk in the process."

I lean close and make direct eye contact. "You did not do this. Andy did it because he was fucked up and refused to take responsibility for his shit. Period."

Pop shrugs. "What's done is done."

Storm clouds roll in and I hurry home. As I pull into the driveway, the first few raindrops begin to fall. I've barely stepped into my house when my cell phone rings. It's Candace. In no mood for her crap, I let the call roll to voicemail. She leaves a message followed by a text. I don't listen to the voicemail, but I read the text message.

Candace: *Plz answer your phone. We need to talk.*

I haven't talked to her since the night of the Club's party and she's probably going crazy as a result. I'm in no mood to hear how much she misses me, but if I don't respond, she'll just keep bugging me.

Me: *It's been a bad day, Candace. I'll catch up with you later.*

Candace: *This can't wait until later. It's important.*

Me: *Unless it's a matter of life or death, it'll have to wait.*

Candace: *It is a matter of life.*

Me: *Forget it. I'm not in the mood to play games.*

Ten minutes later she texts me a picture. A positive pregnancy test. The message that follows it says: *This isn't a game.*

My blood runs cold and my gut twists with a mixture of anger and fear. Anger that she's lying just to get my attention and fear that it might be true. She calls again and I answer on the first ring. "I'm on my way."

This has to be bullshit. I was always careful. We never fucked without a condom. In a stupefied daze, I drive to Candace's, not quite sure what I'll do once I get there. The rain pelts my face and lightning brightens the sky as I saunter to her door. The door swings open before I have the chance to knock.

I push past her into the living room. "What kind of shit are you trying to pull? There's no fucking way you're pregnant."

She stomps into the bathroom and slams the door. A few minutes later she returns and jams a pregnancy test stick into my hand. The test window shows two pink lines. "I'm pregnant and it's yours."

My heart thuds and I'm overcome with a chill. I can't think. I can't talk. All I can do is focus on the plastic stick of doom in my hand. I drop it and grip the back of my head with both hands. *This can't be happening.*

"Do you have anything to say?" she asks.

"I always wore a condom."

"Remember the night of your party?"

I do now.

The rubber broke.

"You said you were on the pill. Or were you lying?"

"I have never lied to you. I am on the pill."

Bile rises in my throat. On weak legs, I walk to the couch and sit. I rub my face with both hands. "You're sure it's mine?"

"Of course I'm sure. I'm not the one who's been running around with someone else."

I shoot her a dirty look. I'm not running around with anyone. I'm *with* Sophie. At least I am for now. Once Sophie finds out, she'll tell me to get fucked.

Candace returns my glare as she stands before me. "I can't do this alone, Rooter. Like it or not, you're going to be a father. I need you to be around."

I'm going to be a father. Having kids was always an abstract idea. I've never given it much thought until now. I guess I assumed I'd have them one day. But not like this and not with Candace. My eyes zero in on the bowl of M&M's on the coffee table. "I can't believe this is happening."

Candace sits next to me. "I know you're freaking out. So am I. My whole life is turned upside down. I don't know what I'm going to do and I'm scared."

How am I going to explain this to Sophie?

As much as I don't want this to be happening, I can't undo it. And having experienced the pain of being abandoned by my father, there's no way in hell I'd do that to a child of my own. I won't abandon its mother either. I just pray I can find a way to make Sophie understand.

Candace lays her head on my shoulder. "A part of me can't help thinking this is a sign."

I pull away. "A sign?"

"We're meant to be together, Rooter. I feel it now more than ever."

As I sit on the porch waiting for Sophie to get home from work, lightning flashes in the sky and rain batters the porch roof as thunder cracks in the distance. It's a fitting setting for the day I've had.

I reminisce about the times Sophie and I have spent together. The feeling of her lips on mine when I kissed her after her break in. The look on her face when I told her I intended to make her mine. The way she laughs when I say or do something crazy. The passion and trust in her eyes last night.

Now I have to tell her Candace, a woman she can't stand, is pregnant with my child. I at least must assume she is until I can get a DNA test. Candace has never lied to me though. And I don't believe she would. She'd be too afraid of the repercussions. Candace knows I'd never forgive her and she'd be denounced by everyone connected to the Club. I can't imagine she'd take that risk.

I won't tell Sophie about the pregnancy tonight after she's worked all day. I'll tell her tomorrow. The realization that tonight may be my last night with her has my stomach in knots.

My phone rings, the ring tone indicating it's Sophie. A song by her favorite boy bander even though I detest his music. But it's her favorite song, and it makes me think of her. The other day it came on the radio and I found myself humming to it the way she does.

If she's calling this late, there must be a problem. I sit upright and answer. "Babe?"

"My tires have been slashed."

And I thought the day couldn't get any worse. "I'm on my way."

When I pull into The Grand's parking lot, Sophie's car sits on flattened tires. Rain pours as I get out of my truck to inspect the damage. The words bitch, cunt, and whore are scratched into her driver's side door. I hear water splashing and in my peripheral I see Sophie coming my way.

"That bitch did this," she says.

"Who, Candace?" I ask, unable to take my eyes from the words on her door.

"Yeah."

I shake my head. I was with Candace for most of the evening discussing our predicament. Andy is dead, and I doubt it was Ivan. That leaves only one other person. Mike.

"Why are you shaking your head?" She gestures to the door with her hand. "This is her!"

"Get in the truck," I say, reeling from what I've just seen. The cocksucker has fucked with the wrong girl. He's going to pay dearly for it.

"I should say goodbye to Ryan." She turns back to his car.

It's pouring rain and I'm out of patience. She needs to get into the damn truck. I wave at Ryan from where we stand and tug Sophie toward my truck. I open the door and help her into the cab.

Once in the truck I turn to Sophie as I back the truck out of the parking space. "This was Mike."

She shakes her head. "I don't think so. It was that bitch. I know it."

I blow out a breath and count to ten to keep my cool before trying to reason with her. "Candace doesn't know where you work."

She rolls her eyes. "She could've followed me."

"Sophie, I realize you hate her," I borderline shout, "but I'm telling you she did not do this."

"Why are you always defending her?"

My knuckles turn white from squeezing the steering wheel. "I do not always defend her! But right now I am because I *know* she didn't do it."

She gasps and spins in my direction. "How do you know?"

Fuck. "Sophie, Mike did this. Plain and simple."

"Tell me how you know!"

Grinding my teeth, I punch the steering wheel. Thanks to my poor choice of words, Sophie's deduced I've been with Candace today and I won't lie to her. Might as well get it over with. I swerve into the parking lot of a burger joint and slam on the brakes. Sophie smashes into the dash as we come to a sudden stop.

"What the hell?" she asks and grabs her shoulder.

I open my mouth, but can't find the words. I take Sophie's hand and hold it tight as I look into her eyes. My heart stutters as I try to find the words to break her heart. Everything is ruined. I'm going to lose her and there isn't a goddamn thing I can do about it. At this moment, I'm not sure who I'm more pissed at, Mike or myself.

"Rooter, what's going on?"

I turn and look out the windshield trying to summon the courage to tell her about the pregnancy. "This entire day has been completely fucked up. I might as well make it a little bit worse."

"What is it?"

I make a steeple with my fingers, covering my nose and take a slow, deep breath. "The reason I know Candace isn't the one who vandalized your car is because I was with her."

"Why were you with her?"

I turn to Sophie and caress her cheek, possibly for the last time. How many times have I promised to never hurt her? Yet here I am getting ready to shatter that promise. "She texted me earlier this evening. Said we needed to talk. I told her to forget it. That I wasn't playing any more games with her."

I drop my hand and turn back to the windshield. My heart slams in my chest and I feel as though I might vomit. "She texted me a picture," I say and pause, shaking my head with shame, "of a positive pregnancy test."

Sophie gasps and in my peripheral I see her rapidly shaking her head. She breathes in and out in fast, shallow breaths, but doesn't say anything so I continue.

"I went over there to call her out on more bullshit so she took another test. It was positive."

"You're sure it's yours?"

"I can't be sure without a DNA test," I rub the back of my neck, "but there was one time… the condom broke."

Her mouth drops, and she sucks in a breath before flinging herself at me and smacking my face and chest. "How can you be so goddamn stupid?"

I take hold of her hands and shove her against the passenger door to get her to stop hitting me. She may be female, but she's damn strong. "You're right. I am stupid. Sophie, I'm so sorry."

"Take me home." She pushes me away.

The look in her eyes is angry, distant. Nothing I might say will make things better.

We ride in complete silence as Sophie chews her nails and looks out the passenger side window. Although I yearn to talk to her, to make her understand, I don't know what to say. The instant my truck comes to a stop in the driveway she jumps out and makes a mad dash for her house. Luckily, I catch her before she can get inside.

"Sophie, please talk to me," I plead as we stand in the rain.

"I can't. Not right now." Facing away from me, she lowers her head. "Like you said, this day has been completely fucked up and all I want to do right now is sleep. Alone."

"I know you're mad—"

"Mad?" she hollers and spins to face me. Her hands are balled into fists and anger rages in her eyes. "What I am goes way beyond mad, Rooter! There is no word in any language that can describe what I'm feeling right now!"

"I'm not comfortable leaving you alone knowing it was Mike who slashed your tires." It's the truth, but I'm mostly uncomfortable with how angry she is. I'm afraid I'll never see her again.

She stomps up the porch stairs. "Well, you sure as hell aren't staying here tonight."

Overcome with panic I dash past her and block the door. "I'll sleep on the couch. Who knows what that whacked out fuck is liable to try next."

"Then send Bear over, because you're not stepping one foot into this house."

"Promise me you'll talk to me tomorrow and I'll leave."

She rolls her eyes and speaks through clenched teeth. "We'll talk when I'm ready and not before then."

I cross my arms and widen my stance. Although I appear confident, I'm exactly the opposite. "Tell me we'll talk tomorrow or I'm not leaving."

"If you don't leave, I may never speak to you again."

"Tell me you'll talk to me tomorrow."

"Fine! Just leave!"

I speak slowly, "Say you promise we'll talk tomorrow."

She squeezes her eyes shut and sighs. "I promise to talk to you tomorrow."

If I had it my way, we'd stay up all night talking this through until I make her understand how sorry I am and I earn her forgiveness. But that isn't an option. Reluctantly, I step away from the door to let her open it. When she steps inside, I take her hand. This may be my last chance to touch her. "Good night, Sophie."

Without a word, she closes the door.

Please Forgive Me

I can't do this.

I can't lie in this bed less than fifteen yards from where Sophie lies in hers. I need to be with her. If she'd give me the chance, I can make her see that everything will be okay. I can make this right.

Candace is pregnant, presumably with my kid, but that doesn't mean Sophie and I can't be together. It doesn't change how much we mean to each other. Candace may be the mother of my child, and someone I have ties with, but my allegiance—my heart—is with Sophie. I am and will always be loyal to her. I can still be a good man for Sophie. I can still give her the things she wants and needs. I can still protect her and care for her. Having a child doesn't change any of that. I must convince her.

I toss the sheets off, get dressed and go to Sophie's house. Using the hide-a-key I let myself in and creep up the stairs. I tiptoe into her room and slowly close the door behind me. Sophie's blinds are drawn, and the room is pitch black. I can't see her, but I hear the steady rhythm of her breath. She's asleep. Careful not to make any noise, I lower myself to the floor with my back pressed against the door.

Hours pass and the rising sun illuminates Sophie's sweet face. Her dark hair is spread across the pillow and she holds the sheet up to her neck even though it's at least eighty degrees in the room.

Her eyes flutter open, landing on mine, and then close before opening again. She jerks upright in the bed with a furious expression. "What are you doing here?"

"I had to see you."

"Maybe I don't want to see you."

I move over to the bed and crouch before her. She looks me up and down, but I can't read her expression.

"How long have you been here?" She asks with a sleepy voice and rubs her eyes.

"I came in about three thirty."

Sophie looks at the clock on her nightstand. "You've been here for six hours?"

Upon closer study, her eyes are red-rimmed and puffy from crying. That I'm at fault for her pain causes my chest to ache. "I realize this situation isn't ideal. It's not what you wanted. But we can get through it."

"I'm not sure we can."

Panic stricken, I shift forward and clutch both sides of her face. "Don't say that."

She tears away and scoots back against her headboard. "You're having a kid. With Candace. How can you expect me to get past that?"

Aching to be close to her, to show her how I feel, I reach out for her. Her angry glare warns me not to come close. I clinch my hands behind my head. I've never been this vulnerable. But ever since getting the news of Candace's pregnancy, I've been scared and unsure about everything. Will I make a good father? Am I ready to be a dad? Do I have what it takes to do right by my child or will I fail as miserably as my biological father? I don't know how to be a dad. I've never fed or clothed a baby. Never changed a diaper. I've never even held a baby. But if I have Sophie by my side, I'll figure it out. With her I'll have confidence and the strength to best father I can be. Without her, I'll fail.

"I realize I'm asking a lot of you, Babe, but please… I need you. I can't do this on my own."

"You're not on your own. You have *Candace.*"

Her words sting. My body tenses and I shake my head. "She's the last fucking thing I want or need."

"Well, that's too bad because you're stuck with her for the rest of your life."

"Fuck!" I punch the mattress. I can't remember the last time I cried, but I could now. "What have I done?"

"I need time to figure out if this is something I can do." Sophie stands, walks to her dresser and stares at her reflection in the mirror. "You're not just asking me to deal with Candace now. You're asking me to deal with you having a kid."

"It doesn't have to change us."

"But it does change us." She spins around to face me. "It changes you."

She's not even giving me—us—a chance. I jump up. "So that's it? You're done?"

"I—I didn't say that."

"It sure as hell sounds like it."

"I…" Sophie's gaze falls to the floor. "I just need some time."

"If this was happening to you," I place two fingers beneath her chin and lift her face, "I wouldn't bolt. I'd stick by you."

She gasps as she raises her hand to her chest. "Are you seriously trying to make me feel guilty?"

If that's what it takes. "I'm just telling it like it is. I thought you were stronger than this."

Sophie has given everyone else dozens of chances. We have one little bump in the road and she's ready to kick me to the curb. It's not like I cheated on her. This child was conceived before we were together.

"Don't you understand? I'm tired of being strong. I'm tired of being let down and left out."

"Sophie, I didn't do this to you. I did this before you. For what it's worth, I am sorry." I turn and sweep my hands through my hair trying to think of anything I might say to make her understand, but draw a blank. "I'm not letting you down or leaving you out of anything. But if you walk away that's exactly what you'll be doing to me."

Without giving her a chance to respond, I open her bedroom door and leave. My last words were a low blow, but it's how I feel. Yes, the situation is fucked. I am asking a lot of her. It's not an easy pill to swallow, but her response is rather extreme. I would expect her to act this way if I'd been unfaithful, but I wasn't. And I'm not asking her to parent the kid. I'm just asking that she not allow this to destroy us. How is that too much to ask?

As I step into my house, Molly from the repair shop texts to let me know he received Sophie's car. They'll start on the repairs right away.

I text Sophie to let her know what's going on: *I had ur car towed to Molly's Auto for repairs. I can take u to work later, or u can drive my truck. Let me know.*

Sophie: *Thank you for helping me. I'm not going to work today.*

Me: *I'll be here all day if u need anything or need to go anywhere.* Before pressing send I add: *Or if u want to talk.*

I'm surprised when my phone pings right away with her response.

Sophie: *I don't want to fight. Please don't be mad at me.*

Shit. She thinks I'm mad at her. Disappointed, yes, but not mad. I shouldn't have left the way I did.

On my way out of the house, I dial her number.

She answers on the third ring. "Hey."

"I'm not mad at you, Babe," I say softly, standing at her front door. "I'm just mad in general. Mad at myself. And I'm scared. I'm scared of losing you. Of having a kid I didn't plan for with a girl I don't want to have it with."

A few seconds pass. While I wait for her response, I let myself into her house.

"I can't promise you anything, Rooter, but I'm willing to take things day by day."

"That's all I'm asking." The downstairs is empty. She must still be in her bedroom. "Is it all right if I come over?"

"Yeah."

"Good, because I'm in your living room." I chuckle.

"I'll be right down."

I wait at the foot of the stairs, listening to her footsteps above me. A minute passes before she appears at the top of the stairs. At the sight of her, warmth fills my chest and I smile. She walks down the stairs, stopping on the last one. I curl a finger through her belt loop and pull her close, burying my face in her neck. With her arms draped around my neck, she leans into me. We hold each other for a while before I lead her to the sofa to discuss other equally important matters.

"I hate to bring this up," I begin, "but we still have the issue of your car to deal with."

She scrunches her eyebrows. "You said it was at Molly's."

Brushing the top of her hand with my thumb I say, "I'm talking about Mike. He needs to be dealt with."

"What do you think we should do?"

I shake my head. "*We* aren't going to do anything. *I* will handle it."

Sophie glances to a set of pictures across the room. One is of Mike wearing a high school football jersey. The other is of him and Miranda dressed up for a dance. Prom, I assume.

Sophie's posture wilts as she frowns. "Rooter, he's Miranda's brother. I need to know what you plan on doing."

I don't care who he is. He'll get what he deserves. "He may be Miranda's brother, but you're my girl and by fucking with you, he fucked with me. He's going to pay for it."

"Pay how?" she asks, apprehensive.

"I'm going to show him what happens when he messes with me."

"Rooter, I realize you're used to handling these situations a certain way," she takes my hand into hers, "but we have to be careful here. You need to keep Miranda in mind."

"Why? He wasn't keeping her in mind when he did this."

"Because she's my best friend. Mike is the only family she has left." She points to the pictures she was just looking at. "It would kill her if something happened to him."

"It's not like I'm going to kill him. I'm just going to…" Images of all the things I'd like to do him pop into my mind. "Temporarily limit the use of his hands."

"Rooter—" She begins to protest, but I stop her by pressing my index finger to her lips.

"If we ignore this, the next thing he does will be much worse. I'm not willing to take that risk."

"Can't you just talk to him or something?"

I shake my head. "I've tried that. The only way I'll get through to him is by paying him a visit."

"We don't know where he is."

"That's why I need his cell phone number."

She stares at me, chewing on her bottom lip. "If Miranda finds out I had anything to do with Mike getting hurt, including giving you his phone number, she'll hate me forever."

"You don't have to give it to me. Where's your phone?"

"It's in my purse in my room."

I run to her room to get the phone and enter the passcode. A text pops up. I don't read it intentionally, but the words practically jump off the screen. *Hey beautiful. I'm thinking about you.* It's from Hayden, the guy she went on the double date with. My body tenses as anger roars through me. Why the fuck is this assclown texting my girl? Has she not made it clear she has a man? I dart down the stairs. My eyes flit to Sophie's then back to the screen and I toss the phone at her.

"What the fuck is that?"

She reads the text and rolls her eyes, shrugging as though it's nothing.

Her flippant response pisses me off. She bitches about Candace continuously and she's getting texts like this from other guys? Fuck that. I point to the phone. "Put an end to that, or I will and neither one of you will like the way I do it."

She chucks the phone onto the coffee table. "Rooter, it's not a big deal. We went out once. It was nothing. He knows I have a boyfriend."

"Then remind him and make sure he doesn't contact you again."

She cocks her head to the side and crosses her arms. "Wait, so you're telling me you're pissed about a text from a guy I went on one date with and yet I'll always have to deal with Candace?"

We don't have time for this shit. I snatch the phone from the table and punch in her passcode. I scroll through her contacts until I find Mike's phone number.

"What are you doing?" she asks, but I ignore her.

I grab my phone from my back pocket and call Rat, the Club's resident programming genius. "Rat, I need you to run a trace for me," I say and give him Mike's number.

"Should I know what this is in regards to?" he asks.

"Just personal business."

"How soon do you need it?"

"ASAP."

I end the call and toss Sophie's phone back to her. She catches it mid-air and lays it back on the table.

"You gonna call that guy or what?" I grumble.

"Right now?"

My eyes narrow. "Is there a reason you don't want to?"

She kicks out a foot, impatient. "I think we have bigger issues than some guy sending me a random text."

"Call him, now," I demand, "or I will."

She tosses her head back and cackles.

Flames of anger shoot through me. "You think this is funny?"

"You being jealous? I think it's hilarious."

I'm not jealous. Territorial, hell yes, but not jealous. I won't tolerate other men texting and flirting with my woman. She needs to set him straight. "Stop laughing, Sophie."

"I can't! It's just so ridiculous." She wraps her arms around her midsection as she continues to laugh.

"Ridiculous? I'll show you ridiculous." I grab the phone from the table and shove it at her.

"You already have."

"Call. Him. Now."

"He's nobody, Rooter. He doesn't warrant a phone call."

Why is she refusing to call him? Unless she has something to hide…

"Fine, I'll do it myself." I scroll through her contacts and find Hayden's number and press send. The prick answers on first ring. Eager fuck.

"Hey, sweetness."

My hands tremble as my fury boils to the surface. "Hayden?"

"Who is this?"

"This is the guy who will shred your dick with a fork if you ever text or call Sophie Holt again."

"Look man, I don't want any trouble. I won't contact her again."

"Good," I say and end the call, but I don't feel any better.

"That was so unnecessary." Sophie jerks the phone from my hand. "And how do you know my passcode anyway?"

I shrug and fall back onto the sofa. It's not like I went a secret mission to figure it out. "I've seen you enter it a thousand times."

"And you remembered it?"

"Is it a problem?"

"Of course not." She folds her arms over her chest. "*I have nothing to hide.*"

"Are you insinuating that I do?" I've hidden nothing from Sophie with regards to Candace or other women. I've always been one hundred percent up front. When she's asked me to talk to Candace, I have. When she asked me to let her read or listen to Candace's messages, I did.

"Suspicious minds are often the result of a guilty conscience, and with your slutty, pregnant exes and all..."

She did not just say that. I lift my hips to take my phone out of my back pocket and toss it to her. "Code is zero-nine-two-six."

Sophie's eyes get big and I know why. My passcode is her birthday, and it's not a coincidence. I also changed the alarm code to my house to the same number.

"I don't need your code," she snipes.

I slip the phone back into my pocket. We need to get a couple things straight. "It's one, not plural. And she isn't my *ex.*"

She rolls her eyes. I hate it when she does that. "Yeah, it's hard for her to be an ex when she's still around."

I groan and drag my fingers through my hair, tired of fighting about Candace. Exhausted with arguing in general. "I thought you said you don't want to fight."

Sophie blows out a breath and drops back against the couch. "I don't. You started it."

I guess I did. I scoot closer until my thigh rests alongside hers and clasp her hand. I overreacted, but in my defense, I couldn't help it. She was right about me being jealous. It got the best of me. "I'm sorry. I lost my shit when I saw that text."

She asks, "Do you really think I'd cheat on you?"

That's a loaded question. I don't think she'd cheat, but I wouldn't be surprised if she left me for someone better. "No Babe, I don't." I lay my head on her shoulder. "I'm just crazy right now."

She hangs her leg over top of mine and squeezes my hand. We sit for a few minutes in complete silence. Having her close is comforting. But my calm doesn't last long. My thoughts quickly wander to what's coming next and how on earth our relationship will survive Candace's pregnancy.

And then my phone rings.

It's Candace.

No Win Situation

I can never catch a break.

All I want is a few minutes of peace. I should know better than to think that could ever happen. As the phone continues to ring, I glance at Sophie. "Should I answer it?"

"She'll just keep calling if you don't."

I hold the phone to my ear. "What's up?"

"Something isn't right." Candace's voice shakes.

I jolt forward. "What do you mean?"

"I'm cramping. I think I'm having a miscarriage."

"Do you want to go to the hospital?" I ask and look to Sophie who's hanging on my every word.

"I don't know what to do. My friend says cramping can be normal early in the pregnancy. Can you come over?"

I screw my eyes shut. Sophie won't be happy, but I've no choice. "Yeah. I'm on my way."

Sophie rolls her eyes and throws a hand in the air. "Here we go."

"I'm sorry," I say and tuck my phone into my pocket. "It's shitty timing, I know, but she says she's cramping."

"Yeah, I bet."

"Babe, I have no way of knowing if she's lying, but if she isn't I should be there."

She nods. "Yeah."

"I can give you the keys to my truck if you need to go anywhere."

"Don't worry about it," she stands and puts her hands in her front pockets. "I'm just going to stay home and chill out."

"I'll call you later, okay?" I stand and lean in for a kiss. She kisses me back, but barely. "I'll be back as soon as I can and we'll spend the rest of the day together."

She looks away and her voice is skeptical as she says, "Okay."

"Babe," I say and turn her face to mine, "I wish I didn't have to leave."

"Me, too."

The sadness in her voice tugs at my heart. I hate leaving her this way. Clutching the sides of Sophie's face, I kiss her deep and hard, trying to convey just how difficult it is to leave her. When I pull away, I search her eyes for understanding. "I'll be as quick as possible. I promise."

I knock on Candace's door, and she hollers for me to let myself in. When I enter the living room she's sprawled out on the couch in a white tank top and panties. Her hair and makeup are perfect. She's even wearing bright red lipstick. This is not the look of a woman who's scared for the life of her unborn child.

"I won't be played Candace."

"What are you talking about?"

"I'm not an idiot. Look at you."

"It's hot in here and it's not like you haven't seen it before."

"Whatever. I'm out of here." I spin around to leave. "I'm not playing this game."

"It's not a game, Rooter." She shoots up from the couch and grabs my hand. "I called you because I'm scared. I'll put some clothes on if it'll make you feel better."

"It would."

She bats her eyes. "Too tempting?"

"Don't start Candace or I'm gone."

She holds her hands up in surrender. "Geez, don't get your boxers in a twist. I'll get dressed."

Five minutes later she emerges from her room wearing a pair of booty shorts and a midriff baring t-shirt. She could've just stayed the way she was. She sits next to me on the sofa and takes a drink of soda.

"Have you talked to a doctor?" I ask.

"Yeah. I have an appointment scheduled for Monday."

"Do you want me to go with you?"

She shakes her head. "No need. There won't be anything to see yet."

"How are you feeling now?"

"I'm crampy, but you being here relaxes me."

I look around. The place is a pigsty as usual with dirty dishes and clothes everywhere. It smells like wet dog and incense. "Is there anything you need me to do?"

"You're doing it. I just need you here."

It's bad timing, but I need to make one thing clear. "At the risk of sounding like a dick, I need for you to understand I can't be here all the time. I'll help with whatever you need and I'll be here as often as possible, but I have the shop, the Club…"

She flips her hair. "And your princess."

I grind my teeth, but try to keep my composure. "The fact of the matter is, you and I aren't together. We lead separate lives."

"I don't know how this is going to work," she says and takes another drink, "but the one thing I know is we can't live completely separate lives anymore. This baby has to be your first priority."

"It will be."

"No. Not will be." Her eyes bore into mine. "This baby needs to come first *now*. It's more important than your job, the Club, and it sure as hell better come before your precious girlfriend."

I throw a hand in the air. "I'm here, aren't I?"

"Yeah, but only because you have to be. You see this as an obligation, a burden. But it's so much more than that." She grabs my hand and puts it on her bare belly. "This is your son or daughter."

"I get that, Candace. You don't need to lay a guilt trip." I yank my hand away and drag it through my hair. "My life changed literally overnight. I'm still in shock, trying to wrap my mind around it all."

She shifts back and stares at me with visible offense. "My life changed too. I wasn't planning on this. Now I have to consider how I'm going to make ends meet. I can't dance once I start showing. How will I pay the bills? How will I provide for our baby? I'm scared as hell."

Guilt hits me square in the chest. I've been so caught up in how my life is changing that I hadn't thought about hers. "Don't worry, I'll make sure everything is taken care of."

"You can't put a check in the mail and call yourself a dad. I need you to be here."

How can she say that to me? She knows me better than that. I smack my thighs. "I said I would be here. How many times do I need to say it?"

She sighs and falls back onto the couch. "Coming over every couple days to check up on us isn't enough. When the baby comes home, I'll need you here to help me."

"We'll work it out."

She groans and shakes her head. "You're not getting it."

"What am I not getting? You said I need to be here and I've promised I will be."

"You refuse to admit it, but you know as well as I do, us being together is what's best for this baby."

I shake my head. I knew she'd do this. "Us having a kid doesn't mean we should be together."

"Yes it does, Rooter. It's a sign. Are you really so blind that you can't see it? We're *meant* to be together."

Exasperated, I stand and pace the room. "Forget it, Candace. You're not going to use this pregnancy to guilt me into a relationship."

"Is it really so wrong that I want to bring our baby into a real family?"

No, it isn't wrong. But it's not her true motivation. "It'll have a real family, Candace. Me, you, my parents, the Club. It'll have a huge family."

"You refuse to see things the right way."

I come to a halt. "And you refuse to see things for what they are."

She didn't call me over cramps. She called to get me over here to lay a guilt trip on me and try to convince me to be with her.

She stands and rushes to me. "Because it shouldn't be this way!"

"I can't talk about this anymore. I gotta go." I turn to the door, but she grabs my arm.

"Are you going to walk away every time shit gets tough?"

"You're making shit impossible!"

Candace leans forward and cries out as she clutches her belly.

My gut instinct tells me she's faking it, but what if she's not? "Are you okay?"

"Bad cramp." She slowly stands upright.

"We shouldn't fight. It isn't good for the baby." I lead her back to the couch and sit next to her.

She looks at me with pleading eyes. "Please don't be mad at me, Rooter."

"No worries. We'll figure this out and everything will be okay."

In a perfect world, all children would grow up in homes with a mother and father present. But this is an imperfect world. Candace's pregnancy isn't the result of a man and woman in love. It's the result of poor decision making. So, while Candace isn't completely off-base to want us to be together as a family for the sake of the baby, it'd never work. I'm not in love with her and I don't believe she's in love with me. I think she loves the *idea* of me and her together. She loves the idea of being tied to the Club in a more substantial way. I can't give her that and I never offered it. But now I'm being made out to be the bad guy because I won't give it to her.

While I'm not angry with her over the pregnancy, I am irritated that she refuses to accept that we won't end up together. It'd be one thing if she and I had been in an actual relationship and shared romantic feelings. Maybe then I'd be inclined to give us a shot. But that wasn't the case as I've reminded her time and time again. How long before she accepts it?

It's Friday, and I've barely seen Sophie. Between the shop, the Club, Candace, and Sophie's schedule at The Grand, there's hardly any time. We spend the nights together because it's the only time we really have, but the tension between us is palpable. Sophie's body language screams "hands off." I get it though. As long as she doesn't completely shut me out, it's okay.

Spread out on the couch with Dopey on my legs, I flip through the cable channels when there's a knock on the door.

"Hey, man," Bear says when I open the door. It's not like him to just show up unless there's an emergency.

"Hey, what's up?" I ask and step aside so he can walk in.

"Miranda's still putting on her face. Thought I'd wait here if that's all right."

"Of course." I assume my earlier position on the couch.

"This is an odd sight," he says and takes a seat on the chair to my right.

"What's that?"

"You sitting around on a Friday night. You sitting around at all, for that matter."

I sigh. "I needed a little quiet time."

He arches a brow. "Since when do you need quiet time?"

"Since Candace got pregnant." I swing my legs over the side of the sofa and sit upright. "Between her, the Club, the shop, and trying to be with Sophie, I haven't had five minutes to think."

"*Trying* to be with Sophie?"

"She's not happy. I don't know what the fuck to do." I rub my face with both hands. "She's staying at Ryan's tonight. Said they're going to have a couple drinks after work and she doesn't want to drive. But I'm not stupid."

"You think she's lying?"

"She's staying there to get some space from me."

"What makes you think that?" Dopey nudges Bear's knee with his nose to get him to pet him.

"She's pissed." I blow out a breath and rub the top of my thighs. "We got into it over Candace calling and texting all day and night. She's convinced Candace is lying about the cramping to get my attention."

"She might be right."

"Yeah," I agree, "and I told her I have my doubts as well, but I can't ignore Candace in case she's telling the truth."

"What did Sophie say to that?"

"She flipped out and accused me of giving Candace too much control. I tried to reason with her and get her to see it from my point of view, but it made shit worse."

Bear shifts forward and rests his elbows on his thighs. "You're in a tough situation, man."

"It's not tough. It's impossible."

"Miranda doesn't tell me a whole lot," he sits up straight, "but she says Sophie really cares about you. She's trying to work through her feelings about the situation."

"I just wish she'd try to see this from my side." Candace could be lying, but I have no way of knowing. Since she could be telling the truth, I have to do the right thing and be there to support her and the baby. It's frustrating that Sophie can't understand that.

"Give her time, Brother."

"I'll give her all the time she needs, but if things continue on like they have, she'll probably just say fuck it and walk. I'm surprised she didn't Wednesday."

Wednesday night Sophie and I had a huge blow up. We were in bed watching a movie when Candace called asking me to bring her some fried chicken. Evidently, she hadn't eaten all day due to morning sickness. The sickness had finally passed, and she was starving, but was exhausted from puking all day. I felt bad for her. As a result of carrying my child, she was sick all day. I couldn't say no.

Needless to say, Sophie was pissed. She said it was just a ploy to get me over there. I agreed it was a possibility, but what choice did I have? To ease her irritation, I offered for Sophie to go with me, which she did. As my shit luck goes, Sophie was right. Candace opened the door wearing red lingerie. Sophie barely spoke to me for the rest of the night.

"You're in a no win situation, for sure," Bear agrees. "You could assume Candace is lying and blow her off to make Sophie happy. But if it turns out she's telling the truth…"

"I'd be the biggest asshole on the planet, and worse yet a deadbeat, absentee father. I refuse to do that regardless of how much I care for Sophie."

Bear nods. "On the flip side, if Candace is lying you could lose Sophie."

My stomach churns at the thought of losing her, but it's a real possibility.

I talked with Mama yesterday and asked her what I should do. One thing about Mama, she doesn't beat around the bush to spare anyone's feelings. She said I screwed up. Getting involved with Candace was a mistake. Now, I've let both women down and put them in unfair positions. If I'm determined to be with Sophie, I must find a way to do right by both. But that'll be tricky because I have to make Candace and the baby my top priority. As the father of Candace's baby, it's my duty to stand by her. However, I also have a responsibility to Sophie. I'm asking a lot of her. It's not easy being with someone who's having a baby with someone else. It's only natural that our relationship is strained. I need to give Sophie the time and space she needs to be sad and angry while making it clear that I'm here for her when she needs me.

As for the possibility that Candace is lying, Mama doubts she would. Candace knows what the repercussions would be. She'd lose everything and everyone who matters to her. That said, Mama wouldn't put it past her to exaggerate the situation to her benefit.

But, Mama stressed one point in particular. The most important person in this equation is the baby. The precious, innocent life I created—albeit accidentally—is a lifelong commitment. Every choice I make must be in his or her best interest. I must do whatever it takes to be the best possible father. Even if it means running to Candace every time she calls. Maybe it'll be more than Sophie can handle and she'll end our relationship. If she does, I'll have to get over it. But under no circumstances can I let my child down.

However, it isn't as simple as it sounds. My commitment to be a good father doesn't make it easy to hurt someone I care about. Seeing the disappointment in Sophie's eyes when I take off to Candace's causes me physical pain. She's been disappointed by everyone in her life. I wanted to be the one person to never let her down. Hurting Sophie goes against every fiber of my being. All I want is to protect and keep her safe, but I can't even save her from myself.

Hours pass as I lie in bed. I've grown accustomed to having Sophie in my arms at night. I can't get comfortable enough to drift off to sleep without her. I pick up my phone from the nightstand and check for a text I know she hasn't sent. She said she'd text me to say goodnight, but it's three in the morning and I still haven't heard from her. I send a text: *Can't sleep without u next to me.*

I hold the phone and stare at the screen waiting for a response that never comes. I tell myself she's asleep, but it doesn't make me feel better. She probably wouldn't answer if she was awake.

Complications & Arguments

I've always had shit luck. In my life, if it can go wrong, it does. And things never come easily for me. So, when I look to my right and see Mike in the parking lot of the local gym, I can't believe my eyes. Another odd stroke of luck is that I'm in my truck. I'd been on my way to the hardware store to pick up shelves for the garage.

I slam on the brakes and skid into the parking lot. I stop the truck and jump out. Mike sees me running at him and takes off for his car, but it's too late. I lunge, knocking him to the ground and elbow him in the jaw as I pin him to the ground.

"Stay put, fucker, or I'll make this a lot more painful." I hoist him up and draw my gun, jamming it into his lower back. "We're going for a ride."

In the truck, I open the glove compartment and retrieve a black bandana and tie it around his head as a blindfold. En route to the Club warehouse, I call Sophie's phone, but it goes straight to voicemail. "Babe, call me as soon as you get this."

Once inside the warehouse I remove the bandana and point my nine millimeter in Mike's face. His eyes bulge from their sockets as he looks from me to the gun and back to me.

"I'm sorry, man," he cries. "I didn't mean to do it. I was fucked up. I wasn't thinking. I'll pay for the damage."

"Shut up!" I give him a shove and motion with the gun for him to walk down the hallway.

"Please man. Please," he begs as he stares down the long, dark hall. "Don't do this. I'll do anything you want."

I put the gun to Mike's forehead. "What I want is for you to shut the fuck up."

The fear in his eyes is exhilarating. I've been waiting for this moment for so long. Only question is, what will I do with the opportunity? I'd like to tie him up and torture him for days on end. Provide him just enough food and water to keep him conscious while I torment him with acts such as prying off his finger and toe nails and driving nails into his knee caps. But before I do anything, I need to get a hold of Sophie.

Once again, I call Sophie and it goes to voicemail. With a scowl, I squeeze the damn phone and consider throwing it through the wall. Instead, I take a deep breath and remind myself to give her the benefit of the doubt.

I lead Mike to the back room and shove him against the wall and onto the floor. "Did I or did I not tell you to leave Sophie and your sister alone?"

"I'm sorry." His lips tremble. "I was high. I wasn't thinking."

"You think that lame ass excuse is going to save you?"

"I'm just so fucked up," he cries. "I lost my mom, my dad, my sister. I got nothing. No one."

I have no sympathy for this prick. I grab him by the neck and press him to the wall. "Motherfucker I don't give a shit what your problems are! You don't fuck with my girl."

Hours pass as I wait for Sophie to return my calls. I've called at least a dozen times and texted just as many. I pace the length of the hallway outside the room, cursing under my breath. It's going on eleven o'clock, why hasn't she called? I know damn well she's awake by now, yet her phone is still off. She must be avoiding me. There's no other excuse.

I sent Sparrow to her house over an hour ago, but he hasn't seen her. If I knew where the hell Ryan lives, I'd send him there to collect her. I can't believe I let her stay the night there without getting the address. I'd thought about asking for it, but decided against it. Under normal circumstances, boyfriends don't demand the addresses of their girl's friends. I didn't want to add to the reasons for her to reconsider our relationship. I assumed she'd be safe at Ryan's and that I'd see or at least talk to her this morning.

If Sophie will be spending time there, I need to know where it is. I can't protect her if I don't know where she is. What if Andy was still out there watching her? What if someone else is watching her because of me? There are too many variables at play she isn't aware of. Sophie has no idea how important it is that I know where she is and that I'm able to reach her, but she's about to find out.

Forty-five minutes later she calls. My patience is long gone. I take a deep breath and count to ten to calm myself before answering. "Where are you?"

"Home," she answers flippantly which infuriates me even more.

"Why haven't you returned any of my messages?"

Mike moans as he comes to. Earlier he was crying like a pussy and begging me to let him go so I knocked him out with the butt of my gun.

"Is Mike with you?"

She must've heard him, but Mike's being with me is beside the point. I leave the room and close the door behind me. "Yeah. Why haven't you called me?"

"My phone died. Where are you?"

I pinch the bridge of my nose and exhale sharply. "Sophie, I need to be able to reach you at all times. Do you understand that?"

"I told you my phone died," she snaps. "How is Mike?"

Unable to control my emotion, I shout, "He's fine! Tell me you understand that I need to be able to reach you."

"Yeah, yeah, I get it. Where are you?"

"I can't tell you that." Not that I don't want to. Only Club members are privy to the location of the warehouse. Otherwise, I'd tell her to get her ass over here.

She screams loud enough that I have to hold the phone away from my ear. "The hell you can't! I need to know what's going on!"

"I have it under control. He'll live. I promise."

"Rooter, dammit! What did you do?"

I cast an evil smirk in direction of the room Mike's in. "Not much… Yet."

"Don't. You. Dare. Hurt. Him." She demands, taking me by surprise.

What the fuck? Has she forgotten who she's talking to? "Sophie, he's going to pay for what he's done."

"That isn't your decision to make. It's mine. And I'm telling you, you will not hurt him."

Not my decision? She's my girl, and he fucked with her. As a man— as *her* man—it's my duty to protect her. To make sure he doesn't fuck with her again. "Sophie—" I begin my argument, but she cuts me off.

"No," she asserts. "If you're smart, you'll listen to what I'm saying."

It takes every ounce of my strength to remain calm. "Since when do you care what happens to this piece of shit?"

"I don't need to explain anything to you. But you are going to listen to me."

Did I hear her right? "What?"

"I'm done with all this shit," she says in a deep monotone.

My heart thuds as panic tears through me. What does she mean by done? "Sophie?"

"You don't get to dictate everything anymore. It's not all up to you anymore. I get a say in what happens."

I pace the hallway. "What is this really about?"

"It's about you! And me! And how everything is completely fucked up! My life is more fucked up now than it was before I met you!"

"I'm on my way." I secure the padlock on the room Mike's in.

"Not until you let him go."

"I'm not letting him go."

"Then I won't be here when you get here."

"Babe—" she cuts me off yet again.

"Do. Not. *Babe*. Me. Just shut the fuck up and listen."

I come to a stop just before the door. The hair on the back of my neck stands and my skin tingles. I can't mask the shaking of my voice as I speak. "I'm listening."

"I'm sure you've already done more than enough to scare him. Let him go. Then you and I are going to talk."

I've not allowed anyone to tell me what I will or won't do. This is a bitter pill to swallow.

"Did you hear me?"

"I heard you," I grumble.

"Are you going to do what I've said?"

I glance down the hallway to where Mike is, enraged by all the trouble he's caused Sophie. I yearn to make him pay. But if I don't do as she says, it could mean the end of us. "Yes. I'll be there in a half hour."

The entire way to Sophie's house I vacillate between fear that she'll break up with me and frustration over her protecting Mike. Speeding and blowing through stop signs, I arrive earlier than I predicted. The truck is barely in park before I kill the engine and run to her house and barge in without warning. The room is dark from the storm brewing outside. A flash of lightning illuminates the room followed by the crack of thunder. Sophie's sitting on the sofa, relaxed—too relaxed—with her legs crossed.

"Babe?" I ask, standing before her.

Her voice is a low monotone, "Did you let Mike go?"

I clench my jaw and remind myself to stay calm. "Yes. Are you okay?"

"No, Rooter, I'm not okay," she answers through gritted teeth. "What did you do to him?"

Why does she even care? "Nothing much. Smacked him around a little, threatened him, and then you called."

"I think you should sit down." She points to the chair on her left.

I sit. "Babe, you're freaking me out."

"Good! You should be. Because I'm beyond done with all the bullshit."

There's that word again. Done. I don't like it. "Done? With me?"

"If things don't change, yeah."

That's not happening. I close my eyes and take a deep breath. I need to get to the bottom of what's really going on here. "Is this about Candace?"

"Mostly, yeah," she admits, "but it's also about how you've treated me through this. It's like I don't even matter."

"Of course you matter." I bring my hand to my chest. I can't believe what I'm hearing. Everything I do is for her. "How have I made you feel otherwise?"

Whenever she's really upset, like right now, she waves her hands in the air like a crazy woman. "You run to her constantly. She could call you over a hang nail and you'd go rushing over there." She looks away. "It's getting to the point that I'm thinking your feelings for her are more than you've admitted to."

I hurl forward in the chair. "I can promise you they're not. But what am I supposed to do? Ignore her? I can't do that. She's pregnant with my kid."

"Maybe," she rolls her eyes. "How do you know it's your kid?"

Oh my God, how many times are we going to have this conversation? "I have to assume it is until it's born and I can get a DNA test."

She drags her hands back and forth across the top of her legs. "Fine. I can accept that. But I can't accept her calling every hour on the hour and you running over to her all the time. She's pregnant, not dying. Women get pregnant all the time for shit sake. It's really not that big of a deal."

I cock my head to the side. "What if you were pregnant? Would that be a big deal? Or should I ignore you?"

"Like I could even get pregnant!" She sighs and throws a hand in the air. "At the rate we're going, we'll never get an opportunity to have sex in order for me to get pregnant because you'll be with Candace all the damn time!"

"What do you want me to do?" I yell, holding my hands in the air. "I'm trying, all right! I don't know what the fuck to do." I jump up and pace the room, holding my hands behind my head. "Do you think I *want* to go running to her every damn day? Do you think I *want* her calling me constantly? Because I don't. I don't want her to be pregnant, but I can't undo it. And I can't hide from it. And I won't ignore it, even if I want to, and trust me, I *do*!"

"I'm not asking you to ignore the baby. I'm asking you to stop giving in to her over every little whimper and whine when there's absolutely nothing wrong with her." She leans forward with her elbows rested on her knees and puts her head into her hands. "If we're going to be together, you need to make time for me. For us. It's like she knows exactly when to call so you'll run to her and leave me hanging, which you do all the time now."

I come to a halt. I can't be mad at her. She's right. I do leave her hanging. Frequently. It isn't fair to her and I hate doing it. But I have a good reason.

It's time I tell her the truth about me. I take a breath and sit on the coffee table so we're face to face. I cup her face and gaze into her tired, sad eyes.

"All I fucking want is you. You're all I've wanted for as long as I can remember." I swallow and pause a moment before continuing. "You want truth? I'll give it to you. The truth is it would be so easy to choose you over the kid. It would be so fucking easy for me to walk away from both of them for you. The only thing stopping me is that's what my dad did to me and my mom. And I don't want to be like him."

She scrunches her eyebrows and blinks. "What are you talking about?"

I pull away and drop my gaze to the floor. I hate talking about this. "Mick isn't my real dad. Or rather I should say, my biological dad. My bio-dad abandoned me. He walked out on my mom when she was pregnant. Left her for another woman."

"Oh my God, Rooter. I'm so sorry," Sophie's voice is filled with surprise and sympathy. She takes my hand into hers.

When I look up at her I'm met with a pair of understanding yet shocked blue eyes. "Mom was just like Candace, trying to get by as a stripper. Had no family. She had one friend… Candace's mom." I blow out a breath and rake my fingers through my hair. "Mick was already in love with her. He took her in when she could no longer dance. He told her he wanted to take care of me and be my dad. She eventually fell in love with him, too. He raised me like his own. Loved me like his own. There's no differentiation between me and Isa to him. To him, I am his blood. And if the kid Candace is carrying is mine, I'm going to love him or her just the way Mick loves me."

Tears well in Sophie's eyes, and she squeezes my hand. "I'm so very sorry."

Jesus, I'm fucked up. What am I doing? I have no right to do this to this girl. Sophie has been through enough bullshit in her life. All I've done is add to it. I've been so determined to have her that I've refused to do what I know is right.

Bottom line is, I can't give Sophie what she deserves. I can't give her the relationship or life she wants. With a kid, I'll always be split in two. Candace will never let up when it comes to being with me. It's inevitable that I will lose Sophie. I might as well get it over with. Spare her more pain and disappointment. "I know the situation is fucked up and that I'm asking way too much of you. I should let you go. This isn't fair to you."

"Rooter, no. You can't let me go because I'm not going anywhere." Her eyes bore into mine and I sense a hint of panic. "I won't abandon you when you need me most."

"I do need you. But you're right." I have to turn away. It hurts too much to see her face and say these words. "We can't go on like this. It'll never work."

She grabs me by the chin and forces me to face her. "Then we don't go on like this. We figure out a balance. Together."

There's nothing I want more than to be with Sophie. Now that I've had a small taste of having her in my life, I can't imagine being without her. But with all my baggage, I'm not sure I can make her happy. I've failed thus far. It's in her best interest that I let her go.

I should end this right now.

Just get it over with.

But…

If I walk out of this house right now, I'd just come crawling back.

And Sophie would take me back.

After failing to respond, she continues, "But you need to work with me."

We're probably doomed to fail, but she'll have to be the one to walk away because I can't even though I should. "I can do that, Babe. I can."

"I would never ask you to abandon your child. I'm only asking for you to make a little time for us."

In my back pocket my phone rings. I don't have to look at the screen to know it's Candace. I screw my eyes shut and shake my head. Candace will have to wait. Right now, I need to give Sophie my undivided attention. "I will make time for us."

"Uninterrupted time."

"Uninterrupted." Somehow, someway, I will make it happen.

"And there's something else."

The change in the tone of her voice worries me. I wait to hear what she has to say.

"You need to give me a say in things that concern me. Like the situation with Mike."

"He deserves to pay for what he did."

"Yeah, but you don't get to decide the price on your own."

This is where we will never see eye to eye. "He deserves worse than he got."

Sophie sighs with frustration. "Maybe so. But Miranda doesn't and she will feel any pain you inflict on him."

I nod. Miranda doesn't deserve to be hurt, and she's been hurt plenty by Mike. I'm just trying to make sure it doesn't happen to either one of them again.

Sophie continues, "Promise me, going forward we'll make time for each other and we'll make decisions that affect us both, together."

"I promise." I lean my forehead against hers and pray I can keep my promise. "I'm going to get this right."

Unbalanced

Sophie's sleeping peacefully, so I slide out of bed slowly so as not to wake her. I left my phone on silent all night, something I never do. But Sophie and I needed a break from the drama. I think I only checked it once for messages in the middle of the night. On my way downstairs to let Dopey out, I see Candace has texted three times and left one voicemail. After listening to her voice message, I text her back and tell her I'm busy, but will check my messages throughout the day.

I'm going to devote this day to Sophie. She has requested uninterrupted time, and that's what I'm going to give her. As long as I don't get called away on Club business, I'm hers for the day.

I hear the creaking of the stairs and watch as Sophie shuffles into the kitchen. She's still in my t-shirt, her long hair is tousled from sleeping. Sophie wakes up hard and is kind of cranky in the morning, which she tries to hide from me. She usually doesn't say or do much until she finishes her first cup of coffee. It's adorable.

She wraps her arms around my waist. "Good morning," she yawns.

"Morning, Beautiful. Coffee's on."

"Thank you."

I lift her chin and look into her eyes. "Sleep well?"

"I always sleep well here."

"Is it just my bed or me?"

She wrinkles her nose when she smiles. "A little of both."

I bow my head and kiss the tip of her nose. Lightning strikes outside and a boom of thunder shakes the house. "Gonna be an ugly day."

"I love storms."

I love learning new things about her. "Yeah?"

She backs out of my embrace, walks to the coffeemaker and pours coffee into the mug I set out for her. "Something about the sound of the thunder and the darkness soothes me."

"I'm not a big fan of rain," I admit and open the door for Dopey and dry him off.

"I love it," she smiles and adds vanilla creamer to her coffee. "When I was little, I'd sit on the porch with my coloring books when it stormed. I loved playing in the rain, but I always got in trouble for it."

"It was just the opposite for me," I follow her into the living room. "Rain always made me feel cooped up. Going for long rides on my bicycle was my favorite thing to do growing up, and I didn't like riding in the rain."

Sophie sits on the couch and tucks her legs beneath her. "I would have if I'd been allowed. Or if I had a bike. My mom wouldn't let me have one so I had to wait until I could come over to Miranda's. The Franks had a bike here for me to ride."

Sitting next to her, I gently stroke the top of her thigh. Rather than responding to the fact that her mother often deprived her, I focus on the kindness of the Franks. "That was nice of them."

"They were great." Her smile is sad. "I don't know what I would've done without them."

"I'm glad you had them." Who knows what would've happened to her had they not been in her life.

She nods. "I miss them."

My phone pings from within the kitchen. My mom's ring tone. Not a great time for an interruption, but that's the story of my life. One untimely disruption after another. I give Sophie an apologetic smile before going into the kitchen to check the message.

"Mom wants to know if we're coming to dinner tonight," I say as I walk back into the living room. "But I was thinking we could spend the day just the two of us."

Her eyes light up with surprise. "Really?"

I nod and take a seat next to her. I stroke the side of her face with the backs of my fingers. "Today there will be no talk of Mike or Candace or of what went down yesterday."

"Fine with me."

"We're not leaving this house," I say and draw her into my chest. "We're going to hide from the outside world and spend the day cuddling and vegging out."

"Veg out? You?"

"I enjoy a lazy day every once in a while, and today is perfect for it." I draw back and gaze into her happy eyes.

"Maybe you'll dance in the rain with me?"

"If that's what you want, that's what we'll do."

The great thing about the day is all of Sophie's tension seems to be gone. She's relaxed and happy. There's a near constant smile on her face.

We lounge around, talk about everything and nothing. We watch movies and play a game of cards. I haven't played Gin in years so Sophie beats me every single hand. Evidently, she used to play the game with Miranda's mom, Loraine. It was kind of their thing. They'd play for hours on end while Miranda sat and whined that she was bored because she hated the game and refused to play. Sophie hasn't played the game since Loraine passed away so it's a bittersweet moment for her.

Before dinner I take Sophie outside to play in the rain. Dopey thinks it's a good idea to roll around in a mud puddle. We spend a good hour cleaning him and the mess he makes in the house, but I don't mind. The look of pure joy on Sophie's face as she stood looking to the sky as the rain fell on us was worth it.

Candace calls and texts throughout the day despite my telling her I'm busy. Hell, that's probably why she's bugging me. I'm sure she knows what I mean by "busy."

She claims she's still cramping and wants me to come over and keep her company for a while. I don't know if she's lying, but she's been claiming cramps for a while now and nothing has happened. She told me her doctor said everything looked good with the pregnancy. Unless I get a text or voicemail saying she's going to the hospital, I'm staying put with my attention focused on my girl.

Wracked by guilt, I hardly slept last night. While lying in bed together after our perfect day, Sophie thanked me for spending the day with her. She *thanked* me. A girl shouldn't have to thank her guy for spending time with her. If I had been doing right by her, she wouldn't have. I laid in bed all night beating myself up for being a shit boyfriend and trying to think of ways to make it up to her. A simple candlelit dinner with flowers won't cut it. I want to blow her mind and remove all doubt as to how important she is to me. I called Mama earlier to ask for help.

Mama sits me down in her living room and asks me a series of questions. What are Sophie's favorite foods? Likes and dislikes? Hobbies?

"Sophie's a simple girl," I answer. "She doesn't expect or want much. She spends all her time working and in school so she doesn't have many hobbies. She likes to read. She spends most of her time with me or her friends."

There's a pause as Mom processes the information. I'm not giving her much to go on. "Does she ever talk about her dreams or goals?"

I remember a conversation we had early in our relationship. "She loves the beach. She's always dreamed of living in a small cottage on the lake."

Sophie dreams of a quiet, comfortable life. She said when she pictures herself as an older woman, she sees herself in a rocking chair looking out at the water, listening to the waves crash on the beach. She even described the house—a white cottage with a huge porch that wraps around the house and "lots and lots" of windows.

Mama's lips spread into the biggest smile. "I have the perfect idea!"

"What?" I ask and my phone rings. It's Candace. She's texted three times in the past hour. She wants me to come by to talk. I haven't responded yet.

"I know a—" Mama starts, but I hold my finger up to stop her so I can send Candace a text telling her I'll call within an hour.

"Sorry about that," I say. "Go ahead."

"I know a woman who owns rental properties on the lakeshore. Your papa and I stayed in one a couple years ago for our anniversary."

"That would be perfect, but do you think she has anything available now? I want to do this soon." By soon, I mean tomorrow.

"I'll call and ask." She pats me on the leg. "Either way, I'll find something Sweetie. Leave it to me. I'll take care of everything."

We discuss a few more details, things I'd like to do during the trip. We enlist the help of Isa for a few of the details and before I leave, they promise me everything will be perfect.

"Hey," Candace greets me with red rimmed eyes. For the first time ever, she's dressed modestly. She wears a pair of black shorts that cover her entire ass and a flowery blouse that covers most of her cleavage.

"Hey. What's up?"

She sits on the couch and sighs. "Are you in this with me?"

What kind of question is that? "Of course I am."

"It doesn't feel like it."

I join her on the couch and turn to face her. "Candace, we talk every day."

"Talk," she scoffs. "Barely. I have to leave a thousand voicemails and send a gazillion texts before you call me back."

"The only time I don't answer is when I can't."

"You mean when you're with *her*," she spits, "which is all the time."

"That's not true." The place is a mess, as usual. If she's going to raise my kid, she'll have to provide a clean, safe environment. I won't have any kid of mine in a dump like this. "The shop and the Club dictates my time."

Candace points to her stomach. "This baby needs to dictate your time."

"The baby *will* when it's *here*."

"The baby needs you now."

I groan and drag my fingers through my hair. "I'm giving everything I can to you and the baby, Candace."

"It's not enough."

I meet her hard stare. "Nothing I do will ever be enough, Candace. Not unless you and I are together."

"We should be together!"

"I'm not having this conversation." I get up to leave but she grabs me by the arm to stop me.

"Yesterday, I had the worst cramps yet. I was scared to death, and you ignored me!"

I throw a hand into the air. "I didn't ignore you! You said you weren't going to the hospital, and you never said you were scared. If you were so afraid why not go to the damn hospital?"

"Because they never do anything for me!"

"Then there must not be anything wrong."

"You just don't fucking get it!"

"You're right! I don't." I inhale deep and blow it out, counting to ten to calm myself. I sit back down on the couch. "This is all new to me, Candace. I'm doing my best. I can't be in three places at once. I still have a job to do and a life to live."

"That's just it! You're more concerned about your precious girlfriend than you are this baby!"

"That's not true. I'm here all the time. We talk every day."

"We don't talk every day," she argues. "We text every day. There's a difference. That won't work when the baby is here."

"I already said, the baby will be my top priority. I'll be around for my kid. You should know me well enough to know that."

"I do know you, Rooter. I know your life. I know what the Club life entails. It consumes a lot of time." She scoots close and her expression softens. "You won't have enough time for work, the Club, our baby, and *her*. Something has to go. It obviously can't be the Club, the shop or the baby."

I crack my neck. "Candace, you are not going to tell me how to live my life."

"Someone has to. I'm surprised your mom hasn't said anything."

I stand and pace the room. These are things I've thought about. I'm not sure how I will manage it all. I'll do my best. And I have spoken with my mom about it plenty of times. She says it'll be hard, but I'll manage. With the help of my parents and the Club, it'll all work out. People have kids every day with people they aren't in relationships with and they make it work. I'm used to shit being difficult. I'll figure it out. It's not fucking rocket science.

But that's not what this is really about. Candace wants us to be together. She thinks if she can talk me in to breaking up with Sophie that there will be a chance for me and her.

Not happening. Ever.

Candace walks over to where I stand. "Do you honestly think you can work at the shop, be in the Club, have a relationship *and* be a good father?"

I grind my teeth. "I'll do the best I can. It's all anyone can do."

She places a hand on my bicep and looks at me with a soft, understanding expression. "I know you'll do your best. That you would *never* do anything to let your child down. Not after what your father did to you."

"No, I won't let my kid down." I pull away and go to the other side of the room.

"I'm just asking you to consider what I'm saying. You'll just end up letting her down in the end. She'll always come last. Eventually, she'll get tired of it."

She already has. Facing away from Candace I say, "I'll be a good father, no matter what. But my relationship is none of your business."

"Rooter, you know I'm in love with you. You know I believe we're meant to be together." I hear footsteps and a moment later, Candace is facing me. "But more than anything, I just care about what's best for you and our baby. This isn't me playing a game. I genuinely want what's best for you. You say we're not going to be together. I'll learn to accept that. But you can't spread yourself so thin. Something has to give. You know it as well as I do. You're preoccupied all the time. No matter where you are, your mind is somewhere else. It's dangerous. You can't handle Club business if your mind is elsewhere. You'll end up dead."

"I'll handle my business and I'll be fine. I don't need you telling me how to manage my life. You can hardly manage your own."

I'll find a way to make everything work. I have to. Giving Sophie up isn't an option.

I love her.

As scary as it is, I'm finally admitting it. Yeah, our relationship is new, but it doesn't matter. I love Sophie—every little thing about her. I think I loved her before we were even together. If I lost her now, everything would fall apart because I would fall apart. Sure, it'll be difficult trying to balance it all. There will be times when someone gets let down. But without Sophie, I'll be a terrible father because I'd be miserable. She's my strength when things get tough. She's my comfort and my peace in the midst of the chaos that is my life.

The Surprise

I don't know how my Mom pulled it off, but she found the perfect lakefront cottage in a little town called Ambrose about two hours north of Halsey. I drove up yesterday to check it out. As soon as I walked in the door, it was a done deal. I signed on the dotted line and handed over the cash. The place is ours through the weekend. We leave tonight.

For the next three days, Sophie is all mine. I'm so freaking excited that it feels as though my insides are vibrating. I don't think I've ever been as thrilled about anything in my life. Not even the day I bought my first Harley.

I'm leaving Dopey, and my phone, with my parents. I picked up a burner and only they have the number. Candace will be pissed, but Mama offered to take care of whatever she might need while I'm away.

Part of me worries this will throw Candace into a full-blown hissy fit and potentially cause problems for the baby. Then again, I'm not one hundred percent sold on the fact that there's anything wrong with the pregnancy. As a precaution, I'm not telling her where I'm going or with whom. I'm making it sound like I'll be away on Club business. Everyone's under strict instructions not to tell her otherwise.

A few minutes ago Molly called to let me know Sophie's car is ready to be picked up. I wasn't planning on picking it up today, but I can make it work. I shoot Sophie a text to let her know I'm on my way.

I let myself into her house without knocking and find her asleep on the sofa. She looks so peaceful and serene that I don't have the heart to wake her. I'm exhausted, too. I haven't averaged much sleep the last few nights. After staying up waiting for Sophie to get home at night, we usually lie awake talking and don't fall asleep until two in the morning. Because we're going away, I've been getting up at six to go into the shop early to get as much done as I can. With a long drive ahead of us, a fifteen-minute power nap will do me good.

I'm woken by the sound of a creaky floor board and look up to see Sophie tip-toeing by my chair.

"Hey, Babe." I smile.

"I'm sorry," she whispers. "Go back to sleep."

I shake my head and pull her into my lap. I glance at the clock on the wall. I slept much longer than I planned. "It's too late to get your car. Molly's is closed now."

"I can have Ryan take me to pick it up in the morning."

I smirk and shake my head again. *This will be fun.* "You won't be here in the morning."

"What?" Her eyebrows squish together. "Where will I be?"

I slap my hands together and rub them back and forth. "You and I are going away for a few days."

Surprise sparks in her eyes before her expression turns to one of disappointment. "But I have to work."

I shake my head and smirk once again. "I already talked to Randy. He's giving you the next three days off."

She leans away with big eyes. "What? When did you talk to him?"

"Earlier today. He was totally cool with it."

Skeptical, she arches a questioning eyebrow.

I wrap my arms around her hips. "Trust me. It's all good."

"Are you sure?"

"Call him. He'll tell you."

Sophie takes her phone from her back pocket and dials the restaurant. After a brief conversation, Randy confirms that she has the next few days off.

Sophie ends the call and pokes me in the chest. "So, Randy says you are very persuasive. Care to tell me a little about that?"

I shrug. Where there's a will, there's a way. When I want something bad enough, I'll do whatever it takes to make it happen. "I convinced a couple of your co-workers to work in your place. Hannah and Emily, I think their names were."

"Exactly how did you convince them?" She crosses her arms.

"I'm paying them."

"You're paying them? Why isn't Randy paying them?"

"He is." I clear my throat and pray she doesn't make a big deal out of it. "I agreed to double their earnings for each night."

She gasps and holds her hand over her mouth. "Oh my God, Rooter. You can't do that. They could earn as much as four hundred bucks each!"

"No worries, Babe." I squeeze her thigh affectionately. "We need this time away together. I don't care what it costs."

She giggles and shakes her head. "You're crazy. I can't believe you did that."

"Do you remember me telling you there's very little I wouldn't do for you?" I press my face into her neck. "I'm trying to make things right so we can get back on track," I say and place a delicate kiss on her lips. "I never want you to doubt your importance to me. You are priceless."

She draws in a sharp breath. "I don't know what to say."

"Don't say anything." I chuckle and slap her on the ass. "Go pack a bag woman. We need to get on the road."

"We're leaving tonight?"

I glance at the clock. I had planned on already being on the road. "Yep, and we need to get going."

"Don't you need to pack?" she asks as I follow her up the stairs.

"I packed yesterday. All I need to do is load it into the truck."

"Oh." She walks to her closet, biting the inside of her cheek as she stares inside. "What should I pack? I don't even know where we're going."

"It's a surprise. All I'll say is to pack that yellow bikini you were wearing the day we met." I wink and her cheeks turn pink.

"That doesn't help much."

"Don't worry about it." I wave a hand in the air. "If you need something when we're there, we'll buy it."

"You are too much."

"No, I'm not." I gaze into her beautiful eyes. "Sophie, there's no such thing as too much when it comes to you and from here on out, I'm going to prove it."

After two hours and nineteen minutes of driving, I pull my truck onto the brick driveway and park next to a red Mercedes.

The place is picturesque with its red shutters and wrap around porch. The setting sun casts an orange glow all around us. Through the picture windows, you can see the sun streaming throughout the house.

Sophie's jaw is slack as she takes in our surroundings.

"Welcome home, Babe," I say and she gasps. "For the next three days, anyway."

She blinks in disbelief. "We're staying here?"

"Yep," I give her a quick peck on the cheek. "Wait until you see the back."

"You've been here?"

I nod. "I rode up the day before yesterday to check it out." I open my door and step out. "Stay here a minute."

I rush to Ella, the owner, who's standing on the porch with a kind smile on her face. She's an older woman, likely in her late fifties, with blonde hair. She's a bit overweight, but it suits her.

"Hi Ella," I return her smile. "Sorry we're a little late. I hope it wasn't an imposition."

"Not at all. It gave me time to enjoy the back deck." She hands me the keys. "I love it here."

"I can see why."

"The housekeeper was here today. Groceries and packages were delivered as your mother requested. Everything should be all set."

"Thank you for working with us to coordinate everything. I'd like you to meet my girl, Sophie."

Sophie opens the truck door as we approach and I help her out.

"Ella, this is Sophie," I drape my arm proudly around Sophie's waist. "Sophie, this is Ella, the owner of the house."

With a smile, Sophie extends her hand. "Nice to meet you, Ella. The house is beautiful."

"Thank you. I hope you have a lovely stay."

"I'm sure we will."

"I'll get out of your hair," Ella says and turns to me. "If you need anything, please call me. My phone is on twenty-four hours a day."

"Will do," I say.

Once Ella pulls out of the driveway, Sophie and I walk hand in hand to the house. My insides buzz with anticipation. Sophie looks around, taking everything in as we reach the front door. I open it and stand to the side to let her enter first.

My eyes are glued to Sophie as she walks into the great room. Her eyebrows raise and she draws in a long, deep breath as she scans the room. Even I have to admit the place is beautiful. As a guy, aesthetics mean little to me, but I appreciate a nice house when I see one.

The interior is decorated in a nautical theme with light colored furniture and white walls. The ceiling is vaulted and the floors are a dark, wide plank wood. Sophie moseys over to the sofa and brushes her hand across the material. Her smile widens, and she turns to me and jumps up and down.

"I can't believe you brought me here."

"You like it?" I ask, although the answer is obvious.

Her eyes sparkle as she drapes her arms around my neck. "It's amazing, Rooter. Thank you."

"You deserve this, especially after everything…"

She quiets me by pressing her index finger to my lips. "Let's not talk about any of that."

She pulls me in for a kiss. I wrap my arms around her waist and draw her to me so that the line of her body is pressed against mine. First, I kiss her top lip then her bottom, pulling it into my mouth. Jesus, she tastes sweet. I slide my tongue into her mouth and kiss her slowly. Heat radiates from her body as she sweeps her fingers through my hair. I reach for her ass and the kiss turns into wild passion. I need to pull away now otherwise, I won't be able to. And I doubt she'll stop me. As much as I want her, I don't want to ruin what I have planned for us. For her.

"We need to stop," I pant.

"No, we don't." She grabs the waist of my jeans and pulls me back to her.

The heat of her fingertips sears my skin, but when she licks those perfect lips, it's torturous. The desire swimming in her eyes makes it hard to think straight, but I'm determined to stick to my plan.

"Remember what I said on our first date about anticipation?"

"You're not playing that game with me again." She tugs on my belt.

I chuckle and reach for her hand. "It's not a game, Babe. I'm not going to put my hands on you again until I know it's right, and the moment is perfect."

"Fine, don't put your hands on me. I'll put mine on you." A devious grin spreads across her lips as she grabs my ass.

"You'll thank me later."

"I doubt it." She sticks out her bottom lip.

Jesus, I can't believe I'm saying no to sex with Sophie. The girl of my dreams—the only woman I've ever loved. It's not easy. Images of her naked body against mine, the sounds she'll make as I touch her, and the way it'll feel when I move inside her…

I've never been one to delay gratification, but being with Sophie isn't about pleasure. It's about showing her how much I care for and love her. Sure, if I took her into the bedroom right now and made love to her, it'd be the most incredible experience of my life. But it's not about me. It's about her. I want our first time together to be perfect for her. I want it to be unforgettable.

To distract Sophie, and myself, I give her a tour of the property. I guide her through the kitchen to the french doors that lead to the backyard deck. As we step outside, her lips part and the smile she's already wearing broadens as she presses a palm to her cheek. I lead her across the huge deck to the pool and jacuzzi and past the outdoor kitchen. At the far end of the deck we come to a stone path and I guide her to the top of the stairs that go down to the beach.

"We have our own private beach," I say, "a boat, and a pair of jet skis. You once said you wanted to try paddle boarding. There's two of those as well."

She gasps. "Rooter, this is beyond perfect."

"But it gets better."

"I don't know how it possibly could."

"Notice how my phone hasn't rung since we got on the road?"

She nods.

I retrieve the burner phone from my back pocket and hold it up for her to see. "This is a burner. Only my mom and pop have the number. I left my phone with them."

Sophie throws her arms around me and squeals. "Oh my God! Rooter, you do not understand what this means to me."

"Yeah, I do," I chuckle at her enthusiasm and pull away. Placing both hands on the sides of her face, I gaze into the sweetest blue eyes

I've ever seen. "Babe, the next three days are for you and me alone. No world. No distractions. Just the two of us."

I place a delicate kiss on her forehead followed by the tip of her nose and her lips. I've never seen her this happy. This is exactly what I was hoping for. As we kiss, Sophie's fingers sneak under my t-shirt, skating across my torso and the sensitive skin just above the waist of my jeans. I moan into her mouth as she presses the entire length of her body against mine.

"You're not going to make this easy for me, are you?" I pant, my resolve nearly obliterated.

"No way."

I place another kiss on the tip of her nose. "Come on, let's go see the rest of the house."

Once inside, Sophie suggests a drink and wonders if there's anything in the house. I open the wine and booze cabinet. I had Ella stock it with Jack Daniels along with champagne and other things I think Sophie might like. I tell her to pour us a couple glasses while I bring our bags into the cottage.

Once I'm back inside, she hands me a glass and holds hers up for a toast. "To the best three days ever."

"To making things right with my girl. And being a better boyfriend." I vow from this moment on to do just that. Sophie will never be happy about my predicament with Candace. As long as I make uninterrupted, quality time for the two of us, she can be and will be happy with me. It's all about balance, as my mom always says.

I show her the rest of the house including a spare bedroom, bathroom, theatre room, and a billiards room. But I save the best for last. The master suite.

We stand before an impressive set of closed double doors. My heart races as I turn the handle. I remember the first time I saw the room. I knew it was the place I wanted to make love with Sophie the first time. I open the doors and motion for her to walk in ahead of me. Again, her expression is one of astonishment and wonder.

The room is stunning with the backdrop of the sunset from the floor to ceiling windows. There's a large wood burning fireplace, and on the wall facing the king size bed, there's an enormous flat screen television with built in surround sound speakers. There is also a built-in bookshelf. In front of the windows, on the far side of the room is a fancy, light gray couch. The light-colored furnishings are a perfect contrast to the gleaming, dark wood floors.

Sophie sets her drink down on the bookshelf then leaps onto the bed. Her hair falls around her face on the white comforter. She looks like an angel. I jump onto the bed next to her and kiss her palm.

"This is perfect," she murmurs and turns to me. "It's the most beautiful thing I've ever seen."

"It's not even close to the most beautiful thing I've ever seen." I roll on top of Sophie, straddling her legs. Her chest rises and falls and her glassy eyes vacillate from my eyes to my mouth as she licks her lips. I fantasize about what is going to happen right here on this bed. It's just a matter of time before I make her mine, completely.

"I want you," Sophie murmurs huskily.

Those words are like magic to my ears. Unable to resist, I claim her mouth hard and fast. Her sweetness is mixed with the taste of the whiskey. Like an automatic reflex, my hand moves to the hem of her shirt to lift it over her head. But I stop myself before I do and quickly roll off the bed.

That was close.

She turns to me with a ridiculously cute pout and I laugh and hold my hand out for her.

"How about a swim?" I suggest. Cold water would do me some good. Then again, maybe not. Sophie in a bikini could be my undoing.

She looks at me as if I'm speaking a foreign language. Her eyes travel the length of my body, lingering for a moment on the bulge in my jeans. "How about we stay right here," she pats the bed where I was just lying, "and play I'll show you mine?"

An image of Sophie's perfect naked body assaults my mind. I swallow and beg myself to stay strong. The memory of her nipples in my mouth and my hand slipping into her panties… I shake my head to clear the thoughts. "Not tonight, Babe."

"Are you sure? I'm wearing that black and red bra and panty set you like so much."

Christ. She'll be the death of me. "You're killing me."

"You know you want to." She bats her eyes and points at my crotch. "I can see how much you want to."

"Yes, I do. And we will. But not tonight." I grab her by the hand and pull her up from the bed. If we don't get the hell out of here… "Let's swim."

The Seduction

My internal clock won't let me sleep in, much as I'd like to. I slide out of the bed, careful not to wake Sophie and go to the kitchen to make a pot of coffee. While it brews, I get the ingredients out for french toast. Once the coffee is finished, I take Sophie a cup along with a note to stay put until I return.

A half hour later, I carry the tray of french toast with powdered sugar, fresh fruit, and a vase holding a single yellow rose into the bedroom. The flower is from one of the rose bushes in the backyard. I spied it yesterday when I was giving Sophie the tour of the property. Yellow is her favorite. As soon as I saw it, I knew I would give it to her with breakfast.

Sophie's sitting upright, holding the coffee mug. She stares at me, with big eyes as I place the food tray in the middle of the bed.

"Good morning," I say and give her a gentle kiss.

She presses a hand to her chest. "Breakfast in bed?"

"You like french toast, right?" *Please say yes.*

She touches one of the flower petals. "I love it."

"Good."

"Have you been up long?"

"Just long enough to make breakfast." I hand her a fork.

She cuts a piece of toast and moans the instant she puts it into her mouth. "This is delicious."

Growing up, french toast was my favorite breakfast. This is the first time I've had it in years. Being with Sophie has wreaked havoc on my strict diet, but it's worth it.

"What do you want to do today?" We can do whatever she wants to do during the day, but I have the evening all planned.

"I think I want to try paddle boarding."

"Okay." I wink to watch her cheeks flush.

"New rule. You're not allowed to wink at anyone but me."

I chuckle. "Why?"

"Because it's ridiculously hot."

"Oh yeah?" I wink again.

"Like you don't know." Her expression turns sullen, and she breaks eye contact.

Taken by surprise, I watch for a moment as she drifts away with her thoughts. When she finally looks back to me, she says nothing. I need to know what she's thinking.

"Where'd you go just then?"

"Nowhere." She smiles, but it doesn't reach her eyes.

"Don't lie. You went somewhere, and it didn't look like a very happy place."

She hesitates. "I'd rather not say."

"Sophie," I lace my fingers with hers, "I want you to be able to talk to me."

"I know I can talk to you. But sometimes I think things that are really... Stupid."

"Things like what?"

She looks down and blows out a breath. "I sometimes find myself jealous of the girls before me."

She wouldn't be jealous if she understood the depth of my feelings for her. No one before Sophie meant anything to me. It was all wasted time. Me sowing my oats, so to speak. I honestly can't remember a single experience that came before her. Yet I can remember, in vivid detail, each and every time I've kissed and touched Sophie. With my index and middle finger, I tilt her chin up so that our eyes meet. "Babe, there's nothing to be jealous of. There was never anyone before you. It was just…"

I stop before the word escapes my mouth.

Sophie nods, knowing what I was going to say, but the look in her eyes tells me my words don't make her feel any better. She twists the comforter between her fingers, revealing a deep insecurity.

"Sophie, you're the only one who has ever mattered to me. What you need to realize is," I motion back and forth between us, "this has never happened with anyone else."

"I know that," her voice is so small. "But I still get jealous."

I understand. I have insecurities too. No way will I ever be good enough for Sophie. I'm completely fucked up and I'm having a kid with another girl. Sophie deserves so much better than me, and one day, she might find it. "If it makes you feel better, I get jealous over guys who don't even exist."

"What?"

"Every day, especially lately," I drag my fingers through my hair. I could choke on my vulnerability. But if I expect Sophie to open up to me, I must do the same with her, "I worry someone better will come along—someone without all the baggage I have—and that he'll steal you away from me."

Sophie gasps and shakes her head. "That's not even possible. You're the only guy I've ever wanted. Even with everything… I couldn't want anyone the way I want you."

Her words are comforting, but I'm still afraid. If I continue to let Sophie down, I could lose her. She still might decide the baby is too much and break up with me. Candace might never back down and push Sophie to the brink that she walks away. Or, perhaps she'll meet a better man and kick my ass to the curb. But for now, she's mine and despite the odds that are stacked against us, I'm determined to keep it that way.

I lean in and stroke her cheek. "And I have never and will never want anyone the way I want you."

I've seen people on paddle boards. They make it look so easy.

It's not easy. At. All.

For what seems like the fiftieth time, I've lost my balance and fallen into the water. Sophie laughs as she stands, gracefully atop her board. She fell a couple times in the beginning, but before long was paddling along like a champ. I feel like a fool. Probably look like one, too. My pride is officially in the toilet.

"Can we try something different?" I whine as I wade in the water, hanging on the edge of the board.

"Fine by me. Your turn to pick though."

"Jet skis." I can ride the shit out of a jet ski.

As we put the boards away Sophie says she's never been on a jet ski. I offer for her to ride with me, but independent as ever, she shakes her head.

I put Sophie on one of the jet skis and show her how to start it up, then I explain that the throttle is very touchy. Just barely touch it to get going or she could throw herself off the ski. The more I think about this, the more I wish she'd ride with me. But, she's an intelligent, capable woman. She'll figure it out.

Once I'm confident she understands the basics, I hop on the other ski and we take off along the shore. Sophie rides alongside me at ten miles per hour for a while. When she speeds up, I stay beside her.

"I love this!" she hollers.

"Want to go a little faster?"

Sophie nods and I speed up to thirty miles per hour. She keeps up with me, but it's a windy day, and with the tall waves, she catches a lot of air. Scared she'll get hurt, I make her slow down.

"I'm going to do a couple tricks," I say before pulling away.

She watches as I jump waves and do donuts in the water. I like jet skiing almost as much as riding my Harley. After twenty minutes of playing around, we cruise up the shoreline, checking out the scenery and mansions. I'll never be able to afford a big, extravagant house on the lake, but maybe one day I'll get a little fixer upper. I can see Sophie and me, in our forties or fifties, finding a small cottage. Me and the guys will do the hard labor renovations. Sophie can help me paint and we'll decorate together.

I can envision a future with Sophie. I can see us getting married one day and even having kids. We could have such a great life together. I'm going to do everything I can to make sure we do.

"That was so much fun," Sophie squeals after we tie the jet skis up to the dock. Her eyes squint as she smiles.

Now is the moment of truth. The moment when all of my meticulous planning comes together to reveal my big surprise. My heart races and my chest is tight. I'm more nervous than excited. This is new territory for me. I've never made a grand romantic gesture to seduce a woman. Never had to. Never wanted to. Until now.

Hand in hand, we walk up the stairs to the cottage. I'm so anxious I could puke.

"Did you have fun?" she asks with discernible concern.

"Of course." I bring her hand to my lips.

"You're being quiet."

"Am I?" The closer we get to the top of the stairs, the harder my heart beats.

"Yeah. Is everything okay?"

"Everything is perfect." I hear soft music playing. A few steps more and we can see the backyard.

Sophie gasps and holds her hand to her chest. "Rooter, this is…"

It's exactly what I asked for. Red and white rose petals are scattered along the pathway to the deck where a table is set for our dinner. There are vases of red and white roses placed sporadically around the deck. And just as I requested, there's a giant arrangement of long stem red roses in the center of the table. Along with the vases of roses, there are just as many candles strewn about, although they've yet to be lit. Vic and Martha, the husband and wife caterers my mom hired, are working in the outdoor kitchen preparing our meal.

"Why don't you go inside and get a shower?" I propose. "I need to talk to Vic and Martha."

I don't really need to talk to them, but dinner should be ready soon and we need time to get ready. After checking in with them, I head to the second bedroom to get showered. I hear the shower running in the master bedroom. I open the door to make sure Sophie has received the package containing her outfit for tonight—a dress Isa helped me pick out complete with jewelry, shoes, and lingerie. The lingerie was Isa's idea. She explained that I needed to make sure Sophie had the right under garments to wear under the dress. Fine with me. I was more than happy to pick out lingerie for Sophie to wear.

Before leaving the room, I scribble a note asking Sophie to wear her hair down. She's always beautiful, but I love it when her hair is down. On my way out, I pause and listen to her in the bathroom and wonder if she's half as excited as I am.

I've worn a suit exactly three times in my life. Each time was for a funeral. I hoped I'd never have to wear one again, until now. Tonight, I'm actually looking forward to wearing this monkey suit. It's charcoal gray and I've paired it with a black shirt and tie. It's a tad snug. The last time I wore it was over a year ago, and I've packed on a considerable amount of muscle. It looks okay though. Not too small. Thank God, because I hadn't thought to try it on before now.

Standing in front of the full-length mirror on the back of the closet door, I fidget with the tie trying to make it perfect. I'm not the best with ties, but it'll have to do. It's not like I can call Sophie in to help.

Sophie.

I can't stop thinking of her. The anticipation of seeing her when she emerges from the bedroom is killing me. Through the wall, I hear her moving about. Is she dressed already? Is her makeup done? Does she like what I bought for her? How does she look in the white bustier? I shake my head on the last thought.

It could be awhile before she's ready so I pour myself a shot of Jack and go outside to wait. About a half hour later I hear the clacking of heels on the wood of the deck. I stand from my seat at the dinner table and turn to see my girl.

The sight of Sophie is like being hit square in the chest by a wrecking ball. I can't get to her fast enough. Everything moves in slow motion. A new word needs to be created to describe how incredible she looks. She's beyond beautiful. Beyond perfect. The woman has robbed me of all oxygen. I literally have no breath. The white, strapless dress clings to her in all the right places and shows off her second best feature—those long, long legs. As I requested, her dark hair hangs in loose waves over her shoulders.

"You are gorgeous," I say and reach for her hand.

Her eyes travel the length of my body and she whispers, "So are you."

"I clean up all right." I pull out a chair for her to join me at the table. I'm trying to stay cool, but the way she's staring has me amped up.

"I think I need one of those," she says, referring to my glass of Jack.

I fill a glass with ice and pour the whiskey. After handing her the drink, I raise mine for a toast. "To a perfect night with the most beautiful woman I've ever seen."

"To you, and what is sure to be the best night of my life."

Damn right it'll be the best night of your life. By the time this night is over, there won't be an inch of your body I haven't tasted.

Without breaking eye contact, we each sip our whiskey. All I can think about is my tongue on Sophie's skin. Everywhere. Fuck dinner. I'd rather taste her.

Sophie licks her lips and her desire filled eyes travel from mine to my lips to my chest and back up. She sucks in her bottom lip. I'd give my last dollar for her to tell me what she's thinking right now. She raises her hand to her throat and licks her lips again.

"You're going to have to quit looking at me like that," I lean forward and breathe her in, "or we'll never make it through dinner."

"That's fine by me." She takes another sip of her Jack.

Tempting. But I'm still determined to play this out according to plan.

"You'll need to eat with what I have planned for you." I wink and it causes her to choke. "You all right?"

"Mm-hmm." She shifts in her seat. She's every bit as affected by me as I am her.

"Do you like the dress?"

"I love it."

I reach down and take a piece of her layered skirt between my index finger and thumb. "When I saw it, I knew it was the one."

"When did you go shopping for all this?"

"On Monday." I lean back in my chair. "Isa went with me."

Sophie shakes her head. "You really went above and beyond with all of this. But what if I hadn't been ready for... this?"

I know what she's asking. With everything that's happened, what if she had decided we needed to take a step back and wait a little longer? I don't need sex to be happy with Sophie. I still would have brought her here to spend quality time together. And I would've been just as happy to be with her as I am right now. "Then tonight would've gone a little differently."

She raises her eyebrows. "You had a plan B?"

"I always have a plan B, Babe." I sip my Jack.

"Of course you do." She pauses. "Would you have been disappointed?"

With everything that's happened, even as I planned this getaway, I knew there was a chance she might change her mind about sex. And that would be okay.

I shake my head. "No. That's not what this trip is about, Sophie. It's about you and me reconnecting. If we make love, that'll just be a bonus."

She arches a brow. "If?"

"I never assume anything." We haven't had the best track record.

"And yet you've made all these arrangements." She waves at our surroundings before looking down to her dress.

"I said I don't assume not that I don't hope." I wink again and watch as her face turns pink.

Martha comes to the table and asks if we're ready for dinner. I tell her not yet and she says she'll check in with us in a few minutes.

Sophie swallows the rest of her shot and I refill it. I want her to be relaxed, but I don't want a repeat of the night of Miranda's birthday party. I won't make love with her when she's trashed and I don't want her passing out on me. That definitely isn't part of the plan.

"For a guy who's never had a girlfriend, you do romance very well."

Never thought a woman would say those words to me. "I can't take all the credit. I had help."

"Yeah?"

"After you told me I needed to make uninterrupted time for us, I came up with the idea of getting away. But I wanted to make it special." I skim the top of her hand with my thumb. "I don't know what girls want so I went to my mom. We talked about you and the things you like. She helped me find this place and got me in touch with Vic and Martha. Isa gave me the idea for the dress."

"I'll be sure to thank them when we get back."

"My mom loves you. Said you're the best thing to ever happen to me." I drag my hand through my hair at my next thought. "She was so pissed when I told her Candace is pregnant. She smacked me upside the head and cussed me out in Spanish." I laugh, nervous.

Sophie doesn't respond. Just stares at me.

I hadn't planned on talking about Candace, but there are things I need to say. "Sophie, you were so mad. Honestly, I was afraid too much damage had been done. That things would never be the same with us. It scared the shit out of me. It still scares me."

"Things have changed." She shifts in her seat. "There's no denying that. But, my feelings for you haven't changed."

And for that I am grateful. "We haven't been together very long, but I knew I wanted you a long time ago. I had it so bad that I'd sit in my room at night with the light out and watch you study in yours."

"Stalker," she giggles. It's the cutest sound.

"I knew being with me wouldn't be easy for you, even without Candace and a kid. But I just couldn't stay away from you any longer."

She takes my hand into hers. "It took you long enough to change your mind."

"You deserve so much better than me. I struggle with that knowledge every day because I want better for you, but I want you for myself more."

"I already told you. You're all I want."

"I can't imagine why. But now I have you, I'll never let you go."

"I hope not."

I lean forward and motion for her to give me her other hand. "I need to be real with you right now."

"Okay."

"I'll try to give you everything you want and need. But life with me isn't going to be like the life you had planned."

"I don't care about those plans. I made them before I knew what I really wanted."

I smile, but continue. I need Sophie to be absolutely sure that a life with me is what she wants. She needs to know exactly what she's getting into with me and I need to know she can handle it. "I'm going fuck up and piss you off… a lot."

"I'm beginning to figure that out. But even after everything that's happened, this is still where I want to be."

"Babe, I'll never do anything to purposely hurt or upset you. I'll never lie or cheat. But I am what I am. You understand?"

"Yeah." She nods. "You're complicated."

I tilt my head to the side and sigh. "That's putting it mildly."

"Just promise me no more Candace's or surprise babies."

"I can definitely promise you that." I look down at the table and inhale deeply. This is the scariest, most vulnerable moment of my entire life. I pray she doesn't freak out. "You own me Sophia Noelle Holt. My heart is yours."

Sophie gasps, but I continue before she can speak. I have to get it all out. "I started falling for you way before that first conversation in your back yard. But that first moment I looked into your eyes, there was no going back." I take another breath. "I'm in love with you."

A tear falls from her left eye down her cheek. I wipe it away with my thumb. "Rooter, I—"

I place my fingers on her lips. "I don't know what you're getting ready to say, but if you're getting ready to tell me you love me, don't say it. Not yet. I haven't earned it."

When she nods, I lower my hand.

"We'll have tough days," I say, "but I promise to make more days like this for you."

Sophie's eyes are still glossy, but they are filled with excitement and happiness. "I don't expect days like this. All I wanted was a little time for you and me."

I know she doesn't have high expectations. She'd be happy to just hang out watching a movie or going for a ride on my Harley, but this is what she deserves. She deserves to be cherished like the precious treasure she is.

Martha clears her throat to let us know she's returned. Dinner was done a while ago. If we wait much longer, it'll be ruined.

"Ready to eat?" I ask Sophie. "I don't think the food will keep much longer."

"Sure."

I'm nowhere near ready to eat. On the way here, I was starved. But after confessing my love and thinking of what lies ahead of us tonight, my stomach is spinning. But I wasn't kidding when I said Sophie needs to eat for what I have in store for her. If things go my way, and I believe they will, tonight's going to be a long night.

After dinner, Martha and Vic begin cleaning up. It'll be a while before they're finished. Overly excited and anxious, I need a distraction. Perhaps a walk on the beach will cool me down. I stand and take my suit jacket off. I kick my shoes off and remove my socks before crouching in front of Sophie and removing her sandals.

"Walk with me?" I stand and extend my hand.

"I'd love to."

The sun is starting to sink below the horizon as we stand at the edge of the water on the beach. It's a balmy night. Even with my jacket and shoes off, I'm hot. Sophie closes her eyes and takes a deep breath as her hair blows in the breeze. I'm mesmerized. I never imagined I'd ever care for someone this deeply. It almost hurts.

"Stop staring," Sophie says before turning to catch me in the act.

"I can't help it. I like seeing you happy and relaxed." I sit in the sand and motion for her to join me.

"I'll get my dress dirty."

"You won't be wearing it much longer anyway."

She acts appalled. "I thought you said you don't assume things."

"What?" I play innocent. "All I said is you won't be wearing the dress much longer. That's not an assumption, it's a fact. It's not like you're going to sleep in it."

"Mm-hmm, we both know what you meant."

I tug her onto my lap. "Hey, I'm a guy. I can always hope."

"You don't have to hope. I'm a sure thing."

I lean into her neck and moan. "God you smell good."

Sophie brushes my hair with her fingers. "You didn't really want to go for a walk, did you?"

I shake my head. If it wasn't for the fact that Vic and Martha are back at the cottage cleaning, I would be in full seduction mode right now. "Is it that obvious?"

Sophie holds her hand up with her thumb and index finger measuring less than an inch. "Just a little."

I laugh. She sees right through me. "Vic and Martha need time to clean up. I was going to try to play it cool like it was part of my plan to be romantic but…"

"You know what they say about anticipation." She wags her eyebrows.

"Fuck anticipation. This is agony." We laugh.

"How long are we supposed to wait?"

"An hour," I groan again.

The time drags. And drags. And drags. We sit mostly in silence listening to the sound of the waves. I check my phone too often. I can't help it. I'm about to bust. I try to calm down by telling myself I've waited what seems like forever to be with Sophie. Another few minutes isn't the end of the world. But damn. Ten minutes feels like ten hours. When the sun has completely set, I check my phone again.

I kiss Sophie on the temple. "We can go back now."

The closer we get to the top of the stairs the faster my heart beats. I'm breathless and lightheaded. My chest feels like it's swelling. And Sophie smells so good and looks even better. It's hard to not throw her over my shoulder and go straight to the bedroom. I'm sure she wouldn't complain, but I want to do better for her. I plan to seduce her until she can't take anymore.

As I requested, Vic and Martha left a few candles burning. On the table where we ate dinner is a bottle of Dom Perignon with a pair of crystal glasses.

I pop the cork and pour us both a glass, not filling them quite to the top. Sophie doesn't like wine. She may not like champagne. I hand her a glass and clink it with mine. She lifts the glass to her lips for a sip before drinking almost the entire glass. I smile, happy that she likes it.

"You really thought of everything," she says.

"More?" I ask and hold the bottle up.

"Please." I fill her glass to the top and she takes a sip. "This is really good."

I show her the label. "It's supposed to be the best."

"You're spoiling me."

"You deserve it." I wink on purpose.

Sophie's face flushes and her lips part. Her eyes are locked on mine. She fidgets with her hair and her dress. She wants me, and is ready for me to make my move. But I'm going to take my time and drag this out as long as I can.

I step up and pull her against me. "We're going to take this slow. So slow that you'll be completely satisfied before you even feel me inside of you."

The First Time

Sophie's chest heaves with fast breaths. She stares at my lips, her eyes begging for a kiss. I can almost see the naughty thoughts streaming through her mind. I lean in and brush her lips with mine before pulling away with a smirk. Her reaction is exactly what I want—pure dissatisfaction. I step back, swallow what's left of my champagne, and take Sophie by the hand to lead her into the living room.

With only one lamp on, the room is nearly dark. Martha has put on the music I asked for. I draw Sophie to me so that our bodies are flush and move to the beat of the slow, seductive music.

"By the time this night is over," I start, "I'll have made love to every inch of your body."

I caress her long, soft neck with one hand as the other sneaks down to her backside. She moans and tilts her head to the side as I suck the delicate skin just below her jawbone.

How can anyone taste so good?

I back away and do away with my tie. The sexual tension between us is palpable. Sophie chews on her bottom lip as I pop open the top two buttons on my shirt. As incredible as she looks in her dress, I want it off. Now. If I wasn't determined to take things slow, I'd tear the damned thing off this second.

I gesture for Sophie to finish her champagne. After she empties the glass, I take it and set it on a nearby table. We resume dancing and she wraps her arms around my neck as I place a series of kisses from her collar bone to her neck. I take her earlobe into my mouth and flick it with my tongue.

Damn, I want her mouth on my body. Anywhere. Everywhere. I kiss her fast and hard as I imagine her mouth on my neck, my waist… My cock. The thought of being in her mouth is almost too much to bear.

"You make me so hard." I grind against her.

"I can feel you," Sophie murmurs.

You haven't felt anything yet, Babe. Just wait until I'm inside you.

I spin Sophie around so her back is to my front. As we dance, my hands slide up from her hips to her breasts. My mouth waters as I fantasize about sucking them. I brush her hair to the side and lick the silky skin between her shoulder blades up to her neck.

"You taste amazing." Unable to wait a moment longer, I reach for the zipper on her dress. "I want to see you."

Sophie's breath catches as I pull the zipper down, bit by bit. The dress falls into a pile on the floor and I draw in a breath. Christ almighty, I am the luckiest bastard alive. "Perfect."

I palm her pert, bare ass and take my time walking around her so I can take in every curve of Sophie's flawless body. If I was ever unsure of God's existence, I'm not now. Only He could create something, someone, so magnificent. And he designed her specifically for me. The vision of my sweet, innocent Sophie in the see-through bustier sends electricity through my entire body. I caress her left breast, grazing the tip of her rose colored nipple with my thumb. Her eyes roll back in her head at my touch.

"I love the color of your nipples." I pinch the nipple though not hard enough to hurt her. "You're so fucking hot in this. I might not take it off."

Her eyes flit open. "But how will you put your mouth on me?"

"Don't worry. I'm going to put my mouth on every millimeter of your body."

She whimpers in pleasure when I squeeze her nipple again.

"You like that?" I ask and tweak the other nipple, recalling how much she liked it that day in her bed.

She doesn't answer, but unbuttons my shirt and drags her fingernails down my chest to my waist. She slides the shirt over my shoulders to remove it, but the cuffs are still buttoned and it gets caught around my wrists. I unfasten the cuffs and drop the garment to the floor.

Sophie's fingertips are lava hot as she traces the tattoo on my side, up my shoulder and down my arm. The hair on my forearm raises at her subtle touch. Desire rages inside me—a fire I can't contain. I pull her to me and crush her mouth with my own. We are like an explosion, hands and mouths everywhere.

And then her hand finds my cock. She grips me. Just. Right.

Jesus.

It's too much.

If I don't slow this down, I'll be inside her in zero point one seconds. It's almost impossible, but somehow I find the strength to peel her fingers away.

I bring her hand to my mouth and whisper, "Slow."

"But I want to touch you."

She's all but begging. I can't believe I'm putting on the brakes.

"And I want you to touch me, but if you do it now, I'll lose control."

"That's okay with me."

"Eager, are we?" I wink.

"Wink at me again and *I'll* lose control and you won't be able to stop me from putting my hands on you."

"Is that right?" I wink again.

"That's not fair. Do you have any idea what that does to me?"

I know exactly what it does to her, but I shake my head. "Why don't you tell me?"

Before she can answer, I bring her wrist to my mouth and slide my tongue along the delicate skin up to the inside of her elbow. When I blow on the wet skin, she shivers.

"That's what I'm going to do to your entire body." I say and turn Sophie toward the hallway to the bedroom and point. "Walk."

Sophie's hips roll and her ass sways back and forth as she walks. My entire body is taut with need. My dick is painfully swollen. My fingers ache to touch her again. We reach the bed and I command her to turn around. My eyes land on her hardened nipples. Desperate for relief I take my cock into my hand. "Lay back on the bed."

Sophie slides onto the bed, staring at my bulge, as I unfasten my belt. I drop my pants to the floor, but keep on my boxer briefs. Sophie continues to stare, panting. Waiting. Wanting. The yearning in her expression matches my own. But I refuse to satisfy my need until I've tasted every inch of her skin.

I bring her foot to my mouth and drag my tongue along the instep. She tries to pull away but I keep hold of her and lick again. She cries out with delight. I crawl onto the bed and lick from her calf up to her inner thigh. "You taste so good, Babe."

Sophie's chest rises and falls with fast, shallow breaths. I recall the sight of her ass as I followed her to the bedroom and flip her onto her stomach. I place an open mouth kiss on her right ass cheek, nibbling the soft skin before moving to the left side. She moans and squirms as I suck, nibble, and kiss the length of her leg before licking the instep of that foot.

"Does that feel good?" I ask.

"So good."

I roll Sophie over again and situate myself between her legs. I press my hardness into her center and moan at the sensation. Fantasies of sliding inside her flood my mind. If not for my boxers and her panties, I wouldn't be able to resist pushing inside her. But I'm determined make this great for her. I kiss and nibble her left arm up to her shoulder, across her collarbone, to the right shoulder and down that arm. "You're beautiful, Sophie."

Her breasts taunt me through the sheer lace of the bustier. I see, but can't feel the soft, supple skin. I lift Sophie's arms above her head and begin untying the laces. It takes decades to get it open. I place my hand on the satiny skin between her breasts. Sophie's tongue rolls with mine as my hand glides from her chest to her waist before caressing her left breast. She's so warm, soft, responsive. I roll her hardened nipple between my thumb and index finger and she arches her back.

"I love how you respond to my touch," I whisper before taking her breast into my mouth.

Sophie cries out, whimpering and squirming as I nibble, suck, and tease her with my tongue and teeth. I pull back and blow cool air onto her wet skin and watch as goosebumps form on her skin.

Fucking beautiful. And you're mine.

I take the skin beneath her nipple into my mouth and suck to leave a hickey. When I'm done with that breast, I move to the other. I want to leave a reminder of where my mouth has been. Not just for her, but for me. I get off knowing I'm the only one who can touch her this way. I look into Sophie's smoldering eyes and brush my tongue across her nipple.

She twists beneath me as I leave a smattering of kisses from her chest down to her waist. Sophie moans and drags her fingers through my hair. Her body trembles as she waits for me to move lower. Anticipating the moment I reach her sweet spot. I cast her a knowing smirk before lifting her legs and placing a wet kiss on her inner thigh.

God, I love teasing her.

Her legs relax and fall open as I skim the velvety flesh alongside the fabric of her thong. The scent of her arousal is sweet, feminine.

"Touch me, please," my sweet girl pleads. Her chest rises and falls with fast breaths.

As you wish, my love.

I flick my tongue against the soft skin next to Sophie's panties. I yearn to touch her where only I can touch her. To make her feel things only I can make her feel. But I also enjoy teasing her. I continue to nip and lick as she quivers and writhes beneath me.

When I'm sure she can't take another moment of my torment, I press my face to her entrance and inhale deep. Her panties are soaked with evidence of her arousal.

"You smell so fucking good," I say. "I bet you taste even better.

With my thumb, I stroke Sophie's covered slit. I massage up and down and around causing her to call out for God. I slide the thong down her legs and toss them to the floor. On my way back up, I pepper the inside of her thighs with kisses before spreading her legs wide.

The sight of Sophie completely bare sends my desire into overdrive. I need to taste her now. But before I do, I need to make sure she's comfortable. I gaze into her eyes, wordlessly seeking her approval.

"Please," she murmurs.

Sophie watches me intently as I stroke the smooth skin on the edge of her pussy. She whimpers and moans as I inch my way closer to her center. The instant my thumb finds her clit she bucks from the bed.

"You're so wet, Babe."

I continue to work her, rubbing up, down, and around. Sophie's eyes squeeze shut and her body trembles. She's moments from release.

"Rooter," she cries out.

Hearing her call out "Rooter" in the throes of passion seems wrong. I stop touching her.

"Please don't stop," she begs.

"Look in my eyes, Babe." I wait until her eyes are on mine. "When we're making love, I want you to call me Jace."

She scrunches her eyebrows, confused. I'm just as surprised. All the times I imagined her screaming my name, I never once heard her calling out "Jace." But now that we are here in the moment, that's who I want to be to her. Given the way I earned my road name, I don't want to be Rooter when I'm making love to her. I intend to make her scream "Jace" all night long.

Sophie's eyes are still on mine as I brush the tip of her clit with my thumb. Her eyes roll back into her head and I sink the tip of my middle finger inside her.

"I want to hear you say my name, Baby," I rasp before pressing my tongue to her swollen clit. She tastes incredible—sweet and feminine.

"Jace!"

The sound of Sophie screaming my name unleashes something wild and primal inside me. I've never wanted to make a woman come undone as much as I do right now. Sophie grabs my head and hollers my name again as I slide my tongue up and down her slit. I slip my tongue inside her as I continue to circle her with my thumb.

She moans deep and throaty and her body trembles and becomes rigid. Her clit is rock hard. She's so very close. I want her orgasm to linger so I slow my pace and lick languidly, waiting for her to come in my mouth. It doesn't take long. A few more sweeps of my tongue and her body falls slack. She sings my name over and over until it's barely a whisper.

It's a heady, valiant feeling, making Sophie come with my mouth. I lie next to her, watching with a smile as she holds her hand to her chest, trying to catch her breath.

Desperate for her touch, for my own release, I roll on top of her and grind myself between her legs. If it wasn't for my boxers, there'd be nothing to keep me from sinking into her. Just the thought of it makes me want to burst. I lean in for a kiss and she doesn't resist although my lips are covered in her wetness. She wraps her legs around my waist and skims the length of my back with her fingertips. Her feather-like touch is spine-tingling. But I have an urgent need for her hands to be elsewhere.

I sit up on my knees. Sophie's greedy eyes follow my hands to my cock. I grip my length and watch her watching me stroke myself on top of my boxers. She licks her lips and fondles a breast as I continue to massage myself. She never once averts her gaze. I hook my thumb in the elastic of my boxers and pull the material down, bit by bit until my cock breaks free. Sophie's eyes go wide and her hand moves subtly in my direction, but stops short of touching me. As I grip myself with one hand, I use the other to wrap her fingers around my shaft.

"Fuck that feels good," I groan, using her hand to stroke myself.

I revel in the pleasure of Sophie's hand pumping me. After a few moments, I get up from the bed to dispose of my boxers. Her raw desire is evident as she watches my every movement. That lust filled stare sets my blood on fire. I yearn for Sophie to touch and explore me the same as I have done with her. I slide into the bed beside her and lie on my back. I take her hand and place it on my shaft again, but this time I let go. I want her to touch me on her own.

She slides her hand up and down like I showed her. It's fucking sublime. Just as I close my eyes to savor the sensation I'm stunned by the warm wetness of her tongue on the tip of my cock. My eyes fly open.

"Fuck, Babe," I hiss as she swirls the head of my dick with her tongue before taking me into her mouth.

I'd hoped for this. Wondered if Sophie might take me in her mouth. But I wouldn't ask or even suggest it in any way. Some girls like it, some don't. But being that Sophie's inexperienced—for all intents and purposes she might as well be a virgin—I figured it'd take her a while to warm up to the idea. This goes beyond any of my fantasies.

Sophie licks me from base to tip, flicking the sensitive patch of skin on the underside of the head.

"Fuck yeah," I moan and grab a hold of her hair. I have to fight not to come in her mouth as she massages my balls while sucking me off.

My sweet, chaste girl is giving me the best head of my life. Her head moves up and down as she works me with her mouth. I've never been as turned on as I am in this moment. And then she looks up, holding eye contact as she continues to suck.

"I love the way your lips look wrapped around me."

Oh shit. I'm close.

Right. On. The. Brink.

And the idea of coming in Sophie's mouth... Of her swallowing.

Oh. My. God.

But this isn't what I planned.

My balls are tight, the pressure intense. It's almost painful. If I just let go, I'd find sweet release.

In a few seconds it won't matter. I'm spiraling out of control.

I'm going to come.

Just as the first shock wave of impending orgasm hits, Sophie halts. If she so much as licked my tip, I'd explode.

"You taste so good," she says and continues to massage my sac.

I can hardly breathe. "That was amazing, Babe. Come here."

I've never had virgin head. I hadn't expected it could be so... outstanding. I can't help but wonder if maybe she's done it before. I'm not her first boyfriend, after all.

A chill shoots through me. I don't want to know. As far as I'm concerned, my dick is the first to be in her mouth. Furthermore, it'll be her last and only.

My heart is still racing and I pant for air as I kiss Sophie hard and fast. She grabs my ass with both hands as I roll on top of her and situate myself between her legs. I rub my hardness up and down her wet pussy and she moans with pleasure.

"I can make you come this way," I taunt as I nibble and suck her neck.

"I know."

I stare into her eyes as I continue to grind against her. My need is immense. All-consuming. I can't wait any longer. "I need to be inside you. Are you ready?"

"Yes."

I kiss Sophie's lips, soft and sweet before reaching for a condom on the nightstand. Her eyes vacillate between the foil packet and my swollen length. I tear the package open with my teeth and wink. She watches intently as I roll the condom down my shaft.

"Look at me, Sophie." I command, gently.

She looks at me with her big, beautiful blue eyes.

"If at any time you're uncomfortable or want me to stop, tell me. Okay?"

She nods.

"I need the words, Babe."

I need Sophie to understand beyond a shadow of a doubt she's safe with me. That as much as I want this, as much as I desire her, she can change her mind anytime. If she doesn't like it or gets scared, I will stop and I won't be disappointed or angry. I love her and I'd do anything for her.

"I'll tell you."

By the confidence in her tone and the comfort in her expression, I'm convinced she's telling the truth. I lean in for a soft kiss. Only moments ago, I was revved up, eager as hell to slide into her. To feel her from the inside. And though I'm still excited, I'm no longer impatient. I remember this isn't about me and my needs. It's about Sophie. It's about showing her how much she means to me. That her trusting herself with me isn't something I take lightly. It means everything to me.

In Sophie's eyes is a mixture of adoration, excitement, and nerves. I thrust forward, entering slowly. She closes her eyes and squeezes my arms as I push all the way inside. God in Heaven, nothing has ever felt this good.

"You okay?" I kiss her cheek.

"I'm okay."

I give her time to adjust before pulling back and sliding in at the same slow pace. She moans, low and throaty. I push again, this time a little faster.

"You feel so good," I thrust a little harder and faster. I hope it's not too much. I'm trying so hard to restrain myself.

But she grabs my ass and pulls me inside with force. "You don't have to be careful. I'm okay."

I couldn't hold back if I wanted to now. I groan and sink into her swiftly, urgently again and again. She meets my thrusts, pulling me into her, every bit as desperate as I am.

"You're so tight," I moan.

When she arches her back, I take a breast into my mouth. She elicits a cock-hardening whimper as I clamp down with my teeth. The scent of sex and sweat mixed with her perfume intoxicates me. I can't get enough of her slick heat. Lost in the moment, I slam into her hard and fast. She scrapes my back with her fingernails and it revs me up more.

"Rooter!"

Right now, I'm not Rooter. "Jace. Call me Jace, Baby."

"Jace!" Her body quivers and she holds me tight.

"Come for me Baby. I want to feel you come around my cock."

Her pussy constricts around my shaft and she cries out my name with her release.

Watching her fall apart pushes me over the edge into oblivion. "Fuck, I'm going to come. You're gonna make me come, Babe."

My orgasm tears through me like a bolt of lightning, sudden and intense. I feel weightless. Being inside Sophie as I come is transcendental. It's the greatest pleasure I've ever experienced. It's as though we are one person sharing the same soul. I'm pouring my love into her as she gives hers to me.

Completely spent physically and emotionally, I can't hold myself up. I fall onto Sophie and try not to crush her.

I don't know how long it takes for me to catch my breath. Sophie's face is still flushed, our bodies are drenched. She's wearing a smile of pure satisfaction and I put it there. I kiss her cheek and roll off her with a smirk.

You're going to be wearing that smile for the rest of your life, Babe.

After discarding the condom, I climb back in bed to cuddle with my girl. I've never cuddled after sex. Never wanted to before Sophie.

"That was…" Sophie starts then pauses. "There aren't words to describe how good that was."

I caress her cheek. "Babe, you did so good."

She raises a brow.

"I don't mean to be condescending," I kiss her lips. "With what you've been through, I didn't know if you'd freak out or…"

She nods.

"You didn't seem scared or nervous at all."

"I wasn't. I trust you."

"I love you, Babe."

She peers into my eyes. "I wish you had been my first."

"I was." I draw her into my arms. "I was the first man to make love to you."

"Yes, you were." She kisses my chest.

"And I'll be the last." As much as I was her first, she was mine. She should know it. "You're the only one I've ever made love to, Sophie."

She doesn't respond right away. "You surprised me when you told me to call you Jace."

I clear my throat. "I surprised myself."

"Did you like it when I called you Jace?"

"Yeah. A lot."

"Should I call you by that name all the time?"

I shake my head. "Only when we're making love, Babe."

She holds herself up on her elbow. "If you don't like the name, why do you want me to use it when we're making love?"

I roll onto my back. "It's not that I don't like the name. It just represents a different side of me."

"A different side?"

"Jace is the person I want to be for you. Rooter is who I am."

"That's confusing." Her eyebrows squish together.

"Jace is pre-club. Innocent. Good. Like you."

"I don't need you to be innocent."

"I know." I stroke her cheek.

Sophie accepts me for who I am. She recognizes my faults and flaws and she cares for me despite them. Not too many women would be able to. I love her for it.

"So, are you ever going to tell me how you got the name, Rooter? Have I earned that," she makes air quotes, "privileged information?"

I laugh and drag my fingers through my hair. "I was hoping you'd forgotten about that."

"No chance." She chuckles and pokes me in the side.

"I don't think this is the time for that discussion." I pull her onto my chest and twist a lock of her hair.

"Why not?" She sticks out her bottom lip.

"Because I want to lay here and bask in the afterglow of making love to my woman."

"Yeah right," she chortles and tries to push away. "You don't want me to know how you got the name."

I squeeze my eyes closed. "You're right."

"Now you have to tell me."

"Keep in mind this was years ago."

"Okay."

I clear my throat and take a deep breath. I've never been embarrassed by this story until now. "Bear's dad is Australian and in Australia rooting means fu—having sex. When I first got into the Club, they were always finding me in the back room…" *God, this is humiliating.* "One day, Bear was looking for me and he asked his pop where I was. His pop told him I was in the back room pouring the root to some girl. Bear knocked on the door and said, "Hey, Rooter we need to get going." It stuck with the guys and I've been Rooter ever since."

Sophie's mouth hangs open. "That's not the story I was expecting."

"I bet not." Neither of us speaks for a minute. "What were you expecting?"

"Well, when you say Rooter the first thing that comes to mind, for me anyway, is Roto-Rooter. So I always thought you got the name because you caused a lot of plumbing trouble." She cackles.

My heart stops and I become nauseous. I want to hide. "What? Please tell me that's not what you've been thinking this entire time."

She laughs harder.

"Oh my God. I should've told you the truth a long time ago."

She stops laughing. "I think I prefer the Roto-Rooter story."

"Sophie, I'm not the same guy I was back then. You believe that don't you?"

"I do. But if you're not that guy anymore, why continue to go by the name?"

"It's a part of me now. And while it may not have the same connotation it used to… Let me put it this way, what we just did, I plan on doing a lot more of." I wink for effect. "Therefore, I am, in fact, still Rooter."

"And yet, you don't want me to call you Rooter while we do it." Her voice is thick with sarcasm. "Makes sense."

Back To Reality

It's our last night here at the cabin. Sophie and I are sitting on the back patio, basking in the evening sun, enjoying the lake view. She holds her camera up to take a picture of the scenery before taking a selfie of us kissing.

This must be the hundredth selfie she has taken of us. Just as with the others, she posts it to her social media page for all her friends to see. She adds the caption, "Best weekend ever with the best boyfriend in the world." I love that she's proud to be my girl and wants to show off our relationship. But the last selfie she posted was post-coital with the caption, "I can't get enough of this sexy beast." You couldn't see below our shoulders, but it was obvious we had just gotten busy.

Sophie scrolls through her friend's posts and comes across one from a girl announcing the birth of her baby. She can't be any older than Sophie. Sophie posts her congratulations and puts her phone away.

"That's the third girl from my class to have a kid this year," she says. "She's my age and already married with a kid."

This piques my interest. "Do you think that's a bad thing?"

She shrugs. "I try not to judge. To each their own. But she's so young. I can't imagine being married with a kid right now."

My stomach knots up. We're together and I have a kid on the way. I don't expect Sophie to parent my kid, but I want her to be a part of its life. She's the woman I intend to spend my life with. We've talked about the baby. She said she supports me. She even went with me to look at furniture for the nursery. But perhaps she hasn't been one hundred percent open with me.

"Are you sure you're okay with my situation?" I ask. "You understand I don't have any expectations of you where my kid is concerned?"

"Of course I know that and I'm okay with everything. I just mean, I can't imagine getting pregnant and having a kid of my own right now. I'd be too scared. And there are so many things I want to do with my life. The last thing I'm thinking about is being a mom."

I know Sophie wants to get her degree and build a career. She wants to be independent. But we haven't had the "What do you want in life" conversation. Does she even want marriage or kids?

"Do you want to be a mom, one day?"

She smiles, shy and way too cute. "One day, sure. What about you?"

I scrunch my eyebrows. "Kind of too late for me. I'm having a kid, ready or not."

"I meant, before the pregnancy, did you want kids?"

That's a tough question. I blow out a breath. "Honestly, the thought of having a kid scared the shit out of me. It still does. I'm worried I'll fuck up like my bio-dad." I twist a lock of her hair as I look deep into her eyes. "But I always knew if the situation was right and I was with the right woman, I would do it—get married and have kids."

She glances away and clears her throat before leaning into me resting her head on my shoulder. "You'll be a great father, Rooter."

"I hope you're right, Babe." I kiss the top of her head.

"I know I am. You're a good guy."

"That's debatable."

She shakes her head. "No, it's not. I wouldn't be with you if you were a bad person."

"As long as you think I'm a good guy, that's all that matters to me."

She pulls away to look at me. "Rooter, it's important that you see the good in yourself. Tell me you do."

"I've done some good things, but I've done bad things too."

"So, you're imperfect." She shrugs. "Everyone is. Myself included."

"Tell me, have you ever fired a gun at another human being? Have you ever beaten someone and left them unconscious at the side of the road?"

She blinks. "No. But I'm sure if you have, you did it for a good reason."

I nod. "Have you ever truly wanted to beat the life out of someone? Have you ever, deep in your soul, wanted another human being to die?"

She's quiet a moment. "Yeah. I get angry and I wish bad things for people sometimes. It makes us human, not bad."

It's not the same as what I'm trying to convey to her. I don't wish bad things. I do them. And most times, I enjoy it. Or at the very least, it doesn't weigh on my conscience. "I guess I'm just worried I don't have what it takes to be a good father."

"I promise, you do." She grazes my lips with hers. "You'll be great."

In the truck, Sophie stares out the window, chewing on her bottom lip.

"What are you thinking?" I ask.

She turns to me and smiles. "How perfect the weekend was."

The weekend has been perfect. Just the two of us with no interruption and no drama. Besides calling to check on Dopey a couple times, I haven't spoken to anyone. It's been a nice change of pace.

The best thing is, I feel more connected to Sophie than ever. We've talked about anything and everything. We've laughed until we cried. We've chased each other around the house, had a food fight, napped on the beach. We've made love more in two days than most couples do in a month.

But now we are on our way home, heading back to reality. I'll be back to trying to balance my commitments to the shop, the Club, Candace, and my relationship with Sophie. I just hope these last few days have erased any doubts Sophie had regarding my devotion to her. While I have every intention of making as much quality time as possible for the two of us, I may not be able to give her as much as she wants.

"Yeah, it was." I rub the top of her thigh. "But the look on your face wasn't a happy one."

"It wasn't?"

I shake my head. "Didn't appear to be."

"I was just deep in thought." She's clamming up and trying to hide it.

"About anything in particular?"

"About how nice it was to have you at my beck and call."

I'm not buying it, but I'll play along. "I make a good beck and call boy?"

"The best," she giggles. "Very attentive."

Lord knows I tried to be. The woman has an insatiable sexual appetite. Sophie's definitely the girl for me. Not that I ever had any doubt about that. I assumed we'd be compatible, but it turns out, my sweet innocent Sophie is a freak. She likes it rough with plenty of dirty talk. Last night she told me to fuck her "hard enough to make it hurt."

"I never thought I'd say this," I reach between my legs to adjust myself, "but Babe, I think I need a couple days off. My junk feels like hamburger.”

She chuckles. “What about your tongue? That still intact?”

My jaw goes slack. “Do you ever get enough?”

“I’m thinking not.”

“Damn woman,” I laugh. “Am I not doing the job well enough?”

“The problem isn’t you not doing it well enough. It’s that you do it too well.”

“Well, that I can’t help.” I wink.

She points at me. “See that right there is what gets you in to trouble.”

“Dually noted.” I lace my fingers with hers.

Sophie looks to the clock on the dash and takes a deep breath. “I don’t want to go home.”

I knew she was thinking about something else. “It’ll be okay, Babe.”

“I just don’t…” She doesn’t finish.

“Don’t what?” I skim her knuckles with my thumb.

“We’ve come so far these past few days. We’re in a really good place and I’m afraid something will ruin it.”

“Look at me,” I wait until she faces me. “Nothing can ruin this. It’s you and me, Sophie. I won’t let anything come between us.”

An hour later, we pull into my parent’s driveway to pick up Dopey. Candace’s Mustang is here.

“You’ve got to be kidding me,” Sophie complains.

I put the truck in park and squeeze my eyes closed. I have such shit luck. We couldn’t make it ten minutes without something coming up. There’s no reason for Candace to be here unless something is wrong. “Here we go.”

I take Sophie by the hand and give her a reassuring glance before entering the house. The instant we step inside, Candace is in our faces. The girls glare at each other so I step between them.

“What are you doing here Candace?” I ask.

"I'll answer that as soon as you tell me where the hell you've been!"

Pop ushers Mom and Isa out of the room.

"It's none of your business where I've been," I answer.

With a hand to her chest, Candace steps closer. "Do you have any idea what I've been through these past few days?"

"Oh, please," Sophie groans from behind me.

"Shut the fuck up, bitch!" Candace yells. "This is none of your business."

"The hell it isn't!" Sophie charges at her, but I pull her to my side and hold her in place.

"Stop it!" I holler at both girls. "What's going on Candace?"

"If you'd been here, you would know." She crosses her arms and juts out her hip.

"I'm here now," I say as calmly as possible. "Tell me."

Candace shifts her weight to the other foot and puts her chin in the air. "I'm not talking to you with her around."

"Well, she's not going anywhere. So either talk or leave."

"That's how you talk to the mother of your unborn child?" Candace gripes. "The child she almost lost yesterday because of the stress she's under?"

"What?" I gasp.

"Yeah, that's right. While you were holed up in a hotel somewhere fucking your little princess," she motions to Sophie, "I've been here trying not to lose our baby."

"What happened?" I could be sick. I didn't expect my going away to put the baby in danger. And why didn't my parents get in touch with me?

"I got fired because I've been too sick to work. Now I'm going to lose everything and be homeless. With all the stress I started cramping really bad and had a little spotting."

"Jesus Candace." I need to sit. I lead Sophie to the couch with me. Candace sits in a chair off to the side. "Did you go to the doctor? Is the baby all right?"

Candace rolls her eyes. "You don't even give a shit about this baby. All you care about is her."

"Of course I care about the baby. I'm sorry I wasn't here."

Candace laughs, sarcastic. "Yeah, right."

"I mean it. I shouldn't have cut contact with you. It was wrong of me." I lean forward, resting my elbows on my knees. *I'm such a thoughtless piece of shit.*

"Rooter," Sophie says, "she's playing you. Do you really not see that?"

"You seriously need to mind your own business," Candace snipes.

"He is my business," Sophie growls.

"Sophie, stop," I demand, impatient.

"You better stop with your fucking games!" Sophie shoots up from the sofa and lunges after Candace. I leap up to stop her, grabbing her by the arms.

Candace doubles over, clutching her abdomen. "Get her away from me!"

"Goddamn it Sophie!" I holler. "What are you doing?"

I dart to Candace's side and kneel before her. Mom, Pop and Isa rush into the room.

"What's going on?" Mama asks.

Candace points at Sophie with one hand while the other remains on her stomach. "She started to attack me! Get her out of here!"

I stand to address Sophie, but Candace clutches my arm.

"Don't leave me," she cries with fear in her eyes.

"I'm not leaving," I promise Candace and hold the truck keys out to Sophie. "Take the truck home. I need to handle this."

Defiant as ever, Sophie crosses her arms. "I'm not going anywhere."

"Sophie," I mutter, "you need to go. Your being here is making things worse."

"How have I become the bad guy?"

"No one said that." I squeeze the bridge of my nose and blow out a breath. "I can't have this conversation right now. Please, go home. We'll talk later."

Sophie yanks the keys from the palm of my hand. "Fine. But do me a favor and consider the fact that this is all an act to get your attention." She turns and glowers at Candace. "Like everything else she's done.

Once Sophie leaves I take Candace to my old room where we can talk in private. Candace sits on the side of the bed as I pace the length of the room.

"She was actually going to attack me," Candace says. "Thank God you got to her first."

I shake my head trying to make sense of what just happened. I can't believe what I just saw. Did Sophie really intend to hit Candace? It sure looked that way and I can't ignore it. "I'm sorry."

"You're not going to let her get away with it, are you?"

I honestly don't know. "I'll talk to her later."

"You'll *talk* to her?" Candace shakes her head, exasperated. "If anyone else had come at me like that, you would've knocked them flat on their ass."

She's right. As the mother of my child, it's my duty to protect Candace, even from Sophie if need be. But I never thought it'd come to that. Even given what I just witnessed, I've a hard time believing Sophie would hurt Candace. At least not while she's pregnant.

"I'm just as shocked as you right now," I say.

"Rooter, I don't want someone like that around my baby. If she'll hurt me while I'm pregnant, what's to stop her from hurting the baby once it's here?"

"Sophie would *never* hurt a child, Candace. I can guarantee you that."

"Can you? You saw what she just did."

She has a point. But I truly believe Sophie would never hurt a baby. "Don't worry, Candace. I will never let anyone hurt the baby."

"I don't want her around me or the baby anymore Rooter. She scares me."

I clutch my head with my hands. Candace has a right to say who will and won't be in our child's life. But this is complicated. I sit next to Candace and lay my hand on her leg. "You don't have to be afraid, I promise."

She nods. "Rooter, please don't pull another disappearing act on me. I get that we're not together, but I need you."

I rub my face with both hands. "I won't disappear again. I made a mistake. I should've told you I was leaving. I just figured you'd give me a hard time about it."

"I probably would have, but only because you're all I have." She glances down at her belly. "I've been scared every day with this pregnancy. I'm so scared I'll lose it. I know you don't want this baby, but I do. I love it so much already. I wish you did too."

"I do, Candace. I do. I promise I'll do better."

I just made this same promise to Sophie. I feel like a rubber band being pulled in opposite directions. How can I possibly give each of these women what they need from me?

Candace cradles her still flat stomach.

"Are you feeling okay?" I ask. "Cramps?"

"They're better, but haven't stopped."

"I can take you to the hospital."

She shakes her head. "I'm tired of hospitals and doctors. They never help anyway."

"I'd feel better if you got checked out."

"The cramps are getting better and I'm not spotting right now. I'll just go home and take it easy for the rest of the day."

"If you won't go to the hospital, I want you to stay here where I can keep an eye on you. I'll ask mom to whip up something for dinner while you rest."

I stand and pull the blanket back for her to lie down.

"Rooter?" She clutches my arm. "Thank you for staying and making sure I'm okay."

"You don't need to thank me. You're pregnant with my kid. Of course I stayed."

Choose Carefully

At the sound of a bang, my eyes shoot open. I take a second to get my bearings.

I'm on my couch and Sophie is standing by the entryway to the kitchen picking up her keys from the floor.

I got home in the middle of the night and found Sophie asleep in my bed. If I'd woke her she'd hound me with questions about what happened after she left my parent's. Too tired to rehash it all, I crashed in the living room.

"Sophie." I sit up.

She fiddles with the keys. "Sorry, I was trying not to wake you up."

"Are you leaving?" I rub the sleep from my eyes.

"Yeah. I was going to get showered and let you sleep awhile longer."

"I'm up."

"What time did you get in?" she asks and steps in my direction.

"About three." I check the time on my watch. It's seven-thirty. "I didn't want to wake you so I stayed down here."

She cocks her head to the side. "You know I wouldn't have cared."

I nod. I know better than lie to her. "I was exhausted and didn't want to talk about what happened with Candace."

"How about now?"

I still don't want to talk about it, but is there any choice? No point in delaying the inevitable. "We should talk."

Sophie sits beside me. "What happened? Is she okay?"

"She's really stressed out. Scared of losing the baby."

She rolls her eyes. "Don't you think she's exaggerating a little?"

I grit my teeth. How can she be so damned insensitive? "She's been sick, she's lost her job, and she's been cramping. So no, I don't think her freaking out over me being gone is exaggerating."

"She could be making up the cramping part."

I blow out a breath, already exhausted with this conversation. "Could you give her the benefit of the doubt for once?"

Sophie gapes at me, dumbfounded. "Excuse me for not trusting her after everything she's done. Did she even go to the doctor?"

I hesitate. She'll use my answer as ammunition in her argument against Candace. Finally, I shake my head.

"See!" She throws a hand up. "If there really was something wrong, she'd have gone to the damn doctor."

"She thought everything would be okay once I got back and she could relax."

"Oh please. And you buy that shit?"

"What choice do I have?"

"You're the father! Make her ass go to the doctor if something is wrong."

"I tried!" I jump up and shoot her a glare. "I spent the entire night trying to convince her."

"And it didn't work, did it?"

I shift my gaze to the window. Again, I shake my head, knowing the answer will feed her fire.

Sophie leaps from the couch. "Of course it didn't because there's absolutely nothing the matter with her!"

"You know what?" My neck stiffens as I try to control my anger. "I hope nothing is wrong with her. Do you have any idea what it would do to me if something happened to that kid, and I wasn't here?"

"Oh my god." Her eyes widen. "Her guilt trip actually worked. She made you feel guilty for going away with me."

I fall onto the sofa and look to the floor. "What I did was irresponsible. I left the mother of my child with no means of getting ahold of me."

Sophie sits back down next to me. "Your mother had your number. I'm sure she would've called you if she thought it was important."

You're not getting it! I smack my thighs. "It's not up to my mom to decide what is and is not important."

"Camilla doesn't believe her shit either does she? That's why she didn't call you."

"Sophie," I groan, "it doesn't matter if we believe her or not. If Candace says something is wrong, and she needs me, I'm obligated to be there. Don't you get that?"

Sophie's nostrils flare. "As long as you're with me and not her, there will *always* be something wrong with her. Don't *you* get *that?*"

Yes, I get that. But it doesn't fucking matter. Candace is pregnant with my kid. I have an obligation. "Fuck!"

I kick the coffee table across the room. Dopey whimpers and scurries to the other side of the room with his tail tucked between his legs. Sophie leaps off the couch, away from me. My chest tightens with guilt. I shouldn't have done that.

"I knew this would happen," her voice is small. "I knew she'd find a way to come between us when we got back. You said you wouldn't let it happen."

My phone rings. Worst timing ever, as per usual. I snatch the phone from my pocket and answer. "What?"

"We got a problem with the McDaniel build," Pop says. "We need you here."

"I'm on my way." I jam the phone back in my pocket.

Sophie sighs. "And now you have to go."

"It's the shop. There's a problem with a build." I stand and take her hand. "I'm sorry if I scared you."

"I wasn't scared."

I hope she means it. I kiss the top of her hand. "Remember those bad days I said we would have?"

She nods, but won't make eye contact with me.

"This is one of them." I tilt her face to meet mine. The sadness I see in her eyes is like a punch to the gut. "But it doesn't mean I'm going to let anything come between us. I love you, Sophie. Nothing will change that."

A tear falls down her cheek.

My chest constricts. It's painful to see her cry, especially knowing it's my fault. I pull her close and wrap my arms around her. "It's going to be okay, Babe."

After straightening out the issue with the McDaniel build, I stay at the shop to catch up on paperwork. When the lunch hour rolls around, I go to Candace's to check up on her. She seems in better spirits but is freaking out about finances. She only has enough money saved up for a month's worth of rent and bills. I tell her not to worry, I will loan her the money she needs. She probably shouldn't be working right now anyways. It might be best she doesn't work until the baby is born. And once the baby is here, I don't want her going back to stripping. I know enough people in Halsey that I can get her hooked up with a clerical job somewhere.

By the time I get home at seven, I still haven't showered and I'm completely spent from the stress of the past twenty-four hours. I will myself to get cleaned up and when I'm finished, I have no energy left to play with Dopey. I fall onto my bed and pass out as soon as my head hits the pillow.

I wake just in time to greet Sophie in the driveway after her shift at the restaurant. Moments later, I slide back into the bed with Sophie in my arms.

"Do you regret going away?" she asks.

I take a moment to think. I want to give her an honest answer, but I don't want to hurt her feelings. "Yes and no. You and I needed the time together and I'm glad we had it, but I regret what it caused."

"Do you wish we hadn't gone?"

I wouldn't trade what we shared over the weekend for anything. But the thoughtlessness in the way I handled it with Candace could've hurt my unborn child.

"No, but I wish I'd handled it different." I brush her hair with my fingers. It always helps her to fall asleep.

"It's like we took one step forward and three steps back."

I lift her face to make eye contact. "You and I will be fine, Babe. I promise."

"What about Candace? Are you going to be back to running to her every time she calls?"

I probably will until things calm down with the pregnancy. But the last thing I want is to start a fight at one in the morning. I glance at the ceiling and sigh. "I'm just going to take it call by call, day by day. That's all I can do."

It's life as normal for the next two days. I work days, Sophie works nights. After work, I go to Candace's and spend my evenings with her. Sophie stays the nights at my house after her shifts at The Grand. I'm on autopilot, living the same day over and over again. I can't do anything to change it, but this is definitely not what I would've chosen.

I worry that Sophie and I won't be able to maintain our relationship at this rate. The majority of our communication is via text. We have no time or energy to really connect. We haven't made love since coming home. When Sophie texts me in the afternoon that she needs some "Jace time" I resolve that come hell or high water, that's what I'll give her.

But there's a problem. Candace texted me asking what time I'd be over after work. She expects me to be there as I have been the last couple of days. When I tell her I won't be there tonight, she's not happy. Evidently she saw her doctor today, and the news wasn't stellar. She goes off on a tangent about me putting Sophie first over the baby. She knew it was only a matter of time before it happened.

To try to smooth things over, I leave work early and go to Candace's for a short visit. It doesn't go well. The doctor's visit really shook her up. She's a mess. She begs me to stay, but I tell her I can't.

As I pull into my driveway, I'm torn. Perhaps I should've stayed. But I made a promise to Sophie. I've barely seen her these past few days. I've spent a lot of time with Candace. It only seems fair that I spend Sophie's night off with her. I'm trying to juggle my responsibilities as best I can. I'm failing, just as I expected. There's no way I can keep both women happy.

I walk into the kitchen just before six and toss my cut to the floor. I pull Sophie into my arms and exhale with relief. "Coming home to you is the only thing that got me through this day."

"Everything okay?"

"It's fine now." I take her face into my hands and kiss her lips. "It smells fantastic in here."

She pours a glass of Jack and hands it to me. "I made chicken alfredo. Garlic bread is in the oven. I also made a salad."

"Sounds perfect. I'm starved." The whiskey burns as I damn near drink the entire glass in one gulp.

Sophie and I make small talk through dinner. She tells me a story about something that happened with Ryan, but I can't recall a word of it. Candace is across town feeling angry and abandoned. Have I abandoned her? Perhaps I made the wrong decision. I'm cloaked in guilt.

"Are you sure everything is okay?" Sophie squeezes my hand.

I can't answer. Everything is most definitely not okay. How do I tell her I shouldn't be here? That I'm a piece of shit for abandoning my kid and its mother.

"You can tell me." Her eyes are gentle as she squeezes my hand again.

"She went to the doctor today." I rub the back of my neck. "She's still cramping and bleeding. Her blood pressure is through the roof. The baby is okay for now, but the doctor said absolutely no more stress or she could miscarry."

Yet I left her in complete distress. What kind of ass am I?

"I'm sorry." Her voice is sincere.

"She's a wreck which isn't helping anything. She insists she needs me there with her. That it's the only way she'll get the stress under control."

Sophie rolls her eyes.

If I had to work at the shop or had Club business, Candace wouldn't have cared that I'm not with her. She's only mad that I'm with Sophie instead of her. I continue, "I realize part of it is her and her games, but I saw the paper from the doctor. This is real. I don't know what to do, Babe."

"Were you with her before you came home?"

I nod.

"She probably wasn't too happy when you left."

Staring at my plate, I shake my head.

"And now you feel guilty."

That's putting it mildly. I glance at Sophie.

"Do you think you should've stayed?" she asks.

I rub my eyes with my thumb and index finger. "I feel split in two. I should do whatever I can to help the baby, but I don't want to risk losing you."

"If your being with me makes her so stressed that she miscarries… I can't let that happen."

My adrenaline spikes and my body tenses. "What are you saying?"

"I'm saying you should go back there and get her settled down."

I exhale sharply and take her hand. I thought she was breaking up with me. "Shit, you scared me."

"I'll clean this up and let Dopey out before I go home."

I don't want to be without Sophie tonight. I could just run over to Candace's, spend a little time there and calm her down. Then I'd come back and spend the rest of the night with Sophie. I can give her plenty of Jace time. "You don't have to go home. Bear's there with Miranda and I seriously doubt they're playing scrabble."

"I need to catch up on laundry. I can always put my iPod on."

"Do you want me to come over when I get back?"

She shakes her head. "We could both use a good night's sleep."

We've slept just fine the last couple nights. "You're mad."

"I promise I'm not."

I follow her into the kitchen. "Then why won't you stay?"

"Because I need a little me time." She rinses her plate and puts it in the dishwasher. She walks toward the dining room, but I stop her.

"Earlier you needed Jace time."

"Candace needs you more." Sadness flashes in her eyes.

I have a split-second debate with myself.

If I go to Candace's will it really make anything better?

Will it damage my relationship with Sophie if I go?

Even if it didn't, she'd be deeply disappointed with me.

Candace is only upset that I'm with Sophie. If I run back to her, she will do this every time I try to spend time with Sophie.

Either way, I'm taking a risk.

My decision is made. "I'm staying."

She wriggles away from my hold on her shoulder. "Rooter, you need to go. I'll see you tomorrow night."

"I refuse to leave things like this."

"Things are fine." She carries more dirty dishes to the sink.

When a woman says things are fine, they are never fine. I've seen it with my mom and pop. I draw Sophie into my arms. "I love you. I'm staying."

My phone rings. Candace's ring tone.

Sophie backs away. "You should answer it and tell her you're on your way."

I answer the call, "Yeah?"

"You don't care about me or this baby at all!" Candace cries.

"Of course I care, but I can't be there every second of every day."

Candace hollers, "You care more about your princess than you do your own kid."

"This is exactly why you're in this condition," I say. "You refuse to accept the situation for what it is and you're getting yourself all worked up."

She screams like a mad woman. "You're the one who refuses to accept the situation! You better man the fuck up, Rooter! You're a father now. You better start acting like it or I'll make sure you never lay eyes on this kid!"

The phone goes quiet. I look at the screen and put the phone back in my pocket. "She hung up on me."

"Don't you think you should go?"

"I honestly don't know, Sophie." I drag my fingers through my hair. "I'm worried about the kid. But my going there won't fix anything because the same thing will happen tomorrow and the next day and the day after that. She won't be happy unless she and I are together and that isn't happening."

"I agree, but if you stay you'll spend the entire night worrying."

I lean on the counter and look to the floor. "My pop once told me that ninety-nine percent of the things we worry about never come to pass. That I shouldn't drive myself crazy worrying about all the things that could go wrong."

"What if something happens and you aren't there?"

"I don't know." I gaze into Sophie's eyes. "All I know is that I need to pick my battles wisely. Something may or may not happen with Candace and the baby tonight." I go to Sophie and take her hands into mine. "But what I'm sure of is if I leave you'll start giving up on me. So I'm going to stay here and believe everything will be okay with the baby."

"If something happens…"

I place my fingers on her lips to hush her. "The only thing that's going to happen tonight is you and me cuddling in bed and talking until we pass out."

At two in the morning, I'm jolted awake by a nightmare. My heart is pounding and I'm gasping for air. There's an indescribable pain in my chest and my face is wet. At first I think it's sweat, but it's not. I was crying in my sleep.

In my dream, the baby, a boy named after me, is born. The court has decided I will lose all parental rights to my son if I don't marry its mother. That isn't how the law works in real life, but in dreams anything can happen. In my dream that was the law. I had to end my relationship with Sophie and marry Candace. I was with Sophie in her living room telling her about the court's ruling. I couldn't be with her anymore. Sophie wailed as she beat the walls and furniture with her fists. She choked on her sobs as tears fell down her face. I was in pure agony at the sight. But there was nothing I could do. I had to let her go. And if I didn't do it within twenty-four hours of the ruling, I would lose all rights to my child.

I roll over on my side and place my hand on Sophie's hip and take deep, long breaths to calm myself. But it isn't easy. The nightmare seemed so damn real. The pain of losing Sophie was crippling. I always expected it would hurt if I lost her, but now I know just how crushing it would be.

After a few minutes my heart rate and breathing slow and the pressure in my chest eases. But the anguish of saying goodbye to Sophie is still there, buried deep inside.

Even though she's right beside me, she's nowhere near close enough. There's only one thing that will calm this ache. I need to be as close to her as physically possible. I need her body pressed against mine as I move inside her.

"Mm, that feels nice," she whispers as I wake her with kisses on the small of her back.

"I've been dying to do this since I gave you the back rub," I say with a chuckle to hide my desperation, "but I was trying to be chivalrous."

I yearn to slam into her this instant. Despite my urgency, I try to take my time to love her the way she deserves. I sweep my lips across her skin from her lower back up to her neck. She starts to roll over to face me as I nibble her silken skin.

"Stay just like this," I say and press my hard shaft against her backside.

I take a breast into my hand and tweak her nipple until it's hard, squeezing just enough to make her whimper. I grind myself against her as I lick and suck the skin of her shoulder and neck. Just as I lower my hand between her legs, she reaches for my cock, pumping up and down.

Fuck the foreplay. "I need to be inside you."

I yank her panties partway down with my hand and finish the job with my foot. I grab a condom from the nightstand and roll it on in record time. I drape Sophie's leg over mine to spread her wide. She moans in pleasure as I slide a finger inside.

"So wet already," I murmur.

I push inside bit by bit, reveling in the heat of her tight, slick cunt. I pull back and thrust again at the same leisurely pace, stroking her clit as I continue to move inside her.

"I love you, Sophie." I push in once more and come to a stop, still circling her clit. "I want to feel you come like this, while I'm still inside you."

I nibble and suck her neck as I continue to work her pussy while I'm seated deep inside her.

"That feels so good. You're so big inside me."

"That's right, Baby. Talk to me. Are you getting close?"

"Yeah."

Her pussy is like a vice grip around me. I could come right now even though I'm completely still inside her. "Say my name when you come."

I don't move an inch as I circle her clit faster and faster. Sophie whimpers and moans as she gets closer and closer to release. She grabs my hand and slows my fingers. Her entire body shudders as she screams my name.

"Oh yeah, Baby," I murmur, "You're so tight around me."

I wait until I'm sure her orgasm has passed before slamming into her hard and fast. I feel more like a savage, wild animal than a man. With every thrust, I claim her, mark her, remind her that she's mine. I'm her male, and she's my female. I can never be without her.

The familiar pressure mounts. My heart pounds. I can hardly breathe. I want her to come again, but I'm right on the edge. I bite my lip and continue to pound.

Her body tenses. She's close.

The first surge hits me.

Then the second.

Sophie hollers my name as she comes.

A third wave strikes as I reach the point of no return.

Fuck yes.

I stop moving.

I Can't breathe. Can't hear. Can't see.

I can only feel as I succumb to the violent pleasure ripping through me.

I groan an expletive and clutch Sophie tight as my body shudders. "I love you so much, Sophie."

It's Over

It's been an almost perfect day. Sophie and I spent the evening at my parent's house for Sunday dinner. Mama had been adamant that we be there after missing the last few. Her exact words were, "If you're not here by four, I will come to your house and drag you out by your ear." She meant every word. She's done it before. I'll do anything not to experience it again.

The only drama was when Candace called. She was upset she wasn't included at the Sunday family dinner being that she's pregnant with my kid. For obvious reasons that won't work. She and Sophie can't be in the same room. Even if the situation was amicable, it would be awkward having my girlfriend and my baby mama at the weekly family dinner.

Sophie and I are now lying in my bed, snuggling after making love. Her hand is pressed to my chest, my hand rests on her hip. I live for moments like this, just the two of us completely at ease.

"Tell me something about you I don't know," she says.

There are a million little things she hasn't learned about me yet. For instance, I haven't told her how I got the scar on the back of my leg. I hate basketball. I refuse to play ever again after breaking my ankle eight years ago. My favorite candy bar is a Kit Kat. But she's not asking for mundane facts. She's asking me to open up to her about things that make me who I am. There's a huge fact I haven't confessed. Not because I've tried to hide it, but because it's an uncomfortable truth.

"I have a younger brother and sister by my biological father. Thomas and Ashley. He was named after my dad." Saying the word "dad" regarding my sperm donor makes me cringe. "Thomas isn't even a year younger than me. Ashley's your age."

She gasps. "Wow."

"I met them a couple years back. They didn't know who I was."

"You didn't tell them?"

"Nah," I shrug. "They didn't seem very interested in me."

"They probably would've been if they knew you were their brother."

"I doubt it. They were every bit as stuck up and shallow as their father."

Sophie caresses my cheek. "I'm sorry."

"A glutton for punishment, I went to his house—my dad's—when they were all there. I watched him with them." I swallow. My chest is heavy. I hate that this bothers me so much. "The fucked up part of it all was that he seemed like such a good dad. The way he looked at them with love and pride. One big happy family."

"That had to have been difficult to see."

"Yeah. I think I'd rather he was a deadbeat dad to all of us. As fucked up as that sounds." I rub the back of my neck. Perhaps I should have chosen a different conversation. Too late now. "But the hardest part for me was that I felt like I'd betrayed Mick. I went there to see what I'd missed out on when in truth, I haven't missed out on anything because Mick has been a phenomenal father. I wouldn't change that for anything in this world. I'm glad Thomas O'Shea abandoned me. I love Mick and I'm glad to be his son."

I'm proud to be a Russo. I can't even fathom having the last name O'shea. Yeah, it bothers me that my biological father abandoned me. But I couldn't imagine not having Mick as my father.

"You're right," Sophie agrees, "you didn't miss out on anything. You have a wonderful family. I wish I had a family like yours."

Her words tug at my heart. "Babe, you do. You have my family now. The more they get to know you, the more they love you."

Her eyes glisten with unshed tears and she nods. "The feeling is mutual."

The lump in my throat threatens to choke me. She needs to understand something. "I don't just love you, Sophie. I consider you my family. You're a part of me now. You always will be."

"When do I get to tell you I love you?"

How I wait for the day to hear those words. I know she feels it, but I need to be sure I'm deserving before she says it. I kiss her hand. "I'm still working on earning it, Babe."

I'm waist deep in receipts and bank statements when my cell phone rings at a quarter to nine in the morning. It's Sophie. She never calls when I'm at work. We have an understanding that unless it's urgent, just send a text.

"Babe?" I answer.

"Candace was just here," she huffs, out of breath.

I squeeze the pencil in my hand. "What? What was she doing there?"

"Trying to talk me into leaving you." Her voice is panicked. "Rooter, she fell."

I jump from my seat. "Fell? Is she okay?"

"I think so. She wouldn't let me help her."

"Shit, I better call her."

"You can't. I threw her phone into the street."

"Dammit, Sophie!" I punch the desk. "What happened?"

"She was playing a recording of a conversation you had with her and it pissed me off. I swear to God I didn't touch her."

"Fuck." This situation just goes from bad to worse. "I need to find her. Stay put. I'll call you later."

I hang up and run to my bike. Bear and Sparrow holler at me, trying to find out what's wrong, but I don't have time to explain. I need to find Candace and make sure she's okay.

There are three hospitals in town. Mercy is closest to Sophie's. Halsey Memorial is near Candace's. But it's possible she's fine and hasn't gone to the hospital. I make a quick decision to ride out to her place and see if she's there.

When I arrive, there's no sign of her. I sit on her front porch stairs and consider my options. If something was wrong, Candace would call me. Even without her phone, she'd find a way to reach me.

Why did Sophie have to throw her damn phone?

To be safe, I call all three local hospitals. Candace hasn't checked into any of them which calms my nerves. Still, I'd feel better if I could talk to her. I scroll through the contacts in my phone and call a few of Candace's friends. No one answers so I leave messages telling them to call me if they see or hear from her.

I wait nearly an hour to see if she shows up, and when she doesn't, I go back to the shop.

I'm at my desk less than an hour when Candace finally calls. She's sobbing so hard she's choking, but I'm able to make out four gut-wrenching words, "I lost the baby."

Candace lies on her couch in an oversized t-shirt and yoga pants, hugging a pillow to her chest. Her friend Brittany, a stripper at the same club, sits at the end rubbing her feet.

I hurry to her and crouch at her side. "How are you?"

She squeezes her eyes shut like she might cry. "Our baby is gone."

"I know." I take her hand into mine.

"That bitch killed our baby!"

"What happened?" I ask.

Brittany snipes, "You girlfriend pushed her down the stairs."

I look to Brittany then to Candace. "She pushed you?"

Candace nods. "I was just trying to talk to her, but she freaked out and pushed me down the front porch steps."

I shake my head. I want to ask why she was there, but does it even matter? The damage is done. The baby is gone. My child… our child… is dead. And Sophie… my Sophie is to blame.

But Sophie said she didn't touch Candace. Sophie has never lied to me. I can't wrap my mind around it all.

Candace squeezes my hand, her lip trembles. "I can't believe the baby is gone."

I need to say or do something helpful, but what? Nothing will undo what has happened. It won't bring the baby back.

"Is there anything I can do?" I ask. "Are you in a lot of pain?"

"They gave me painkillers, so the pain isn't too bad right now."

"I need to know what happened." I turn to Brittany. "Can you give us a moment to talk?"

Brittany stands and addresses Candace. "I have a few errands to run, but I will be back in a couple hours."

"Thank you for being here," Candace tells her.

Brittany bends down and kisses her forehead. "I'll be back soon."

Once she's gone, I pull a chair up to the couch so I can face Candace.

She closes her eyes and takes a deep breath. "Last night, I got to thinking." She pauses. "I've always been considered part of your family. It really hurt me not to be invited to the Sunday dinner, especially being pregnant." She grimaces.

Candace is considered family, but she's never been invited in the Russo Sunday dinner. It's always just been Pop, Mama, me and Isa. I guess I can understand why she thought that would change when she got pregnant.

"I'm sorry, Candace. We weren't trying to hurt you."

"I know that. And that's why I went to Sophie's today. I wanted to talk to her, one on one to try to fix things. I figured since you're with her and I…" she swallows, "*was* pregnant, that we needed to find a way to get along for the sake of the baby and the family."

"That's not what Sophie said. She said you went there to try to convince her to leave me."

"What?" she hollers. "That's not true! She wouldn't even hear me out. She just chased me away."

"She said you played a recording of you and me talking and it upset her."

"A recording of what? I don't have any recording."

"I don't know, that's just what she said."

She sits up to face me directly. "And you believe her over me?"

"I didn't say that."

"But you're questioning me."

"Please calm down." I place a hand on her shoulder. "I'm just trying to get the facts."

"The fact is, I went there to call a truce, and the bitch flipped out and killed our baby. Now, she's lying about it."

"So you went there to talk to her, and she lost it and pushed you down the stairs?"

Candace nods. "That's exactly what happened. Ask a neighbor, I'm sure somebody saw it."

I don't want to believe what I'm hearing. It had to be an accident. Sophie wouldn't push her. Would she?

"Rooter, look at me." She leans in close, eyes locked on mine. "Have I ever lied to you?"

I shake my head. But to my knowledge, neither has Sophie.

"You've known me forever. You know I would never lie to you." She reaches for my hand. "This may be hard to hear, but I'm telling the truth. Your girlfriend pushed me down her stairs. She was mad. She probably didn't mean to hurt me. Or, maybe she did. I don't know. All I know is I just spent the morning in the hospital having a miscarriage."

I put my face in my hands. I desperately want to believe Sophie. But Candace is right. I've known her for years. Much longer than I've known Sophie. Candace has always been loyal to the family and the Club—always been honest with me.

Just the other night, I watched Sophie charge after her. I convinced myself she wouldn't have hit Candace. Now I see that wasn't true. Sophie hates Candace. She hated that Candace was pregnant. Even if she hadn't meant to hurt Candace, the fact that she could hit a pregnant woman shows Sophie had no regard for the baby. *My* baby!

I've no choice but to believe Candace.

I leap from the chair and pace the room, my hands clasped behind my neck.

But why would Sophie make up the story about a recording? And she did call to tell me Candace fell. She even sounded concerned.

Maybe she wasn't concerned, but rather scared. Scared of what I might do if I knew she pushed Candace down the stairs. But she had to have known Candace would tell me her side of the story. That their stories wouldn't match. Did she assume I'd side with her over Candace?

To be honest, I'm not sure I believe Candace was there to "call a truce." I believe she'd go there with a recording to piss Sophie off. But what kind of recording could she have that'd be so upsetting? I haven't said or done anything out of line since being with Sophie.

The scene plays out in my mind. Candace was there, for whatever reason, and it pissed Sophie off. Sophie chased Candace away causing her to fall down the porch steps. Perhaps Sophie pushed her without thinking because she was so angry.

Either way, Sophie is the reason Candace lost the baby.

My baby is gone. Dead.

My gut churns—a mixture of anger, sadness, and disbelief. Initially, I hadn't been excited about the pregnancy, but I ache for the loss. I'd gotten used to the idea of being a dad. In my mind, I was already a father. So many times I pictured being in the delivery room and holding my child for the first time. I'd tried out different names in my mind. I'd been hoping for a boy and was planning on asking Candace if we could name him after Mick. As scared as I was about being a good dad, I was also looking forward to it. I'm just now realizing it, but I was already in love with my child. Now, he or she is gone. I am no longer a father.

My whole life has just changed once again. And it hurts.

"I'm so sorry, Rooter." Candace puts a hand to my cheek. "I shouldn't have gone there."

In Candace's eyes is such sorrow and regret. The indescribable pain of a woman who has lost a child. She loved the baby so much. It was all she talked about. She fought so hard for it and for us as a family. And now it's gone. The hollowness in my chest can't compare to the level of grief she must be experiencing.

I was too damn headstrong. I insisted on keeping Sophie. Insisted that I could make it all work. I was so damn selfish! Candace told me again and again about the stress she was under—the cramping and the fear she had she would lose the baby. I pushed it all aside for my own agenda. If anyone is to blame, it's me. I allowed my selfish desires to hurt Candace and our innocent child.

I'm every bit as worthless as my sperm donor. But I didn't just walk out on my kid. What I did is worse. My choices led to my child's death. I will never forgive myself.

The more time that passes, the deeper my anger and sorrow become. This morning, I woke a happy man with the woman I love in my arms. Now, mere hours later, my unborn child is dead because of said woman.

Candace is asleep on the sofa as I throw back a fourth shot of Jack Daniels. If only I could drink myself numb. Instead, the booze has the opposite effect. The more I drink, the more my fury boils to the surface. I'm furious with myself and with Sophie. Candace was wrong to go to Sophie's. I've told her time and time again to never go there. However, Sophie should have kept her emotions in check. But, she lost her shit, as she always does, and it cost the life of my child.

My heartbeat pounds in my ears as I sit, watching the clock, waiting for Brittany to return so I can go to Sophie's. I don't want to hear her side of the story, but I've got plenty to say.

I've sat here watching an inconsolable Candace cry for hours over the loss of our baby. She keeps telling me how sorry she is and how guilty she feels. That if she hadn't gone there, our baby would still be alive. It's the most heartbreaking thing I've ever witnessed.

I've never been so infuriated, hurt… *betrayed* in my life. I trusted Sophie completely, and she has taken something dear from me. That it was her deepens my pain and anger. It may have been an accident. Her rage got the best of her. But it's no excuse.

There are consequences for losing control and she must pay. No one has ever taken something this precious from me and gotten away with it. I won't hurt Sophie. I would never lay a hand on her. But, I refuse to betray my dead child by excusing what she's done.

I hear the rumble of a Harley followed by a knock on the front door. When I open it, Bear stands before me.

"Hey, Brother," he says and pulls me in for a quick hug.

"Hey, man. Thanks for coming."

Bear steps into the living room and looks around the room. "Candace still asleep?"

"Yeah. It's better that way. She's a wreck."

"I bet."

My phone rings. It's Sophie. I don't bother to answer. What I have to say must be said face to face. Not long after the phone stops ringing she sends a text: *Please call when you can.* I slide the phone into my pocket without responding.

"Candace is saying Sophie pushed her?" Bear asks.

"Yep." I sigh.

"Do you think she's telling the truth?"

"I think that whether Sophie pushed her or not, she's responsible for what happened."

He watches me carefully. "What're you gonna do?"

"I'm gonna let her know how I feel about what she's done."

He arches a brow. "Let her know?"

"I'm not going to hurt her."

He eyes me again. "When do you plan on talking to her?"

"As soon as Brittany gets back."

"Rooter, look at yourself." He points to a mirror on the wall across the room.

I glimpse my reflection. I stand rigid, hands balled into fists at my sides, the vein in my forehead protrudes.

Bear continues, "You aren't in any condition to *talk* to her right now."

"She needs to know what she's done."

"I've never seen you like this, Rooter. I think it's best if you wait until you've calmed down."

"Calm down?" I scream. "I'm never going to calm down, Bear! My kid is dead!"

"I know, man, and I'm sorry. But if you go over there like this…" he puts his hand on my shoulder, "something bad could happen."

"Something bad already happened." I grit my teeth. "And Sophie's responsible. I want her to see me like this! I want her to know exactly how I feel!"

"I just don't want you to do something you regret."

"I've already done something I regret."

By the time Brittany arrives, I'm completely blinded by my rage. The entire way to Sophie's house, I keep seeing Candace balled up in fetal position on her bed, sobbing over our dead baby. I keep hearing the anguish in her voice when she cries, "I'm not a mommy anymore."

Candace has recounted the story a dozen times. Each time I hear it, the more I believe it. Though Sophie may not have intended to hurt Candace, she is responsible for the death of my child.

I want to see the look in Sophie's eyes when I tell her. Will she be surprised? Will she feel remorse? She'll be sorry when she realizes she has betrayed me in a way that there's no coming back from.

When I pull up to her house, Bear's Harley sits in the driveway. Miranda is still at work, so he isn't here for her.

I should have known he'd come.

I barge in through the front door. Sophie's on the sofa and Bear sits in the chair to her left.

"What are you doing here?" I ask Bear.

"Just trying to keep things on an even keel, Brother."

Sophie jumps up from the couch, but my icy scowl keeps her from coming close. "Bear told me about the baby," her voice trembles, "I'm so sorry."

"Don't you dare say you're sorry." I step forward, hands clenching and unclenching. If it was anyone else standing before me, I'd choke the life out of them. "You are not sorry."

Sophie holds her hands out in front of her. "Rooter, I swear I didn't lay a hand on Candace."

"That's not what she said."

She steps toward me. "How many times has she lied? Do you honestly believe her over me?"

"I saw the way you went after her the other night!" It's all I can see. Sophie charging after Candace. Sophie pushing her down the stairs.

"I'd never hit a pregnant woman. It was an accident. We were arguing. She said things. I got in her face and screamed for her to leave," she motions to the porch "she lost her footing on the stairs and fell."

The woman standing before me is no longer my Sophie. This woman is the person responsible for the death of my child. "So you admit you are to blame."

"No." She shakes her head. "I don't admit to that. She came here and got in my face. She did this."

She has a hell of a lot of nerve to say this is Candace's fault after just admitting her guilt. I charge toward her, stopping a couple feet away, and point in her face. "You got in her face, you were going to hit her and she fell down the stairs! You did this! You killed my kid!"

"No," she cries. "No, I didn't. You have to believe me."

Her tears mean nothing to me after spending the day watching Candace grieve the loss of our baby. They just infuriate me more. My entire body shakes as I stare her down. She's lucky I don't hit women.

Bear gets up from his chair and steps in between us. I shift to the side so I can see Sophie. Or rather, so she can see me as I speak. "I'll never believe another word you say. I never want to hear your voice again." I point at her again. "If you're smart, you'll stay away from me and you sure as hell better stay away from Candace."

"Rooter, please don't do this," she pleads and tries to get to me, but Bear holds her in place. "Please. You know I'd never do anything to hurt you. I love you."

The words I once longed to hear make me want to throw up. "I can't even stand to look at you," I growl. "I could never love someone who could take the life of an innocent child. I never want to see you again. If you have half a brain, you'll make sure I don't."

Sophie's desperate pleas have no effect on me as I storm out of her house and slam the door behind me.

Revelation

Three days have passed since the miscarriage and my break up with Sophie. Candace is staying with me while she recovers. I figure I owe it to her since I'm mostly to blame for what happened.

Last night Candace told me she has nothing left to live for now that the baby is gone. I tried my best to convince her it isn't true, but it didn't work. That I can do nothing to ease her pain leaves me feeling helpless. And my guilt is overwhelming.

My feelings about Sophie, her involvement in the miscarriage, and our breakup are complicated to say the least.

Bear was right. I should have waited to talk to her. I was far too upset to be rational. I'm ashamed for the way I behaved. I regret the hurtful things I said. If I could take them back, I would. But I was and still am angry about what happened.

Now that I'm thinking clearly, I don't believe she pushed Candace. However, I have a hard time believing she's completely innocent. I think Sophie had a hand in the incident by scaring Candace and causing her to fall down the stairs. If Sophie had just kept her cool, Candace wouldn't have lost the baby.

But I won't lie. I miss Sophie. I haven't seen or spoken to her since I walked out on her that day. I've not gone this long without seeing or talking to her since we started seeing each other. Though it's for the best, it gnaws at me.

I thought coming to work would help calm my mind by giving me something else to focus on. But I've been staring at the computer screen for over an hour and haven't accomplished a thing. I huff and slump into the chair.

The office door opens and Bear steps inside. "Have a minute?"

I nod and wave him in. He takes a seat in a chair across from me. Though we've seen each other here at the shop and the clubhouse, we haven't spoken about the incident at Sophie's. He spends a lot of time with Miranda so I know he's seen Sophie. I'm itching to ask about her, but refrain from doing so because I don't want it to get back to her. I don't want to give her false hope.

"I was getting ready to head out," he says. "Thought I'd check in and see how you're doing."

"It's been a tough few days," I admit with a sigh.

"I can imagine. How's Candace?"

"Hanging in there… barely."

"We would all understand if you took some time off."

"Pop said the same thing, but I need something to occupy my time."

"Makes sense." He taps his fingers on the arm of the chair. "Can I ask you a question?"

My stomach tightens. I nod, dreading what's coming next.

"Have you thought about Sophie?"

"Of course I have…"

"She's a mess, Rooter. She cries all the time. Hardly comes out of her room."

I close my eyes and take a deep breath. It doesn't please me to hear Sophie's hurting, but I'm stuck between a rock and a hard place. I must be careful with how I respond. I can't be too remorseful, yet I don't want to come off as a heartless dick, either.

Bear continues, "You said some nasty things to her, Rooter. She thinks you hate her."

"I know I did." I hang my head. At some point, I will apologize to her, but for now I need to keep my distance.

"Do you still hold her responsible?"

"All three of us are responsible."

"She swears she didn't push Candace."

I pinch the bridge of my nose. "Maybe she didn't, but she admitted she got in Candace's face."

"If Candace hadn't gone there—"

I cut him off, "You think I haven't thought this through a million times? Because I have. Candace shouldn't have gone there, but she did. Sophie should have kept her cool, but she didn't." I drag a hand through my hair. "I made this happen because I insisted that I could make it work—that I could be with Sophie and still be there for Candace and the baby. It was a recipe for disaster."

"You're being too hard on Sophie, and yourself. What happened was awful, but it was an accident, Rooter. A very unfortunate accident."

I slam my palm on the desk, enraged. "An unfortunate accident? My kid is dead, Bear! That isn't an unfortunate accident, it's a fucking tragedy!"

"It is a tragedy," he agrees, ever calm. "But laying blame won't ease anyone's pain."

"Yeah, well sweeping it under the rug won't either."

"I'm not telling you to sweep it under the rug. I'm trying to tell you not to make it worse by alienating the girl you love."

I shake my head. "There's no chance for her and I now. Not after this."

"I'm sorry to hear that because I've known you a long-time Rooter, and I've never seen you as happy as you were with Sophie."

Because I've never been that happy. Not even close. Probably never will be again.

I shut my computer down. There's no way I'll get any work done today.

"Candace is a fixture in my life, for better or worse. Especially now. There's no way to make it work."

"If that's the case, you might as well just be with Candace. Because as long as she's a *fixture* in your life, you won't be able to have a relationship with anyone else. She'll never allow it."

"I guess I'll have to deal with that when the time comes, but it isn't my priority right now."

Bear shakes his head, obviously exasperated. "When this storm passes, you're going to regret your decision. Sophie's a good girl. She loves you and I'd be willing to bet every dollar in my bank account you still love her."

It would be a safe bet. Uncomfortable, I shift my gaze to a blank spot on the wall to my left. "Did you come in here just to make me feel guilty about breaking up with Sophie?"

"No, but if you do feel guilty, maybe that should tell you something."

"It tells me I should've never been with her to begin with. None of this would have happened if I'd just stayed the fuck away like I knew I should. Like I will from now on."

He leans forward. "You could just as easily say, none of this would've happened if you hadn't gotten involved with Candace."

I hate it when he's right. "Either way, it's a moot point. I did get involved with her *and* with Sophie. Now everything is completely fucked and there's no fixing it."

A few more days pass. I've done a good job of avoiding Sophie thanks in large part to our conflicting schedules. But it was only a matter of time before our paths would cross and the time has come. As I unload groceries from my truck, she is walking to her car to leave for work. Her gaunt appearance is horrifying. She's a sickly gray color with dark circles under her eyes. It appears she hasn't eaten a single meal or had a minute of sleep since we broke up. And when her eyes meet mine, I'm eviscerated by the sorrow that I see.

Bear said she was having a hard time, but this… this is too much. To see her in this condition is an indescribable agony. This is my fault. I have never detested anyone as much as I do myself right now. If I could kick my own ass, I would.

Perhaps I should have reached out to her as Bear suggested.

But what good would it have done? I stand by my conviction that she and I can't be together. If I'd gone to talk to her, nothing would've stopped me from begging her to forgive me and take me back. The temptation of being near her would be too much to overcome.

What kind of asshole would I be to get back together with Sophie while Candace is sitting in my house grieving the loss of our baby? And as powerful as my feelings are for Sophie, my anger and grief over the miscarriage is equally strong. I'm not sure when or if I'll ever get over it.

It's best that I leave well enough alone. Let Sophie move on and help Candace heal.

By Monday, I've hardly slept. Like a zombie, I'm just going through the motions. Since seeing Sophie, she is absolutely all I can think about. I'm worried about her. I can't stand knowing she's in pain over me. It has taken every bit of my willpower to stay away when all I want to do is barge through her front door, take her into my arms, and kiss away her hurt and sadness.

Bear and I are eating lunch at the picnic table outside of the shop when his phone rings. He holds up a finger to pause our conversation to take the call.

"Hey, darlin'," he answers with a crooked smile.

It must be Miranda. I push the chicken and rice around my plate. My appetite is in the toilet.

"You did the right thing," he says. "This is the best thing for her."

My ears perk up. Are they talking about Sophie?

"If she needs help moving anything, tell her to text me. I'm happy to help."

I put my fork down and stare at Bear. *What the fuck is going on?*

The instant he sets the phone on the table I ask, "What was that about?"

"Sophie's moving out."

Utterly un-fucking-prepared for this and panic stricken, I jump up from my seat. I must get to her.

Bear grabs my arm, halting me. His expression is fierce. "What are you doing, Rooter?"

"Let go," I bark.

"You suddenly want her back now?"

"I said, let go."

"What about Candace being a fixture in your life? You said it can never work between you and Sophie. Has that changed?"

My expression is murderous as my eyes bore into his. I don't want to go up against my best friend, but if he doesn't back off, I will. "I said let go."

"You have no right to go over there. You destroyed her," Bear growls, gripping my arm tighter.

I tear my arm away, seething, "This is none of your business, Bear."

"Wrong. What she does is none of *your* business. Not anymore."

I stalk away, but he has the nerve to step in front of me and stop me once again. "Get out of my way, man."

"Rooter, I love you like a brother. I'd take a bullet for you," he jabs his index finger into my chest, "but I will not allow you to hurt that girl again. If you go over there that's exactly what will happen. Candace is living in your house, still recovering from the miscarriage. What do you think will happen if you make up with Sophie?"

I look to the ground, my hands balled into fists. He's right. "Fuck!"

"I'm sorry, man."

Not as sorry as I am. I'm nothing but a sorry piece of shit.

I have to let Sophie go. Give her a chance to move on.

But I don't want her to move on. The idea of Sophie not loving me is a punch to the gut. It's torture.

But I can't offer her anything. I may never be able to. I have too much baggage.

The fair thing is to keep my distance—something I should have done from the beginning.

Days creep by, getting harder as I go along. If I could turn back time, I would handle things with Sophie differently. I shouldn't have blown up at her. I should have taken time to think and sort out my feelings. But that's never been my style. One of my many, many faults. I'm so fast to react. Too fast. I let my emotions control me. I have to change. But even if I do, and I will, it won't change the past.

The only way I can get through the day with any sanity is by telling myself that maybe one day, Sophie and I can be together again. Without that hope, however far-fetched it is, I wouldn't be able to function.

Bear doesn't tell me much, out of respect for Miranda and Sophie, but he has told me she's living with Ryan. It's a relief knowing she's with him. I like Ryan and I trust him with her. If anyone can get Sophie through this, it's him.

Candace isn't showing much improvement. All she talks about is the baby and the plans she had. She was positive she was having a boy. She wanted to name him after me, Jace Alexander Russo Jr.

She asked if I might consider having a baby with her in the future. She believes it's the only way she'll get over the loss of this baby. The answer is an emphatic no though I didn't say that. I simply said I can't think about future children until I've grieved the loss of this one.

But that isn't really true.

Obviously, I'm sad about losing the baby. But I'm much more heartbroken over losing Sophie. I talked with Mama about it. She says it's normal. The baby was more of an abstract idea in my mind while Sophie was a tangible loss. She's a living, breathing person whom I shared an intense relationship with. Her explanation helps assuage my guilt though not entirely.

Staring at the computer screen in my office, my eyes grow heavy. Lack of sleep this past week is finally catching up with me. I close my eyes and lean back in my chair when Bear bursts into my office.

"We have to talk," he says and closes the door behind him.

"What's up?" I ask, assuming it's a Club issue based on his anxious demeanor.

"I just got a call from Miranda."

My heart palpitates. "Is Sophie okay?"

He nods. "Miranda just overheard Candace outside on the phone. Rooter, she lied. She was never pregnant."

"What?"

"She faked the whole fucking thing. All of it."

"What?" I repeat.

"This was her plan all along. Fake a pregnancy and pin a miscarriage on Sophie to break you up."

My already racing heart speeds up. I can hear the pounding in my ears. But I must stay steady. Collect all the information before I react. I've learned my lesson. "You're sure Miranda heard her, right?"

"Rooter, she said Candace was laughing about how easy it was and how she has you in the palm of her hand."

I sling my computer monitor across the room and let out a guttural roar. "That cunt is dead!"

I tear out of the office. Everyone's eyes are on me as I race out of the building. My initial instinct is to rush to Sophie and tell her what's going on. To take her in my arms and never let her go. But blind rage leads me to Candace. I want that lying bitch out of my house and my life, now.

I hadn't even realized Bear was following me until he pulls into the driveway behind me. It's a good thing he's here, otherwise I might murder the whore.

I charge into the house through the side door. Candace is at the dining room table eating leftover chinese from last night. Fear flashes in her eyes as I barrel toward her.

"You fucking, lying bitch!" I yell.

She jumps up from her seat and tries to run away, but I catch her, pinning her against the wall, crushing her until she cries out in pain.

"Rooter, you're hurting me," she whimpers.

"You'll be lucky if that's all I do to you," I snarl. "I know what you did."

"Take it easy," Bear warns.

Candace's face is ashen, and she looks everywhere but in my eyes.

"You goddamn bitch." I may have been raised never to hit women, but I might not be able to resist the urge.

"I'm sorry," she whispers. Her lips tremble and tears well in her eyes. "I never meant for it to go this far."

Poor choice of words on her part. Now I'm even more pissed. "This far? Just how far did you intend for it to go?"

"I love you so much, Rooter. I was crushed when you broke up with me."

"We were never in a relationship Candace."

"Yeah, you say that, but you did things that made me believe otherwise."

"Bullshit."

"It's true," she chokes. "I've seen you with other women. You were different with me."

I loosen my grip. "Different how?"

"You brought me dinner on my work breaks, we texted every day. We hung out together, went to movies, had dinner together. We talked like two people in a relationship talk about life and dreams. You never did that with anyone else."

I could argue some of that. I only took her dinner at work when she asked, never just because. And she's the one who initiated the majority of our texting. We went to one movie together. As for talking and hanging out, we were friends. I've known her forever. We'd done those things before. I didn't see the big deal. Apparently, it was a big deal to her. Maybe I had led her on without realizing. I guide her to the sofa in the living room and motion for her to sit. Too amped up to be still, I remain standing.

"I never meant to lead you on, Candace." I drag my fingers through my hair. "I told you the score. It was just sex for me."

"But it wasn't for me," she sobs. "It killed me when you ended it. Next thing I knew you were with someone else. At first, I thought she was just another fling, a distraction. But then I saw you way you were with her. So gentle. So unlike *you*. And you were *always* with her. You even spent the night with her. You let her sleep in your bed. You never did that with me." Her eyes fall to the floor. "I couldn't understand what she had that I didn't. What she gave you that I didn't. And when I tried talking to you, you just shut me down, wouldn't listen."

Perhaps giving her an opportunity to explain herself was a mistake. The longer she speaks, the more I want to strangle her.

"That's no fucking excuse for what you did!"

"I was desperate. I didn't know what else to do. I assumed if you thought I was pregnant, that you'd finally realize you love me, that we belong together."

I laugh, sarcastic. "You've got to be kidding me. What did you think would happen when I learned the truth?"

She looks away, unable to look me in the eye.

"You weren't planning on me figuring it out," I answer for her. "You were planning to fake a miscarriage the entire time."

She keeps her eyes cast down.

"Son of a bitch!" I grab the lamp off the end table and throw it across the room. It hits the wall and breaks into pieces on the floor. Dopey whimpers and runs up the stairs.

"I'm so sorry, Rooter," Candace cries. "Please forgive me. I'm begging you, please. Imagine how much you say you love Sophie. I love you so much more than that. You are everything to me. Everything. I know what I did was wrong—"

"You don't know a fucking thing about love!" I charge toward her. Bear gets up from the chair and stands beside us. "You don't hurt the ones you love! You don't lie to the ones you love! You sure as hell don't ruin their lives!"

"I wasn't trying to ruin your life. I would never want to do that."

"But that's exactly what you did." I point in her face. "Not only did you hurt me, you hurt the girl I love. No one hurts Sophie and gets away with it!"

My breaths are fast and shallow, my entire body tingles. I want this lying, manipulative slut to feel the pain she's inflicted on Sophie and me. I want to watch her bleed. I wrap my fingers around her skinny little throat. Just as I apply pressure, Bear yanks me away. Candace tries to scramble away, but I grab her by the hair.

"Take it easy, Rooter," Bear warns.

It's a good thing he's here.

I haul Candace upstairs as she cries, begging my forgiveness.

"Shut up, cunt," I holler and drag her into the guest bedroom. I go to the closet and throw her clothes and shoes at her. "Pack your shit!"

A shoe hits her in the face and she scurries to the far corner of the room and cowers on the floor.

There are no boxes or bags to put her stuff in so I open the window and toss it out to the driveway. Just when I think I've gotten it all, I find something else. How did all this shit get here? I only brought a few boxes of her stuff here. She must've been making trips to her house to get things. She obviously planned on being here long-term. When everything is gone from the bedroom, I head to the bathroom to get her crap out of there. I don't want a single trace of the skank in this house.

Once I'm sure the house is clear of anything belonging to her, I grab her by the hair and drag her to the door.

"Your ties to me and the Club are gone," I growl and shove her outside. "By the end of the day, everyone will know what you've done. If I was you, I'd get far, far away from Halsey. If I ever see your face again… there's no telling what I might do."

Life Or Death

I start for my bike when Miranda calls my name.

"Sophie isn't home," she says as she walks toward me. "I told her what happened. She figured you'd go looking for her and left."

"Do you know where she is?"

Miranda shakes her head and hands me her phone. On the screen is a text from Sophie: *Yeah, I just don't know what to say. I'm glad he knows the truth, but it doesn't change anything.*

I hand the phone back to her. "If you find out where she is, let me know?"

"Yeah," she agrees.

"Thanks."

Candace is crying as she loads her car with her things.

I turn to Bear. "Help her? I want her gone ASAP."

I go inside my house and ring Sophie's phone, but it goes to voicemail. I call right back. Again, it goes to voicemail. This time, I leave a message.

"Sophie, please talk to me. I'm so sorry for everything. Please answer the phone…"

Not knowing what else to say, I hang up and consider calling again. It'd be useless. She won't answer. But I can't give up. If I have to call and text all day and night, I won't stop until she talks to me.

I send a text: *Please answer. I know you have ur phone. I saw ur text to Miranda. Sophie, I'm so so so so so sorry. Please talk to me.*

I'm surprised by her quick reply: *I can't talk to you. Not right now. I need time.*

No way am I giving her time. Not until she hears me out. I call again. Voicemail. I send another text: *I'll just keep calling and texting until u answer.*

Sophie: *I'll block your number.*

Does she really think that'd stop me?

Me: *I'll get another phone, and then another, and then another. Just answer and talk to me.*

Sophie: *I'll change my number. Leave me alone.*

Me: *Just hear me out and if u still want me to leave u alone, I promise I will.*

Sophie: *I can't.*

Me: *I don't want to do this, but if u don't answer I'll be at The Grand tomorrow when u get there. Either way, we're talking. We can either do it now on the phone or tomorrow in person. U pick. If u don't call I'll assume u want to talk in person.*

Two minutes later, my phone rings. "Baby, I'm so sorry."

"Rooter, this doesn't change anything." Her voice is resolute.

"How can you say that? It changes everything."

"No, it doesn't. What happened still happened. I scared her and she fell down the stairs. If she had been pregnant, she could've lost the baby, and you'd still hate me."

I pace my living room. "But she wasn't pregnant, Babe. She set us up. This is all her fault," my voice falters. "I never hated you."

If only Sophie knew how miserable I've been without her. How I haven't been able to think about anything but her…

"Yes, you did. I saw it in your eyes. I heard it in your voice. You meant it when you said you never wanted to see me again."

"Babe, I was mad. I lost it and said things I didn't mean."

"Let me ask you something. This morning, before you found out the truth, how did you feel? Did you hate me this morning?"

No, I didn't hate her, but the anger and sorrow was still there. "This morning, I was still grieving the loss of a child, but I've missed you every second you've been gone."

"You moved on rather quickly for someone who misses me. You moved her in the very next day."

How can she possibly think that? "It wasn't like that, Sophie. She was staying in the guest room. I was helping her recuperate and get back on her feet."

She sighs. "Too much damage has been done. There's no coming back from this."

Her words break me and a sob escapes my lips as tears fall from my eyes. I have no shame. I want her to know how very sorry I am and how much she means to me. "No Baby, don't say that. I can make this right. I can fix it. I'll do whatever you say. Just come home."

She speaks through tears of her own. "Rooter, do you care about me?"

More than anything in this world. My body is wracked by tremors as I cry. "Baby, I love you so much that it's breaking me in two. And you love me."

"If you love me, let me go." She's crying so hard, her words are barely coherent. "Please just let me go."

No, Baby, no. Please don't do this. Give me another chance. Those are the words I want to say and I almost do. But I don't deserve another chance. "That's what you really want?"

"It's what I need."

"I'm so sorry I hurt you. I'll never forgive myself." If anyone else caused her this much pain, I'd slaughter them.

"I have to go. Goodbye, Rooter."

This is it. Our final goodbye. I've lost my only love forever.

"Goodbye, Sophie."

I drop to the floor on my knees. The pain cuts deep. It's unbearable. I can't do this. I can't be without Sophie. I wrap my arms around myself and scream.

Laying on the floor, I cry until the anger overtakes my sadness. I want to kill something, anything, maybe even myself. I pick up the coffee table and throw it as far as I can. It ends up on the dining room table where I see Candace's food. I slam it against the wall before grabbing one of the dining room chairs and chucking it through a window. Anything and everything in sight gets obliterated in my wake.

A pair of strong arms grab me from behind. Bear speaks, but I can't make out what he's saying. I try to wrestle out of his grasp, but he's a strong son-of-a-bitch.

"Let me go!"

"Calm down, Rooter!" He takes me down to the floor. "Destroying your house won't bring her back."

It's been three agonizing days. I've tried to do as Sophie asked and let her go, but being without her is like being deprived of food and water. She is my nourishment, my life.

Yesterday, I rented a compact car—something Sophie would never believe I'd drive—in an attempt to be inconspicuous. Earlier, I followed her and Ryan to a flea market. Ryan did his best to make her smile and laugh, being the great friend he is. But even when she smiled, her sadness was evident. She's every bit as miserable as me.

Now, I'm parked across the street from their place, in full stalker mode with binoculars in hand. I'm cramped and claustrophobic in this ridiculous contraption they call a vehicle, but if I get out I'll risk being seen. The discomfort is a small price to pay to be able to see Sophie's sweet face.

To pass the time, I listen to music—Sophie's kind—and play games on my phone. Before I know it, it's evening. I just now realize

I haven't eaten today. Oh, well. Doesn't matter. I'm not hungry, anyway.

Sophie and Ryan come out and get into his car. I follow behind, keeping my distance. They pull into the Red Door parking lot. Rather than pull in after them, I circle the block. By the time I make it back around, they're already inside. I wait fifteen minutes to make sure they've gotten settled before going in.

There's no doorman tonight and no cover charge to pay. It's busier than I would imagine for a Sunday. A good thing as it offers me cover. I'm less likely to be noticed.

There's a dark area in the back of the bar where hardly anyone ever sits. There's no one there now. I take the long way there, along the perimeter of the bar. Sophie is off to the far right, close to where we sat the night we were here together.

Memories of that night bombard my mind. Sophie in her dress. Us on the dance floor. Making out on the ride home. The strip tease. Waking up with her body draped across mine. Definitely one of the best nights of my life. All of my nights with her were the best of my life.

Three beers later, I need to hit the John. But Sophie's out on the dance floor with her friend Abby. She's sexy as ever. I'd give anything to be out there with her, feeling her body move against mine. I don't want to miss anything, but my bladder protests.

When I exit the men's room, Sophie's nowhere to be found. Ryan's still here, so she must be as well. Unless she left with Abby… Both girls have had a lot to drink. Surely, Ryan wouldn't let either of them drive drunk.

Before I can panic, the girls emerge from the hallway I just came from. They must've been in the ladies room. That was a close call. We could have come out at the same time.

Ryan is on the dance floor with Sophie now, but Ryan's guy friend, date, whatever, comes out and wants to dance with him. Sophie looks for Abby who's flirting with a guy she appears to have just met. Sophie starts to walk off the dance floor, but a guy approaches her and asks her to dance. My heart skips a beat.

Please say no, please say no.

Thank God she turns him down. If she hadn't, I would be on that dance floor cutting in.

The night winds down. The bartender asks if they'd like another round and they say no which I take as my cue to leave.

After following Sophie around for a few days, I return the rental car. I feel pathetic and more than a little creepy. Following her just makes me miss her more. It's awful being near her, but unable to speak with or touch her. It reminds me of what I can't have.

Later that evening, Bear stops by the house before he and Miranda leave for dinner. He's asked me to meet him for drinks a couple nights this week and I've refused. He's worried I'm becoming a "shut-in." If only he knew I've spent the last few days in a car spying on Sophie. He'd be more concerned.

"You want to join us?" he offers. "Miranda won't mind."

"No thanks, man. Me and Dopey are going to gorge on junk food and watch reruns."

"You can't spend all your time in this house. Come with us."

My phone rings.

My heart stutters as Sophie's name flashes on the screen. "Sophie?"

"Mike's here," she whispers, her voice laced with fear. "I'm scared."

I hear pounding and the sound of Mike screaming in the background.

"Oh my God," she whimpers, "he's kicking the door."

That motherfucker is dead.

I put the phone on speaker and motion for Bear to follow me as I grab my keys and run for my truck.

"Stay on the phone with me," I tell her as I fire up the engine.

"We're on our way."

"I'm at Ryan's. He lives on—"

"I know where it's at."

Mike screams something about making her pay. Bear sends a text to Miranda to tell her there's been an emergency and that he's with me.

"I don't know what to do," Sophie's small voice shakes.

I'm scared for her, but I must stay calm. If I freak out, she'll be even more afraid.

"Grab your gun and lock yourself in a room," I tell her. "The more barriers you put between you the longer it'll take him to get to you."

Less than a minute later she tells me she's in Ryan's bathroom.

"I can hear him screaming," she says. "He's going to break in."

There's no way I'll get there before he gets in.

"Stay where you are and keep your gun at the ready. If he gets into the bathroom before I get there you fire immediately. Do you hear me?"

"Yes," her voice cracks.

My hands tremble, a mixture of fury and fear. Is she capable of defending herself against him? Or will their history prevent her from doing what needs to be done? "Sophie, he's dangerous. He isn't the Mike you used to know."

"I know."

"I'm only ten minutes away," I say, but ten minutes feels like forever. Please God, keep her safe until I get there. "Hold on, Babe. Everything will be okay."

I hear a loud noise followed by Mike's voice. He must be in the house.

"He's inside the house," she cries.

"Stay calm, Sophie." I keep my voice steady and smooth although I feel the opposite. "Remember the night when those guys broke into your house? You were so calm and collected. I need you to be that way now."

"I was only calm because you were there."

There's more banging followed by Mike hollering.

"I'm driving as fast as I can," I say. "Just hold it together until I get there."

"Please hurry," she begs.

"Baby, I'm coming."

There is a loud thud followed by more of Mike's screaming. He has no idea what's coming for him. I should have ended him when I had the chance.

"He's kicking Ryan's bedroom door," Sophie mutters.

"I'm going to fucking kill him."

There's another loud crashing sound and Sophie cries out. "Oh God, he's in the bedroom."

"He's probably going to make it to you before I get there. Do not hesitate to shoot him."

I hear Mike say, "Sophie, if you make me bust through another door, I'll be really pissed off."

"Tell him I'm on my way," I seethe.

"Rooter's on his way, Mike," Sophie says. "He'll be here any minute. You better leave before he gets here."

Mike laughs. "Yeah right. He doesn't want anything to do with you. He left you high and dry like I knew he would."

"I'm serious Mike," Sophie says. "I'm on the phone with him right now."

Mike tells her it won't matter because she'll be dead before I get there. Ice runs through my veins. If anything happens to her…

"If you hurt me, he'll kill you!" Sophie screams.

I'm going to kill him, anyway.

Mike laughs again and says it doesn't matter.

He probably doesn't care about his life, and probably won't give a damn when I unload every round in my gun into his head.

"Mike, please don't do this," Sophie cries.

I'm so close, yet so far. I silently beg for God to let me get to her before it's too late.

I hear a series of loud bangs.

Sophie sobs. "He's going to break the door down.".

"Put the phone down and aim," I command. "You shoot the moment he comes through the door."

I hear her moving about as the banging continues. I pray she has the strength to do this. Seconds tick by slowly.

"I have my gun," she yells. "I swear I'll shoot you."

Mike laughs followed by the sound of a gunshot. Sophie screams. Terror rips through me.

"Sophie! Sophie!"

Several shots are fired. My body tenses with each one.

"Sophie! Pick up the phone Sophie!"

"I shot him through the door," Sophie pants, breathless. "I can't hear anything."

"I heard over five shots. Are you okay?"

"Yes. He didn't hit me."

I exhale a breath of relief. "I'm almost there. Can you see him?"

"He's on the floor, not moving. I think I killed him." She hyperventilates. "Oh my God, I think I killed him."

"It's okay, Sophie." I fly down her street. "Stay put until I'm with you."

"O-kay," she chokes.

We finally arrive, and I slam on the brakes and throw the truck into park. With my gun in hand, I sprint to the open front door.

"I've got your back, Brother," Bear says.

"Sophie!" I yell as I enter the premises, following the path of destruction to a back room.

"Rooter!" Sophie screams my name.

I round the corner into the bedroom. Sophie's eyes lock with mine. I start to run in her direction when I see movement.

It happens so fast.

On the floor, Mike has his gun aimed at Sophie.

"Sophie!" I scream.

I reach for her, pull her to me and spin us around.

Splintering pain tears through me.

Sophie screams my name.

The fog lifts.

I hear beeping and strange voices.

And then I remember.

Mike. His gun. He was aiming at Sophie.

My eyes open. The room is bright. Too bright.

I'm in a hospital.

I look around, frantic.

Sophie's not here.

"Sophie!" I try to holler, but my voice wavers.

"Sophie!" I holler again, this time a little louder.

An unknown voice tells me to calm down. The nurses hold me down, but they don't understand. I need to get to Sophie. I need to know if she's all right.

"Where's Sophie?" I struggle to sit up, but they won't allow me.

"We need you to calm down Mr. Russo," the male nurse says.

"Where's Sophie? Is she okay?"

"We need to examine you, Jace," another nurse says. "We'll bring your family in when we're done."

"No! I need to know where Sophie is!" I fight with all my might to get up. If they won't tell me where she is, I'll find her myself.

They push me down harder. "Lie still!" the male nurse demands.

"No goddammit! Where is Sophie?"

I scream her name, again and again, all the while fighting to break free.

I tug at the wires connected to me and the nurses yell at me to stop, but I don't care.

"Sophie! Where's Sophie?"

And then I hear her angelic voice. "I'm here."

I calm at once. "Sophie?" I lean over to see around one of the nurses. Every movement sends searing pain through me, but I don't care.

"I'm here," she says, "it's okay, calm down."

My beautiful girl is safe. I sigh in relief and pull her close. "Babe, you're okay."

Her hand is soft and warm as she strokes my cheek. "You saved me."

"Will you relax now?" The male nurse asks, breathless.

I nod and everyone except Sophie leaves the room.

"I've never been so scared in my life," I say and pull Sophie so that she's sitting next to me on the bed.

"You?" She shakes her head. "You have no idea what fear is. You were shot and have been sedated on a ventilator since last night."

"He could've shot you." My eyes well up as I recall the scene.

"It should've been me."

"No. Never say that." I wipe away her tears.

"You could've died."

"Better me than you." If she would've died, I would've been right behind her. I could never live without her.

She shakes her head. "I'd rather be dead than live in a world where you don't exist," her voice cracks. "I love you."

My lips spread into the widest smile. Everything is right in the world once again. "I love you, too."

Sophie rests her forehead on mine and whispers, "Please don't leave me again."

"I'll never leave you Baby." She need never worry about that. I take her face into my hands and press my lips to hers. "I swear to fucking God, I will murder anything and anyone who tries to come between us."

Three days later, I'm released from the hospital early. Evidently, I'm a faster healer than most. I've still got a long way to go for a full recovery, but I'm well enough to go home as long as I have someone staying with me. Sophie graciously offered. If I have it my way, she'll be living with me permanently.

As we lay in bed, a rerun of I Dream Of Jeannie is playing, but I'm not paying attention to it. Instead, I'm gazing at my girl, running my fingers through her hair. There's a content smile on her face.

"I don't want you to call me Rooter anymore," I say.

Sophie stares at me, her mouth hanging open. "What?"

"I want you to call me Jace from now on."

"You do?" She rolls over to face me.

I place a delicate kiss on her hand. "I haven't been able to talk about it before now, but losing you did something to me. It changed me. When you called me that night… When he pointed his gun at you I knew nothing in this world means as much to me as you do. The only thing that matters is making you happy and being what you need."

She cups my face with her palm. "You are what I need. You do make me happy. You don't need to change."

"I'm not changing." I assure her. "Rooter will always be my alter ego. Hell, I'm sure the guys in the Club will always call me that. But when you look at me that's not what I want you to see. I want you to see the good in me."

Her eyes soften. "I've always seen the good in you."

I pull Sophie to me and kiss the top of her head. "I never felt pain like I felt when you asked me to let you go. And it wasn't just the pain of losing you. It was knowing the pain I caused you." I pull back because I want to be looking in her eyes when I say the rest. "I know I made this promise before and failed, but I swear I'll never hurt you again, Sophie. You're everything to me. I love you."

"I love you, Rooter," she cries.

"Jace, Baby. Call me Jace."

BOOKS BY TEIRAN SMITH

Double H Romance Series
Rooter
Becoming Jace

Standalone Romance Novels
What the Heart Wants

ABOUT THE AUTHOR

Teiran is obsessed with the written word. When she's not writing, she's reading. She can get so lost in a story, be it one of her own or someone else's, that she won't even break away to eat, drink, or sleep. By the time she gets up from a story, she's usually dizzy from low blood sugar, and suffering blurred vision.

Whenever she's not writing or reading, you will find her working in her art shop. Her spare time is spent with her husband, Scott, and their four legged child, Lada.

Please visit:
Author website: www.teiransmith.com
Email: teiransmith@gmail.com
Facebook: www.facebook.com/TeiranSmith